RESCUING MELISSA

The Guardians: Hostage Rescue Specialists

ELLIE MASTERS

JEM Publishing

Copyright

Image/art disclaimer: Licensed material is being used for illustrative purposes only. Any person depicted in the licensed material is a model.

Editor: Julie Cameron

Cover Artist: Ellie Masters

Interior Design/Formatting: Ellie Masters

Published in the United States of America

JEM Publishing, LLC

ISBN-13: 978-1-952625-10-7

Dedication

This book is dedicated to my one and only—my amazing and wonderful husband.

Thank you, my dearest love, my heart and soul, for putting up with me, for believing in me, and for loving me.

You pushed me when I needed to be pushed. You supported me when I felt discouraged. You believed in me when I didn't believe in myself.

If it weren't for you, this book never would have come to life.

Books by Ellie Masters

The LIGHTER SIDE

Ellie Masters is the lighter side of the Jet & Ellie Masters writing duo! You will find Contemporary Romance, Military Romance, Romantic Suspense, Billionaire Romance, and Rock Star Romance in Ellie's Works.

Sign up to Ellie's Newsletter and get a free gift. https://elliemasters.com/RescuingMelissa

YOU CAN FIND ELLIE'S BOOKS HERE:

ELLIEMASTERS.COM/BOOKS

Military Romance

Guardian Hostage Rescue

Rescuing Melissa

(Get a FREE copy of Rescuing Melissa when you join Ellie's Newsletter)

Rescuing Zoe

Rescuing Moira

The One I Want Series

(Small Town, Military Heroes)

By Jet & Ellie Masters

EACH BOOK IN THIS SERIES CAN BE READ AS A STANDALONE AND IS ABOUT A DIFFERENT COUPLE WITH AN HEA.

Aiden

Brent

Caleb

Dax

Patton

Rockstar Romance

The Angel Fire Rock Romance Series

EACH BOOK IN THIS SERIES CAN BE READ AS A STANDALONE AND IS ABOUT A DIFFERENT COUPLE WITH AN HEA. IT IS RECOMMENDED THEY ARE READ IN ORDER.

Ashes to New (prequel)

Heart's Insanity (book 1)

Heart's Desire (book 2)

Heart's Collide (book 3)

Hearts Divided (book 4)

Hearts Entwined (book5)

Forest's FALL (book 6)

Hearts The Last Beat (book7)

Billionaire Romance

Billionaire Boys Club

Hawke

H.R.H. Richard

Brody

Contemporary Romance

Firestorm

(KRISTY BROMBERG'S EVERYDAY HEROES WORLD)

Contemporary Romance

Cocky Captain

(VI KEELAND & PENELOPE WARD'S COCKY HERO WORLD)

Sweet Contemporary Romance

Finding Peace

Romantic Suspense

The Starling

~AND~

Science Fiction

Ellie Masters writing as L.A. Warren

Vendel Rising: a Science Fiction Serialized Novel

Contents

ONE

Contracts

MELISSA

Melissa Patterson's tenth wedding anniversary should have been a happy occasion, a milestone of marital bliss, not this soul-shattering death. She stood in her kitchen, gripping the stack of papers, and held back the tears as she stared at the top page.

Two simple scratches of ink were all it had taken to negate ten long years of marital terror.

Ten years ago, she'd been the proverbial blushing bride. The fairytale wedding had been the social event of the season—a perfect start to her first day in hell.

The divorce had been her lawyer's idea as if she could separate herself from Scott Patterson's name. The world believed she'd been complicit in his crimes. Her lawyer said she deserved to be free.

Her shaky hand had scrawled a much less elegant mark than her husband's. Even on death row, Scott lost none of his confidence. The elegance of his signature mocked her hurried scratches, precise and controlled like the killer inside. What had gone through his mind as he'd penned his name? She'd never know, and he'd die with his arrogance fully intact. Maybe then, she'd be free.

Melissa scrubbed the tears from her cheeks, glanced at the dirty dishes on the counter, the dried food needing to be scraped, and the silverware cluttering the sink. She made the conscious decision to leave the mess for later. Scott would have never allowed such a thing, but this wasn't his house, and she didn't need to obey his rules.

Not anymore.

A run would clear her mind. Melissa tossed the divorce papers onto the counter next to the dirty dishes and went to change into her running gear. Her pink and purple barefoot running shoes didn't match the blue and yellow of her outfit. Not that it mattered. She had long since abandoned the need to maintain a perfect appearance. Scott's punishments were no longer something to fear, and after today, he would be gone for good. Her greatest fear was whether his harsh voice would still whisper admonishments in her head after his death. He'd done it from prison for three years, and she had no reason to believe that would change.

She yanked her hair into a lopsided scrunchy, and could almost hear Scott scolding her sloppiness. Gritting her teeth, she silenced his reprimand with a yank on her messy bun. Melissa grabbed her keys and locked the front door.

On the front porch, the headline of the morning newspaper screamed the top news:

Stay of Execution Denied for Fairytale Killer

She sent the paper flying off her front porch with a swift kick, where it splashed in a muddy puddle on the lawn, then placed the key under the mat.

Gray clouds threatened. Maybe the rain would wash away the memories, drown out Scott's incessant nattering in her head, or cleanse the ache in her heart. A storm would be a perfect match for her mood.

A 10K run should do the trick.

Two kilometers in, the acidic burn of a fast-paced run heated her muscles. Her chest expanded, pulling in air with every third strike of her foot. She'd taken up running during Scott's trial, a long-drawn-out process lasting more than a year. Beating up her body had been precisely the therapy she had needed to endure the media circus imposed on her life. Every day of that year was a living hell. The two years with him on death row had been only a little better.

By the halfway mark, her legs ached, and her breathing deepened. Endorphins flooded her body. With the famous runner's high achieved, she relaxed into her stride.

Overhead, the gloomy sky darkened and dumped rain. One kilometer left. She welcomed the fat drops. The musty smell of the downpour invigorated her, even as the rain soaked her clothes. A thunderclap sounded overhead, a sharp sound, followed by a low, throaty rumble she felt more than heard.

Hail followed the thunder. A glance at the darkening clouds rewarded her with a bolt of lightning shattering the sky. The answering thunderclap followed a second later. The lightning was closer than was safe. She needed to get out of the weather.

The moist air ahead of the storm gave way to cooler temperatures, chilling her to the bone—time to find shelter. Lightning crackled through the air, striking a tree across the park. Smoke spiraled into the sky as the tree sizzled.

Pea-sized pellets rained down from the heavily laden sky. Lightning flashed, syncing to the beat of a memory—blinding pain when Scott struck with his belt. PTSD, the therapist said. It would fade with time, he said. Her therapist said a lot of things Melissa didn't believe.

Five bolts of lightning struck in quick succession. Resounding peals of thunder followed. It reminded her of the whoosh that preceded the strike of Scott's belt. Her heart skipped a beat, and the massive blast had her tripping over her feet.

Ten years of her life wasted. She screamed her frustration into the clouds and ran as the force of Mother Nature answered her cry.

The jogging path met with a road a quarter-mile down where the neighborhood park ended. She needed to get to one of the businesses on Main Street, where she could wait out the storm. Time to pick up the pace.

The sky took on a greenish cast. Clouds dipped low, roiling as the storm whipped them to a froth. The wind beat at her. Hail slammed into her, first from the right, then the left. It lashed out, as if unsure how to best launch its attack on her delicate flesh. Her heart rate spiked, not from running, but from the sickening hue cast in the sky. Tornados, while rare, weren't unheard of in the small town of Fort Walton.

Melissa had never seen a tornado and didn't want to start now.

She quickened her pace, muscles protesting, and lungs burning. The storm raged, building around her as if feeding off her turbulent emotions. Like Scott had done too many times to count, the storm lashed out at her, furious and raw, beating her until her skin stung. She stumbled, afraid for her safety, and angry she'd been foolish enough to go running during a storm.

She turned onto the sidewalk that edged the tree-lined Main Street. Down the road, through the sheets of driving rain, a coffee shop's "Open" sign flashed a welcome beacon. She ducked her head and sprinted for safety.

Electricity filled the air. The tiny hairs on her arms lifted. A flash of molten light burned to her left. Her skin tingled. A concussive force slammed into her as she ran.

She tumbled from the sidewalk into the street, arms and legs spinning in a wild tangle of limbs. Before her head hit the blacktop, twin headlights of a black SUV blazed in her eyes. The screech of tires had Melissa cringing for an impact that never came. Her vision dimmed, and she lost her fight to stay conscious.

TWO

Twister

CJ

A PETITE BRUNETTE LAUNCHED HERSELF INTO THE STREET. CJ slammed the brakes of his rented SUV, tires squealing over the wet pavement. The car's windows rattled with the storm, and his vision sparked with afterimages from a lightning strike.

He swerved, turning the wheel to avoid a spin. Steering through it, he tapped the brakes to regain traction. A large piece of hail landed on the front windshield, splintering the safety glass into a spider web of cracks.

"Fuck, fuck, and double fuck!"

He came to a stop and jammed the transmission into park. The woman sprawled across the pavement. Had that lightning hit her? Was she dead? No way to know unless he got out of the car, but she wasn't moving. Shit, what was that noise? Sounded like a freight train.

He glanced left, peering through the sleeting rain. A funnel cloud snaked toward the ground less than half a mile away.

"Shit!" He unbuckled and vaulted out of the car. Every nerve in his body came alive. Fear over whether the tornado would touch down, and concern for the lifeless woman, spiked through his veins.

Thank God he'd stopped.

Sprinting to the unconscious woman, he knelt at her side and felt for a pulse. A faint beat trembled against the pad of his finger. Still alive then.

After he checked for injuries, CJ pulled her over his shoulder, praying she didn't have a neck injury. He didn't have time to stabilize her cervical spine, not with a whirling beast trying to touch down.

Time to move.

Racing back to the car, he opened the hatch, thinking there'd be more room there, and set her down with as much care as possible. With another curse, he shut the back hatch as the growl of the tornado approached. Dirt and debris spun in the air.

Too damn close.

He scrambled to the driver's side and jumped inside. A roar filled the air as the tornado touched down and churned toward him.

With the windshield cracked into a thousand pieces, he couldn't see shit. He leaned back and kicked at the window until the sheet of safety glass crumpled outward.

Debris lifted by the wind hit him in the face. They had little time. He slammed his foot down on the gas. The tires screeched on the wet blacktop, slipping for a heart-stopping moment before launching him and his unconscious passenger forward through the thickening cloud of grass, dirt, and other debris.

Across the street, most of the local businesses were closed. A face peered out the window of a coffee shop. He prayed the person in the coffee shop sought shelter somewhere in the interior of the brick and mortar façade. He headed to a garage he'd passed a hundred yards back. It should provide more protection against a tornado than a building.

If memory served, the ramp angled down, going below ground. He shifted his foot, tapping the brake to spin the car in a 180-degree arc. The tornado ripped up the ground behind him, destroying the manicured park. It rumbled down the street, chasing him.

"Fuck!"

Rain blinded him through the missing windshield, and twigs slapped at his face. He blew through a red light. Everyone except him, and the crazy lady out for a jog, had taken shelter.

Something big slammed into the back of the car, lifting the rear wheels and making him swerve.

He regained control, thankful he'd been hit in the back instead of on the side or front. If the airbags had deployed, he would've been toast.

The parking garage came into view. He skidded, drifting the curve, and pulled into the entrance.

Sticks turned into branches and tree trunks. An awning from a local business cartwheeled in the air.

He barely heard the squeal of the tires over the freight train of destruction hurtling down the street. Turning the corner, he headed down to the next level; his ears popped with a sudden pressure drop. He had only a passing glimpse of the funnel as it brushed past the entrance, sucking parked cars up into its vortex.

He stopped another level down, pulling into a vacant space. His breathing was ragged, and his pulse thrummed along at a steady clip.

Behind him, the woman moaned.

He sighed. On leave, and he was still saving lives.

The storm continued to rage, but the tornado moved on to play with other victims. CJ exited the vehicle to check on the woman's injuries.

The rental was ruined. In addition to the missing windshield, dents littered the roof and hood, and flying objects put deep gouges in the quarter panels. Oh, and the rear bumper was missing.

He yanked on the back hatch, trying to open it. Whatever hit the car twisted the frame. He tugged a few times, but it wouldn't budge. Thank God he purchased the extra insurance the rental agency strong-armed him into buying.

He'd have to drop the back seat and pull her out of the car through the back door. Since he didn't know how severe her injuries might be, he was a little reluctant to move her again. He fished out a flashlight from his luggage and climbed in the back.

Airway, breathing, and circulation intact, CJ moved to the secondary survey looking for other injuries. He ran his fingers through her matted hair. There was a lump beside the messiest ponytail he'd ever seen. Her hair was wet from the rain, but there didn't seem to be any blood. Her relaxed features made her look so fragile. Fuck, but she was breathtaking.

What the hell was he thinking? The woman was hurt and unconscious. He was supposed to be a professional, but damn, he wasn't dead.

She had a strong, steady pulse, and her chest rose and fell in a natural rhythm, both were reassuring signs. The tight exercise clothes she wore distracted him. They clung to her curves and pulled his eyes away from his professional assessment. Goosebumps prickled the skin of her arms.

Shit, the poor thing had to be freezing.

Her pained moan snapped him back to business.

Her left arm was bruised, no more lumps on her head, and no apparent broken bones. A medic by trade, he was suspicious of internal injuries. He continued with his assessment, lifting her shirt and lowering the waistband of her running pants. He grimaced at the deep bruising over the left side of her chest, which extended to her hip. She might have cracked her ribs, but since her breathing wasn't labored, he wasn't concerned about damage to her lungs. Her abdomen, on the other hand, worried him.

He needed to call 9-1-1 but didn't have reception. The chance ambulances were running was low, and complicating matters, he didn't know where the local hospitals were located. He needed to get to the street to make the call, maybe even search for hospital locations and take her himself.

She didn't appear to be in immediate danger, although the bruising on her side suggested internal injuries. He'd feel better if she woke up.

He pulled off his jacket and covered her to keep her warm. Sharing body heat would be more efficient, but he could only imagine what she'd think, waking up in a stranger's arms.

Instead, he made her as comfortable as possible. He crawled back over the folded rear seat and grabbed his duffle. He was cold too, drenched to the bone by the rain. The adrenaline coursing through his veins faded, leaving him with shaky hands and chills.

Damn, the sleepy little town of Fort Walton was full of surprises. He came for an execution, and now he'd survived his first tornado.

CJ stripped and changed into something dry.

While he waited, he pulled out the local daily paper and re-read the headline for the hundredth time:

Stay of Execution Denied for Fairytale Killer

He planned to watch a monster be put down. His sister would finally have justice, and he'd find peace.

THREE

Mint Cookies

PIERCE

Two Girl Scouts greeted me at the front door. A little girl in an adorable Brownie vest held hands with another girl wearing a green sash. Their pressed outfits beamed with neatly sewn badges.

"Well, hello." A grin stretched across my face. Little girls were full of such promise for the powerful women they would one day become. A strength I would challenge until they broke beneath me.

I crouched down, getting eye-to-eye, where I would be less threatening. The Brownie had a lock of hair curling at the corner of her eye. My fingers twitched with the need to brush the hairs away from her face. A woman supervised the girls from the curb, probably the mother. My fingers clenched, and then I raised my hand to wave. She returned my wave with a shy one of her own.

So friendly and trusting.

So naive and stupid.

Her children were younger versions of herself and turned my thoughts in delectable directions. I couldn't have the girls—they were too young, and I had standards—but the woman held promise.

"What can I do for you?" I surveyed the gathering clouds, wondering why two little girls would be out when it was about to storm.

The girl in green grasped her sister's hand. "We're selling Girl Scout cookies, sir. Would you like to buy some?" She glanced up at the gray sky. "Mama says we have a little while before the storm, and we have a…" Her face scrunched up, "…q-quota to reach."

I loved the way her mouth worked out the unfamiliar sounds of such a big word.

"A quota? I'd love to." I pitched my voice high and brought my hands over my heart, knowing it would make the girls smile.

The Brownie giggled.

I gave her a wink. "I love Girl Scout cookies. Please tell me you have Thin Mints. I love them."

The older girl's expression brightened, but it was her sister with the brown vest who answered.

"Yes, s-sir. We have Thin Mints."

I wanted to tweak her nose, but the watchful mother might not appreciate me touching her daughter. The little girl was so damn adorable with her pigtails and innocent eyes; her cuteness factor was off the charts. I couldn't help myself and leaned close to inhale her warm, innocent scent.

Her older sister drew back, but I expected the reaction. As charming as I was, some females, the smart ones, pulled away, acting instinctively for self-preservation. I sensed great intelligence in my green-sashed friend.

"May I please have ten boxes?"

"Ten boxes, ss-sir?" The little girl's brown eyes brightened. She jumped up and down.

"Oh, yes. Ten." I fished for my wallet and pulled out two crisp, fifty dollar bills. "Here, this should cover it."

The little girl screwed her face up as she tried to do the math, failed, and referenced a card in her hand. "It's five dollars a box, sir. That's fifty dollars." She stared at the money and pulled at her ear as she worked out the math. "That's too much."

I couldn't resist. I tweaked her nose.

She grinned and gave me the most delicious giggle.

"Fifty for the cookies and fifty for your troop." I pointed to her mother standing on the curb. "You tell your mama to take you somewhere extra special. Good girls deserve special treats, don't you think?"

The advancing storm darkened the sky. I loved thunderstorms in springtime. The musty smell of fresh rain reminded me of the delectable scents below the house.

"Oh, yes, sir." The little Brownie clapped her tiny hands.

Her older sister glanced over her shoulder. "I need to check if we have ten boxes."

I offered the Brownie the cash, but her sister yanked the money out of my hand. That little girl needed a spanking.

"I'll wait here," I said. "Go get my cookies while I chat with your sister."

The older one wrinkled her nose and twisted her lips, "Anna, you get the cookies. I'll wait here." She handed Anna the cash.

My little Brownie, Anna, twisted her mouth into a pout, but she turned and obeyed at the stern look from her sister. Why was it women always felt the need to tell others what to do? Anna's sister needed to mind her own business and let Anna do what she wanted.

As Anna ran to her mother, I made small talk with her sister. "How old are you?"

"I'm eleven." Her arms crossed over a blossoming chest.

Girls seemed to mature at younger and younger ages. Still, this girl was too young for my tastes. Maybe several years down the road—after she grew those tiny nubs into breasts—I'd take her as one of my princesses. Anna's sister had a backbone.

I loved a challenge. She probably got that quality from her mother.

The girl and I traded silence while Anna skipped down the path to the curb, stopping to pick up an earthworm and toss the poor creature in the grass.

Her mother's lips formed an 'O' in surprise after the Brownie handed over the cash, and my attention focused hard on that mouth.

I had no use for the girls, but there were several ways I could use their mother.

Anna's sister shifted a step back, placing more distance between us. We waited for their mother to get the cookies out of the trunk of the car. Little Anna balanced ten boxes of Thin Mints in her arms as she carefully walked back to my door.

"Sir," the little girl said with pride, "your cookies."

I relieved her of her burden. My fingers skated across the buttery smoothness of her skin, and a shiver worked its way down my back. I straightened and waved to the girls' mother, raising my voice so she could hear me. "Thank you. I'm so happy you stopped by."

A light pattering of rain fell.

"You better hurry," I said to the girls. "You want to beat the rain."

The little Brownie flapped her hand goodbye. Her sister spun in a huff.

I needed to introduce myself to their mother.

The sky dumped rain, and I stayed under cover of the porch. The girls squealed as their mother waved them to the car.

Ah, another time then.

The girls ran down my sidewalk, screeching as rain saturated their clothes. I waved goodbye to their mother and closed my front door.

Thin Mints were best served cold, but I'd never been good at denying myself. I ripped open a pack and shoved two cookies into my mouth. My eyes closed when the minty chocolate melted on my tongue.

For a moment, I wondered if my princesses might appreciate the cookies, but they hadn't behaved today.

Treats had to be earned.

Lightning flashed, followed by peals of thunder that rattled the kitchen windows—time to get back to my princesses. The storm would make them uncomfortable and scared, and they depended on me to keep them safe.

The wind whipped through the street and hail bounced and skittered on the lawn. My attention shifted back to the kitchen counter where the morning paper rested. I re-read the headline for the hundredth time.

Stay of Execution Denied for Fairytale Killer

Today, the world would lose a great man, but I would carry on his work. He would find peace while I created a masterpiece.

I went to the door leading down to my basement. I opened it, walked through, and turned to fasten the lock behind me, checking to make sure it was secure.

One. Two. Three. Four. Five. Six.

There was another door at the bottom of the stairs. I hummed as I unlocked and then refastened this lock, counting out loud. "One. Two. Three. Four. Five. Six."

Through my basement and past the racks holding my wine collection, I hummed with anticipation. A third door was hidden from view behind the stacks of wine.

I checked the lock.

One. Two. Three. Four. Five. Six.

Best not to make a mistake.

He hadn't been so careful and would pay for that error with his life. That would never happen to me. I was too methodical and smarter than my mentor.

Satisfied all was well, I pushed aside the rack of wine to reveal the third door. This door had a combination lock, and I spun the dial six times then stepped into the tunnel.

The ceiling was low here, and I stooped to avoid hitting my head. The rich scents of earth and loam greeted me, and I breathed in deep. The musty smell reminded me of home. A long passage extended before me, years of work hacking a tunnel out of the dirt. Rough-hewn timbers braced the walls and ceiling. A string of bulbs lit the distance.

This was my slice of heaven, a kingdom for a prince, and his most precious possessions.

Six sacred obligations all modeled after the great work of my mentor.

The key in my pocket opened the last door with a soft snick of metal on metal. I flicked on the lights, and my dungeon greeted me with a welcoming glow and the whimpers of my princesses.

I straightened to my full height and stretched. Split roughly into thirds, the modified survival shelter held the king bed closest to the door. Eight cages occupied the middle third of the room, four on each side. I kept an open space in the back where I'd anchored chains into the stone wall and hung my toys against the wall.

Unlike the tunnel, I'd braced the insides of this room with metal sheeting and steel supports. While dirt was an excellent insulator, I'd nearly lost my first two princesses to hypothermia. I hadn't realized how cold they would get living underground.

I'd installed a raised wooden floor. And in addition to lights, I granted them the luxury of heat. How comfortable they remained depended on how well they behaved. They had their chamber pots, and a chore rotation to keep the place neat and tidy.

I swore I'd never again risk the health of my princesses because of my stupidity.

A princess was waiting for my return. I'd left her chained to the king-sized bed. But first, I needed to lock the door from the inside.

One. Two. Three. Four. Five. Six.

I sighed. We were once again whole: a prince and his princesses.

Cinderella should have greeted me with a smile, but she glared at me instead.

A muscle ticked in my jaw. "Is this how you greet your Prince Charming?" I slapped her face, leaving a red handprint.

Always the noisy one, Cinderella screamed.

My cock responded, throbbing with anticipation and thickening with need.

I slapped her again because it felt good.

Whimpers sounded from the cages, but I didn't spare a look for my other princesses. This was Cinderella's moment.

The others would serve when it was their turn.

Today, I celebrated the end of a great man's life. I would take my princesses in the same order He took his; a memorial of sorts to a man I admired.

Cinderella's brilliant blue eyes brimmed with tears and flicked to mine before jerking away. She knew better than to gaze upon my face. Her tears fell in fat juicy drops, speeding up my heartbeat and stiffening my aching cock. She struggled to hold back her sobs and failed.

I drank in her terror, letting it stoke my desires, feeding that primal need inside.

"Tsk, tsk," I chided. "You're a mess."

The tears had ruined her makeup.

I held a mirror to let her see how she'd smeared her lipstick and how her mascara had run.

Under the glow of the incandescent bulbs, black rivers streamed down her cheeks. That last slap smeared her ruby lipstick, and the smudge left a streak two shades brighter than the ones made by my palm.

Golden curls spilled over her shoulders and rested upon her bare breasts. I couldn't resist. I took her nipples and squeezed, drawing out a hiss from between her gritted teeth. The sound made my fingers dig into her soft flesh, where they left dark splotches on her pillowy breasts.

"Are you allowed to make a sound?"

We had been through this before. I was tired of repeating myself. Training was such a difficult task, but fortunately, I had plenty of patience.

"My Prince," she cried. "Forgive me."

My arousal throbbed. I had finished with the first princess less than an hour ago. The potency of my purpose settled in the ache of my balls. I'd taken medication to make sure I would be able to service all six before midnight struck.

"Remember, no teeth scraping my skin." I unfastened my pants.

Ah, I'd almost forgotten. Leaning to the side of the bed, I flicked on the video camera. My journey needed to be documented.

With a grip on her hair, I pulled her head forward. Her chains clinked and rattled.

Behind me, Red Riding Hood sobbed. I ignored her. She had been placed back in her cage after a satisfying beating. A sniffle came from Sleeping Beauty strapped in the corner. Goldilocks remained quiet, but then, I had gagged her. Gretel was still passed out in her cage. She had been the first I'd taken today. She'd fought my dominance, and I took her harder than I would have liked.

Belle, my beautiful Belle, shuffled in her cage. She remained quiet while I made use of Cinderella. Unlike the others, I didn't chain her when she was in her cage. She was the perfect princess and understood how to behave.

She'd been my first, but I would take her last.

Cinderella's delicious mouth sought my pleasure. My release gathered at the base of my spine, tickling my balls, then exploded outward in a rush. I crumpled over Cinderella as my vision dimmed. I hated it when I passed out.

I roused a minute or two later—my one flaw. I'd been teased about it before, but that never happened anymore.

Cinderella deserved a reward.

A legend died today, but I would carry on my mentor's torch. He thought my plan fitting and had given his blessing.

I would have my Queen.

FOUR

Pink Lace

MELISSA

Melissa's skull felt like it would explode. She dragged a hand to her temple, and a wet tangle of hair greeted her exploring fingers. She cracked an eyelid. Why is it dark? Where the hell am I?

Her ribs ached. Her left hip throbbed. And her arm…hurt. She groaned against biting pain.

"Shh…" An unfamiliar voice spoke. "You're safe."

Her vision adjusted to the dim light.

She remembered nothing.

Something crinkled over her body. Thin, but warm, she knocked it off, trying to sit up—wrong move. Pain lanced down her side, and a chill air brushed against her skin, making her shiver.

Light filtered through windows of a…car? How did she get in the back of a car?

A roaring of blood pounded past her ears, and she clamped her hand to her head as pain blossomed anew.

"Try not to move," the gentle voice said. "You might have a concussion, and I'm worried about your ribs. There was a tornado, but you're safe in a parking garage."

There was that crinkling noise again. A hand touched her shoulder.

"Don't touch me." She flinched.

"Darlin' calm down." The man's voice sounded warm and safe.

"Don't call me darling." She tried to scoot away, but overwhelming pain pulled her up short.

Scott had used that name. What was it with Southern men and the annoying habit of calling every woman darling? She wasn't some silly girl. She was a grown woman, strong and self-sufficient. She also found herself trapped in the back of a stranger's car with no memory of how she'd gotten there.

She wasn't as cold as she thought she should be, considering her clothes were soaked. Her toes squished in her five-toed running shoes, the only part of her body which didn't ache.

"Okay, what do you remember?" The man's deep voice filled the air with sultry tones.

The words dripped like liquid silk from his tongue, splashing over her, and exerting a calming influence. The thick drawl relaxed her as it filled the too-small space of the car with a pleasing warmth, which meant he was far too close.

The faintest scent of sandalwood, musk, and rain hung in the air. There was a click, and a light shined in her eyes. She flinched and cried out from the movement.

"Sorry," he said.

He turned the light on himself, revealing the sharp angular lines of a smooth, square jaw, a close-cropped military hairstyle, and brilliant blue eyes. He regarded her with intense interest. His eyes sparkled in the light, and his smile touched the edges of those baby-blues. Her heart may have stopped for the briefest moment, but then fear kicked back in, jolting her into a frenzy.

She scooched back, fighting the pain.

He reached for her. Prominent veins climbed the muscles of his forearm and twined around his bicep like vines on a tree.

"Charles James Rowan, Jr., at your service, ma'am, but my friends call me CJ. What's your name?"

She didn't take his hand. "Mr. Rowan, can you please explain what I'm doing in the back of your car?"

He winked. "Please, call me CJ. My father was Mr. Rowan. I never had a particular fondness for him."

She tried to sit—bad idea. A throbbing in her head came moments before a wave of dizziness. She hissed and settled for curling on her right side, which seemed to be the least offensive position.

"Whoa there. Don't move around like that."

"Why not?"

"Weren't you listening? You may have a concussion, and your side's all bruised up. As soon as it's safe, I'm taking you to a hospital."

"I don't remember anything."

"Don't worry; it'll come back to you."

"I must look a mess." Scott would be furious if he found her in the back of a car with another man. Wait, she didn't have to worry about him anymore, but she still felt wrong breaking a rule, and uncomfortable for not looking her best. Scott always insisted she put her best face to the public.

Another soft laugh warmed the surrounding air.

"I've seen worse messes. But I'd have to say; you make a drowned rat look positively stunning."

She closed her eyes and pressed her lips together. The man was honest to a fault.

"Gee, thanks."

"While we wait for the storm to pass, let's see if I can jog your memory. You were running…"

Yes, she'd been out running. Pieces of the morning came flooding back. The signed divorce papers making her once again single. Lightning followed by thunder. Rain, hail, and the greenest sky she'd ever seen. And finally, there had been a crack of lightning. She'd been thrown into the street. The screeching of tires was her last memory.

"Do you usually set out for a run in the middle of a thunderstorm?" he asked.

"Not my best decision."

His grin brought a smile to her face.

She watched him carefully. His attention never once wavered from her face. Most guys would have ogled her breasts by now. She'd always been self-conscious about the size of her breasts. She pulled the crinkly blanket tighter around her body.

"You said there was a tornado?"

He saved her from more than a lightning strike. She prayed her neighbors were safe. "How bad is the damage? Was anyone else hurt?" She clutched the blanket in her cold hands and shivered.

His lips pressed together. "I don't know. I scooped you off the pavement and raced into this garage."

"You saved me?" She sounded like a fool stating the obvious.

"Looked like you needed a helping hand." He gave her a wink, letting her know he was teasing.

What could she say to that? 'Thank you,' seemed trite.

"What kind of blanket is this, anyway? Feels like I'm wrapped in tin foil."

"It's an emergency blanket. You were shivering. I put my jacket over you, but it was soaked. I keep an emergency kit in my gear, although I've never used the blanket." Mischief sparkled in his eyes. "I figured it was better than the alternative."

"What was the alternative?"

"Sharing body heat."

"Oh…" That silenced any more questions.

He got out of the car.

"Where are you going?" She didn't want him to leave.

CJ chuckled. "I want to get to the street and call an ambulance." He paused for a second, his gaze turning to her chest. Leaning in, he extended his hand. "Here, let's get you out."

If she didn't move too fast, the throbbing in her head kept to a minimum. The entire left side of her body protested as she moved forward with CJ's help.

His strong hands gripped under her arms, and he pulled her free of the vehicle. He lifted her and placed her on the ground, where she weaved on unsteady legs and panted against the pain.

"I'm so cold."

He wrapped an arm around her waist and pulled her against his chest to steady her.

Into her ear, that honeyed voice murmured, "Give yourself a chance to get your balance. Head all right? Dizzy? Nauseous?"

She shook her head, causing a wave of dizziness to wash over her. She leaned against him and clutched at his forearm. "Um…dizzy. Definitely, dizzy."

He whispered words of comfort into her ear. "Take it slow. The dizziness will pass. We need to warm you up and get you out of these clothes. You're a popsicle."

"I'm fine," she said, but she leaned into him, loving the warmth of his body. He was dry as a bone while she was two shakes short of dripping wet.

"Fine my ass," he muttered. "Damn, I should have shared body heat."

The thought of him curling up to her sent a tingly sensation surging through her veins. Her entire body shook with the chills.

"Okay, we're getting you out of those wet clothes." He turned to a duffle bag resting against the rear tire and rummaged around inside. When he stood, he held a pair of black sweatpants in one hand and a shirt and sweatshirt in the other.

"No time for modesty." He came toward her looking like he would strip off her top.

"No way!" She clutched her arms across her body.

"Trust me." He set his lips into a determined line.

"I don't even know you."

His eyes crinkled. "Don't worry; I'm a trained paramedic. You have nothing I haven't seen a thousand times before. Now strip."

No way, but the grim set of his jaw told her he wouldn't be taking no for an answer. Fine, but she wouldn't let him undress her, except her left arm was stiff and didn't seem to want to work.

She twisted around, turning her back to him. That seemed to be the only modesty she'd be allowed.

CJ lifted her shirt, his warm fingers pressed against her cool skin. He raised the wet fabric over her head, even guiding her arms through the sleeves until she was left standing naked above the waist except for the pink lace of her running bra.

She was standing in front of the side mirror. It gave him a perfect view of her breasts.

He caught her gaze in the reflection and tipped his head. "I'm a professional, but I'm not dead." He lowered the shirt he'd pulled out of the duffle bag over her head.

The sleeves hung well past her fingers, and the hem brushed her knees. Shapeless, the shirt was warm and dry, much better than her wet running gear. Thankfully, the shirt was black, because the water from her bra seeped into the fabric.

CJ bent to his knees, his intent clear.

She stepped away. "Oh no. I can do this on my own. You go stand behind that pillar."

"No can do. You're swaying on your feet. I don't want you falling over. Besides, my shirt hangs down to your knees. I won't see anything you don't want me to see."

"Like my breasts?"

"Your breasts were covered by that lacy pink bra. Technically, I haven't seen them yet."

Yet? Did that mean he wanted to see them? And did she want him to? She was dizzy, but this time it was for a different reason. That reason stared up at her with sky-blue eyes from where he knelt on the ground.

"All right." She nodded, conceding he might be right.

His hands touched her outer thighs, and his fingers walked up beneath the shirt to the waistband of her tight running pants. He curled his fingers over the edge of the fabric and pulled the clingy spandex down over her hips. His shirt, as promised, kept her covered.

With CJ's help, she stepped out of her running pants. He covered her in reverse, helping her step into each leg of the black sweatpants and lifting the pants over her hips.

"Nice shoes," he commented. "Do you like running in them?"

"I only bought them a few months ago, but they're comfortable."

"Not many people like running in those." CJ stood, still gripping the top of the sweatpants in his hand. "Here, hold on to the waistband. My sweats are big on you."

She glanced at him. "Well, you have about a hundred pounds on me. How will they stay up?"

He lifted a belt. "With this, but I have to find my knife and poke a hole in it. Your waist is tiny. I bet I could wrap this around you twice."

Not true, but kind of him to say.

The belt bothered her, though.

She stiffened. During her marriage, she'd developed an aversion to a man holding a belt in his hands. One day, she wouldn't be plagued by memories of her soon to be dead husband—ex-husband.

And after today, Scott could no longer touch her. It would finally be over, and she could move forward with her life.

"I don't want to ruin your belt."

"Well, let's see. If you wouldn't mind lifting the shirt."

"You just want another peek at my bra." She teased him, then froze at the uncharacteristically forward comment.

"I wouldn't mind it." His comment heated her cheeks.

He wrapped the belt around her waist while she held the fabric of the shirt. He poked a hole to make the belt fit, and, despite what he said, it didn't wrap twice around her waist.

His calloused palm touched her bruised side. "This looks nasty. I'm worried there may be internal bleeding with the amount of bruising you have." He looked closer. "Seems to have spread."

"It's sore, but I'm okay."

"No, you're not."

Already, her body was warming up, and his clothes smelled incredible. She resisted the urge to pull the fabric close and sniff.

"Okay, let's call for that ambulance. I'll help you walk."

When they got to the street, the amount of damage outside surprised her.

The tornado had carved a path of destruction down Main Street, leaving wrecked cars and debris in its wake. Shattered glass and storefronts littered the street. They didn't see any people, but that wasn't a surprise. It was almost noon and a Sunday. Most people would've been at home, or worshipping at church.

"Tell me more about the tornado," she said with awe.

"Touched down moments after you launched yourself into the street."

"I didn't launch myself into the street. I was tossed."

"Launched or tossed, next time you want to get a man's attention, there are far safer ways."

She bit her lower lip, trying not to laugh. "I wasn't trying to get your attention. I was struck by lightning."

"Almost," he corrected. "If you'd been hit, we wouldn't be having this conversation."

On that sad note, he fished out his cell phone.

Filtered gray light shone down on the town. A faint gusting wind and a sprinkling of rain were all that remained of the massive storm.

A grim expression fixed his face. "A tornado hit the county hospital. They're diverting to St. John's in Clear Creek. All the ambulances are busy."

"That's over twenty miles away. Maybe you could just take me home? It's not far from here."

He shook his head. "No. You need to get checked out by a doctor. I'll drive you to Clear Creek. Car's a mess, but it might get us that far. Do you know how to get there?"

She did.

He went to collect the car, loaded her up, and took off down the street, following her directions. They had to swerve around debris. Driving over the smaller stuff had her gritting her teeth against the jarring vibrations.

A hundred questions flashed through her mind. He seemed attracted to her, and, for a moment, she wondered if he would be interested in seeing her again, but she shelved that thought.

While she'd been able to hide from most of the media blitz, Melissa Patterson was a tainted woman. Scott's infamy fouled her life, seeped into the cracks and crevices, and nothing could ever remove the stain he had left.

If CJ would have realized who she'd been married to, he'd have put her back on that road and let the tornado have her.

She wrapped her arms around her waist and gave herself the only hug she would ever get. For the thousandth time, she cursed Scott for ruining her life.

FIVE

Emergency

MELISSA

Saint John's Community Hospital buzzed with the disorganized chaos that followed a natural disaster. Melissa's knight in shining armor parked in the emergency parking lot and carried her inside the building. She hadn't protested, although she should have; there was something heartwarming about being carried in a strong man's arms. The last time that had happened she'd been wearing white—the color of innocence and the beginning of hell.

Thinking about Scott ruined the moment with CJ. In a poor attempt to reclaim it, she wrapped an arm around his neck and leaned against his shoulder. The steady rise and fall of his chest, the solid thump, thump, thump of his heart comforted her on a soul-healing level.

CJ's overprotectiveness touched her deeply. The attention he lavished on her made her feel special, but she worried about the inconvenience she was causing.

No one had been around the past three years to lean on, let alone hold her close. She basked in the warmth of this stranger's compassion, wishing for something more, yet knowing the moment was only a transient thing.

CJ barreled through the crowd in the lobby and strode up to the front desk where a woman managed the line of patients and soothed worried family members. The middle-aged woman's bun was lopsided on her head. Strands of hair worked their way free and stuck out in all directions. Bags drooped under her eyes as they pinched against the task of handling an overwhelming crowd.

The long line of patients gave CJ nasty looks.

"Victim of a near lightning strike." He spoke with an authoritative air. Like a man used to being in charge. "Concussive blast tossed her in the air."

The nurse gave him a hard look. "That's quite a story."

"She can't stand because she's dizzy, and she has bruising along her left side, which is getting worse. I'm worried about internal bleeding."

Bleeding? Surely he was being dramatic and trying to justify why he cut to the head of the line, but she did feel light-headed. And the room seemed to be spinning.

The nurse's eyes widened. "You're serious?"

He nodded. That sent the overworked nurse into action.

In less than a minute, the staff had Melissa stretched out on a gurney and whisked into a treatment room. CJ never left her side, except when they took her to get a CAT scan. He waited outside while technicians imaged her with practiced efficiency. They wheeled her back to the emergency room and said a doctor would be by soon.

Soon? She didn't believe that. Other people needing help inundated the emergency room.

A young doctor rushed in moments later. A wrinkled white coat covered even more rumpled scrubs. Deep furrows lined his face, and the bags under his eyes revealed more than stress.

He glanced at the chart. "Miss Doe? Is that your real name?"

"We didn't have time for paperwork," CJ answered.

"Ah." The doctor looked at Melissa.

She wasn't sure what her name was now. With the divorce papers signed, she guessed her maiden name would suffice. "Melissa Evans."

The doctor turned to CJ. "Well, Mr. Evans, your wife sustained a serious injury to her spleen. There are several cracked ribs and one that's broken on the left side. She needs surgery and might lose the spleen. Best case, the surgeons control the bleeding and leave the spleen intact. If all goes well, we'll keep her for a couple of days and do serial scans to make sure the bleeding is controlled." He barely looked up from his chart.

"And if she loses her spleen?"

"It will take longer."

Melissa stared at the doctor while he rattled off the extent of her injuries. She tried to process the information but failed. All she understood was something was wrong with her spleen. Even with the beatings, Scott had given her, she'd never needed surgery, and that bruising had been far worse than this.

CJ gripped her hand. Her attention turned to the heat of his touch.

"What about her head? I'm worried about a concussion. She's dizzy and has trouble with her balance."

She dropped her head onto the pillow and allowed her eyes to close. Exhaustion pulled at her, and she wanted nothing more than to sleep.

The doctor continued, speaking more to CJ than to her. Her mind focused on what CJ was doing with his thumb, drawing lazy circles over her inner wrist. Now that she was being taken care of, would he leave? Would she ever see him again? Asking for his phone number seemed too forward. Hell, the ink on her divorce papers was barely dry.

"There's evidence of a mild concussion." The doctor's voice droned in Melissa's head. "Considering she avoided the lightning, we should be thankful things aren't much worse. Gabby said you were near a twister?"

Melissa cracked open an eye. She didn't know a Gabby.

"Yeah." CJ let out a breath. "Out-raced one and took shelter in a parking garage. I never saw a tornado before and never want to go through that again. It was practically on top of us."

"Five twisters touched down around town. That's the most we've seen in over a decade. One took out County General."

The local hospital. Melissa sent a prayer for those caught in the path of that tornado.

The doctor continued. "Another wiped out a trailer park."

"Oh, that's horrible," CJ said.

CJ's concern for others warmed her heart. He kept stroking her arm, providing much-needed comfort. When she winced against the pain, he gripped her hand.

"Well, don't worry too much about your wife. We'll take good care of her."

Her gut twisted at the mention of wife, but Melissa caught CJ's wink and relaxed.

"She'll go to the surgical floor after surgery. You can wait for her there."

"Could you give us a moment?" CJ's touch raised goosebumps on her skin.

"Sure." The poor doctor looked worse than she felt.

CJ smoothed her hair. "See why I wanted to bring you to the hospital?"

"Thank you."

Surgery? Loss of her spleen? Concussion? Those frightened her, but she remained calm with CJ standing over her. She looked into his baby blues and caught him smiling.

Again.

His presence made her feel less alone.

"I never said thank you…for saving me." She managed a pathetic thank you. "You're very courageous."

He smirked. "What was I going to do? Leave you in the street like a fried and drowned rat?"

She laughed and then splinted against the pain. "Poor rat. Glad you decided to help."

He brushed the hair off her forehead. "Like there was ever a question." He gave another of his infuriating winks.

She switched subjects, afraid to take the tenderness of the moment further.

"You told him I was your wife."

He rubbed the back of his neck. "Hospitals are particular about sharing medical information with non-family members. I didn't want to get kicked out until I knew they were taking care of you. They assumed—"

"And you didn't correct them." She should have been upset but found herself more amused than irritated.

He leaned down and kissed her forehead. His lips were soft and gentle, and oh so wonderful. What would those lips feel like against her mouth? For a moment, she thought she might find out, but he shifted to place a second kiss on her cheek.

"It's been a real pleasure, Mrs. Evans."

She put her left hand on his forearm. "Thank you. I owe you my life." The words 'Will I see you again?' waited on her lips, but she held them back.

He stared at her hand, then turned toward the door. She'd hoped he might stay, but he spoke the words which ended everything. "I have to go. I'm supposed to be somewhere else."

"Thank you." She struggled with her feelings, straining to keep them from showing, but did he have to leave?

This time he brushed his lips over hers. "Take care of yourself, Melissa."

Her last moments with CJ passed in the blink of an eye. First, he was lightly brushing her lips with a kiss that wasn't a kiss, and then he was gone.

She ran a finger over the spot where his thumb had drawn circles on her inner wrist. His touch lingered there, and she swore she could feel the heat of his skin.

Her wedding ring flashed in the harsh glare of the fluorescent lights. The three-carat diamond sparkled with a brittle light.

He had called her Mrs. Evans.

Oh no!

She tugged at the ring, but the damn thing wouldn't slide over the swelling of her knuckle. Why had she never taken it off? She was still struggling when a technician came to take her to surgery.

Maybe that's why CJ had left. If she'd learned anything about him in their brief time together, he was a gentleman. Now, she had no way of finding him to explain she no longer belonged to any man, let alone a serial killer.

SIX

A Superhero

CJ

CJ LEFT SAINT JOHN'S EMERGENCY DEPARTMENT. ONE GOOD DEED down. If Melissa Evans hadn't been married, he would have asked for her number. They'd connected. He hadn't misread the vibe between them. But she was married, and he respected that.

Shame, he'd never see the pretty jogger again.

A truck came to a screeching halt in front of the emergency department, nearly running CJ over.

"Help! I need help!" A man hopped out of the beat-up truck.

"What's up?" Years of training kicked in. CJ didn't even question his actions.

"In the back." The man flailed his arms.

Blood saturated the man's shirt, and a nasty wound on his neck oozed. Adrenaline was probably the only thing keeping him upright, but he didn't seem concerned about his injuries.

Wide eyes and a crazy stare spoke to the man's fear, and he looked to be in the early stages of shock.

CJ moved to the side and looked in the bed of the truck.

Holy crap!

He flipped down the tailgate and jumped inside.

A woman about six or seven months pregnant laid beside a hunting dog. A metal rod pinned the dog and woman to a large chunk of wood. It looked like the side of a barn. With a whimper, the dog's tail wiggled when it smelled CJ. One arm of the U-shaped metal rod had been shoved through its leg and had trapped the dog to the wood planking. The other end of the rod punctured the woman's shoulder. CJ couldn't tell if the piece of metal had gone through muscle or had pierced her lung.

He felt for the woman's pulse. Thready, but present. She was breathing, but unresponsive.

A horrific scene of the woman and dog trying to outrun a tornado flashed through his mind.

"Easy boy." He stroked the dog's muzzle, letting the animal smell him.

If the dog moved, it might worsen the woman's injuries.

It whined and beat its tail. The poor thing tried to lick his hand but couldn't lift its head.

How the man loaded his wife and dog into the back of the truck amazed CJ. The man's wounds, cuts, scrapes, and gouges down to muscle were as severe as the woman's.

CJ attempted to reassure the man. "She's breathing."

The labored rise and fall of the woman's chest said she didn't have much time.

"Oh thank you, Jesus." The man swayed on his feet. "And the dog?"

Country boy was going to pass out any minute.

"Get help." When the man didn't move, CJ added. "The dog's okay."

His command proved unnecessary because emergency personnel spilled out of the entrance, running to the truck. Someone inside had been watching. Overwhelmed perhaps, but this staff was kicking ass.

CJ pointed to the man, worried he'd be overlooked once they saw the pregnant woman. "Someone take care of him before he collapses." For good measure, he added, "You're going to need a lot more help than that." How far was the nearest vet?

A nurse in purple scrubs gave him a strange look and then instructed the others what to do.

A man in green scrubs gathered the husband into a wheelchair and bustled him inside. The nurse pinched her lips when she saw the gory scene of the woman and dog. She had to have previous military experience or trauma training because she didn't seem shocked by the extent of the woman's injuries. Small hospitals didn't see this kind of trauma. She pressed her fists to her hips and took in the scene.

CJ read her identification badge.

Florence Reynolds was a doctor, not a nurse.

His training kicked in, and CJ gave his report. "She's breathing, and her pulse is thready…weak. Can't tell if the rod is in muscle or pierced her lung. Breathing is labored, and she's unresponsive."

"You know them?" Doctor Reynolds jumped into the bed of the truck.

The pregnant woman moaned.

"No. I was leaving when he pulled up."

"You a paramedic?"

"Yeah." That was but one piece of his particular skill set. As an ex-Green Beret and Delta operative, it served him well in the military. As Guardian, it continued to prove useful.

She eyed him. Legally, she shouldn't allow him to touch her patient, but the emergency room was overrun. She nodded as if deciding her next move.

"Okay, Mister?"

"Rowans. CJ Rowans."

"Mr. Rowans, are you willing to help me get her out of this truck?"

"Yes, ma'am."

"Good." She signaled to her staff who had brought out two gurneys and an orange bag of medical supplies. "We need to move them as a unit and deal with separating them later."

This woman knew her stuff. He breathed out a sigh of relief.

"Get to the front and push while my team pulls them onto the gurney. What the hell are they stuck to?"

"I think it's siding from a barn." He moved into position.

Four staff members waited with the gurneys. Dr. Reynolds checked vitals on the pregnant woman, and the dog then jumped down. It took more work to get the pregnant woman and her dog out of the truck than he'd anticipated

"Thank you, sir. We've got it from here." Dr. Reynolds stuck out her hand to CJ.

"My pleasure."

"Can you move the truck?" she asked. "Park it in the lot and drop the keys at the desk?"

"I'll take care of it. What about the dog?"

Dr. Reynolds cracked a smile. "Don't worry about the dog. I'll make sure he's taken care of."

He moved the truck, turned in the keys, and went to see if his hotel had survived the storms. Before heading to the prison, he wanted to wash and change clothes.

He'd thought of little else in the past three years. He needed to be there when the last breath left Scott Patterson's body. The bastard deserved worse than death, but CJ would take death by lethal injection.

As he searched for his hotel, his thoughts wandered back to the brunette with the mismatched running gear and lacy pink bra.

If he didn't have to be at the prison, he would've stayed.

Overhead, deep blue skies looked down on him; the calm after the storm freaked him out. Some parts of town had been scoured off the face of the earth while other sections remained untouched.

He stopped three times to help others in distress before pulling into the hotel parking lot. It had survived without a scratch. As he grabbed his gear out of the back, a cell phone rang.

Not his.

Looking for the source of noise, he found a phone in the back of the car. It must have fallen out of Melissa's pocket, although he had seen nothing resembling pockets in her tight running gear.

An unregistered number flashed on the screen. The phone rang six times before the person on the other end gave up. Maybe it went voice message? Less than a minute later, the phone chimed again—same number. Persistent caller.

It might be a family member looking for Melissa, or the husband—lucky bastard.

He pressed the button to accept the call. "Hello?"

"Hello—Hey! Who the fuck is this?" An angry voice rasped. "Where's Sissy?"

"Sorry dude, you have the wrong number."

"This is Melissa's cell. I know my wife's phone number."

CJ frowned. "Melissa Evans?" The man's voice sounded familiar, but CJ couldn't place where he may have heard it.

"Evans my ass," the bastard on the other end said. "You tell my wife to keep her fucking legs shut. Or I swear I'll shut her legs myself. I don't care what she told you, she's mine. Do you hear? That bitch belongs to me!"

"I don't like your tone of voice." No man should speak about his wife with such disrespect.

"She better not be fucking you."

The guy was crazy.

"I met your wife today."

"Then why the fuck are you answering her phone?"

"Because, I dropped her off at Saint John's. She's having emergency surgery. I suggest you settle down before visiting her."

How did a pretty woman get involved with such an ass? If this guy could be abusive to a stranger, what was he capable of behind closed doors?

"Like that's fucking possible, asshole. How do I know you're not lying?"

"You don't." CJ fisted the phone until his knuckles turned white. He regretted telling the bastard Melissa was in the hospital.

"This conversation is over."

A string of profanity ripped through the phone, colorful in its depth and breadth.

Maybe he should get back to Melissa's bedside and stand guard against this creep?

SEVEN

Let's Play

PIERCE

THE PARK BUBBLED WITH THE NOISY CRIES OF CHILDREN, SQUEAKING and squealing as they clambered up, over, and around the playground equipment. My ears hurt listening to them.

This part of the town fared well after the severe weather from the previous day. There were a few fallen branches, but nothing serious. Even the playground equipment and surrounding grass were nearly dry. Overhead, the sky shimmered with a deep blue.

Watchful mothers parked themselves on benches, minding strollers, purses, and the ever-necessary stash of kiddie box drinks and baggies of Cheerios.

Thank God I never spawned a tiny human. They were, as a group, a waste of breath.

Ignoring the children at play, I considered my approach. I'd stolen a yippy dog, Terrier or Scottie. I didn't know and didn't care. He was sniffing my pocket, where I'd stashed treats to entice him. At least he wasn't sniffing my crotch. The dog was a tool, and I'd let the little mutt go when I was through. He yipped again, and I decided to call him Yip for the day.

It had taken time to track down the little girls who'd come to my door. An Internet search for local Girl Scout troops led me right to their home page.

Idiots.

They had nothing secure on their page. I clicked right through their password protection and found and opened the file with their home addresses.

I'd been surprised they didn't live close by. Those girls had one determined mother. I could only imagine what would push a mother to drag her daughters all over town selling cookies. But I liked it. I loved her ambition. It promised much in the days to come.

I turned my attention to the playground and the kids running amuck.

The little Brownie's sickly-sweet laughter floated through the air. And her curls bounced every time she skipped or ran.

Her older sister, the one carrying the frown, chased little Anna. Despite the twist in that girl's lips, she looked lovely with her long, flowing hair. Sunlight glinted off the straw-colored tresses, beckoning my fingers to comb through that perfection, to pull, to twist…to yank until her frightened eyes widened for me.

But, I wasn't here for the girl. I wanted the mother.

Anna squealed as her sister chased her down the slide. She ran around the monkey bars, trying to get away.

Our eyes met, and my heart leaped at the flash of recognition. But then her sister caught up to Anna, tagging her, and then Anna was off at a run; her turn to chase.

Across the playground, their mother sat on a park bench with a book propped in her hands. She pretended to read, but her eyes followed every movement of her children at play.

I sauntered over, taking my time. Yip led with his nose, smelling everything and lifting his leg along the way to mark territory he would never own.

The method of my approach mattered, and I had planned every detail. I wanted this woman to join my collection very much.

She wasn't a beautiful woman by conventional standards, but she wasn't ugly either. Her hair glistened in the bright noonday sun, two shades darker than that of her children. Her broad nose didn't fit the delicate features of her heart-shaped face, but the brilliance of her eyes balanced everything out.

And the way she adored her children made my heart ache, but I wanted her gaze for myself. With practice and training, she would worship me.

I stopped at the opposite end of her bench, keeping a stranger's distance, and gave her a friendly smile when the dog licked at her shins. She didn't recognize me. I reeled the pooch in. Yip danced at the end of the leash, eager to explore the world.

Putting my foot on the bench, I retied the laces of my shoe, then reached into my pocket, pretending my cell phone had gone off. I pressed the phone to my ear. With another easy smile, I turned my back and sat on the edge of the park bench.

The dog jumped onto the bench, barking and sniffing the air. I scratched his neck while I palmed the phone to my ear.

I twisted around to face forward, pretending I was listening hard to whoever had called. This way, I could see her reaction out of the corner of my eye.

For the next few minutes, I carried on a conversation with myself and made sure she heard every word.

"Chrissy, stop." I shook my head and put a concerned expression on my face.

The mother didn't move away, but she watched me with a wary eye. I didn't blame her. If I were a woman, I'd be suspicious if a strange man sat next to me at the park, especially one with no children of his own. But I had the dog, and I relaxed his lead.

She reached out to let the mutt sniff her hand while I ignored her.

I continued my fake conversation. "No, you'll be okay. They got the guy. He's not getting out. Not for a long, long time." I shifted, pulling the dog to my side. I gave a silent apology for my dog's misbehavior. In front of us, Anna and her sister carried on their game of tag, recruiting two other children into the fray.

"Come to my classes, Chrissy. You know I'm the best. I'll teach you everything you need to know. I'll even give you a discount if you come tonight."

My gaze met the mother's beautiful blue eyes. I shifted away as if I was trying to keep my conversation private. I even covered the phone and lowered my voice, but my whisper was loud enough. She could still hear.

"Yes, you can bring your friends. Self-defense training is the most important skill a young woman can have."

I pivoted so the mother could see more of my face. So far, there still had been no hint of recognition. You would think a man who gave an extra fifty dollars for Girl Scout cookies would leave an impression—thankless bitch.

Yip licked her palm, and now she was scratching the top of his head.

I interjected appropriate pauses into my conversation. I needed to make it look like I was listening to Chrissy on the other end, just as I made sure the woman sitting next to me heard every word I said.

"You can't learn to defend yourself overnight. It takes hard work and dedication."

The mother's eyes widened, and she leaned forward the tiniest bit, cocking her head to hear—nosey, but good for me. Curiosity killed the cat, but I had no intention of taking this woman's life. Lucky for her, I wasn't like Him.

I don't remember what I said next. Chrissy wasn't real, but the mother was, and I had her attention. By the time I finished my fake conversation with fake Chrissy, all of the mother's unease from having a stranger share her bench would have dissipated.

Time to reel her in. I gave the dog enough leash, and Yip crawled into her lap.

Seriously, women made it too easy.

Anna came racing out from under the slide, screaming at the top of her lungs, laughing as a little boy gave chase. She made a beeline for her mother.

"Sss…safe!" My little Brownie stuck her tongue out at her pursuer. "Oh, look at the doggy!" she squealed.

"Only babies run to their mommies." The boy pinched Anna's arm.

"Ow!" Anna rubbed at her arm and kicked the boy. "I'm not a baby."

Her mother yanked Anna away before the boy could retaliate.

I couldn't have asked for a better introduction if I'd coached the little monster myself. To my delight, he reached out and pulled one of Anna's curls.

Before her mother could react, I stood, using my height to intimate the little snot.

"Young man, that's no way to treat a lady."

Yip emphasized my point with a bark.

My scolding had the boy's eyes widening.

I made sure I didn't touch him, but I had a performance to deliver. I exchanged a look with Anna's mother and shook my head. "Where is your mother, young man?"

My demand made the poor little boy look like he would jump out of his skin. Every time the dog barked, he flinched. His face paled, but then he fisted his chubby fingers and puffed out his tiny chest. At that moment, I respected him.

His chubby finger pointed at Anna. "She's a cheater, and she's a girl, not a lady." He pressed his fists to his hips and stared at me with indignation. The little growler would grow up into an asshole.

"You pinched me." My Brownie whined and rubbed at the pink spot on her arm.

"Now children," the mother soothed. She gave me one of those knowing looks adults use around children. "We need to use our words and not our hands."

I let Anna's mother lecture the children and sat; this time a little closer. She worked the magic only a female can accomplish with children. Within a few moments, everyone was friends again.

Anna hopped off the bench. She pointed at me. "Don't I know you, mister?"

My heart fluttered in my chest. I encouraged her with my voice, pitching it two octaves above my usual tenor. "I'm not sure." I tried to sound unsure, non-threatening.

Anna tugged on her mom's sleeve. "Mommy, he's the one who gave us the fifties. The nice man. He bought the cookies!"

Anna bounced to her feet. She launched herself into my lap, hugged me, and then jumped back to the ground. I was still enough of a stranger for her to keep the physical contact brief.

"Kids?" I turned to my prey with a shrug and a disarming smile.

Theater class and the drama club had always intrigued me in high school, and I'd studied enough about acting to make this work. I lifted my finger and pointed to Anna. "Why yes, I remember you now." I let a trace of surprise lace my words. "You're that little Brownie who came to my door."

Anna jumped up and down, clasping her hands in front of her chest…a very flat, pre-pubescent, and boring chest. "Yes! Yes! You bought cookies."

"Didn't you have a sister with you?"

Anna pointed to the playground. "Angela's playing hopscotch."

"Well, you tell her hello for me. I loved my cookies. I ate them all up."

"You shouldn't eat cookies all at once." The expression on Anna's face made me smile. "It makes your tummy hurt. That's what Mommy says, and she knows everything."

Her words had me laughing. I turned to her mother, who gave me a children-will-say-the-darndest-things expression. "I know, but I was never good at following rules."

Anna giggled and ran to the playground. Her interest in me had run its course. She'd even ignored the dog. A moment of silence passed between her mother and me, punctuated by the mutt's sniffing sounds.

Her mother cleared her throat. "I'm sorry about Anna. She can be precocious." Her cheeks flushed as she stared at me.

I gave her my best Prince Charming grin and watched a spreading blush fill her cheeks. "Well, at least she listens to what you say. But, you may need to speak with her about stranger-danger." I gestured, referring to the hug Anna gave me.

The woman gave a nervous smile, and then silence befell us again. I wondered how long it would take before she broke it.

In less than a minute, she turned toward me. "So, is Anna right? Are you the one who gave my girls extra money?"

I nodded. "I'm a sucker for Girl Scout cookies."

"It was very generous of you."

"Well, I remember how hard it is to sell the dang things."

She took a moment and then made the wrong assumption. "Your daughter sells Girl Scout cookies?"

"No, my sister did." I let her assume my sister no longer did because she'd grown up. "I thought the girls didn't go door-to-door anymore?"

Her lips pinched. "They're not supposed to, but I always buy a bunch extra. I like to contribute to the troop. The girls get merit badges and prizes if they reach a certain level of sales."

She leaned back. Her attention no longer focused on her children.

"Maybe I should stop? I tire of walking the neighborhoods with them, and then I'm nervous when they knock on the doors. I mean, you never know who will answer. Or if they'll be safe."

I laughed. "Well, that's why I can't help buying them." I leaned back, mirroring her movements, and laced my fingers behind my neck. "Some moms just let their kids go. They don't watch over them." My mother had failed in that sacred task.

"They want to go out on their own, but I won't let them. I don't want to be a mother hen, but I worry. I let them go to the doors on their own, but I watch from the street."

"Yes, I remember my mother watching my sister."

"Right. What does your sister do now? Is she still involved in the Girl Scouts?"

I turned to the woman, leaning an inch or two closer, and made ready to sing my sob story. I even had a tear or two ready.

"No. My sister died. She wasn't much older than Anna when it happened." An over-share, but I had her full attention now.

"Oh my." Her hand flew up and covered her mouth. "I'm sorry."

As I weaved my story, I reeled her in like an expert fisherman. She had an odd name, Henrietta. Too old for her, it reminded me of my grandmother. It would be the first thing I changed.

I turned the subject from my kid sister's death to something more cheerful, like how incredible Thin Mints tasted and how they reminded me of my sister.

Our words danced in the air as we traded life stories. I learned more than I cared about her two little girls, the father who died fighting for freedom in the desert, and her plans. I tried not to stare at her breasts too much, but they were plump and begging to be squeezed. She pretended not to notice, just as I pretended not to stare.

With her long blonde hair, brilliant blue eyes, and rosebud lips, this woman would have made a wonderful princess a decade ago. Fortunately, I didn't need a princess. She would fill a different role.

Henrietta would be our Fairy Godmother, and I would give her a gilded cage. Her hands would fit in the spare set of steel cuffs in my chest. I knew how I would bind her and how I would take her our first time together.

A Fairy Godmother would soothe my princesses' fears. I shifted on the park bench, hiding my growing arousal from Henrietta's observant eyes. She'd given me her name and sealed her fate when she brushed lint off my shoulder.

Henrietta continued to watch her precious girls play chase, but her gaze kept turning back to me.

I gave her my best smile. "It has been such a pleasure meeting you…again, but I must go. I only get so much time off from work. And, I need to get Yip home."

Her expression fell to a frown. That made my heart leap with joy.

"It was nice chatting with you."

What a perfect day; the longing in her voice was brilliant. I placed my hand on her knee and paid close attention to her reaction. When she didn't pull away, I gave it a slight squeeze.

"If you still have some of those Girl Scout cookies…" I winked, and her cheeks flushed again. "You could bring them over. I wasn't lying when I told your daughter I ate them all."

Henrietta waved her hand in a dismissive gesture. She had yet to pull away from my hand, resting on her knee. "Well, Anna was just say—"

"She was just repeating what any good mother would tell her child." I lifted my brows with mischief. "But, you and I are adults. We don't have to listen to our mothers anymore. One perk of being a grownup is we can be as good or as bad as we want."

She laughed. "Well." She hesitated, then continued, her voice husky and sinfully seductive. "That's true."

I almost had her, and the anticipation had me leaning closer than I should, but I couldn't help it. "If you can't come over, I understand, but I would like a chance to get to know you better." I removed my hand from her leg and smiled at her surprised expression.

"Oh, I can bring some by." Her lashes fluttered. "I'm sorry, but I don't remember where you live."

I gave her the address.

"The girls get off school at three. We can stop by after that?"

I shook my head. "I'm sorry, but I work the graveyard shift at a garden center, and I'm asleep by then."

"A nursery has a graveyard shift?"

"It's a large operation, and most of the prep work and arranging is left to the night crew. I work in the floral department. I deliver, too." Women were suckers for flowers.

A beautiful play of expressions paraded across her delicate features as she considered her options.

I loved it when they came willingly. It made the surprise so much more delectable when they realized they'd delivered themselves into my hands.

Henrietta glanced at me, looking through her lashes. "I could come sooner? But the girls won't be able to give you the cookies themselves."

I gave half a laugh. "Henrietta, as darling as your children are, I'm much more interested in getting to know you."

I stressed the word 'know.' Henrietta knew what she was coming over for, and it wasn't to deliver cookies.

"Lunch at ten?" My question hovered in the air between us, and my pulse quickened, waiting for her reply.

Her eyes flicked to mine. I was thrilled to see a banked heat smoldering in their depths.

How perfect of a day was this for me? A mother and a widow?

She said it had been a year since GI Dickhead's death. It might be fun to take her in my bed before bringing her to join my princesses. She would live with the knowledge she'd given herself freely for the rest of her life.

In my head, I'd already fucked her in every way imaginable. My pants were so tight that my cock ached to be free—time to wrap this up.

"Are you offering to cook for me?" She was such an idiot.

"I'm a fabulous cook."

She bit her lower lip, considering my offer of food and sex.

I leaned over and pecked her cheek. "I'll expect you at ten... tomorrow? Bring Thin Mints for dessert."

Her hand flew to her cheek, cupping the spot where my lips touched her skin. She bowed her head, and her lashes fluttered again.

Before she could consider backing out, I was off the bench, careful to turn my body to hide my arousal. "It's a date."

She nodded but didn't look up. "Y-yes. Tomorrow."

The resolve in her tone sent shudders through my spine.

Tomorrow I would add a Fairy Godmother to my collection. All that remained was collecting my Queen.

EIGHT

Broken Towers

CJ

When CJ arrived at the prison, the string of expletives streaming from his mouth would have made a sailor proud.

The triple fencing surrounding the front, and one side of the massive structure, was missing. A swath of destruction a hundred yards wide marred the ground for half a mile. Aiming straight as an arrow, trees, grass, and the top layer of soil had all been scoured from the earth.

Bits and pieces of twisted metal littered the area; parts of cars and other wreckage were vaguely recognizable. A bumper lay crumpled in the arms of a tree. A car's hood folded itself around a telephone pole. There was even one car, a little Fiat, perched on top of an old oak tree. The majestic giant had weathered the storm well, with only a few splintered branches beneath the car decorating its canopy. In the parking lot, several cars lay on their sides. A few rested on their roofs, and their tires pointed to the sun.

All around, diligent guards stood watch, weapons ready, while other men in dirty orange jumpers stacked debris into piles. A forklift moved shredded lengths of fencing. A bulldozer growled at the edge of a field, stacking twisted metal into a massive heap.

This bullshit had better not fuck with the execution.

He'd taken time off from the Guardians, pulled himself off an active case to be here. It meant leaving Delta Team in the capable hands of his second in command, Jenny, a feisty woman climbing the ranks within Guardian HRS. She had her eye on his command and would probably get it soon. Jenny's ambitions aside, if that bastard still pulled breath by the end of the day, CJ would have words with someone.

He pulled up to the gatehouse. The small structure stood untouched despite the devastation less than ten feet away. The guard, a massive Black man, raised a hand and held his palm out, commanding CJ to stop. He lowered the driver's side window, an unnecessary move considering he no longer had a front windshield.

"Sorry, no visitors." The guard rested a hand on his weapon while his gaze took in CJ and the damage to his car.

"I'm not here to visit. I'm here for the execution." And he would be late if this guy didn't get a move on. He had to check in by five for the six o'clock execution.

The guard rubbed a hand over the back of his neck. "Family or press?"

"Family." Thoughts of his sister flitted in his head. Her laughter. Her smiles. The touches of her anger when he didn't let her have her way. All of it was gone.

"I see." The guard twisted his mouth. "I've got bad news."

"Bad news?" CJ pounded the steering wheel. The guy better not say it. His blood heated with anger and frustration pulled at his chest. He gripped the steering wheel and tried to calm himself before he said something stupid.

The guard spit on the ground. "Been postponed."

"Postponed?" He closed his eyes and counted to three.

The guard placed his free hand on the doorframe of CJ's car and leaned in. "I'm sorry, but…"

"Did the bastard get a stay of execution from the Governor?"

"No."

"Will it be rescheduled?"

The guard waved at the destruction around the prison. "Twister took down all the power lines. Hit one of our backup generators. Warden had to delay it."

CJ's knuckles turned white, and his teeth ached from clenching his jaw. There was a strange quiver in his gut, an unsettled feeling twisting him from the inside out.

The guard looked unsure. "Don't think this kind of thing happens too often. Might be considered an act of God. If that's the case, then…"

"Acts of God don't cancel executions, at least not anymore. So what do I do now?"

He'd taken off a week from work. One day to drive to this godforsaken town. One to witness the execution. Two days to drive to his sister's grave and pay his respects. Two days to drive back. The final day was for him, time to de-stress before returning to the rigors of his job as a Guardian.

"Don't know, except I've been told to tell all the family and reporters of the delay. Someone will be in contact with you." The guard pointed to a TV news crew setting up their satellite antenna. "Those bastards aren't upset by the delay. Twister taking out a state prison is just as good of news as an execution."

CJ gave the guy a non-committal grunt.

"Looks like you saw action." The guard gave a pointed look to the missing windshield.

"Hail," CJ said.

The guard's brows drew together. "Looks like more than hail." The guard huffed a low laugh. He gave the poor SUV a once-over with his eyes. "I thought we had it bad. Looks like you did, too."

With a sharp nod, CJ answered. "Hid in a parking garage."

"Then you know what it was like?"

The guard pointed to a tower at the corner of the field. Huge chunks of the brick walls were missing as if someone had taken a bite out of the stone. The roof was gone.

"I was in that tower when the twister hit. Ducked into the stairwell. It sucked up the roof like it was candy. Almost took my buddy Randy, but Abel and I held onto him."

"Held him?" How could two men hold a man during a twister?

"Twister tried to suck him into the sky. Dude, you cannot imagine…" The guy's gaze traveled along CJ's rented SUV. "Well, maybe you can. About shit my pants. Randy pissed his, but I guess when you're saying goodbye to your life, that's allowed."

"Randy's lucky."

"Not quite. Popped both of his shoulders out of their sockets as we held onto him. And his legs got shredded by the debris. Sent him to Saint John's. Heard they're busy."

"They are."

His mind turned to Melissa. She should be in surgery by now. Who'd be there when she woke? Would that bastard at the other end of her phone hurt her? Or would she wake to an empty room, afraid and alone? God, he felt like such an ass for leaving.

The guard continued to ramble. "Yeah. We grabbed Randy's arms and just held on. Longest twenty seconds of my life."

Twenty seconds?

"You counted?"

The guard shrugged. "Guessing. Seemed like forever."

With an easy-going attitude, the guard was hard to shut up. CJ didn't like the way the guard's finger kept tapping the trigger guard of his weapon. He'd seen plenty of men like that. The stress of a traumatic event made them jumpy and dangerous.

It was time to leave, except his senses screamed something wasn't right.

The one thing his time in the Army had taught him was to listen to his gut. He wasn't a superstitious guy, but you didn't live long in his line of work if you ignored your Spidey-sense. And, his was yelling in his ear.

He glanced at the damage done to the tower. "Did it cause any damage to the prison?"

The guard paused a beat too long before answering. "Nothing…serious."

CJ didn't like the hesitation in the guard's voice or the way his eyes had cut to the high-security area. Something was up.

His vision clarified, narrowing down to one small point. He pulled in a breath, held it, and then slowly let it out. This feeling, he knew all too well.

More information was required, but this guy wasn't going to let him dig around a prison in chaos. What he needed was best done over drinks.

He read the name tag on the guard's uniform. "Officer Reynolds, how long have you been on shift? You look like crap."

"Been here since night shift began."

With a low whistle, CJ struggled to find something to say.

Chatty Reynolds made things easy. "My shift was ending when that storm blew through. Couldn't leave, and now I have to wait for relief. National Guard is on its way. As soon as they get here, I'm heading for a drink."

"Do you know Grady's pub back in town?" CJ couldn't have asked for a better lead-in.

"Heck yeah, best pub in town. The only place that serves beer in the morning. Me and the guys usually unwind there after our shift."

"Well, Grady's is still standing. Why don't you and your buddies stop by when you get off? I'll buy a round, as thanks for what you're doing here." He leaned forward, making a show of looking around. "You know, if you need an extra hand, I've got experience."

"Prison's on lockdown," Reynolds said with a shake of his head. "Go back to your hotel, and someone will get in contact with you."

"How about that drink?" Damn, he wanted to poke around the prison, and see what had everyone on edge.

"After the day I've had? Shit, that sounds damn fine." Reggie glanced up the road, and a broad smile lit his face. He pointed to a convoy packed with National Guardsmen. "Looks like the cavalry has arrived."

"Well, there you go, Officer Reynolds."

"Shit, call me Eggs, everyone does."

CJ nodded. "Charles Rowan, Jr, and my friends call me CJ."

"Cool. Don't know how long this song and dance will last CJ, but I'll be there for drinks for sure."

"Like I said, first round's on me." CJ's eyes narrowed as he watched the trucks approach. That was more than a little help. Something was up.

CJ pulled forward until he could turn his car around. The men in the convoy looked serious, grim expressions were plastered on their faces. They were kitted out too, with bullet-proof vests and weapons. Ten trucks were a significant force, more than should be required to guard a prison—even when the outer fencing had been ripped to shreds.

Noting the small things kept him alive. It's what made him an excellent Green Beret. It's how he got recruited as a Delta operative, the most elite force in the military. Eggs' hesitation, and the too many National Guardsmen, were both questions he'd have the answers to after buying Eggs and his friends a couple of rounds of beer. In particular, he wanted to know what was up with the high-security area.

Shared tragedy, heroism, and plenty of booze loosened men's tongues. Fortunately, he had the perfect story to share.

NINE

Yellow Lace

PIERCE

MY FAIRY GODMOTHER ARRIVED AT MY PLACE AT 10 AM. I PEERED through the slats of my kitchen blinds and watched her approach. Henrietta hesitated, glanced back at the street, and then back toward the house. I guess she was deciding whether to go through with our rendezvous. The brave woman clutched a box of Thin Mints in her delicate hands.

Henrietta wore a lacy yellow dress. Prim and pretty, it wasn't something a woman wore when she intended to have sex.

That worried me. I didn't want to force our first time together. That would come later. Hmm, I had an idea.

Her yellow heels gave her some trouble on the uneven walkway, but she came to me with a determined stride.

Excitement itched along my skin as I watched through my kitchen window.

My preparations were in order. The kitchen was spotless, except for what I had set out for lunch. Through the archway, the living room was neat and tidy. The loveseat stood ready and welcoming, with throw pillows and a soft cover-up. I'd piled the two wingback chairs full of books. We were to sit together, not apart. I had even changed the sheets on my bed. It would be the first and last consideration I gave Henrietta.

I'd hidden a video camera in the spine of one of the books. I had it primed where all I had to do was hit one button. Afterward, I'd make her watch the video over and over again. I intended to keep it looping beside her cage—a constant reminder of her willing participation and how eagerly she'd given herself to me.

Energy sizzled through my body, making me jump when a hesitant knock sounded on the door.

My heart hammered beneath my breastbone. I was so excited to welcome her home.

I didn't answer.

The silence stretched until she knocked again. Pressing my forehead against the door, I stared through the keyhole.

She was damned adorable chewing on her lower lip. I waited until she raised her hand to knock a third time and then pulled the door open.

I took her raised hand and kissed it.

The richness of her scent, light and floral, had me grinning ear to ear. She was perfect. Older than what I usually collected, but still innocent and naïve.

"Oh my," she exclaimed, as I let my arms wrap around her waist.

Henrietta endured a much more intimate welcome than she may have expected, and, to my delight, she didn't pull away. It gave me an opening to kiss her cheek and keep my hands wrapped around her waist.

"Hello," I murmured in my most seductive voice.

She flushed and tried to stand on her own, but I pulled her across the threshold, keeping her in my embrace. It was one of those open, awkward holds you only saw at the beginning of a first date. But, she'd have to get used to my touch. Might as well start now.

"Come in, Henrietta. Sorry I didn't get to the door sooner. I was preoccupied." The first of many lies I would tell. Truth was for later.

I released my hold on her waist and took the box of Thin Mints out of her hand. She didn't pull away.

Henrietta took a moment to compose herself, but pink dusted her cheeks. Even her breathing was uneven.

I tried to remember how long ago her husband had died. When was the last time this woman had been held down by a man and truly fucked? No wonder she was nervous.

I gave her a most charming smile. "Holding a beautiful woman in my arms is the perfect beginning to a long day." I lifted my brows for the briefest moment to confirm I was interested in more than a simple lunch.

Now was the time for her to decide whether to stay or go.

If she had any sense, she would run back to her car. Instead, she followed me to the kitchen.

Her gaze passed over my prep bowls. "Looks like you know what you're doing."

I nodded. "I went to culinary school for a few years." The monotony of cooking soothed me.

"Are you a chef? I thought you worked for a florist?"

"I was a chef for a time, never a job that panned out. And, now, as you know, I work nights in the floral department at a gardening center. I'm a man of many talents. I can arrange a bouquet and whip up a delectable feast." I was a woman's wet dream and her worst nightmare.

"I couldn't imagine sleeping through the day. Must be strange."

"I black out the curtains in my bedroom, and I invested in soundproofing on all the walls." That was true, but not for the reasons she thought.

She nodded. Poor thing had no idea.

I gestured to a stool. "Sit. Do you like red or white wine?"

"It's ten in the morning," she exclaimed. "I rarely drink this early."

I gave a false laugh. "Sorry, my days and nights are messed up. For me, it's late evening. I usually have something before bed." I lifted a bottle of white wine. "You sure you won't drink with me?"

She did that thing with her lip again. Total turn on. I intended to make use of that mouth after we ate. For now, that tiny sign of her nervousness made the swelling in my pants all the more uncomfortable.

She hesitated for what seemed like forever. I turned my back to her to hide my irritation. If she didn't say yes soon, I would slap her stupid face and carry her downstairs.

Fortunately, she agreed.

Good thing.

I was hungry and wanted to eat before we had sex. I poured two glasses of wine, using my body to block what I was doing as I added a white powder to her drink. It would make her pliable without drugging her too much.

I handed her the wine. "Cheers!"

"Cheers," she repeated. "Um, to new friendships?"

Oh, we would be more than friends. "To new possibilities."

Her flushing came easily. I loved how transparent her emotions were. She must have felt brave because she lifted her glass a second time. "To…new possibilities."

We drank to new possibilities while I decided how I would fuck her first.

I drank from my glass, watching her take two deep swallows. Time to lower the heat, make her comfortable, and tone down the references to our pending sex-fest. I would lose her if I was too aggressive, even with the drug in her system. I wanted her pliable and lucid, not passed out.

For the next forty minutes, we chatted while I made lunch. I boiled pasta and whipped up a cream sauce, which I let her taste, teasing her as I did. A few minutes later, her words slurred, and her lids drooped.

I asked her to prep the salad, and she accomplished the task without complaint or further direction. She poured a second glass of wine for me and then put a generous amount into her cup.

The more the wine bottle emptied, the less inhibited she became. I took advantage of every opportunity to touch her, lengthening my caresses as the morning drew on. As I finished my Alfredo sauce, I had her taste one last time. I purposefully dripped the sauce on her chin. When I leaned in to lick it off, she grew still as a statue, but she didn't push me away.

I didn't kiss her, although I wanted to. I nearly came right there, tasting the sweetness of her skin. Instead, I took her hand and led her to the table. "Come, let's set the table."

A look of disappointment flickered across her face.

I was getting to that.

She helped with the table, and I told her to have a seat while I served our plates. She complied, following my direction. That would serve her well in the days to come.

Lunch proceeded rather innocently. I sat across from her, and we traded nothing of consequence for most of the meal. As I poured her a third glass of wine, we gazed into each other's eyes, and then her foot tentatively touched my shin. She looked at me through her lashes, her eyes glazed from the wine and the effects of the drug.

I smiled. "Maybe we should retire to the living room?"

Henrietta wobbled as she stood. "I'll clear the table."

I came around and put my arm around her waist. "The table will wait. I can't."

Her eyes darted to the empty couch and then to the hallway leading deeper into my home.

"I've never…I mean…"

I placed my finger over her lips, silencing her. "We won't do anything you don't want to do. Come, let's sit on the couch and talk. There's no rush."

Her eyes flicked back to the hallway and then to the couch. She wanted to go to my room, but I steered her to the living room instead. She would think well of my control later.

"It's just…" Her hands trembled, and her voice shook. "I haven't been with anyone since Joe's death."

I pulled her close. "Let's just talk. Time enough for more, later."

The tension in her body eased at my words. I settled her on the couch and sat beside her. With an arm wrapped around her shoulders, I pulled her close.

"Tell me about your husband."

She sniffed and tensed. "No, Joe's not here anymore, and it's past time I moved on." She turned to face me. "Will you kiss me, please? Like really kiss me?"

TEN

Round Of Beer

CJ

CJ WAS DEEP INTO HIS SECOND BEER BY THE TIME EGGS AND A FEW of his co-workers arrived at Grady's Pub. He called out to the tired men and ordered two pitchers of beer, a platter of wings, chips, salsa, and loaded potato fries.

Eggs saw to the introductions. "This is Tony."

CJ shook hands with a young man. He had a neck as thick as his biceps, and a skull perhaps a few inches thicker.

"You ex-military?" CJ had been out of the military for years, but he hadn't given up the signature buzz cut. He could always tell who was ex-military.

"Yeah." Tony's grip was firm. "Four years in the Marines."

Perfect. That connection would bond them. Now for a few drinks to loosen Tony's tongue. "I spent four years with the Green Berets and then another tour with Delta Force."

"Badass," Tony said.

"Told you he was cool." Eggs continued the introductions. "This here is Abel."

Abel thrust out his hand. "Nice to meet you, CJ."

"Eggs told me you saved a life."

Abel was an older gentleman and still thick with muscle. His face was deeply pockmarked, and CJ knew all about Abel's wife, five kids, seven grandbabies, plus two more on the way within twenty minutes.

Talk about Abel's kids had Eggs pulling out a photo of his son, a seventeen-year-old star of the football team. Stories flowed from there, growing louder and wilder as the day continued. CJ bought more beer.

Conversation flew from one topic to the next in a rapid-fire barrage of boasting, laughing, and general competitiveness for the most outrageous tale. The men traded insults as CJ ordered the fourth round.

The volume around the table escalated.

Eggs hit CJ in the arm. "Tell us your story. I want to hear about your tornado."

"No fucking way." Abel tossed back his beer and flagged their waitress down. "You saw one, too?"

Eggs leaned forward and pressed his finger to the tabletop. "That's not something I ever want to see again."

Abel and Eggs shared a moment. Having had a close call with a tornado himself, CJ could only imagine what the two of them had endured.

Tony sighed. "I was stuck inside the walls. All I heard was something like a freight train bearing down on us, and then there was that explosion."

"Explosion?" CJ leaned forward and refilled everyone's cups.

"Yeah, when the generators blew," Tony said. "Caused a bit of damage, and then the…"

Abel reached out and smacked Tony on the back of the head. "Shut your trap, asshole."

Something had happened at the prison, and the men weren't supposed to talk about it. CJ would have to dig deeper.

"Aw, CJ's cool." Eggs took the pitcher from CJ and emptied the last of the beer into his mug.

Abel stared at his beer. The alcohol had turned his cheeks rosy and made his eyes unfocused.

CJ was already counting out cab fares home for the men.

Tony turned to CJ. "Eggs said you outran a tornado. Tell us your story."

He wanted to hear more about the damage at the prison, but if he pried too hard, the men would clam up.

Their waitress stopped at the table and distributed shots that Tony ordered. He gave the girl a fat tip and a smack on her ass. She left with a roll of her eyes and a smile on her face.

"It started with a bolt of lightning…and a woman." CJ lifted his shot glass and raised it for a toast. He began his story with the smack of his shot glass thudding on the table.

"No shit," Tony said. "Was she hot?"

"Very," CJ said. "Even hotter after I got a look at the pink lace of her bra."

"No fucking way," Tony said with a hoot.

"I needed to see her injuries. That's why I had her strip."

"Seriously?" Eggs said.

"You rescued a woman and got her out of her clothes in the middle of a fucking tornado." Tony slapped him on the back. "Dude, you're my hero."

CJ shook his head. "It wasn't like that."

"Did you get her number," Tony asked.

Not her number, but he had her phone.

CJ shrugged. "Nothing happened. It turns out she's married and to a royal ass." He described the odd phone conversation.

"Wait, so you have her phone?" Eggs gave CJ a look.

"She lost it in the back of the car."

They wanted to hear more about the tornado, and he obliged. As time wore on, his thoughts turned back to Tony's comments about the explosion. The number of National Guardsmen he'd seen in that convoy had him wondering if something more was up.

He challenged Tony to a game of darts. The music climbed higher. Laughter roared, and the boasts became more spectacular. This wasn't CJ's first dance party.

He threw alcohol at the men, and they guzzled it down. Meanwhile, he sipped at his drinks, switching to Long Island Iced Tea, which the barkeep made virgin after a few hushed words and a fat tip.

At the end of the night, he called for two cabs. Eggs and Abel rolled into one and headed off down the street. Tony lived on the other side of town.

CJ held out a hand and shook Tony's. "Hey, good thing those National Guard troops came when they did, right?" He needed to know what had happened at the prison.

Tony's speech slurred. "Yeah, gotta get manhunts started as quick as possible." He wobbled. "Don't worry. Only two got out." Tony staggered into the cab. "Guardsmen will have them returned in no time."

He needed to confirm what he feared. "Yeah, especially when it involves inmates on death row, like the Fairytale Murderer. What's his name?"

"Ain't that right?" Tony swayed on his feet. "That's why they're keeping it hush-hush. If people knew…" Tony blinked and shut his mouth.

Not confirmation, but pretty damn close.

Tony piled into the cab, and the car took off.

Patterson had escaped. CJ felt it in his bones. With no evidence, except the damage at the prison and the drunken slur from a guard, CJ's blood ran cold.

He needed to make a call.

ELEVEN

Yellow Tulips

MELISSA

HOSPITALS SMELLED WRONG. THEY WERE TOO CLEAN OR PERHAPS not clean enough. A pervasive odor of sickness hung in the air, something even the best disinfectant couldn't hide. The staff was obnoxiously loud. Their conversations, all day and night, kept Melissa painfully awake.

And the lights!

She couldn't wait to get away from the harsh fluorescents. She'd barely slept in the past two days, and what sleep she caught had been filled with pain.

Hospitals were the worst place to be if you wanted to get well, and she couldn't wait to be discharged.

She shifted in her bed. Everywhere ached. Even her hair hurt. After two days on the soft mattress, her back screamed to be in its comfortable bed at home. The bruising over her left side was spectacular. Every time she moved, her body begged for her to stop. Three tiny bandages marked her belly, and a rainbow of bruises marred her side. But, she moved as much as she was able. Her ticket home depended on getting up.

She'd undergone emergency laparoscopic surgery. The procedure was supposed to have been less painful than cutting her open with a knife. Three small holes had been punched in her belly, one for a camera and the others for surgical ports. The surgeons inserted tools through the ports that controlled tiny knives, scissors, and other things she didn't understand.

Her healing was supposed to take far less time than if they'd opened her up. Still hurt like hell. Pain medication took the edge off the worst of it, but the pills made her foggy.

To make things worse, all the air they'd injected into her belly had her looking five months pregnant. She'd been assured her body would return to normal. In the meantime, she ran her fingers over the three tiny bandages, which also made her skin itch.

Every color of the rainbow represented itself over her left side, from deep purple and blue to a softening yellow, orange, and even sickly greens. From hip to shoulder, the bruising reminded her how close she'd come to death.

Her thoughts turned to CJ and his smile. Her chivalrous knight, with his chiseled jaw, thicker-than-thick biceps, and sculpted chest, had the softest eyes and biggest heart she'd ever run across. His sky blue eyes had twinkled with mischief when she'd caught him peeking at the lace of her bra. But, he hadn't made her feel self-conscious. She'd been vulnerable, and he'd made her feel safe.

She shouldn't think about him, but couldn't stop doing just that. He'd blown in and out of her life with the same speed and devastation as that tornado. Wreckage remained in his wake because he'd stirred up an aching loneliness she'd suppressed since Scott's arrest.

In the three years since her ex-husband had been taken away, she'd not once thought about the possibility of another man.

CJ's interest, as small as it had been, had her hopeful. His touch stirred something deep inside. Something she hoped to explore, but she was realistic. He'd been nothing more than a fantasy.

Her fitful dreams had been filled with the real-life superman that was CJ. The funny thing was her life had needed saving, but not from a tornado.

She'd wanted to thank CJ, but the nursing staff had no information about the man who'd dropped her off in the emergency room. Her hero had become a ghost.

But, it was a time for new beginnings. Scott was gone. She had a new life stretching ahead. It was time to heal. In body, mind, and soul, Melissa vowed to take back her life.

Her nurse breezed into her hospital room, followed by a deliveryman carrying flowers.

"Got something for you, Miss Evans." Charles comforted Melissa. His massive size, rather than intimidating, conjured images of a squishy teddy bear. Everything he did made her feel better. It was in the tiny things, like the way he fluffed her pillow, held the straw so she could sip her water, and even in how he maintained her dignity while exposing her body to care for her wounds. He soothed her fears about needles when he had to stick her arm, distracting her with jokes and silly songs.

"Special delivery!" The deliveryman held out a bouquet of tulips with an expectant expression. Nearly as tall as Charles, the man had the lean build of an athlete, like a runner or a cyclist.

Her heart missed a beat, and she stifled a gasp. That message was one she knew all too well. But, there was something new nestled within the blooms.

A flash of crimson drew her attention to the single blood-red rose gracing the yellow tulips.

Her stomach heaved, and she grasped the bed rails as blood pounded in her veins. This couldn't be happening.

The florist reached into the flowers and pulled out the red rose. He brought it to his nose, inhaled, and then presented it with another grand gesture. There was a raw beauty about his features, and something disturbing about the intensity of his gaze.

Rimless glasses framed a long narrow face. His gaze shifted between the rose and her hand—a brittleness out of synch with the friendly gesture.

She reached out, hand trembling, and took the rose.

"Who did these come from?" She knew the answer but had to hear the truth. Her voice quivered, showing a weakness she thought long buried.

She hadn't seen the execution. Scott had demanded her presence, but she'd refused. Her lawyer was to let her know of Scott's death, but in the confusion of the storm and her hospitalization, her lawyer didn't know where she was, and she'd lost her phone.

She placed the rose on her lap without smelling it and hid the tremors shaking her hands. She had nothing to give the delivery man for a tip and hoped he'd take the hint and leave.

He gave a curious look, a frown framed with irritation.

Charles moved around the room, methodical while he worked. He hummed a tune while he strung new fluids in the IV pumps beside her bed, a full bag of clear liquid to replace the one which had emptied into her veins.

Charles paused. "Beautiful arrangement. Are tulips your favorite?"

Memories she'd tried to forget surfaced with a wave of anguish, bringing with them a clamminess she couldn't ignore. Dizziness caused her to clutch at the side rails of her bed. If she hadn't been confined to the bed, she might have collapsed.

How had Scott sent flowers? Was it some sadistic torture he planned in the days leading to his execution?

Charles plucked the card out of the flowers. He handed her the envelope. "Maybe it's from your hero?"

"Hero?" The deliveryman's brows scrunched up. "What do you mean, hero?" Disapproval hung heavy in the man's voice.

Why was the deliveryman lingering?

"Miss Evans was saved from a tornado," Charles said.

CJ had pretended to be her husband when he dropped her off in the emergency department. He did it to stay close while they completed her initial assessment. Only after her surgery did she admit the truth to the staff. The hospital still had her listed as a Jane Doe, something she'd been told would be straightened out at discharge when she paid her bill. She shared her story with Charles and may have gushed over CJ with the narcotics floating in her veins.

She tried to steady her hand and clutched the envelope to her chest. Memories of Scott surged with each constricted breath. Was it possible he hadn't died? Knowing how calculating he was, he'd probably arranged for the delivery before his death, a 'fuck you, you're still mine' gesture.

He'd given her three yellow tulips on their first anniversary. Three tulips, he said, one for his undying love, the second for his smoldering passion, and the third for his everlasting loyalty. The following year she received six, nine the year after, and then twelve, fifteen, and then eighteen in that horrible last year when everything had fallen apart.

Three tulips for each year of marriage.

The flowers had been a symbol not of love, passion, and loyalty, but something much worse. They'd been stolen lives.

But in those six years, not once had he given her a rose. The flowers had always been yellow tulips—his favorite, not hers—and always multiples of three.

She hadn't understood the significance behind the tulips, at least not until the trial. But when the prosecutors pulled out the princess outfits, her world, as imperfect as it had been, imploded with horror.

She'd been the first to wear the princess outfits but hadn't been the last.

That story became a thing fit for the tabloids and shared in national news.

Love. Passion. Loyalty.

Might as well have been pain, torture, and death.

She used to joke with him that if he continued adding three every year, he'd have to buy an entire delivery truck at their fiftieth anniversary.

One hundred and fifty tulips.

The tabloids had made connections where there had been none. She'd been as much of a victim as those poor women, but the tabloids vilified her, intimating she had been his accomplice. Twisting the truth brought more sales, and they painted her in the worst light. While they made millions, Melissa struggled to breathe and make it to the end of the day.

Scott had made her into the perfect fool.

After Scott's conviction, the deliveries stopped. She hadn't seen a yellow tulip since and couldn't look at the delicate flower without her stomach heaving.

"I'm going to be sick."

Weak from her injuries, she could barely lean over the side of the bed.

Charles scooped up a trash can and placed it under her mouth moments before she emptied the contents of her stomach. Wonderful man that he was, he held her hair out of the way.

The deliveryman inched back to the doorway. If he was expecting a tip, he would have to wait a long time.

"Since when have you been feeling nauseous?" Charles felt her forehead and then checked her pulse.

"I haven't." It was the tulips, but she didn't want to explain the reaction. The single red rose fell to the floor.

How had Scott orchestrated this delivery? And how had he known to deliver it here? No one knew she had been hospitalized.

"I'm getting the doctor." Charles pressed the call bell located over her bed.

In a few seconds, another nurse popped her head into the room. "Need help?"

"Call Dr. Sims."

"I'll be fine." Melissa protested with a wave of her hand. "It's nothing."

"Nothing, my bee-hind." Charles used his smile to comfort her, but her insides twisted.

"Can you please take the flowers out of the room?"

Charles cocked his head. "Just lay back. Try to relax while we check this out."

She gestured to her belly, drawing a circle over the bandages beneath her hospital gown. "Spleen's all good. Nothing else wrong. I'm supposed to be getting out of here." Even to her ears, she sounded like a petulant child.

"You're not fine. Dr. Sims will make sure everything's okay."

She counted the flowers. Eighteen tulips. Eighteen lives snuffed out of existence.

Scott should be suffering as the devil welcomed him to his eternal resting place in hell. Her eyes cut to the florist when he picked up the rose and tried to hand it to her.

"I don't want the flowers."

Charles cocked his head. "You sure?"

"I'm hypersensitive to their smell."

Charles's forehead creased. "I smell nothing."

"Please, just make them go away. I don't want them."

Charles handed the bouquet back to the deliveryman and ushered him out of the room.

Doctor Sims walked in. "What's wrong?" He pulled his stethoscope out of his white coat pocket.

"Nothing."

Charles returned. "She's nauseous. Vomited. Her vitals are steady."

Dr. Sims placed the stethoscope on her chest. "Take a breath."

While she breathed, he listened, examined her wounds, pushed on her belly, and then ordered a battery of tests.

Charles squeezed her hand. "Don't worry. It's just a precaution." He left to get the supplies required to draw the blood work her doctor had ordered.

Melissa turned the envelope over in her hand. She stared at it for minutes before she found the courage to open it.

My beautiful Queen,
Love to keep us.
Passion to fuel the fire.
Loyalty to bind us.
You belong to me.
Yours to serve.
Mine to rule.
Your loving King

Her lungs pinched as they struggled to pull oxygen past constricted airways. The ringing in her ears escalated until it turned deafening.

He's dead. He can't hurt me. I'm free. Free to live. Free to forget. He's dead.

I AM SAFE!

He can't hurt me anymore.

She repeated the litany until Charles returned with his needles and empty tubes. If she said the words enough times, then maybe one day they would be true.

No, it was true.

It was finally and unequivocally real. The Fairytale Killer had been sent to the pits of hell where he belonged. Scott couldn't touch her anymore. He couldn't hurt her ever again. As Charles prepared to take her blood, the single red rose on the table caught her attention.

She glanced at the note again. Scott had asked her to call him many things in their years of marriage. She'd always been his fairytale princess, and he was her prince charming. Scott had never once called himself a King. A tremor worked its way up her spine, and she jumped as Charles inserted a needle into her skin.

"Sorry." He worked with brisk efficiency, collecting the required blood into his vials.

A simple needle stick was nothing compared to what she'd endured at the hands of the man who'd vowed to honor, love, and protect.

"Charles?"

"Yes?"

"Can you check on something for me, please?"

"Sure thing."

"I need to know about my husband."

"Your hero?" Charles gave her a big grin.

"No, not him. My ex-husband."

If he was still alive, she needed to know. And if he hadn't sent the flowers, then who had?

TWELVE

Stains

CJ

The tornados made national news, but CJ didn't care about the fucking tornados. He flipped channels trying to find a story about the prison break, but all the newscasts seemed silent on that account. Nothing about an explosion, missing inmates, or a manhunt made its way to television, print, or internet news.

How was that possible?

For three hours, he scanned channels and surfed the net, getting nothing but a rehashing of the destruction. Frustrated, he called into work to see if Sam could help.

"CJ? What are you doing calling me? You're supposed to be on leave." The surprise in his boss's voice was unmistakable.

"Listen, I need help with something."

The Guardians were hostage rescue specialists and often contracted with the FBI, assisting with off-the-books hostage extractions. Sam had strings in high places. CJ hoped Sam could dig up something about Patterson.

"How'd your personal business go?"

"That's what I want to talk about. It didn't."

"How's that possible?"

"The execution didn't happen."

A long stretch of silence passed on the other end of the line. CJ let it hang. Sam had never let him down.

Sam cleared his throat, a prolonged rumble, then spoke in a firm voice. "What do you need?"

CJ needed confirmation. "You heard about the storm down here?"

"Who hasn't? They're blasting it on national news like it's a national disaster zone. Were you near any of it?"

"You could say."

"Did you see any of the twisters? News is saying there was a bunch."

Five to be exact, but he didn't elaborate. "Yeah, up close and personal."

Melissa came to mind, falling in front of his car, shivering under the emergency blanket, the lace of her bra sitting over the ivory perfection of her breasts. Damn, his trousers grew tight with inappropriate thoughts about a married woman.

"You there?" Sam's deep voice boomed.

"Sorry."

"Not like you to drift off like that. What's up?"

"Nothing," he said.

"Then why'd you call?"

He tried to dislodge Melissa from his mind and focus on more pressing matters, but he couldn't get the brunette out of his thoughts.

"I need you to check something for me. I can't get anything out of the news. A tornado hit the prison. News isn't reporting any problems, but the guards are telling a different story. One of them said there was an explosion, and the National Guard arrived to search for Patterson, but it's not being publicized."

"Is it him?"

"If I can trust the words of a drunk guard, then yes. Any other prisoner and they'd be blasting it on the news to get people to keep an eye out. But him?"

Scott Patterson's crimes had been beyond horrific. CJ was surprised something hadn't leaked to the press.

"Probably trying to cover their asses," Sam said.

"I think so, which is where you come in. I need to know if the bastard got out."

There were many reasons to keep quiet about the escape. None of them good. Panicking an already stressed population might be one of them.

"If Patterson is free, the more eyes looking for him, the better. Whoever is in charge is an idiot."

"Sounds like," Sam agreed.

"I don't know why they haven't made a statement. I could be wrong here. I'm only going on what a bunch of tired and very drunk guards were saying, but if it was him, you know how bad that could be."

Scott Patterson spent the better part of a decade on a killing spree. Each year he'd increased his kills by three, and he'd spent the last three years locked up. The man would have pent up energy to spend.

"I'll look into it," Sam promised. "In the meantime, what are you going to do? Because something has come up, and I could use you."

CJ glanced at the water stains on the ceiling. He should go back to work. Except for visiting his sister's grave, there wasn't anything keeping him here.

"You got a case?"

"Yeah. It's a special one."

"Who were you going to send?"

"Your team, of course. Mac and Jenny are already on their way. By the way, Jenny did well leading Delta team on this last case while you've been out. If you decide you want to step up, she'll be a great replacement."

"And what will you do?" Sam was the battle commander for the four Guardian teams: Alpha, Bravo, Charlie, and CJ's team, Delta. "Forest tagged me to manage the entire operation. He's ready for me to hand over my job to my replacement. You say the word, and it's yours."

Forest Summers, a billionaire on a mission to rid the world of human traffickers, recently acquired Guardian HRS. Everyone was excited by what that meant for the Guardians. Sam moving up to manage the entire operation, left his position of battle commander open.

"I'm still chewing on it." He liked his position as Delta One, lead of Delta team, and wasn't sure if he was ready to step up to take leadership of all four Guardian teams. It was a lot of responsibility and took him a step away from the action. Was he ready to hand over Delta? It was a huge step up, more responsibility, less fieldwork. "Let me finish things out here. I'll give you my answer when I officially come back."

"No rush. You're the only man for the job. Not that I'm pressuring you to take it, but I don't trust anyone else to take this job."

"No pressure."

"Hah, right. No pressure."

"How's our new boss? Is he shaking everything up? Is he a hands-on, in your face, can't get rid of him kind of boss, or is he willing to step back and let us do our job?"

"His vision is impressive. You should see his plans for Guardian HQ. Forest is a bit quirky, but I have to tell you, he doesn't believe in the word can't. There's nothing that man can't do, and you'll like him once you meet him. He's impressive. As far as the hands-off aspect, it's too early to tell. The man is passionate about rescuing innocents. I can say that which brings us back to Jenny. If you have any doubts, I need to know."

"Her skills are top-notch. I'm just not sure I want to step away from fieldwork."

"I get that, but think about it. No pressure, but I'll need an answer."

"If that's the case, why doesn't she take the lead on this case? You don't need me."

"I want your eyes on this case, and I need your experience. It's right up your alley as we have shit for leads."

Wonderful.

"Well, I say keep Jenny on point. She'll either step up or not. I'll back her up as needed and tell you if I think she's ready to lead Delta team." If Sam wanted her to step into CJ's role as Delta One, he needed more time to evaluate her abilities. "How about assigning me to look for Patterson? If he got out, I'm tracking his ass down. If they can't figure out how to kill him, I know a good place to park a bullet."

Sam's long sigh had CJ frowning.

"It's a kidnapping case, with no leads. The mother of two girls went missing yesterday afternoon. The school called the cops when the mother didn't pick up her girls from school. You know how time-sensitive cases like this are?"

Shit, Sam knew CJ's soft spot for kidnapping cases, but this one was fresher than what they usually worked on.

"How did the Guardians get involved?"

Guardian HRS didn't usually take cases unless they were complicated, had already failed the negotiation stage, or required unorthodox extraction techniques. Often, their clients were wealthy enough to pay for the privilege. It didn't make sense why they were involved in this case.

"Personal favor. Widow of a war hero, two young girls, and a lot of guardian angels who were buddies of her husband. They're afraid that with all the storm damage, no one will pay attention to her case. You know how these things go. Mac and Jenny are on their way. The rest of Delta team will follow once they finish up the last assignment."

CJ focused on the water stains. The brown spots made sockets for eyes, and a lopsided grin stared back at him where the water had dripped a little more on one side.

Nothing good ever happened when kidnappers got their hands on women.

"You know I'm better working on Patterson's manhunt, right?"

"Getting you on that case will take time. I'll see what I can manage, but until then, work with Jenny. I want your assessment of how Delta takes to her calling the shots. I need you on this case."

Of course, he'd work the kidnapping. No way he'd turn it down, but he wasn't going to let Patterson's escape go without a fight.

"I'm on it, but see what you can dig up with the Justice Department about Patterson."

"You know I will."

Sam had been the one to notify CJ when they'd discovered his sister's body. He'd been there through the grief and managed CJ's unhealthy obsession during the year-long trial, redirecting his pent-up energy into more useful pursuits, such as rescuing innocent victims.

Oh hell, that voice. The voice on the other end of Melissa's phone.

There was a reason it sounded familiar. How could he forget the voice of the man who killed his baby sister?

He suppressed a growl, but that did nothing to prevent his fist from connecting hard with the wall. Fuck, that hurt. He'd better not have broken the knuckles. Now, he needed ice.

"Send me what information you have."

"Thanks, CJ. These girls have already lost one parent. Check in with me once a day, no exceptions."

"Got it."

"Sending you the files."

His phone blipped with an encrypted file notification.

He'd come to this town for closure. Instead, he'd found upheaval. Patterson still breathed, and CJ could do nothing about it. A gorgeous woman had fallen into and then right out of his life. Had he imagined their connection? Not like him to read a situation wrong. Shit, the air had practically sizzled between them.

Now another woman needed to be saved?

He palmed Melissa's phone. After his team arrived, he would return it while they briefed him.

It pained him to think someone as awful as that had been a part of Melissa's life. Men like that deserved to have their balls cut off and shoved down their throats. The fact Melissa had to deal with such a man put CJ's protective instincts into overdrive.

Shit. With Patterson out, she needed protection. Screw the phone. He had to get to her now. For the moment, the hospital would provide her some degree of protection. If Patterson wanted to get to her, he wouldn't approach her at the hospital. The man wasn't an idiot.

With a calming breath, CJ relaxed. As long as she was there, she would be relatively safe.

A quick text filled Sam in on the problem.

He ached to rush to the hospital, but he had a job to do, and in kidnapping cases, hours could mean the difference between life and death.

A quick type of his security code unlocked the encrypted file. This was what he did. Rescue others. No one had been around to pull him and his sister from their personal hell. He did that himself, and some stains could never be washed away.

He caressed Melissa's phone, aching to rescue her.

THIRTEEN

Locks

PIERCE

I WAS IN A FOUL MOOD WHEN I RETURNED HOME. THINGS HADN'T gone as planned. I had been so excited to meet my Queen, but she treated me like less than nothing. She hadn't even said thank you for the flowers, and that fucking male nurse had shoved them back in my face.

He and I would have words.

I left the rose. The tulips had been from Him, but the rose…the rose had been my gift.

Not that she appreciated it.

I punched a fist through the wall of my kitchen and then stared at my bloody knuckles. Bright red validation, that's what that was. Blood fascinated me. It always had.

The stairs leading to the basement beckoned, whispering dark and filthy promises. I took a step toward the door, my hands fisting as I approached. The pain in my knuckles stopped me. Blood wept from the cuts, and a throbbing kept time with the beat of my heart.

Down the steps, through the cellar, past the wine rack, open the locks, and then through the tunnel to that final door. My precious princesses waited to serve my every need.

But I didn't need them. Not when I desired my Queen.

A roaring filled my head, and I cupped my ears, smearing blood alongside my left cheek. I squatted and rocked, waiting for the moment to pass. All I could think about was whipping my princesses for their Queen's transgression until their tears poured more freely than their blood.

This was why I'd installed the locks. They slowed me down when I got like this. My urges needed to be curbed, especially when they were dark and unpredictable like now.

Control.

A prince had to be a master first of himself, even more so when he desired to be king.

Bad things happened when I lost control. This lesson was one to remember. I slammed the door to the basement, silencing the beast calling me.

Hit. Whip. Fuck. Punch. Kick. Beat.

Their torturous screams would invigorate me and satiate the lust flaring in my gut. My balls ached to spill their seed, and my cock stiffened and throbbed.

Blackness filled my heart to overflowing, demanding bestial release.

Sandra's destroyed face ghosted in front of me. Her features framed in silent agony as her mouth formed a silent scream. The image was forever etched in my mind. I still heard her sobs in my dreams. Back then, I hadn't been in control.

The burning inside, which called me to crush, to maim, to hurt had not been restrained back then. I'd exploded in a firestorm of sadistic lust and made my first and last mistake. Sandra had been my first, my only, girlfriend, and that rage had snuffed out her light forever.

This was where my thoughts spiraled…into the oblivion of past mistakes. I had to regain control before I lost myself to the depravity of my mind.

I wrapped my arms around myself and rocked on the floor, banging my head against the wall until the pain grew to a level of clarity I understood.

Inexperienced in what a body could endure, and bursting with urges I didn't understand, I learned what happened when I didn't rein in my desires.

Sandra's vacant stare was something I would never forget. An enduring lesson and what a mess that had been.

The locks kept my princesses safe from these feral cravings. A prince was foremost a master of himself, and when I couldn't control my urges, I was unfit to rule. The locks kept me out as much as it kept them in.

The mistakes I'd made with Sandra forced me to learn the boundaries between pain and death. I took my princesses to the brink because I liked it, but never once did I make another mistake.

I had more self-control than Him. He'd been weak, whereas I was strong.

God, how I wanted to fuck my princesses now, but they'd have to wait until I calmed down and got my hand stitched up. I wrapped my bloodied hand in towels, grabbed the keys to my delivery truck, and headed back to the emergency department at Saint John's.

His instructions had been specific: deliver those flowers on the day of his death. But, I hadn't been able to find her at her home. I'd camped outside for two days waiting for her return.

It was only because of my job that I stumbled upon her whereabouts at all.

Stuff like that didn't happen without divine intervention, which meant fate intended us to be together.

FOURTEEN

Doors

CJ

A LOUD, PERSISTENT KNOCKING DISTRACTED CJ FROM READING THE files from Sam. When he didn't immediately answer, knocking turned to pounding. Pounding turned to yelling. He palmed his weapon and approached the door only to hear a man and woman arguing on the other side.

"Stop it. You'll wake the whole damn place." Jenny's deep alto was unmistakable.

"What the fuck?" Mac's baritone complemented the lower register of her voice. "Why isn't he answering?" The pounding intensified.

CJ blinked lids heavy with fatigue and peered through the peephole. He rolled his eyes. Ahead of schedule.

On the other side of the door, Jenny smacked Mac in the head with her purse. Mac's head tilted sideways. Jenny carried a Glock 17 in that purse. She wasn't an average woman. A tall beauty, she had a classic majesty, muscled just shy of being manly. Yet, she oozed a sultry seduction nearly as dark and potent as the color of her skin. Men underestimated her. It's why Sam added her to the team.

CJ had been the first of the crew to step wrong with Jenny. They'd all done so, except for Mac. Something smoldered between those two, but as far as CJ knew, they weren't an item.

Mac grunted. "You fucking bitch!" He spun and leaped at his partner.

Jenny jumped back, avoiding Mac's lunge. She placed a finger on his chest. "Don't even think about it."

Before someone from the motel called the local police on them, CJ opened the door. "Can you two keep it down?"

Jenny side-stepped around Mac, not an easy thing, because Mac was built like a Mack truck, thus the nickname. CJ had no idea what Mac's real name was. Everyone had always called him Mac.

"He wishes," Jenny muttered as she shouldered past CJ. "Answer the fucking door next time. Seriously, you'd be dead if we'd wanted to kill you. Since when do you sleep that deep?"

"Maybe he wasn't sleeping. Anyone inside we're going to surprise?" Mac's eyebrows arched.

"I was taking a shit and reading the files Sam sent."

"Bullshit," Jenny said. "It smells like a fucking rose in here." Jenny plopped down on the only chair in the small motel room.

CJ smirked. Jenny never took his shit.

"You two got here quick."

Mac sat on the bed, leaving CJ to stand; he wasn't about to sit on the bed with Mac. He folded his arms across his chest and stared at his friends.

"Sam told us about what happened. Are you good to go?" Jenny's look could cut steel. "I need to know if your head is in the game." There was no compassion in Jenny's expression. Once she had a job to do, the woman got shit done. Emotions were for weaklings.

A product of the slums of Rio de Janeiro, she'd lived a difficult life until a CIA agent crossed paths with her during a sting operation. She'd already killed the five men who'd raped her. Sam recruited her on the spot. According to Jenny, feelings got people into trouble.

Mac was more of the typical hire. Ex-Delta Force, like CJ, his acquisition to the team had been a no-brainer.

CJ gripped Melissa's phone until the plastic cut into his palm. "I've got some business to take care of before we get started." He had a woman to save, or at least keep safe.

"Sam said your business was canceled." Mac leaned against the headboard and put his boots on the covers.

CJ made a dismissive gesture. "Patterson escaped. My business isn't done." He wiggled the phone. "This belongs to his wife."

Mac broke the ensuing silence with a deep indrawn breath. "You know why we're here, right?"

"Kidnapping case."

Jenny's gaze cut up to the ceiling. "We don't have time to fuck around returning a damn phone." She stood and cocked her left hip forward, a pose he'd seen too many times before. It was her do-not-fuck-with-me stance. "You're to stay out of the manhunt."

CJ turned wide eyes to Jenny. "Is that what you think?"

She arched a brow.

He shrugged. "Sam's looking into it, of course, trying to get jurisdiction, but not only do I have Melissa Evan's phone, I know where she is. It's a good bet Patterson will try to make contact."

"So?" Jenny crossed her arms over her chest.

"She's in the hospital." CJ blew out a deep breath. "If Patterson goes after his wife, he'll head to her house. She needs protective custody." The roaring in CJ's ears reached deafening levels.

"Meaning you?" Jenny scoffed. "I see."

"No, I don't think you do. This is small-town America. They have a handful of cops. No one's going to care about her safety."

"Not our job," Jenny said. "Let me remind you that our victim has two little girls. Their dad is dead, and if we don't get a move on, their mom might soon be dead."

"I'm not suggesting we delay anything. The police station is on the way to Saint John's. We have to stop in there and meet with the local authorities. You can do that while Mac and I go to the hospital. Melissa Evans deserves protection."

"Shove it up your ass, CJ," Jenny said. "We're not doing a stopover."

"I'm going to the hospital. All three of us don't need to be there for the meet and greet with the Chief of Police. That's for you as lead." Not that he had to remind her what it meant to be Delta One.

"Fine." Her breath whooshed out as she gave in. "Drop me at the precinct, run your little errand, and then we get to work."

The only reason Jenny acquiesced was because she respected him. She also depended on his recommendation.

FIFTEEN

Daisy

MELISSA

MELISSA'S BODY PROTESTED EVERY MOVEMENT, BUT SHE DIDN'T CARE. The only way out of the hospital was to move, and she needed less help every day. The nurses who'd provided her care were terrific, but she wanted to go home.

"You're being discharged." Dr. Sims boomed his announcement during his morning rounds. At six in the morning, his jovial voice had jolted her awake and left her a grinning fool despite the early hour.

Freedom!

She couldn't wait to sleep in her bed and make food that had taste, texture, and didn't make her want to gag.

The best part? Her favorite nurse was back on shift, and she'd get to say goodbye to Charles. Compassionate caring wasn't a quality she associated with men, but Charles had a heart of gold and healing hands.

"Easy does it, Miss Evans." Charles helped her transition from the hospital bed into the wheelchair.

"You can call me Melissa, you know." She took her time maneuvering her battered body. Her muscles objected, and she guarded her side, bracing against the pain.

"Old habits, I guess." He grabbed a clipboard and tucked it under his arm.

"I can walk," she insisted.

"Hospital policy." Charles gave her one of his easy smiles. "Everyone is discharged in a wheelchair to the curb. Now, you sure there's no one I can call?"

Melissa pursed her lips and crinkled her forehead. Her so-called 'friends' had all scurried under the woodwork after her husband's … ex-husband's …arrest. She needed to stop thinking of him as a husband. He was dead, and she didn't belong to him anymore. By the time Scott had been tried and convicted, there'd been no one left she called a friend. Her parents had passed away years ago, and she'd been an only child, as had her parents. No uncles. No aunts. No cousins. No family. And no friends.

There wasn't anyone to call, let alone someone to take her home.

After three years, she hadn't found a job. No one wanted to hire a serial killer's wife. She lived off Scott's bank accounts and had years left before she'd be forced to work.

In the meantime, she worked toward the marketing degree she abandoned after meeting and marrying Scott.

"A cab will do."

She shifted in the wheelchair, giving a weary sigh. Not for the first time, she contemplated moving from this small town. It'd been her home her entire life, but she'd been treated like a pariah since Scott's case broke. Moving would mean leaving her parents' gravesites behind, and honestly, she didn't have the strength to leave that part of herself behind.

The pain medications messed with her head, making her feel sluggish and distanced from the world. While she'd asked Charles to find out about Scott's execution, he'd been too busy, and she felt terrible asking again. Instead, she'd flipped through the news channels, but the reporters seemed more interested in covering tornado damage than an execution. The first item on her list, call her lawyer when she got home.

"Okay." Charles made sure her feet were in the footrests of the wheelchair. "You ready?"

She wore the only clothing she had, CJ's baggy sweatpants and sweatshirt. It was either his clothes or head home in a hospital gown. CJ's clothes held the lingering scent of him, a hint of musk, the tiniest waft of his laundry detergent, something woodsy and fresh, like eucalyptus leaves.

"Ready as I'll ever be."

Melissa took a breath and blew it out slowly. It had been only a handful of days, but it already felt like a lifetime ago when CJ had rescued her from the tornado. She clutched at the fabric and breathed deeply. Strong and masculine, the scent soothed her.

Her gaze landed on her lap. The harsh fluorescent lights made the diamond of her wedding ring glitter. She twisted the platinum band as she had a thousand times before. With a tug, she tried once more to remove the ring, but the damn thing wouldn't budge. Her swollen skin trapped it there just as Scott had held her captive for so long.

Charles squatted in front of her, holding a tissue. It amazed her how he always seemed to have exactly what she needed. His ability to care for others was a real gift.

She reached out. "Thank you."

He was kind enough not to ask why she was crying.

A shadow passed to the side; she turned at the unexpected movement and bit back a groan at a twinge of pain. The same deliveryman who'd brought the noxious tulips held a bouquet of crimson roses sprinkled with baby's breath. His gaze locked on her as he knelt to present the arrangement with another odd flourish.

Scott hated roses. Could these be from CJ? Her heart leaped with hope.

Charles gave an appreciative whistle. "Now those are beautiful, not like the tulips."

The deliveryman flashed Charles an irritated glare. He turned to her, fixing a smile to his face. "I told my boss you didn't like the tulips. He insisted we replace the arrangement."

That excited feeling in her belly died out. Not from CJ then, but it was probably too much to have hoped for flowers.

"Who ordered the tulips?" She had a million questions. "Can you tell me when the order was placed?"

The man shrugged. "I'm sorry, I don't know. I just deliver them."

His voice held a complex timbre. Smooth and hypnotic, it was bigger than his lanky frame, and magnetic in an unsettling way.

She felt a need to apologize. "I'm sorry you had to come back. The tulips weren't your fault. I was just feeling nauseous after surgery."

"Well, flowers are supposed to cheer a person up. I chose roses. I'd hoped they might make you happy."

She didn't want the flowers, but he seemed kind, and she hated making him feel bad. Besides, he had gone above and beyond to replace the tulips.

"Thank you, they're beautiful."

A look of elation filled his face, more than she would have expected from a simple 'thank you.'

Charles pointed to the bandages on the man's hands, a note of concern edging his tone. "What happened to you?"

"A boxing injury…comes with the territory." The deliveryman shrugged.

"You don't look like a fighter." Charles eyed him dubiously.

"I give better than I get. You should see the other guy." His swagger wasn't convincing.

Melissa hid a frown. She didn't like boxing, didn't understand the need for grown men to beat on each other until they bled.

"I'm sorry, but I don't have money for a tip." She never carried a wallet when she ran. It had made for an interesting conversation with hospital billing, but they'd worked out payment for her hospital stay.

The delivery man made a dismissive gesture. "None required. Your smile is good enough."

"Well, thank you. I appreciate the flowers."

He glanced left then right. "Are you switching rooms?"

"I'm being discharged."

"Oh, that's good news."

"Thanks."

Charles pushed her toward the elevator and jabbed at the down arrow while the man followed. He rode with them and then continued walking beside her through the lobby and to the curb.

"You waiting on a ride?" The lanky man pulled out a set of keys from his pocket.

Melissa looked up. "I've got a cab coming."

"Cab was supposed to be here already, Miss Evans. I apologize." Charles' head swiveled, his gaze casting across the parking lot and the drive leading to the hospital entrance.

The deliveryman shook his head. "You shouldn't have to take a cab."

She shrugged, and the roses shifted in her lap, nearly tumbling to the ground. She grabbed at them and then buried her nose into the delicate petals, inhaling the light fragrance.

"I could save you the price of a fare," he offered. "Where are you headed?"

Charles placed a hand on her shoulder, squeezed, and answered for her. "Thanks for delivering the flowers, but Miss Evans will take the cab."

The deliveryman raised his hands. "Hey, just trying to do a good deed. It's really no problem. I don't mind."

She hesitated, unwilling to appear unappreciative, but he was a stranger.

"Look." Charles' voice deepened, taking the edge of a challenge. "She's not getting into a car with someone she doesn't know."

"I think she can decide for herself..."

"Listen," Charles' tone had gone arctic. "We're not discussing this. Probably time for you to leave."

The deliveryman scowled, but after a glance at Melissa, backed down.

Melissa braced herself and struggled to her feet. Someone needed to diffuse the situation before it got out of hand. Charles and the deliveryman locked stares.

A familiar voice called out.

"Melissa?"

CJ jogged toward her from the direction of the parking lot. Her heart fluttered, and her knees wobbled, making her sway.

Charles gripped her shoulder. "I'm calling another cab." He supported her as a wave of dizziness overcame her. The unsteadiness passed after a few seconds.

Devouring the distance in long, measured strides, CJ's pace quickened. A huge man jogged behind CJ. She blinked. If she thought CJ was a large man, she'd been mistaken. The guy jogging behind him was massive. A head taller, his chest and biceps were twice as broad as CJ's.

CJ stopped his easy lope just shy of the curb. He held a white daisy, pinched between his thumb and forefinger. The poor flower's roots still clung to a clod of dirt.

He thrust it at her. "Um, here."

"It's beautiful."

It was more than beautiful.

Daisies had always been her favorite. Their ivory petals reminded her of better days, innocent times when she'd dared to dream of a future filled with smiling children, a huge family, and a warm bed with a man who protected her from the world.

Her life had taken a decidedly different turn.

"Are you being released?" CJ asked.

She wanted him to pull her against his chest and wrap those powerful arms around her again. She wanted to inhale his rich, deep scent, not the lingering essence of him from his clothes. But, CJ didn't take her into his arms.

"Guess I heal fast." She rushed to fill the silence.

"I thought they were going to remove your spleen." His gaze dipped to her stomach.

She shook her head. "It wasn't as bad as they thought. They did a lapra…lobora…"

"Laparoscopic surgery." Charles finished her sentence.

"Yeah, what he said." The medical jargon blurred into unintelligible nonsense.

"Makes sense then." CJ's gaze swept from one end of the curb to another, taking in the scene. His vision hitched on the deliveryman standing behind the wheelchair and then moved on. "How are you getting home?"

"I'm waiting for my cab."

His brows drew together. "No one came to visit you?"

Odd question.

She brought the daisy to her nose, breathing in the faint scent. "Nope."

"Well, shoot. I'll take you." He dragged a hand over his close-cropped hair.

Charles leaned in to whisper. "Is this him?"

She gave a curt nod. Charles knew all about her disappearing hero.

The huge man standing beside CJ rumbled something unintelligible. From the tone, it sounded like he had a problem with what CJ suggested.

"You're the guy who saved Miss Evans. Nice to meet you." Charles thrust his hand forward and pumped CJ's arm up and down.

"Nice to meet you. Were you her doctor?"

Charles laughed. "No, a common mistake."

"Charles was my nurse," Melissa explained.

CJ gave her a wink. "Well, thank you. She needed someone to watch over her."

"Yeah, that's been my experience," Charles teased. He glanced at the tall, Black man. "Hello?"

"Hello."

CJ grinned. "Sorry. Melissa, this is..."

"Name's Mac. Nice to meet you."

She smiled at CJ's friend. "Likewise."

He scratched his head. "CJ and I work together."

Charles glanced at her. "You okay with him taking you home?"

CJ pulled her to him. When he touched her hand, a bolt of electricity shot from his fingers up her arm.

She gave a brief nod to Charles, letting him know it was okay.

CJ gathered her in his arms. "Can you walk, or should I pull the car around?"

The little daisy got crushed between them.

"I'm good." She wished her voice didn't waver. Charles and CJ both lifted a brow.

"Don't push yourself too hard." Charles touched her shoulder, an affectionate gesture goodbye.

"I promise I'll go slow." She lifted on tiptoe and brushed Charles' cheek with a friendly kiss. "Thank you for taking such good care of me."

He smiled. "My pleasure. Remember, you have an appointment in a week." His tone sounded almost scolding, but the smile reaching his eyes told her he meant well.

"I promise to be a good patient." She gave Charles a final hug. "Thanks for everything."

Charles jockeyed the wheelchair out of the way while CJ picked up the plastic bag holding her paperwork.

Charles blew an exaggerated kiss. She clutched the daisy to her chest and left the roses behind.

SIXTEEN

Rings

CJ

CJ HELPED MELISSA OFF THE CURB. HER BROWS KNITTED TOGETHER the moment her foot contacted the ground. She was still in great pain. He wanted to carry her to the car, but her grim determination held him back. Instead, he offered his arm. She took it with a sigh of relief.

The timing couldn't have been better, and he couldn't believe he nearly missed her. A minute or two later, and she would have been gone.

Color pinked her cheeks. Her face had been pasty when he last saw her last, shock from her injuries. Today, a radiance made her skin glow, despite her obvious pain. Long, chestnut hair flowed halfway down her back, and his fingers itched to run through her curls. He loved the way her hair shifted with red highlights when she moved.

She gazed at him, those beautiful brown eyes alight with hope, and he was happy to return her smile.

His sweats and shirt looked ridiculous, hanging in baggy folds over a body he knew to be divine. While it had been necessary to strip her out of the wet running clothes to avoid hypothermia, he harbored guilt about enjoying the view. Her petite body was the kind that begged to be explored by a man's hands.

But she was married.

"Want me to get the car?" Mac's deep baritone refocused CJ's attention.

After only a few steps, Melissa's breathing became labored. She clutched at his arm.

Odd, how that small contact had his heart pounding. He stopped to let Melissa catch her breath.

"You sure you're all right?"

"Sorry, …tired." She pulled in deep breaths, closed her eyes, and swayed.

"You don't have to apologize. Maybe we should go back?" He was afraid she might pass out.

Her grip on his arm tightened. "I'm…fine." She paused. "I think we're…just…going…too…fast." She pulled in a few more breaths.

"I'm sorry. I shouldn't have been walking so fast." Except he hadn't been walking fast at all. Poor thing was exhausted. CJ dug in his pocket and pulled out a set of keys. He gave a jerk of his chin to Mac. "Yeah, I think you should pull the car around."

"No problem." With a wink to Melissa, Mac trotted off.

She gave a weak laugh and shook her head. "Why does it take…so long…to get fit…but takes so little time…to lose it all?"

He couldn't help but pull her close. He loved how her frame molded perfectly to his. "I can carry you?" Maybe she'd say yes?

She shook her head. "Thanks, but I can make it."

He breathed in Melissa's soft scent, letting his eyes drift closed. He wanted to remember this moment. Her hair brushed against his arms, and he couldn't help but take a few strands and twist them around his fingers.

For a breath, and then another, she folded into him, but then she stiffened.

She put a hand on his chest, probably to steady herself. He soaked in the gesture, loving the feel of her hand on him. The moment lasted but a few seconds, then her hand dropped.

CJ turned Melissa around and returned them both to the curb.

He settled Melissa on a bench. "Better?"

Her breathing seemed to have evened out.

"I'm surprised how easily I got out of breath. I wouldn't think a few days in a hospital could do that," she said. "Your friend seems nice."

"Sorry about bringing him, but we're working a case. Don't let Mac scare you. His social filter is leaky, and the scar on his face can be off-putting, but he's a good guy."

Melissa bumped his arm. "Thanks for coming to see me."

He lowered himself beside Melissa and pulled her to him. She snuggled against him, and he kissed the top of her head. He brushed back the hair from her face, and she glanced at him, her eyes soft and her lips kissably close. How he longed to taste those lips, feel the softness of her skin, and tangle his tongue with hers, but she was married and to the worst possible man.

How could this delicate woman have ever been caught in the thralls of such a monster?

He pulled her deeper into his embrace. She breathed out, seeming content. All traces of her earlier pain was barely evident.

"I thought I'd never see you again," she murmured. She touched his shirt, then dropped her hand. "I never had the chance to thank you." She fingered her ring and heaved a deep sigh. "I'm not married by the way."

Wait! What? When had that happened?

He felt like kissing her right there. If he thought it wouldn't hurt her, he'd have his lips on her now.

This changed everything…most everything. He needed to tell her about Patterson. Hell, he couldn't believe he almost missed her. Mac wasn't happy bringing her along. His partner itched to get back to Jenny, but they weren't in a rush. It took time to work with local authorities to iron out jurisdictional agreements. Besides, Jenny would call when she was ready for a pickup.

Melissa lifted her hand to shield her eyes from the morning sun. The diamond glittered in the light, and she paused to look at it.

"I don't know why I never took it off. My husband…well, we've been separated for the past few years. I divorced him the day you and I met." A frown creased her forehead—so much sadness in a lovely face.

Freshly divorced. He gritted his teeth.

She yanked on the ring, but it didn't budge. "It's stuck now." She fidgeted on the bench and pulled away.

He let her go, giving her the space she needed, even as he wanted to pull her close and never let her go. "I may have a trick to help with that."

"You do?"

"All you need is dental floss."

"I wanted you to know. I didn't want you to get the wrong idea."

His heart hammered a steady beat. "You don't have to explain."

Did this change things? A woman who still wore her wedding ring had unresolved issues. Still, her words gave him hope, even if further complicating the situation. He didn't know if this meant she was available or not, but pushing would be wrong.

He needed to tell her about the odd phone conversation and her ex-husband's escape.

"Hey, I need—"

Her soft palm pressed against his arm. "Listen, I'm thrilled to see you again." She took another deep breath, looking tired and frail. "All I want is to go home."

He should have told Sam to put a watch on her house or reminded Jenny. This town's police force didn't have the resources to work the Henrietta Jones' case, let alone set up a watch on Melissa's home. She looked too frail to process the shock of her husband's escape. He needed to get her to a place of safety, but maybe with his team, he could take her home to grab some things first. He'd figure out how to break the news to her on the drive over.

He gripped her hand, tracing the delicate bones of her fingers. "Thank you for telling me."

She stretched up to kiss his cheek. The gesture was innocent, almost friendly. "Thank you for not taking advantage of me."

What kind of men had she filled her life with that she felt the need to thank him for doing what was right?

"I did what anyone would do."

An uneasiness settled over them for a time. He should tell her how he felt but found himself oddly tongue-tied.

She cocked her head. "Really?"

He fished inside his pocket and pulled out her cell phone. "You left this in my car. I wanted to make sure you got it back."

"Oh." Her hand shook as she turned the phone over in her hand. "Thank you."

"Hey there!" A skinny man ran toward them, carrying a clutch of red roses.

CJ shot to his feet, placing himself between Melissa and the stranger. He tried to keep her behind him, but she pushed him to the side.

"It's okay. It's the delivery man."

There was something off about the guy's face, or maybe it was his eyes. They were beady and set too close together.

"You forgot your flowers," he said with a gasp.

Okay, maybe it was the hunger in his gaze when he looked at Melissa that had CJ's senses spiking. He showed entirely too much interest. CJ shifted, using his body to shield Melissa. With a yank, he took the flowers out of the man's grip and handed them to her.

Melissa lifted the roses to her nose and gave a slow inhale. "Thank you, um, sorry, but I never got your name?"

CJ hated roses. Their pungent floral reek gave him headaches.

"It's Pierce, Pierce Channing," the man said.

Bloody bandages wrapped the guy's left hand. No way was CJ letting that creep touch Melissa.

Mac turned the corner in a black SUV.

"Ride's here," CJ blurted out. He stood a head taller than Pierce Channing and had at least fifty pounds on the guy. With his body language, he made it clear Melissa wasn't to be touched.

The car rolled up to the curb. CJ jerked the back door open and ushered her inside, leaving the delivery man gaping.

As he climbed in to sit beside her, she clutched his dilapidated daisy and placed the roses in the space between them. He squeezed her hand, trying to reassure her for what he wasn't sure.

She wiped a tear from her cheek. "Thank you for returning my phone. It was very thoughtful."

CJ helped Melissa secure her seatbelt and then clicked his in place. That Pierce guy hadn't moved. His too-narrow eyes stared as Mac pulled forward.

"We'll get you home soon," he said to Melissa.

She focused out the window. "Ever wish you could just disappear?"

SEVENTEEN

Field Of Dreams

MELISSA

For a moment, Melissa's heart thrummed with the vitality which came from knowing another person cared, but then a sinking feeling in her gut slammed her back to reality.

The only reason CJ showed up was to return her phone. But what about the daisy? It had been an afterthought; a weed yanked from the ground. She smiled, trying not to let her inner turmoil show. He brought a friend along. She couldn't shake the feeling that returning her phone had been secondary to whatever else he had to do today.

An awkward silence invaded the interior of the car as his huge friend drove away from the hospital. She didn't know what to say, not with Mac sitting so close. Even CJ seemed to prefer the quiet. His good deed done, she assumed he was eager to be rid of her.

But the daisy?

He probably would have done the same for anyone. It's what people did when they visited people in hospitals. But what was she to think about a daisy he yanked out of the ground, root and all? She was a fool to think there was anything special about a damn flower.

Hero worship?

That's the trap she'd fallen into. He saved her, and now she obsessed over him.

She stared out the window because she couldn't bear to look at him, ashamed by how quickly her thoughts turned…romantic. Is that what happened?

Mac asked for directions to her house, and she rattled them off.

"Hey, CJ," Mac said. "Do you mind if we pick up Jenny? She's done."

Another friend?

CJ glanced at her. "Do you mind?"

Melissa shook her head and then focused her attention out the window, content to sit in the oppressive silence.

A few minutes later, they pulled up outside police headquarters.

Melissa leaned forward, curious, but then regretted moving at all. She needed a dose of her pain killers.

The most beautiful woman Melissa had ever seen waited by the curb. Ebony skin, high cheekbones, and a flash of emerald in her eyes created a stunning combination. The woman's flawless skin reflected the sun's rays, making her glow with an otherworldly beauty. Long, narrow braids swished with the woman's every move, falling nearly to her hips.

Jenny opened the passenger door and hopped in. She twisted in her seat and thrust her arm between the gap separating the front and back seats.

"Hey, I'm Jenny. I see you met Mac."

Mac vented a long sigh. "Buckle up already."

Jenny smiled. "This hulking beast has shit for manners, but don't let him frighten you." She punched Mac in the arm. "He's as gentle as a teddy bear."

CJ shook his head. "Melissa, meet Jenny. She can be a bit rough around the edges."

"Um, nice to meet you," Melissa said.

"CJ don't be an ass. It's nice to talk to a woman now and then. Mac is shit for company, and you're not much better."

"Hey!" Mac clutched his chest. "You wound me."

"Whatever." Jenny twisted in her seat. "It's nice to meet you, Melissa."

Melissa couldn't help but smile. This was a woman she could be friends with.

Mac pulled the SUV back into traffic and followed her directions home.

"How are you feeling?" CJ placed a hand on her arm and gave a gentle squeeze.

"I'm fine."

She shifted away and stared out the window. Five tornadoes. The devastation was all around, paralyzing in its ferocity. How had her house weathered the storm? She didn't know what she was going to find at home. People wandered the wreckage, more people than lived here. But that's how it was in small towns. Good Samaritans came to help, clear out debris, gather up lost pets, and hand out emergency supplies.

News crews had satellite vans parked in the areas hit the hardest. Emergency crews and utility companies commanded a decent presence as well. All she wanted was for the ride to end. The sooner CJ was out of her life, the better. Right?

Wrong. She liked her savior.

"You don't look fine," he countered.

"I'm fine." She whipped her head around and dropped her gaze when his eyes widened, and he leaned back. She didn't blame him. He didn't deserve her anger. It wasn't his fault he didn't feel the same about her.

"Sorry." She counted to three. "I'm just tired."

He gave her one of his winks. "You're pretty when you smile."

The simple complement confused her, and her mouth gaped, unable to form a reply.

"Do you always go speechless when a man says you're pretty?" His low throated chuckle filled the car with a warmth she wanted to soak in forever and a day.

The daisy in her hand looked forlorn and droopy, kind of how she felt. She stroked the delicate petals while composing her next words.

"It's not something I hear often."

She focused all her attention on his flower, unable to meet his gaze.

"Well, you are."

"If I remember correctly, last time you commented on my looks, you compared me to a drowned rat."

His laughter filled the car. "I think I did."

"A drowned rat?" Jenny twisted around in the passenger seat, the scorn in her voice palpable. "Not your best pick up line, CJ." She wrapped an arm around the headrest, her attention flicking between Melissa and CJ. "Ignore him, love."

CJ coughed.

Melissa pulled at the oversized sweats. "I think I've gone from drowned rat to baggy-pants lady. I feel like someone stomped on me seven-ways from Sunday. Honestly, I want to get home, take a shower, wash my hair, and put on something clean."

The last part was a lie. She'd wear CJ's sweatshirt until it turned to rags. He'd probably be wanting his clothes back, though.

"I hear you," Jenny said. "Those have to be the ugliest clothes I've ever seen."

"Hey, those are mine!" CJ protested.

Jenny stuck her tongue out, then raised her brows with interest. "Am I allowed to ask how a girl we picked up at a hospital is wearing your clothes? Or do I let that one go?"

Mac huffed a laugh. "Oh, please, Jenny, stop meddling."

CJ's cheeks fill with color. "A gentleman never tells."

"You're no gentleman." Mac chuckled.

Jenny punched Mac in the arm. "Shut up." She looked at Melissa and cocked her head. "Are you going to make me ask?"

Melissa sighed and then told the story about the tornado, how she and CJ had met, and about him putting her in his sweats. She left out the part about him peeling her out of her wet clothes, and all the mixed signals she received.

"So, he gave me the only thing he had that was warm and dry." She turned to CJ. "I appreciate everything you did. If you give me a moment when we get to my house, I can give you the clothes back. Then you can be on your way."

The frown on his face surprised her. "About that…"

Why the hesitation? She pinched the bridge of her nose. "I've never felt so tired."

Jenny flipped around to face forward again, which left Melissa and CJ in relative privacy. Silence descended again, hanging stiff and stifling between them. Melissa passed the time looking out the window and took in the destruction. It was too hard to figure him out, not that she had the time.

Before long, Mac pulled into her driveway.

She moved to get the door, but CJ placed a hand on her thigh. "Sit tight. I'll help you out."

"I'm fine. I can get the door."

"I know, but let me help." He jumped out of the SUV. "Guys, let's check it out."

Mac and Jenny exchanged looks but said nothing as they climbed out.

Melissa waited for CJ to come around. He helped her out, grabbed the roses, and handed them to her.

They walked up the path in silence, not touching, but when she got to the porch steps, she needed help. Mac and Jenny walked a few paces behind.

She tried bending to retrieve the key from under the doormat but found it too painful. It would be days, if not weeks before her body healed.

"Can you get the key for me, please?"

"Please tell me you don't leave a key to your house under the front mat?"

"I always do when I go out for a run."

"Are you a fool?"

She took a step back. The words had been eerily calm and angry.

"Promise you'll never do something so stupid again." He glared at her as he lifted the mat.

There was no key.

She squinted in confusion, sure she left it there when she went for her run several days ago.

"You sure you left the key here?"

She nodded.

He straightened, pulled open the screen door, and made a signal with his hand over his head. Jenny and Mac stepped around Melissa, each with a gun in their hands. Who were these people?

Melissa clutched the roses. "What's wrong?"

Mac took off behind the house while Jenny came behind CJ. He had a gun in his hands as well. Where had that come from? He made another gesture, and Jenny responded with a nod. Reaching down, he twisted the knob of her front door.

She whispered, "I locked it when I left."

CJ placed a finger over his lips, ordering her to silence. She pressed her lips together, moistening them with her tongue.

Something was wrong. A chill hit her body, making her tremble.

He pushed on the door, pointed to the porch, and commanded her to stay where she was. Leading with his gun, he entered her home. Jenny followed.

Melissa ignored CJ's order and stepped inside.

Someone had spread yellow tulips all over her entryway.

He was supposed to be dead.

The bottom fell out of her word, pulling a ragged gasp from her lungs. She weaved on unsteady legs as fear drowned her in horrific memories. Yellow petals covered every square inch of the floor, except the middle where a young woman dressed all in white lay without moving.

CJ's voice turned arctic cold. "I told you to wait outside."

She could barely hear him over the roaring in her ears.

The girl's sightless eyes stared at the ceiling. Her hands had been posed, folded over her chest, clutching a sheaf of papers.

Melissa's heart hammered, flooding adrenaline and horror through her veins. Panic gripped with the sudden need to flee. But to where?

Beneath the body, glistening wetness spread, staining the nearest tulips deep crimson.

Jenny ghosted to the left, moving with incredible stealth into the living room. CJ skirted the edge of the foyer, headed to the dining room.

The paper in the woman's hands was unmistakable. The message was clear as day. One word had been scrawled over the divorce decree.

MINE.

She dropped to her knees, her scream splitting the air, and the bouquet of red roses tumbled to the floor.

EIGHTEEN

Crime Scene

CJ

The scene in Melissa's house was a walking nightmare. CJ had an intimate familiarity with death but had seen nothing as cold as this. Not even when he'd taken his father's life or logged his first official kill. Those moments had been filled with passion, anger over the brutalization of his mother night after night, and fear for what his sister may one day endure. He'd been left with no other option. The next kill had been a snake of a man who'd kidnapped two innocent girls.

Each of those kills had been justified, but irrevocably scarred his heart.

This?

It was pristine, methodical, emotionless.

Which begged the question. What were Patterson's motives?

Fuck, he'd spoken to his sister's murderer on the phone the day Patterson had escaped.

The police responded within minutes of his call. Ignoring all the questions he had, he asked Melissa if she knew who the girl was, but

Melissa shook her head. She hadn't said a word since that bloodcurdling scream.

Someone should've had this house under surveillance. What the fuck were all those National Guardsmen doing? Couldn't one of them have been spared to watch this house?

Jenny and Mac helped him clear Melissa's home. Scott Patterson wasn't inside although Mac had seen a man hopping over the back fence. He'd given chase but returned empty-handed. If Melissa had come home by herself, she would've walked into her husband's madness defenseless and alone. CJ scrubbed a hand over his face, blocking that terrifying scene from his mind.

After recovering from the initial shock, her tears began, and he held her until the police arrived and separated them. At least that part followed standard procedure.

The next hour had been spent under the scrutiny of the police and a barrage of questioning.

He put in a call to Sam. His boss was already all over the case, calling his contacts. Due to the high profile, there was no doubt the FBI would be called in to assist.

Melissa looked nothing like the fragile woman accused of assisting her husband in the deaths of so many girls. She'd been a platinum blonde during the trial. The woman he'd saved from a tornado bore little resemblance to the wife of Scott Patterson. No wonder he hadn't recognized her during the storm.

He kicked a pebble with his shoe. The police had finished with him, and now he listened on the phone while his boss chewed his ear off.

Melissa perched beside Jenny on the porch steps. Even the modest house she lived in was a far cry from the palatial estate Patterson had owned.

Despite all the insinuations during the murder trial stating her culpability, Melissa hadn't been connected to Patterson's crimes. Claims of an abusive relationship came to light, as did the release of her medical history and emergency room visits. The story had been buried under the current headlines of the day. She'd been found innocent, but the wreckage Scott Patterson wrought upon his wife persisted.

It looked like she had done as much as she could to escape her past. Why she remained in the small town which had dragged her through the mud remained a mystery. An even more concerning issue was why she still wore that damned ring?

A detective held a notepad in one hand and pencil in the other while he grilled Melissa. He scribbled down her answers, asking all the wrong questions.

No way had she been involved in the mess inside. He'd already gone over her hospitalization with the detective.

Melissa's eyes were a swollen mess. He could see the puffiness from halfway across the lawn. Her cheeks were wet with tears, and she sat with a rigid spine. Like the rest of them, she wasn't allowed inside where the crime scene was located, nor was she allowed to leave.

He was taking care of that.

The police didn't care she'd been released from the hospital a little less than an hour ago. They had questions and wrote on small pads of paper with the scratching of their pencils. The noise had CJ gritting his teeth.

A second cop sauntered over to where the lead detective grilled Melissa. He rested his foot on the lowermost stair and leaned in, towering over her.

Poor thing wrapped her arms around herself and hunched inward. Her face pinched with pain. She wasn't fully recovered from surgery and now had to deal with the horror of seeing a girl murdered in her home.

He should be over there, comforting her, but instead, he was on the phone, arguing with his boss.

"I want her protected," he said for the tenth time.

"You know the drill. Time is of the essence."

"Look, Jenny finished with the Police Chief; we're going to go over the files and strategize. Jenny and Mac can do that while I make sure Melissa is set up someplace safe. You said the FBI is on the way. Melissa's security detail isn't going to interfere with the Henrietta Jones' case. I promise."

"I know, but I also know you. You're too close to Scott Patterson. I need you focused on Jones' case."

"I am."

"He's making a statement."

"She's our only link to Patterson, and as you said, he wants her. The best way to catch him is to keep Melissa close. Let me do that, at least until the Feds arrive."

"Let the locals see to her protection."

"They're stretched to breaking. They should've had a guard on her the moment Patterson went missing, but the whole town is in turmoil. They couldn't even locate her in the hospital, and they should've had someone watching her house the moment he escaped. I'm telling you, they're not set up for this."

"I know," Sam said with a heavy exhale.

CJ ran a hand over the top of his head. "Do you have an ETA on the Feds? We need someone with half a brain to look at this crime scene before the locals destroy it."

"I don't, but thanks to our new boss, we have an in with the FBI, a man named Ben Chambers. He's working to mobilize a team. The rest of Delta team should be there within the hour. In the meantime, get Melissa Evans to a secure location. Let Jenny run the Henrietta Jones' case, but don't leave her hanging. She needs a good mentor."

He caught Melissa's eye. Torment filled her face, and an aura of hopelessness radiated outward from her small form. He wanted to tell her everything would be all right.

Sam's clipped voice returned. "It's all arranged. I'm texting you the information for the hotel. They have tight enough security; she'll be safe there. Get her settled and then rejoin with Mac and Jenny. Don't fuck this up."

"Thanks, Sam." He marched over to Melissa and pulled her into his arms. "We're leaving."

NINETEEN

Hearts And Flowers

CJ

HEARTS AND FLOWERS WERE FOR SAPS AND WEAK-WILLED FOOLS, BUT slap him silly if CJ wasn't becoming that guy for Melissa. He preferred guns, sweat, hard fists, and even straight-up sex, but it didn't bother him to wrap Melissa in his arms and simply hold her close.

Melissa stared at him, confused after he announced they would be leaving. He entwined his fingers with hers, hoping to reassure her everything would be okay.

She cocked her head. "But the officer…"

He lifted her hands and wrapped them around his neck, pulling her against him. She barely came to his shoulders, and he could rest his chin on the top of her head if he wanted. The woman fit him like a glove. She tilted her head back to look at him, but all he could see were her pink, pillowy, and perfectly kissable lips.

She wasn't married to that psychopathic asshole, which meant he didn't have to keep his hands to himself.

A devilish grin spread across his face.

"I'm taking you to a hotel with a hot shower or warm bath, whichever you prefer. You've got to be exhausted."

"But my things?"

"We'll get whatever you need."

He jerked his chin to Jenny, who'd been watching the whole exchange. She arched a dark eyebrow and cocked her head to the side.

"The cops won't let you inside, but they might let Jenny take a few things." The place was a crime scene, he doubted they'd let Jenny take anything, even with the connections Sam had called, but it was worth a try.

"Yeah, sure," Jenny said. "Is there anything in particular you want?"

Melissa chewed her lower lip, then rattled off a list and told Jenny where to find a suitcase.

Jenny gave him one of those annoying I-know-what-you're-thinking looks. She wasn't a woman who took orders well. Maybe he should have asked before offering her services. Still, he wanted to get Melissa away from the house as quickly as possible.

"Please just do it already." CJ vented an exasperated sigh.

Jenny gave the slightest of nods before heading inside.

"I don't understand how I can leave." Melissa scrunched her forehead. "They said I had to stay and go down—"

"You've been in the hospital. It's clear you had nothing to do with this. They'll have more questions, but you can answer them later. You need rest, and I want to make sure you get stripped out of those clothes and in that shower."

A flush crept into her cheeks. Too late, he realized what he'd said and how she might have taken it. He'd already stripped her down once. The chance to do so again had his mind thinking wicked thoughts and his cock twitching.

"You know who they think did that, don't you?" She pointed back to her house, her voice hesitant and wary.

He nodded. There was nothing to be gained by ignoring the truth. "I do."

She shifted away from him and cast her gaze to the ground. He tightened his grip around her waist, pulling her back to his chest.

"Then you know who I am?"

"I do." But she didn't yet know how he was connected to her ex-husband.

"You sure you want to be associated with the ex-wife of a serial killer?"

His heart broke to see a fresh tear creep down her cheek.

He wiped the moisture away with his thumb, wishing he could have kissed it away instead. "Your safety worries me. I'm concerned he's back out in the world where he can hurt you."

"You're too kind." She brushed another tear from her cheek. "I thought it was over. I thought I'd finally get my life back." More sniffles followed a few choked sobs. "He just keeps coming back."

He hadn't yet mentioned the phone conversation he'd had with her ex-husband, but now was not the time. She was frightened enough.

He tucked her head under his chin, and his hands moved of their own accord, stroking her gorgeous hair and twining it around his fingers. It was so much more beautiful than the short blonde bob she'd once worn.

"He's out there." Another shudder passed through her body. "That girl died because of me."

He kissed the top of her head. "It's not your fault."

"He won't stop. Forever and always, those were our vows. Until death do us part. He'll keep killing until he has me. I should never have gone through with the divorce. I knew what it would do to him, but I thought… I just wanted to be free."

Her fingers clutched at the fabric of his shirt, and her voice dropped to a whisper. "When it happened, I didn't believe the police when they came to my house. I didn't believe it when they showed me the warrant. I still couldn't wrap my head around what was happening when they found the bodies. He told me it wasn't him, and I believed every word."

CJ held her close and rubbed her back. "Melissa, stop. There's no way you could have known."

She shook her head as if trying to dispel the horrible memories.

He'd seen similar behaviors in other victims and did his best to listen.

"I should have known," her voice cracked, "but I was so afraid. I ignored all the odd things he did because I wasn't allowed to question him. I couldn't see what was right in front of my face." Her voice dropped to a whisper. "I married a monster, and everyone thought I'd helped him." She choked back more sobs. Despair hung thick on her words, but in her eyes, the truth shimmered with her fear.

He related to her horror because of his memories.

"After his execution, I thought I'd be able to live again, turn the page on a new life. But, he's cheated me out of that, and—oh God—all the families waiting for justice."

Her comment had him tensing, and he had to force himself to relax.

She pulled at CJ's shirt. "He's coming, and he won't stop until he has me back until he—" She broke down with wracking sobs.

CJ rocked her, not knowing what else he could do. "You'll be in protective custody. He won't be able to touch you."

Jenny walked out of the house carrying a small suitcase. Behind her, Mac followed with a much larger bag. CJ arched a brow.

Jenny shrugged. "Wasn't sure what to pack. You never know what a girl will need."

He shook his head. "Load it into the car. Did you talk to Sam?"

Mac's face broke out into a grin. "Oh, you bet I did. Not sure what you said, but we've got marching orders."

"We good?" He asked.

"Yup, we have some strategizing and planning to do, but this won't hold us up."

CJ blew out a breath. "Well, let's not waste any more time. Take us to the hotel, and we'll get started."

"There's not much to go on until we talk to the girls."

Melissa stiffened. "Girls?" Her raw, helpless gaze tunneled straight to his gut. "Oh, CJ! There are more girls?"

With the slightest press of his lips against her temple, he made a hushing sound.

"No, it's for a kidnapping case we're working. Nothing to do with this." She felt too damn good, cuddled against his side.

"What exactly do you do?" Melissa asked. "I thought you were a paramedic."

"I was… am, kind of." He scratched his head. Explaining what Sam's company did would generate more questions than he was willing to answer. "We work kidnapping cases in consultation with the FBI."

She stiffened. "What kind of consultation work?"

"High profile kidnappings." He pointed to her house. "Sometimes we help with cases like this."

She swayed on her feet, and he steadied her until she regained her balance. "Who are you?"

"I'm a Guardian." He'd explain what that meant later. Eventually, he'd have to tell her about his sister. But that talk could wait.

TWENTY

Setbacks

PIERCE

I COULDN'T BELIEVE MY BAD LUCK.

Collecting my Queen was proving more complicated than it needed to be. I almost had her until that asshole showed up with his friend.

If that stupid male nurse hadn't been so over-protective, she would've been in my car before that asshole arrived. That nurse bugged me. He'd been there when I'd delivered the tulips. I hadn't liked him then, and I loathed him even more for costing me the opportunity to take my Queen.

I don't think he bought my story about boxing.

How dare he tell me what I could and couldn't do. That jerk of a nurse put his nose where it didn't belong. My frustration was building, heating my blood with dark urges I could barely contain. I needed a release before I did something stupid.

While I didn't have my Queen, six princesses were waiting to serve. There was also a very disobedient Fairy Godmother I needed to punish.

A long night stretched ahead of me; all I needed to do was pace myself and work out the demons festering inside of me.

My Fairy Godmother had a nasty habit of biting. It was time to introduce her to a ring gag. Her video was fun to watch. I planned on going over it again with her, pointing out the luscious moans she'd made when she'd ridden my cock. I was going to make her watch her tits bounce, and the explosive orgasm I'd ripped from her body.

Her motherly instincts had flashed when I'd introduced her to my princesses. A perfect Fairy Godmother, a protective streak ran through her veins.

It had been a long time since I'd used my knives. I shied away from them because of the mess they caused. But, her protectiveness had me thinking it was time to bring the blades back out. What lengths would she go to protect the others? Maybe, I could get her to be more willing during our time together.

Yes, that would be perfect.

I'd love to watch those tits bounce. I'd have to work out the placement of the chains. Having her ride me placed me in a vulnerable position, but I was confident I could rig something safe.

The distraction would help while I figured out how to get my Queen.

TWENTY-ONE

Check In

MELISSA

The hotel wasn't super fancy, but it was the nicest in town. Melissa found herself bracketed by CJ and his friend, Mac. They escorted her through the lobby. Each carried one of her suitcases. Jenny remained with the car, stating she had calls to make.

Scott had been in her house. He defiled her home. Her heart raced, and all she wanted to do was run and hide. Go so far away, Scott would never find her. But he would. He would track her to the ends of the earth.

"You doing okay?" CJ cupped her elbow, lending support.

Each step drained energy from her body. Pain surged and flashed, and she was tired of pretending she didn't hurt everywhere at once. She held herself stiffly, afraid to twist or bend, but movement was inevitable and pain unavoidable. As much as her body suffered, it was her heart which pained her the most. Scott had broken it years ago, and killing that woman in her home? He left her heart ripped and shredded to pieces.

"Just overwhelmed." She scanned the hotel lobby, her skin sweating with nerves.

Mac had seen a man running out of her yard. If Scott had followed them, she'd be in no condition to run, let alone defend herself.

She may have stretched the truth with Dr. Sims. Her nurse had been suspicious, and Charles questioned whether she was well enough to go home. He might have been right. Another day or two in the hospital might have been a better choice.

Too late now.

"You don't look good." When Mac spoke, it sounded like the rumbling of distant thunder. "Look like you're about ready to keel over."

Sharp shards of pain lanced through her side as she took another step. He might be right. She bit her lip and hoped no one noticed. Sweat beaded her brow, and her forehead flushed. Breath labored into her chest, tugging in tight little gasps as if her body was determined to make as little movement as possible and minimize the pain.

"I think I just need to lie down for a bit."

She closed her eyes and prayed for strength. All she had to do was make it to the room upstairs. Then she could rest. Spots danced in her vision, and the room swayed under her feet. She blinked against vertigo, forcing her mind to alertness and her body to endure.

I will not pass out.

Despite the soreness of her body, a constant throb, and ache, her mind remained alert. The shock of the last few hours penetrated deep, but she wasn't defeated. If anything, the experience hardened her determination. She wouldn't let Scott break her, no matter how hard he tried.

A quaint three-bedroom, her house was a far cry from the monstrous estate she had lived in with Scott. It had taken her nearly two years after his incarceration to work up the courage to move. The day she filed divorce papers, she shut the door for good. The estate sat empty and neglected now, deteriorating over time.

Selling it hadn't been an option. His family wouldn't allow the sale, despite what their son had done. The Patterson family home now rotted like everything else Scott had touched.

CJ gave her the once over as if making sure she was doing okay. If only he knew how close she was to complete collapse. She smiled, pretending all was well. Nothing could be further from the truth. Somehow, she managed to convince him, because he continued forward, guiding her through the crowds of the spacious hotel lobby.

He said he worked for a firm which consulted with the FBI, and now he knew her darkest secret. Wife of a serial killer, she couldn't be more cursed. Oddly, he hadn't abandoned her to face this horror alone. How long he would be with her, she didn't know but was glad for whatever stolen time she could take.

Now that she knew a little about what he did, she caught the way he surveyed the room. He watched not only her but those around him, his eyes scanning the lobby and keeping a lookout for threats. As vulnerable as she felt, it was nice to know someone trustworthy was looking out for her wellbeing.

Slowly, they made their way to the check-in counter.

All she wanted was to forget who she was or better yet disappear. Years ago, the cops questioned her like they'd done today. Back then, they confined her for two days while the interminable questioning continued. Thank goodness the same hadn't happened today.

Would she ever be free of her ex? He'd been an abusive husband, cruel in so many ways, but she had stood by him. It was expected as a wife, and he told her what he would do if she ever left him.

Her shoulders slumped, and she could barely hold her head up.

CJ glanced at her, concern tugging at the corners of his eyes while he checked in at the registration desk. He handed the suitcase he was carrying to Mac.

"Take this, please." Mac grabbed the bag, and CJ wrapped an arm around her shoulders. "Just a little longer."

It was time to be strong. She'd been through this before and would get through it again. She could get a gun, even hire a bodyguard until she figured out how to leave town. How did someone disappear? Scott wouldn't stop looking. All she had, for now, was CJ. For now, she would trust him and not worry about the details.

But despite CJ's pledge to protect, he didn't know Scott. Her husband never failed once he set his mind to a task. And he meant to punish her for leaving him to die.

The receptionist behind the counter handed CJ the card keys to the room. Mac stepped away to survey the lobby and its attendant guests. CJ guided her to a bank of elevators, pressing his hand to the small of her back. Ever protective, he remained by her side.

"Room's on the eighteenth floor," CJ said.

Mac shadowed them, joining them at the elevator. He put out a hand, preventing a couple from entering the elevator.

The man huffed while the woman gave an indignant snort. When Mac took half a step forward, both their expressions changed. The doors closed, leaving the three of them alone inside the glass elevator.

Mac said. "I'll help you to the room and then talk to security."

"Thanks, I appreciate it. Jenny needs you, so be quick. Sweep the room with me then go. I'll wait until the rest of our team shows up, then call you." He jabbed the button for the eighteenth floor, and they rode up in silence.

She vented a deep sigh.

"You don't look so good." He placed the back of his hand on her forehead. "You feel clammy."

Not wanting him to touch her, she took a step back. She couldn't stand any more kindness from this man, but she wanted it desperately. "I'm fine. Just tired and sore."

From his expression, he didn't believe her, but he didn't press. Mac said nothing and did a great job holding up his end of the silence for the rest of the elevator ride. Heights made her dizzy, so she avoided looking out of the glass to the lobby falling away beneath them. Finally, the doors opened, and CJ strode out, leaving Mac to manage the suitcases.

Melissa swayed on her feet as her vision spotted and dimmed.

Mac leaned over. "You okay?"

"Just dizzy." She flashed him a fake smile. "It's been a long day, and I don't like heights."

He leaned down, tucked one of her suitcases under his arm, and grabbed the other in the same hand. Mac wrapped his free arm around Melissa. "You can lean on me, sugar. You look like crap."

"I'm going to tell Jenny that you guys are horrible at flattery."

He smiled at her attempt at humor. "She knows already, but seriously, your coloring is off. You look pale and a little sweaty looking."

"I'm fine."

Mac helped her down the hall, ignoring her protests. CJ jogged ahead and inserted a keycard into the electronic lock. He drew his gun and opened the door.

She moved to step behind him, but Mac held her in place. "Let him clear the room. Then we go in."

They waited outside while Mac scanned the hall.

"Clear," CJ said from inside the room.

Mac released her and gave her a gentle nudge. "In you go."

Melissa stepped inside an opulent suite. A mini kitchen and sofa suite made up the main room, and a door led off to a bedroom. Mac carried in the two suitcases, shut the door and latched the security bolt.

She walked to the large picture window and pulled up short. "Oh, my. This view is spectacular."

The last time she'd been in a hotel room this large had been ten years ago on her honeymoon. She clutched her stomach as it churned.

"I can't afford this."

"You're not paying for the room." CJ pulled her into another hug.

"I'm not?"

He shook his head. "You're in police protective custody."

"I am?" Silly question, because that was obvious, but that didn't mean it felt real.

"Don't worry." He turned to Mac. "How much longer until her detail arrives?"

"Not long," Mac said. "Should be here within the hour."

"Good, go talk to hotel security and make sure they're briefed." CJ leaned against the small counter of the kitchenette and fingered through the coffee choices. "I doubt he'll try to get to her here."

A chill traveled down the center of her spine. "He's coming for me."

Mac put his hands on her shoulders and turned her to face him. "It only makes sense, but given his history of planning, he's going to need time to figure something out."

"So, what do I do?"

Mac pointed to CJ. "You mind him. Do what he says. Don't leave the room. He's in charge until Jenny or I get back. You open the door for no one else. You got it?"

She could only nod.

"All right, I'm gonna go. Jenny and I have business." He turned to CJ. "Can I have a word with you in the hall?"

The two of them disappeared to the hall, and when CJ returned a few moments later, he made sure the security bolt latched.

She took a step back, unprepared to see the heat in his gaze. It was gone in a flash, though. He banked his expression so quickly she wondered if she'd imagined it. She took in a deep breath and glanced around the living room, uncertain what to do next.

CJ picked up the two suitcases and carried them to the bedroom. "Who knows what Jenny packed. Take a look and let me know if you need anything else. I'll either have Jenny get it from your house or buy it." He put the suitcases on the bed.

She followed, feeling hesitant and awkward. CJ unzipped the suitcases and opened them. He brushed the side of her cheek, then swept a strand of her hair back, tucking it behind her ear.

Such a small gesture, she trembled.

"Trust me," he said, "you'll feel better after a shower."

It infuriated her how he had her entire body shaking with his tender touch. She balled her fingers into fists and fought a tear forming at the corner of her eye.

He pulled her into his arms. "Melissa, you'll be okay."

The heat of his body melted any self-respect she had left. It didn't matter if he was only doing his job. She buried her head into his chest and inhaled his intoxicating scent, musky with the slightest hint of spice. Wrapping her arms around his waist, she let herself believe this incredible man could want the damaged goods she represented. It may not be the truth, but it didn't matter. She needed to be held, to be comforted, if only for a moment.

TWENTY-TWO

His Shower

CJ

CJ BREATHED IN MELISSA'S LIGHT SCENT, LILAC, AND ROSE. SHE reminded him of the breaking rays of dawn, full of promise with the coming of the day. He clutched her tight as if holding her could protect her from the evil permeating her life. If she could find shelter in his arms, then maybe some of the horrors visited upon her could be pushed aside if only for this moment.

How one man could destroy the lives of so many infuriated him. In his line of work, it was easy to believe the war of good against evil would never be won, and the devil ruled the earth.

Whenever he felt this sense of futility, he turned to the victims. Strong and resilient, he admired how they picked up the ruin of their lives and carried on. They reminded him to be strong and to continue the fight.

Scott Patterson destroyed Melissa's life as surely as he stole the lives of his victims. Despite that, or in spite of it, Melissa pieced her life back together, much like CJ continued with his, moving with the pace of each day until a week turned into a month and months became years.

Evil touched too much of his life, taking first his innocence, then his mother, and finally, his sister. Yet, he still believed he could change the world. Holding Melissa had him wishing he could do more. Be more.

What had it been like living with a serial killer, loving him, only to experience the ultimate in betrayal?

A man who fixed things, he vowed to solve her problem. Until then, he would provide comfort and support.

"Go take a shower," CJ said. "You'll feel better. Or soak in the tub."

"I don't want to."

"I know, but there's nothing either of us can do right now." He lifted her chin and forced her to look at him. "The cops are looking for him. The Feds will be here soon. There's nothing to do except get some rest."

"I think I'll just go to bed."

He placed his hands on her arms and lifted her away from his chest, just far enough to gaze into her eyes. "Trust me. A shower will make you feel ten times better."

"I'm so tired."

He gave an easy laugh. "I don't doubt it. I'm surprised you're doing as well as you are." With a tiny shove, he got her moving. "Take a nice long soak. I'll be in the living room. If you don't mind, keep the door cracked. That way, if you need anything, I'll be able to hear."

She made her way to the bathroom, turning to call out to him as he headed to the other room. "In case I forget, thanks."

He settled onto the couch, shifting as he tried to find a comfortable position. It proved difficult, because Melissa was in the other room, stripping for her shower. His pants tightened as he remembered undressing her in that garage.

The swell of her breasts behind the lace of her bra fascinated him, and the flare of her hips begged for his hands to encircle her tiny waist. Those hips were built for a man's hands, designed for traction and to withstand his dominating need. Her breasts were the perfect size, neither too small nor too large. Pillowy soft, they promised comfort and pleasure. He leaned his head back with a sigh and adjusted his growing erection behind the zipper of his jeans.

Soft sobs drifted to his ears.

He jolted to his feet, ready to go to her, but forced his protective urges to the background. Crying was natural and expected after the events of the day. He left her to her grief, giving as much privacy as he could. A moment later, a thud sounded from the bathroom. The timbre of her cries turned frantic. This time, he didn't hesitate.

He found her sprawled on the floor. Steam filled the room, and he had difficulty making out what he saw. She lay in an awkward pile, legs bent, and her arm trapped beneath her naked body. Her long hair covered her face and draped her breasts and shoulders. Heavy bruising covered her body.

Why hadn't she said anything? Shades of red, purple, blue, yellow, and green covered her from her collar bone to her hip. The bruising wrapped around to her back and extended down her buttocks.

"What happened?" An unnecessary comment, but he couldn't think of anything else to say.

Her words were unintelligible. She gestured to her back, but he didn't understand what she was trying to say. He opened the shower door and knelt by her side. The water drenched his clothes.

She was trying to push herself up. Without a thought, he sat beside her, collected her in his arms, and rocked her against his chest.

She curled into him.

After a time, her sobbing stilled.

"I couldn't reach the soap, and then I fell. I couldn't get off the floor. It hurts so much." Her body shook with her frustrated cries. "I can't even take a shower by myself."

"Shh, it's going to be all right." Poor thing was overwhelmed. Hell, he was overwhelmed. Was he really cradling a naked woman in a shower? What the hell was he thinking?

He knew what he needed to do and hoped she understood his intentions were honorable. He set her on the floor, taking great pains to place her with care. The mass of bruising on her body had him concerned. He moved the wet hair out of her face.

"Do you trust me?"

She wrapped her arms around her chest, shielding her breasts from his view, and pulled her knees up to hide everything else. Slowly, she nodded.

He pulled her to her feet, being careful not to cause her too much pain.

"I couldn't get my arm to reach—"

He placed a finger over her lips. "You trusted me once before. Trust me now."

She took in a shuddering breath, and her mouth parted.

He placed his finger under her chin. "I'll be a perfect gentleman. I'll help you soap up, wash your hair, and rinse you off…"

"You won't touch me?"

A smirk lifted the corner of his lips. "I'll have to touch to get you clean. Just think of it as a sponge bath, but in a shower instead."

His gaze cut to the jeans plastered against his legs. "I need to get out of my jeans, but I'll keep my boxers on."

Her eyes widened. "You're taking your clothes off?"

"Not everything. But it'll make less mess to clean up later if I strip out of my shirt and jeans. Unlike you, I don't have a change of clothes."

"You must think I'm a wreck."

"I think you need someone to help you. That's not the same as being a wreck."

"Have you ever washed a woman's hair before?" She kept her arms crossed over her chest, but she did a poor job of hiding her breasts. A pink nipple peeked out between the crossing of her arms.

It took everything for him to keep his eyes focused on her face.

"It's not like running a bar of soap over your head," she said.

He was happy to see some of her spunkiness return. "Hair washing is one of my many skills. When I'm done with you, you'll feel like a new woman."

She bit her lower lip.

"Ah, shit, I didn't mean it like that."

Her gaze darted to the ground. He couldn't help but take another peek at her creamy skin.

"You won't do anything funny?"

"Scout's honor."

"You were a Boy Scout?" The look on her face told him she didn't believe him.

"You're looking at an honest to goodness Eagle Scout. Your safety is assured in my hands." He gave her a four-finger salute.

She readjusted her arms, covering the flash of nipple he'd been staring at.

"I'm not promising perfection, but I promise I'll take care of you." With great reluctance, he brought his gaze back to her eyes.

"Thanks." She shifted her eyes down, looking even more vulnerable.

He wanted to wrap her in his arms and take her pain away.

"Why didn't you tell me you were hurt so badly? If I'd known, I would've taken you back to the hospital."

"I couldn't stand staying in that hospital a day longer. Besides, as long as I don't bend, twist, or move, I'm good." The threat of tears wavered in her voice.

He headed them off by placing his hands on her bare hips and his chin on the sweep of her shoulder. He loved touching her, and the smoothness of her skin reminded him of velvet. The heat of her body made his body answer with a burn of its own.

With a whisper, he tried to soothe her. "Well, let's just get through this shower." As awkward as that may be.

"You said you'd be a gentleman."

"And I intend to honor my word." Not an easy task. He struggled not to stare at the swell of her breasts. "I'm going to take my clothes off now. Do you think you can stand, or are you at risk for falling again?"

"Standing isn't the problem. It's moving that hurts."

Divesting himself of the wet jeans proved more difficult than expected, but he hopped and tugged until he shimmied out of them. He stripped out of his shirt, leaving only his boxers in place. There was nothing he could do about the erection tenting his pants.

She leaned her forehead against the wall, one hand splayed against the tiles, not even looking at him. Her other arm was wrapped around her waist. The rounded globes of her ass had him drawing a sharp breath. His cock twitched at the sight of her nakedness, hungry, needful, and wholly inappropriate.

So fragile.

With only his boxers to cover him, he stepped behind her and placed a hand on her shoulder, needing to touch her, not overwhelm her. He could only imagine the vulnerability she must be feeling.

And the trust she extended him? CJ's heart hammered beneath his breastbone, and he reined in the raging tide of lust surging through his veins.

As awkward as she was when she moved, she relaxed into his touch. That gave him hope.

A shudder passed through her body.

He didn't know how he would make it through this shower. He'd be embarrassed if he broke his word, but he was determined to help Melissa. If he could keep his mind on why he was here, and not on what he wanted to do, he'd make it through. But images of pushing her against the wall and burying himself balls deep kept flashing through his head. He needed to stop that line of thought before he burst.

He needed to focus.

She sighed. "I hate feeling like this."

"Try not to think about it. Here, hold my hand."

Here he was again, stuck in hero-land, worse than the friend-zone as far as he was concerned. At least when he was in the friend-zone, he knew where he stood. In hero-land, he never knew what to expect.

TWENTY-THREE

Her Shower

MELISSA

MELISSA'S HEART STUMBLED, UNSURE WHETHER TO RACE AHEAD OR stop in its tracks. She was in a shower big enough for two with the hero of her dreams standing half-naked behind her.

She felt all of him. His presence enveloped her, wrapped around her, and covered her in a blanket of support and something much more primal. The heat of his skin radiated out from him as if seeking her center and stoking a desire buried deep within. She wanted him. Or wanted him to want her. She breathed deep, certain this was a dream, but knowing it was all too real.

It would be nice to enjoy this moment, except for the excruciating pain.

Of all her fantasies, none held a candle to what was happening now, but this wasn't a sensual prelude to sex. It was a pathetic weakness that brought him near.

Story of her life, and it sucked.

Her body was a twisted mess of muscles strained too far, and she'd seen the bruising when she'd undressed. She thought she could handle something as simple as a shower, but the floor tilted up, and she crashed into it. And as she fell, memories of a more twisted time invaded her thoughts.

The bruises and pain brought back the night of her first beating.

She'd been married less than two years. A thunderstorm raged above her house. Flashes of lightning lit up the sky, and in-between the booming thunder, tornado sirens pierced the night with their shrill cries.

Scott hadn't finished the new tornado shelter. It didn't have a door. She was alone, waiting for Scott to come home. She grabbed the keys to the old shed, the one he ordered her never to go inside.

The entrance to the old shelter was in there, a heavy door she could barely lift, but a door nonetheless. He said it wasn't safe, likely to collapse at any moment, but she feared the destructive force of a tornado more than a cave-in from an old storm shelter.

With the wind roaring, and the sirens wailing, fear gripped her gut. The new shelter wasn't ready, and she had to choose. She raced to the old shed and fumbled to open the trap door leading to safety. It might collapse inward, but it was better than facing a tornado in a shelter without a door.

She didn't hear him yelling until he yanked her back, slapped her in the face, and knocked her to the ground. He kicked her in the ribs and screamed at her to never go inside the old shed.

Scott dragged her back through the storm and across the expansive lawn to the new shelter. He threw her inside, and she crumpled, shivering against the cold concrete floor. Beyond the entrance, the storm howled, and the sirens wailed.

Confused and terrified, yet relieved to have her husband home, she didn't understand his rage. Her relief was short-lived because he ripped screams from her battered body under the fury of his belt.

For your protection, he said. He punctuated each word with the swing of his belt. The old shelter isn't safe, he said.

She would discover that lie many years later. If only she made it to the old shelter before he came home. How many lives could she have saved if she discovered what he hid beneath the shed?

She spent two days in the hospital under observation, and never ventured into that corner of the estate again, not even when the police came four years later with a warrant demanding she open that old shed. She thrust the keys at them, her hand shaking, unwilling to break one of Scott's rules.

Only then did she learn what vile purpose that shed, and the bunker below it, had been used.

Tears ran down her cheeks with the terrible guilt from that night. If only she'd been quicker. If only he hadn't come home when he had. If only she had discovered the girls trapped inside. She could have saved them. She could have saved all the ones who had suffered and died over the next four years.

"Hey, are you okay?" CJ leaned over her shoulder, his powerful hands gripping her waist.

His calming presence helped her breathe away the horror of that night and anchor herself back in the present. Her tears flowed, but he couldn't see the terrible remorse.

Ah hell, what was she thinking? He was in the shower, stripped down to his skivvies, not naked but close enough, and he was trying to comfort her. She pressed her palm against the tile, spreading her fingers in frustration. The rough tile pebbled beneath her fingertips, just as ugly and raw as she felt on the inside.

CJ said a shower would make her feel better. He didn't mention he'd be joining her, not that her falling down had been his fault. But she felt self-conscious exposed to his eyes.

Was he looking at her ass? Did he like what he saw? Had he seen down there? She hadn't shaved or waxed in far too long. He must think her a primitive.

She pressed her forehead against the shower wall and breathed out.

His fingers dug deep into her back. The roughness of his hands caught on her skin, causing tiny shivers to spread out from each of his fingertips. He moved up to her neck, hitting pressure points at the base of her skull.

It hurt like crap, but the pounding in her head seemed to fade.

"Does that feel okay?" He didn't ease the pressure. "Not too hard?"

"It hurts," she admitted, "but whatever you're doing is making my headache go away."

"That's what it's supposed to do. Try not to tense up."

Easier said than done.

His fingers worked magic. He said he would only help her wash up, not give a massage, but she didn't dare stop him. Whatever he was doing felt heavenly.

CJ's fingers pressed into her flesh, kneaded with expert precision, and attacked her knotted muscles with purpose. Beneath his touch, her body melted, taut muscles relaxing, the pain dissipated.

"You've got a lot of knots," he said.

Melissa lifted her shoulders to her ears when he pressed on a particularly sensitive spot.

He stopped rubbing. "Sorry. I didn't mean to hurt you."

"No. It feels amazing." She stretched her neck.

His hands pressed against her skin, and his fingers continued their magical dance. He hit another sore spot causing her to hiss and lift onto her toes. The deep pulls of his breath startled her, almost ragged and raw.

He reached out to steady her. "Sorry."

"No. It's okay."

"I don't want to hurt you."

"You're not hurting me," she said with some protestation. "Okay, it hurts a lot, but it's the good kind of hurt."

"Hm." He collected her hair and straightened it down her back. "I love your hair."

"It's a mess. Boring and straight."

"There's nothing boring or straight about your hair." His fingers pressed into the muscles of her back, causing her to gasp as he hit yet another spot. "Stop?"

"Mm…no." She loved how he paid attention and adjusted the pressure he applied. His touch felt like fire and had her curling her fingers against the tile.

"It doesn't work unless you let the muscles release."

She squinted against the pain. "I'm trying." Her teeth clenched.

With effort, she forced her shoulders down. CJ rubbed her skin, changing the deep muscle massage to a light surface caress. Once she relaxed, his fingers pressed in and held. She gasped in agony.

He placed his cheek next to hers. "Breathe in and out. Give it a moment. The muscle will surrender."

She did. It was difficult. It hurt like hell. And it worked.

As the water poured around them, the muscles in her shoulders relented under his touch. She lifted her head and breathed out, only to arch as he massaged the muscles along her spine.

"Holy crap," she cursed.

CJ paused. "Stop?"

She panted against the pain. It wasn't the good kind either. Tiny jolts of electricity traveled down her spine and wrapped around her ribcage.

"That doesn't feel right." Her body wasn't healed enough to manage that pain.

"Hmm, okay. How about we wash this hair?"

At that moment, the shower turned from slightly sensuous, to mechanical and stale. The metallic taste of disappointment filled her mouth. Her shoulders slumped as the last bit of energy left her body.

"I guess," she said.

Why not? What else were they going to do in the shower? She was naked. He was nearly so, and the long, hard length of him had bumped against her hip more than once. Was she crazy thinking sex might be in the picture? Did he even want her like that? I didn't seem like it, but there was his erection.

Melissa pinched her eyes closed. Good thing they were in a shower. He would never see her tears of frustration.

A coolness spread against her scalp. CJ had squeezed shampoo over her hair.

"You'll need a lot more than that," she said.

"Really? Cause I put on a bunch."

She shrugged. He'd figure it out.

She didn't move. He'd already seen far more of her body than she was comfortable with. She didn't mind if he saw her ass. There was nothing special about her flat ass. Honestly, as far as the sex went, if he tried to put the moves on her, their coupling would be the most uninspired lovemaking in the history of shower sex.

At least CJ had the most divine hands ever created on earth.

The way he massaged her scalp had her head tilting back in ecstasy. He cupped the left side of her head in one hand, scrubbed with the other, and then gently rolled her head to clean the hair on the other side. He added more shampoo, rinsed it, then coated her hair in conditioner.

"Time to wash the rest of you." His gentle tone had heat rising to her cheeks—another reason to face away.

Before she could think how uncomfortable she would be, his hands lowered to her shoulders and drifted down her arms. He rubbed her arms, lathering her skin. His fingers circled her elbows, and he massaged her forearms, continuing the electric touch down to her wrists.

His fingers passed over the backs of her hands, which she held stiff, unclear how she should respond. Then he circled around until their palms connected, and her heart rate spiked. His touch was sure and confident while she trembled.

Their fingers interlocked and folded together. He brought his hands around to the front of her body, just below her breasts, encasing her in the surety of his embrace. Suds covered her, trailing down her skin in rivulets. He leaned against her, his chest sliding against her back. Their skin, slippery with the soap, heated with mutual arousal. His erection pressed against her skin, and she gasped.

"Sorry." He shifted, angling his hips away. "It's, um, a natural reaction."

She screamed inwardly with silent frustration. That's not what she wanted.

"You doing okay?" His question lingered.

She bit her lower lip, not trusting herself to words, and nodded.

"If I make you uncomfortable, do anything that crosses a line, you let me know. Okay?"

She nodded again. The hard length pressed against her hip. She released her lower lip and prayed her voice didn't shake.

"Yes."

"I'm going to wash your front and back, and then I'll wash your legs. I have to touch certain places…"

"It's easier if we don't talk about it too much. Just do it."

He released her hands, and she let her arms drop to her sides. CJ's ministrations became efficient from that point forward. The shoulder rub had been a painful but exquisite experience, delivered with care and consideration. When he washed her hair, she could imagine he lingered because he enjoyed it as much as she did.

When he washed her body, especially her most private places, he did so in a methodical manner. In less than half a second, his hands ran over her breasts. He lifted them like they were nothing and dropped them to move on. There wasn't even an attempt to brush her nipples with his fingers.

He used a washcloth to clean between her legs as if he couldn't bear to touch her down there. Up and down her legs, brusque and businesslike, he continued to her backside with that same damn clinical efficiency.

All the while, she closed her eyes and gritted her teeth as a constant and needy throb made her ache for more. Her cheeks burned, heated not from arousal, or embarrassment, but from a deep frustration.

She couldn't wait to end this agony.

TWENTY-FOUR

Knives

PIERCE

Okay, so the knives may have been a bad idea. At the moment, the fire in my belly had been a thing of legend. I roared with each slash, Gretel's screams pushing me to cut again and again. Thick and luscious blood poured out of her ivory skin, a liquid feast for my enjoyment. Complementing the piercing wails, my princesses' cries crescendoed with each slice. I had punished them, and their fear fueled the adrenaline racing in my veins.

It was like standing at the edge of a cliff. My lungs burned, and I teetered on the precipice of going too far. Blood cooled as it dripped down the handle of the knife to coat my wrist. It dried there, turning sticky, while I reveled in the whole experience.

The metallic tang of blood filled the air. I inhaled it. Tasted it. I couldn't resist taking one lick of the blood on my hand, and then I had another. The dripping crimson fascinated me. I rubbed the glistening slickness between my fingers, drawing designs on my flesh, watching cracks form as the blood dried.

I felt powerful.

Strong.

Like, I could do anything.

All my princesses bowed before me, their resistance melting away before my supremacy. Power beat in my chest, burning along my nerves as it rushed along my limbs.

He must have felt like this when He took his princesses.

And at the end, my essence exploded over her breasts, the ropey white strands mingling with the crimson decorating her flesh.

I had chosen Gretel because I liked her the least. Her straw-colored hair and dull brown eyes completed an uninspired face full of freckles. She was the youngest, not yet eighteen. Her breasts were amazing, the feature which had drawn me to her.

She barely moved, crumpled as she was against the back wall. The chains still bound her, and fine tremors shook her fragile form. Her task had been to teach a lesson to Henrietta, our Fairy Godmother, and she'd served admirably.

Henrietta's training progressed with difficulty. She fought every step of the way. I'd spent a day slapping her around, using the belt and the cane. We were in the early phases and, while I expected resistance, biting my cock had earned this punishment. She would learn her job was to protect my princesses, not subject them to further harm.

She probably thought her punishment would be wrought out on her flesh. How wrong she had been. It was time to see if she had learned.

I had her bound on the bed. The ropes were long enough for her to move about but too short for her to stand. I wanted her to straddle me like she had our very first time.

After the intensity of my release with Gretel, I had collapsed over my poor princess. Only then did I notice her unresponsiveness. I pressed my fingers to her neck and sighed with relief. The flutter of her heart still beat. Anger thrummed in my veins. This was our Fairy Godmother's fault. She had caused me to go too far.

I stalked toward the bed, moving between the cages as my eyes cut left and right, taking in my cowering princesses. My feet pounded over the wooden floor, creaking as I went. I'd almost killed poor Gretel. Perhaps He and I were more alike than I thought.

I turned my thoughts from Him and even from Gretel, who I'd left chained to the wall. I'd graced Gretel with my seed, and the act had left me drained.

Time to replace Henrietta's gag, but first, we had much to discuss.

I slapped her face, then gripped her chin and forced her to look at me. "This happens when you misbehave. A Fairy Godmother sets the example. Your job is to protect them."

"You twisted little man." Her breasts heaved as she spat the words in my face.

She'd already said something along those lines too many times. Honestly, she wasn't very original.

I turned on the video camera and started the playback of our first time together. The clip played on a small television I'd brought down just for her.

"Do you remember this, my dear Henrietta? Do you remember fucking me with such abandon?"

I queued the video to the part where she had been riding my cock in my bedroom. Her breasts bounced. Her head was thrown back in ecstasy. Moans of pleasure spilled from her mouth as she rode me. My fingers clutched her thighs, and my hips jerked with my release. Our first time had been glorious.

Tears leaked from her eyes, and a flush of shame colored her cheeks. I rewound and placed the video on repeat. "You're going to do that again."

It had felt so damn good.

Her sad eyes regarded me, cutting over my shoulder to look at what I'd done to Gretel. "Please, no."

I ran my thumb over her bottom lip. "You will, but first, I'll try out your pretty mouth again." If she bit me again, I would move on to the next princess.

I didn't want to repeat the last ten minutes. My arm burned from the exertion, and the blood was flaking off my skin. I itched and needed a shower.

Her head shook. "Please, just let us go. We won't say anything."

"Tsk, tsk. You know that won't happen. You will serve and show the same enthusiasm as our first time, and you'll never use your teeth to bite again. Do you understand?"

Fear shone in her eyes, and she cast her gaze around the room, taking in the rows of cages. I had six princesses. One Fairy Godmother and one cage left to house my Queen.

As much as I disliked her, Gretel made me proud. She tried not to cry. Tears were forbidden down here. But when I had carved the X between her breasts, she couldn't help herself. I didn't blame Gretel and wouldn't punish her for her weakness. That fault belonged to the proud woman tied to my bed.

"So, let's talk about what's about to happen." The more I spoke to Henrietta, the more my dick grew hard. "I want you to ride me. I want to hear you cry out as you come. You'll enjoy it, and if I come first, we'll move on to Cinderella and then the next."

Her lids drew back, the smell of her fear rising between us.

"Do you understand?"

She broke, her chin tucking to her chest.

"Okay," I said, sheathing my erection in latex. "Let's begin."

She panted with her exertions, but I came before her climax crested. I placed my bloodied hands on her hips and glanced with a smile.

"My dear, Henrietta, did you not understand? You were supposed to come first."

I lifted her off me, removed the condom, and rolled from the bed. I would need time before I could use her again.

Gretel drew my attention, so silent against the back wall. I went to her and cleaned her the best I could. Many of her cuts still oozed, and some went deeper than I'd intended. It looked like she might need stitches.

I returned to Henrietta. "Would you like to say anything to Cinderella before I begin?" It was dangerous having three of them out. I could handle two, but never had I controlled three at once. A glance at Gretel soothed my fears. She was in no condition to cause a problem.

Henrietta's face turned ghostly white. Her mouth gaped as her breath hitched in her throat. "No, please! Please don't. I'll do better." Her choked sobs made it difficult to understand her words. "Please, m-m-my Prince, please, let me try again."

"I want to watch you come."

She knelt on the bed. Her legs quivered, her head sagged, and her arms stretched overhead. I reached out and rubbed at the muscles of her shoulders, knowing how fatigued they must be. Her joints must be on fire. She moaned as my fingers kneaded her flesh. I hugged her, giving the comfort she desperately needed.

Brushing back the mess of her hair, I kissed her temple.

She tensed but didn't pull away, and she didn't nip at me. We were making progress.

I picked up the knife. "Same as before."

Henrietta screamed as I carved an X in the flesh between Cinderella's breasts.

Unlike Gretel, Cinderella never cried out, but I had trained her to endure. I put Cinderella back in her cage and checked on Gretel before returning to Henrietta.

"You know what I want." My hand went down to stroke myself. Her eyes followed my movement.

She bit her lower lip, so sexy and plump. "Please, don't hurt them anymore."

I was spent, and it took time to get me hard. Henrietta did much better this time, grinding her hips. I would have preferred if she hadn't scrunched her eyes closed, but she worked hard to please me. She came long before the first tingle started in my balls. I would reward her effort.

Rewards were important.

The responsibility I had toward my princesses filled my world. I had a duty to them. To care for them. To provide for them. To see to their happiness.

I took Gretel to the shower in the corner of the room and rinsed the blood from her body. I examined each cut, pulling apart the wounds. As I'd suspected, a few sliced into muscle. I would need to close those, which had me thinking of that nurse from the hospital.

Gretel turned flat eyes to me when I finished toweling her dry. "Thank you, my Prince."

My least favorite princess was my most compliant, rivaling even Belle's steadfast devotion. I kissed her on the nose. "You have pleased me very much." Gently, I carried her to her cage.

Her eyes dropped to the floor as I locked her in.

She deserved the best care.

Not much later, I was outside the hospital, wondering if that male nurse was still on duty. I'd never taken a man before, but it shouldn't be a problem. I kept chloroform in my van, along with an assortment of other drugs. I'd been a Boy Scout; being prepared was ingrained in everything I did. Rope and duct tape were stowed in the panels, more than enough to subdue him. If that didn't work, there was always my gun.

I wasn't sure how to get him down to my dungeon, or what to do after finishing with his services. I mean, I knew, but I wasn't sure the best way to go about killing him.

It was hard not to make a mistake when doing that. So much went into planning it.

Here is where my mentor and I disagreed. I liked my princesses. I loved training them and seeing them well-behaved, sharing meals with them, having our little talks, and disciplining them when needed. Fucking was fun, too. That and watching with pride as they struggled to please me. I found killing difficult, whereas it came easy to him.

Belle had been with me for well over three years. Gretel had been around almost two. I couldn't get enough of my princesses and planned to have them for years to come.

On the other hand, my mentor had been wasteful, keeping his for a week or two at most. He hadn't been able to control his urges. His work may have been elegant, pristine even, but wasteful in the killing.

While I had learned much, his weakness had been what finally led to his capture. On the other hand, I had practiced my techniques, learning exactly how far I could push my princesses and how well they healed. It was an intricate dance when we knew our roles and our expectations. There was no uncertainty in my dungeon.

No death.

I vowed not to repeat His mistake and to control myself.

Death was messy but sometimes necessary.

I made a list. Drug store for bandages and antiseptics. The hospital to get the nurse. And I had yet to collect what had been promised. My Queen was still missing.

The universe continued to conspire against me, keeping me from what was rightfully mine. Taken into protective custody, I assumed. Where? They were vague on that and on what happened at her house, but I saw the tulips through the open door.

My mentor was not dead, and he was out there.

He'd better not think to take back my Queen. She was mine, and I didn't share what was mine.

TWENTY-FIVE

If Only

CJ

Washing Melissa's body was an exercise in torture as far as CJ was concerned. Now, his cock was a hard, hot mess requiring attention of a particular nature.

Melissa was exhausted after the ordeal in the shower, and he tucked her in bed, making sure she was comfortable. After checking the outer door was locked and latched, he closed the bedroom door and locked it. Then he headed back to the bathroom to clean up the mess of his clothes.

He peeled off his wet boxers and turned on the shower, letting the steam build again.

With the water spraying against his back, he grabbed the soap, then reached down. His balls hung low and heavy, and his cock throbbed with unspent need. He gripped his shaft and closed his eyes with the first firm stroke.

Not in any hurry, he let his mind wander to what he would have done if things had been different with Melissa. He vented a deep sigh and then leaned his head back to fantasize about how that shower should have gone.

His hand couldn't provide the release he craved, but it served his need for the moment. The hot spray of his come took off the edge, but he was still painfully aroused

Dissatisfied, he stepped out, his gaze landing on his pile of wet clothes. Wrapping a towel around his waist, he searched for his phone, grabbed his clothes, and left the bathroom. A quick search in the closet of the darkened bedroom revealed a cotton robe. With a quick swap of the towel for a robe, he left Melissa to sleep and headed to the main living area of the suite. A quick call downstairs brought a laundry pickup, and an extra tip ensured they would expedite the cleaning. Desperate for a distraction, he thumbed the keypad of his phone. It was time for work.

The phone rang five times before Mac picked up. "What's up?"

"How's it going?" CJ asked.

"Not so good." His partner's voice sounded frustrated.

"What do you mean?"

The robe gaped in all the wrong places, and he gave up any attempt to cover himself, tossing the damp towel over his lap in case Melissa woke and came searching for him.

"Cold trail," Mac said, irritation hung thickly to his words.

"Your leads didn't pan out?" CJ frowned.

"We never had leads."

"What do you mean?" He leaned back and repositioned the towel.

"Got a moment?"

He glanced around the empty hotel room. "Melissa's sleeping, but before I forget, I need a change of clothes. Can you grab them from my hotel and bring them over?"

"What have you been up to?" Mac teased.

"Don't get excited. Nothing happened." He shook his head and shut his eyes against the juvenile ribbing.

"Ah, come on. I leave you in that hotel room with a beautiful woman and nothing happened?"

CJ gritted his teeth. "You're asking if I took advantage of a woman who found a girl murdered in her home? Not only is her serial killer ex-husband alive, but he escaped prison and is coming after her. That's the woman you think I fucked?"

A long stuttering pause followed. Several times Mac said something, but he never strung the sounds into something intelligible.

CJ kicked his heel over his knee. "Just tell me about our case."

"Asshole. Like I said, Henrietta Jones is a serviceman's widow."

"I read that in the files. He's a decorated war hero."

"Well, let's recap."

"Okay." A common technique, they would talk about their cases, never assuming the other knew all the details. It was amazing what the simple act of discussing a case turned up.

Mac continued, "Two days after that storm blew through, she never picked up her kids from school. The principal called the police."

"Right, the Police Chief is a friend of Sam's, and with her husband being the small-town hero, it's a high profile case, but with the storms, they didn't have anyone to work it. He called Sam, who put the Guardians on the case."

"Right. The woman vanished. Nobody knows anything."

"Are you still downstairs in the lobby?"

"Nah, Jenny wanted to talk to the girls."

"Where are you now?"

"Social services group home. The girls don't know anything. Their mom walked them to school every day, did volunteer work, and picked them up when school got out." Mac gave an exaggerated moan. "You should try sitting in one of these kiddie-sized chairs and see if it doesn't pinch your ass."

He couldn't imagine Mac getting half his ass into one of those seats.

Mac continued. "Typical background on the mother. Everyone loves her. She wouldn't hurt a fly, yadda yadda yadda. The perfect mom."

"Any reason to think she would abandon the girls?"

"None."

"Boyfriend? Lover?"

"None anyone knows about."

"So, why are they assuming an abduction?"

"What else could it be?"

"We're missing something." He leaned back and stared at the ceiling, trying to think. "Have they identified the victim at Melissa's house yet?"

"No. These are small-town cops, but the Feds arrived a little while ago. They've got a whole team and are sending samples to their lab."

CJ brushed his hand over the stubble of his jawline. "I need a razor."

"I'll get your stuff."

There was a slight pause while Mac spoke to someone else. When he returned, CJ knew there was bad news by the change in his friend's breathing.

"No-go on the protective detail. The locals are busy with another kidnapping, and the feds didn't bring extra manpower. They can send for some, but it won't be until tomorrow."

"Another kidnapping?" CJ sat up straight, alert. "Patterson's stepping up his pace."

"Not Patterson. A man was taken. Jenny says the cops have no one to put on the hotel. What do you want to do?"

"When's the rest of our team due to arrive?"

"Not until tomorrow."

"Okay. You and Jenny see what you can find out from the girls and keep me informed about Melissa's ex. I'll stay with Melissa. When you're done, I'd appreciate it if you could bring my stuff."

"You gonna tell me what happened to the clothes you were wearing?" Mac teased.

"Not going there." His gaze slid to the bedroom door, and his mind traveled beyond to the sleeping beauty in bed.

Damn.

He was aroused and uncomfortable again. It would be a very long evening and a longer night.

TWENTY-SIX

Only If

MELISSA

Melissa woke up in a cold sweat. Blood-drenched tulips flitted through her mind, the tangled threads of dreams she didn't want to remember.

For a moment, she couldn't remember where she was. Darkness filled the room, and she bolted upright only to gasp against a sharp pain cutting through her side.

Memories returned in a flash of agony. The tornado. CJ. The hospital. Surgery. And finally, her home and a field of tulips stained by death. She wrapped her arms around herself and rocked in bed, crying in the darkness.

Scott was out there. When he found her, would he kill her? Or, did he have other plans for his wife?

There was no sound in the room except her quiet sobs. It looked like CJ left her to sleep. She was grateful for that small courtesy. Privacy seemed to be something she could not guarantee around that man.

For a stranger, he certainly inserted himself into her life. Was he still out there, or had he left? Her gut seized with fear. She didn't want to be alone. If Scott discovered where she was, she'd be in no condition to fight.

A rustling came from the other room, and she tensed.

"Melissa?"

CJ's deep voice resonated deep within her core, striking at something buried deep and long forgotten. A sigh of relief whispered past her lips. He hadn't abandoned her. The longer CJ stayed around, the more of herself she lost in his charms. Such the perfect gentleman.

Stupid. Gallant. Hero.

She hated him for being so perfect.

Careful not to pull her tortured muscles, she twisted and gave the pillow a long hard stare. As welcoming as the soft down appeared, she wanted nothing to do with the dreams it promised. A glance at the clock showed her it was two in the morning. She should be asleep. Her body needed rest to heal. That damn dream, like Scott, had spoiled everything.

The darkness clawed at her, reminding her of evil things lurking in the world. She turned on the light next to the bed.

The door hinges squeaked.

"You awake?"

"Yes."

"Can't you sleep?"

"No."

CJ stepped into the soft illumination spilling from the doorway; his features silhouetted until he moved into the cone of light beside her bed. Her breath hitched in her throat, rendering her speechless as she gazed into the soul of an angel.

He sat on the corner of the bed, tugging at the edges of a white robe. She wanted to touch him. Instead, she kept her arms wrapped around her waist, giving herself a lonely hug.

"You should try to get some rest," he encouraged, moving closer.

She shrugged. "I had a bad dream."

He brushed the hair off her forehead. "What was your dream about?"

"A nightmare." She scooted back. "I feel better now. Thank you for…"

An awkward pause hung between them.

His presence electrified her. When he wasn't beside her, she could convince herself she could resist him, that his magnetic pull wasn't that strong. But when he was close, all her defenses crumbled. This undeniable need surged strong and powerful within her body, and perhaps even her heart. Scott had never had this effect on her.

How did CJ make her feel so alive? Or was she that desperate for affection?

"You don't look better." A grin spread across his face, softening the strength of his jawline.

"Your compliments need work," she teased, forcing a smile of her own, but she wasn't ready to join him in laughter.

"Sorry, but why didn't you tell me you were in that much pain?"

She shrugged. "What was I going to say? I hate hospitals. They keep the lights on all night, and the staff talks the whole time. All I wanted was to go home and get some rest where I could heal."

The smile on his face faded. "I can only imagine if you had taken that cab. You would've been alone."

"Do you think he was at the house?"

His pause made her heart skip a beat.

"Did you see him?"

He shook his head. "I didn't."

"Did Mac or Jenny?"

CJ scooted until he was sitting beside her. He took her hand in his. "Mac thought he might have seen movement at the edge of the property, but we can't know for sure. Your ex took a huge risk going there."

"Because of the manhunt?" She sat a little straighter. "Wouldn't my house have been under surveillance? How did no one see anything?"

"All the damage from the storm has complicated things. Electricity is still out in some parts of town. Most of the police have been diverted to assist in recovery. No one was watching your house, and I'm pretty certain he was waiting for you."

Her heart did one of those free-fall things where the bottom dropped out and sent her on a plunge into oblivion. She hunched over as a wave of nausea threatened to overwhelm her.

Scott had been waiting. He was patient and jealous as hell. What if he saw her with CJ?

CJ enveloped her in warmth with one of his healing hugs, a promise that he would protect her from the world.

She blinked back hot tears, unwilling to show another moment of weakness in front of this man who had shown so much kindness. His fingers tangled in her hair, straightening out the mess. His soft lips pressed against her forehead, and she wished his tender kiss could make all the evil in the world disappear, but that would be hoping for too much.

"I appreciate everything you've done. I really do." An errant tear trickled down her cheek. She brushed at it with irritation. "I don't know how to thank you, but tomorrow I'll figure out how to pay for a security detail. I know you're busy."

She watched him, hoping he would take this way out and extricate himself from the mess that was her life. Instead, he cupped her chin. His baby blues stared at her with such intensity that they burned her from the inside out.

He leaned close, his gaze never once leaving hers. "I didn't come to the hospital because of a stupid phone. I came to see you."

Her breath hitched as he leaned in and brushed his lips against hers. Heat seared her mouth and burned deep to her core. When he deepened the kiss, she couldn't think of anything except to kiss him back.

He paused, pulled away, and broke the spell. They stared at each other, the air crackling with promise, but filled with the weight of her ex-husband's presence.

"I'm here because I want to be." He pressed his finger to her lips when she tried to speak. "You need rest, and in the morning, you and I need to discuss a few things."

He exited the room, leaving the door open a crack.

Her fingers brushed her lips. She tasted him, rich and sultry. Had the kiss been a dream? Or more of a promise?

TWENTY-SEVEN

White Silk

CJ

CJ shouldn't have gone for the kiss. He stormed off to the other end of the hotel suite, shaking out his hands.

Shit. Shit. Shit!

There was so much they still needed to talk about before he confused things with kisses because there definitely would be more. But how to broach the connection with his sister?

He stopped at the large picture window and yanked back the curtains to stare at the city lights.

Street lamps paraded off into the darkness—silent soldiers guarding the night. A clock tower squatted over the town square, keeping time. And off in the distance, floodlights bathed a deserted shopping center in artificial daylight, until the return of shoppers the next day. A few headlights pierced the darkness, illuminating safe passage for the people inside. There were a few areas blanketed by dark, those parts of town where power had yet to be restored. Despite that, the city breathed with a subdued vitality. Hidden between all the light, lurking in the shadows, a killer walked the streets.

What would Patterson's timeline be this time around? Would one death satisfy his need for desecration, or was he even now brushing against innocent lives, choosing his next victim?

CJ wished he was out hunting, doing what he was trained to do, rather than guarding a woman who tangled his thoughts and had him thinking of nothing other than getting her into his bed.

The trip to this small town wasn't anything he'd imagined it would be. He'd planned to close off a chapter of his life, witness an execution, and place a flower on his sister's grave. It was supposed to be over. Instead, his sister's murderer was killing again.

That was one hell of a detour.

He didn't need the additional burden of a woman. Eventually, he'd have to tell her about the link which joined them. There was no easy way to address the small detail of Patterson's rape, torture, and murder of his baby sister. He desperately needed to talk to Melissa before things went any further.

He massaged the corded muscles of his neck, trying to relieve some of the tension building there.

"CJ?"

He spun at the softness of Melissa's voice. Time to deal with the damage of that kiss.

"Melissa."

A silk nightgown draped her slim form, covering her body but hiding none of the details of what lay beneath. His mouth went dry, taken in by her beauty. When she took a step toward him, the fabric of the camisole shifted. He couldn't help but stare at her perfection.

With great effort, he lifted his gaze and met her troubled expression. "You should be sleeping."

The caution of her movements was painful to watch. After seeing the extent of bruising on her body, he was amazed she was even on her feet.

"I can't sleep."

He took an involuntary step back but ran up against the press of the window. The need to run was as palpable as the need to take her. Caught between two warring desires, he found himself paralyzed, afraid even to breathe.

Her eyes closed and she breathed out a long deep sigh as if steeling herself for a difficult task. Her lids flicked open and revealed her determination pinning him in place. She ran a finger along her lower lip, tracing the curve of her mouth.

"You kissed me." Her brows knitted together, confusion forming a deep furrow.

He wanted to kiss her pain away. "Melissa—"

She held up a hand. "You said you didn't come to the hospital to bring back my phone. What did you mean by that?"

His gaze darted between her eyes and the curve of her lips, trying to gauge her state of mind, but he came up empty-handed.

She took a few steps but turned away before she got too close. Her nightgown's white silk hugged the curve of her ass and swished between her long, lean legs.

He checked his robe, making sure it was closed, and tightened the knot at his waist. Nothing was poking out that shouldn't be, but he'd feel much more comfortable if he were dressed.

"Why did you kiss me then leave?"

"Because you need to rest." Because if I stayed, I wouldn't have stopped at a kiss.

"But, in the shower, the way you…so brisk and businesslike…like a chore." A tear trickled down her cheek. "I've never felt so ugly. Why would you kiss me if you felt that way?"

Anguish filled her words. She wrapped herself in her arms, a gesture she did when she felt insecure like she'd become accustomed to being the only person who provided her comfort.

He moved. His powerful legs devoured the distance between them, while his mind replayed her words.

I've never felt so ugly…

He did that. He went to her, but she stepped away, holding out a hand to halt his advance.

"I thought you were teasing about the drowned rat comment. It seemed innocent and funny, but you keep saying things like that. I never thought anyone could be so cruel."

He approached, but her upraised hand stopped him in his tracks.

She scrubbed at her cheeks. "I get who I am, and my life's a mess." She fisted her tiny hands and stiffened her spine. "I'm not asking for anything, but please stop toying with me."

Oh, hell, this was worse than he imagined. How had he messed things up so badly for her to believe such horrible things?

Professionally and personally, he was taking advantage of her vulnerability, but he no longer cared. He needed to feel her lips and taste her sweet mouth. She needed to know how he felt.

"That's not what I think at all."

"Then, why?"

He grabbed her waist and pulled her against him, sweeping down to claim her quivering lips before she could react and pull away. As his mouth brushed against hers, she gasped and placed a hand against his chest, but she didn't push him away. Her fingers curled in the fabric of the robe.

He deepened the kiss, daring to taste her tempting mouth. And while he closed his eyes, he tightened his grip around her waist, trying to be gentle with her bruising, yet desperate to cleave her to him.

She tilted her face back, the soft touch of her lips, raising the hairs on the back of his neck. His cock tightened, fully aroused now, and a tingle of electricity surged through him. He slowed down the kiss, taking time to explore, teasing her to open to him and tangle her tongue with his.

She moaned as he claimed what he wanted, and then he broke the kiss. Not to release her, but to pull her close, and allow her to feel the full force of his arousal pressed between them.

He placed a finger under her chin. "That shower was the hardest thing I've endured in a very long time. I kissed you, but I want to do so much more. I didn't want to take advantage of you."

She gasped.

"You've had a long day, and the last thing I wanted was to make things more difficult. You needed help, and I was trying to help, not push myself on you. I'm sorry if I made you feel ugly."

"It felt like you were washing a dog. My nurse touched me with more interest than you, and I'm pretty sure he's gay."

He laughed. "Have you seen yourself in a mirror? Drowned rat, baggy pants, and you can barely move. You fell in the shower because you had no right taking one alone. A bath would have been the better choice."

The corner of her lip turned up. "I didn't think I could fold my body into that tub."

"Well, what did you think I would do in that shower?"

"I don't know, but did it ever occur to you to cop a feel? Give a girl some hope?"

He threw his head back, releasing a deep belly of laughter. Now that had not been what he'd expected her to say.

"Cop a feel? Did you really just say that? And you could've done the same thing."

"What?"

"Cop a feel. Can't you feel how much I want you?" It was a struggle to remain a gentleman around this woman. He gave her a quick once over. "Do you even know how gorgeous you are?" He gripped her upper arms, settling on the safest place on her body to touch. Grabbing her waist would ensure one of two things. Either he'd cop a feel of her ass, or pull her against his hardened cock. A little friction…he shook his head. She was his assignment—a woman to protect, not fuck. But damn did he want to do just that.

"Honestly, I felt like I was getting a sponge bath by a nun."

"A nun!" Had she compared him to a celibate woman? To hell with Sam and protocol, and screw touching only her arms. He cupped the soft swell of her breast. "Is this something a nun would do?"

She bit her lower lip, and couldn't have given a more perfect answer.

Sometimes life gave something amazing. He kissed her nose while his fingers traced the tight bead of her nipple until it pebbled beneath the silk of her nightgown.

She reached between them and released the belt of his robe. Her fingers skimmed his muscles, her fingertips tracing each ridge. He held himself perfectly still, unable to stop her exploration, and unwilling to try. She stared down at the full length of him, and a sly smile spread across her face, erasing that deep furrow over her forehead.

"You're most definitely not a nun."

He gasped as she gripped him, gliding her fingers up and down his cock. He dug his fingers into her shoulders while she curled hers around his shaft and stroked him root to crown. The path she traced sent bolts of electricity crackling along her nerves. This was not the direction he'd expected this conversation to go. Still, she seemed determined, and he was more than willing to oblige her hunger.

"Melissa." He rocked forward with a groan. "I hope you're not teasing me, because…"

There was a twinkle in her eye.

"How do I look to you now, nun? Do you see a drowned rat, or was it a fried rat?"

He rocked back on his heels while she stroked him. A groan escaped his lips despite his best intentions to remain silent.

"You look like the woman I'm going to fuck. Don't start something you don't intend to finish because I'm warning you, I'm the farthest thing from a nun." He tried to capture her in one of his roguish gazes but found himself unprepared for the desire shining in her eyes. She placed a finger on his nose and gave a squeeze to his dick.

"That's what I'm hoping for." The glide of her hand up and down his shaft wasn't light or tentative. "Is this okay?"

"Okay?" The gasp escaping his lips as she stroked him sounded needy even to his ears. Not the picture of the dominant man he wanted to portray. "It's definitely okay. I have to tell you, I've been trying to be the perfect gentleman since the day you launched yourself at me. It's been very hard not to take what I want." It was time to turn the tables and take back control.

"Take what you want? You do want me?" She sounded hesitant and unsure, even with her hand all over his dick.

"Yes. Does my hard cock in your hand feel like a man who doesn't want you?"

"Even knowing who I am?"

"What does that mean?"

"You know, my—"

He placed his finger over her lips. "All I need from you is to hear whether you want to continue this because if that's a yes, this ends only one way, and that's with me buried balls deep inside of you. Seeing as how your hand is on my dick, I'm taking that as a yes. But I don't play around when it comes to sex. I want you. I haven't been able to think about anything but you since we met. However, I won't take advantage of this situation, and I most definitely won't take advantage of you."

He grabbed her ass, pulling her against his cock, then cupped her chin. His thumb rested at the corner of her mouth, and he dragged a finger across the curve of her lips, then breached them, pressing his thumb inside her mouth.

She curled her lips around his thumb, her tongue circling the tip in a sensuous promise of something more. Her lips were soft, whereas the velvet of her tongue had him groaning and his cock jumping. What would her tongue feel like on his cock?

"So what's it going to be?"

She let out the tiniest of whimpers, and her gaze locked onto his with a look of desperation matching the need rising within him. She gave a slow lick, then released his thumb from the wonder of her mouth.

"I want you to take advantage of me." She gave a soft laugh. "I haven't felt anything like this in my life. Is it wrong to say that?"

"Not at all, but are you sure this is what you want? To be with me?" He picked his words carefully. If she needed only this one night, he'd give it to her, but he hoped this was more of a beginning than a one night stand.

"I do." Her hand brushed against his cock, and her delicate fingers danced along his shaft.

Leaning in, he touched his lips to hers—just a slow, tender lick before taking more.

The contact detonated a spark between them.

"Fuck, there's no turning back now. I want you so damn much." His words came out in a furious growl.

She threw her arms around his neck, pressing her body against his. His hands gripped harder, mindless of her injuries. He lifted her off her feet and carried her into the bedroom. Nothing but silk separated his hands from her body, something he would soon remedy. He needed to feel the heat of her skin against his body.

Her mouth broke away, her head dropping with a sigh against his shoulder.

"CJ…" she breathed, "I want you too."

Slowly, he lowered her onto the bed, bending down to suck on the tender skin of her ear. His hand slipped to rest on her belly, grabbing at the fabric of her nightgown. He sought her softest parts, tracing the curve of her breasts with his fingers and walking a path down her belly to swirl around her navel before heading lower still.

She pulled him down, arching her neck to encourage him. He obliged, licking and tasting from her earlobe down to the corner of her jaw, seeking the warm heat of her mouth while his hand explored. He was desperate to taste every inch of her body.

The nightgown needed to go. He found the hem and slipped his fingers beneath the silky fabric. She wriggled her hips, lifting so that he could uncover the expanse of her creamy skin to his aching eyes. Their eyes locked as he moved the bunched fabric over the swell of her breast, exposing her fully to his determined gaze. Time slowed down as she slipped her arms out of the spaghetti straps and let him pull the fabric over her head.

She lay before him, naked except for the small triangle of fabric covering her pussy. That would come off next.

Her arousal filled the air and slammed into him with a heady intoxication he would soon devour.

"God," he murmured. "I've wanted to do this since the day we met."

Her low laugh had him smiling. "Why didn't you?"

He slapped the side of her ass playfully. "Because, I'm not the kind of guy who takes advantage of an injured woman."

She looked at him with hooded eyes. "What kind of man are you then?"

He was a hunter. A boy who'd killed to save his mother. A man who saved strangers.

"I definitely don't deserve you." He divested himself of his robe, his cock bobbing in the air, eager and ready, but he wouldn't rush this moment. She was a feast he intended to savor.

"Oh, I don't know about that."

"Well, I'm the kind of man who'll make a drowned rat scream." A smile tilted the corner of his mouth.

"We need to discuss your pillow talk." Her lips pushed out into a pout.

"How about this, then?" He brushed a strand of hair away from her face. "I want to fuck you until you lose your voice from screaming until you can't even remember your name. You won't be able to walk for days, and I'll be in you so deep, you'll never forget I was there. And every time you open your mouth, it'll be to beg me to take you again."

Her mouth parted, and her chest heaved. "Oh, my." The soft pink tip of her tongue rested on her bottom lip, then her mouth widened. "That was good."

"Good?"

"Very."

He devoured her, sweeping his tongue inside her eager mouth, claiming her for the night.

His hands wrapped around her waist, his fingers curling under the small scrap of fabric of her panties. Slowly, he pulled it over her hips and down her thighs, enjoying the delicious reveal. He tossed her panties on the ground.

Taking his time, he kissed her chin, then nibbled the soft spot where her neck joined her shoulder. His lips brushed over her nipples, which peaked with arousal. Moving with care, he kissed the worst of her bruising, tracing the angry lines of purple and red with his tongue, trying to determine how sensitive she might be. It would be too easy to hurt her, and his need demanded something rough and raw. He'd be soft and gentle if he had to, but he preferred a harder edge.

She didn't flinch against his touch, her fingers curled in his hair, tentative and unsure as he moved between her legs.

He positioned himself between the smoothness of her thighs, inhaling her rich beauty, and glanced up to catch her eyes.

She released him and pressed her hands to the sides of her head, giving a soft moan and wriggling her hips beneath his hands.

He pressed a kiss to her mound, then another to the apex of her thigh. His fingers brushed her with gentle strokes, increasing the pressure and moving closer to her core. Then he feathered his kisses, his tongue driving against her tender nub until she bucked beneath him.

He wanted hard and fast but needed to make sure she could handle what he had to give. Tracing the seam of her pussy, he licked and kissed until she shuddered beneath him, melting back into the bed. He slid his fingers against her thigh, then pressed one inside her cleft. She groaned in pleasure, her legs opening for him. He sucked her clit into his mouth, stroking her as he slipped another finger inside her channel.

A strangled sound tore from her throat, her hips bucking beneath his mouth. He pumped his fingers in and out, feeling her walls clench around his knuckles. A shudder hit her body as he thrust his fingers into her, teased her G-spot, and pulled out, circling her clit before thrusting in again.

"CJ," she cried out. "I'm…" Her entire body jerked beneath him. "Oh, my God!"

He pressed his tongue against her clit as she came apart beneath him, her breathing short and erratic.

Once she came down from the high of her orgasm, she whispered, "Oh, my God, it's been years…"

Years? He pulled himself up the length of her body; he could do way better than that. They were just getting started. Then, it hit him.

"Fuck!"

"What?" Her lids flew open.

"No, fucking condom." He pressed his forehead against hers and gave a muffled laugh, and then he kissed her lips.

He expected sympathy for their dilemma, but she laughed hard, dissolving into fits and giggles.

"What's so damn funny?"

She pointed at him. "There's a lesson for you. Next time, don't kiss and run."

"Kiss and run?" He glanced down between her legs. "I don't think you can call that kissing and running."

Her fingers traced the swell of his muscles. "Not that! What you did earlier."

He tipped his head and vented a deep sigh. His dick ached, and once again, he'd go unfulfilled.

“Good night, you should get some rest.” She kissed him on the cheek and left him gaping as she rolled to her side.

“Good night?”

“Mm-hmm, I should get some sleep.” Another giggle escaped her perfect mouth.

He gripped his cock, angry as hell for not being able to claim her the way he wanted but pleased to have brought her such pleasure.

“How am I supposed to sleep?”

“Hmm,” she said. “Maybe you should make a run to a drugstore before morning. We can try again when the sun comes up, but I think nothing is open this time of night.”

He smacked her on the ass. “Don’t think I won’t. This isn’t funny.”

She turned back over and cracked one eye open. “Call it payback for calling me a drowned rat.”

“What if I apologize?”

She eyed his engorged cock. “I’m listening.”

TWENTY-EIGHT

Bedsheets

MELISSA

Melissa twisted in the bedsheets, sleepy and satisfied for more than one reason. As frustrating as the shower had been with the sensual-turned-clinical body wash, she reveled in the languid exhaustion from what had been the best orgasm of her life. Her clit throbbed with the aftershocks of CJ and his amazing tongue. She rolled her eyes back, wanting more of that bliss.

More of him.

Scott had never taken her to such a soul-shattering height. He met her basic needs but had never made her fly apart. Scott saw it as a sign of failure if she didn't orgasm during their lovemaking. But those brief twitches—she couldn't call them orgasms—had been tiny blips of sensation, not the toe-curling, eye-rolling, whole body, come-apart orgasm that had been.

CJ was definitely not Scott.

Her stomach knotted with memories of her ex-husband's touch. His murderous hands traveled her body both before and after his kills. She hadn't known it then, but afterward, those gory memories fueled her nightmares.

"Hey." CJ cupped her chin. "Are you all right?"

Her gaze cut to his chiseled body. Broad shoulders, biceps larger around than her legs, and ridges of muscle with V-cut indentations, which angled down to the potency of his masculinity. His hardened cock jutted before her, the head weeping with need.

Oh, the poor thing.

He'd done more than please her. CJ had ended a years' long sexual drought. And she repaid him with thoughts of Scott. With a mental shove, she pushed Scott and her mental baggage to the back of her mind to focus on the man stretched out on her bed.

His eyes held such strength, and his arms brought such comfort. She could lose herself in him forever.

"Hey," he said. "Are you going to answer me?"

He bent down and brushed her mouth with his lips, the slow, gentle press turning deeper with each pull of his breath. He took. She gave. It felt natural and easy, nothing like the forced intimacy with…Stop!

She wrapped her arms around CJ's neck and lost herself within his embrace.

More of this was what she wanted, and wow, he knew how to kindle a blaze of fevered need. Heated lust spread through her body, and she hungered for more. The need to feel him inside of her, stretching her, and filling her up, made her hungry for a lick, a taste, and his touch everywhere. But, the lack of a simple piece of latex would keep them apart.

The things CJ had done. The way he'd taken control. He allowed her to lose herself in the moment. But that moment was gone with the flight of her thoughts. She'd been selfish too, leaving him hanging, but what if…? She gripped his cock.

"Holy fuck." CJ jumped, and she released him, surprised by his reaction.

"I'm sorry. I just thought—" She thought what? To give a handjob to pay him back? Tit for tat? Did he want that?

Ugh, she had been out of this game for over a decade. The ridiculousness of the situation sank in. She was such an idiot. A soft laugh bubbled up and out. She really was a fool.

"What's so funny?" The sternness in CJ's voice turned her giggle into unadulterated laughter.

Ouch. Her incisions pinched with pain. Only a twinge, though. She didn't hurt as much as she thought she should. Maybe CJ had magical healing hands? Or perhaps he relaxed her so much that she was beyond feeling pain?

"You." She pointed at him. "You're funny."

"Me? What did I do?"

Melissa rolled to her side and faced him. She worried her lower lip, biting it to keep another round of laughter from spilling forth. "You jumped."

"What?"

"I put my hand on your cock, and you practically leaped out of your skin."

His brows drew together. "I did no such thing." He glanced at her, a sheepish expression on his face. "Okay, maybe you startled me."

Melissa cupped her head and leaned on her elbow. "Seriously, what kind of man doesn't have a condom stashed in his wallet?"

He poked her shoulder. "The kind who isn't fucking everything on two legs." He rolled to his back. "It's not like I woke up thinking today's the day I'm getting laid."

She ran her fingers over his abdomen and followed the faint line of hair up to his navel. Slowly, she drew a circle and watched his cock bob.

His breathing hitched. The heat of his body radiated in the space between them. She leaned forward and snuggled into the crook of his arm, placing her cheek against his chest. Her fingers wandered, heading down now, retracing her path. She inched closer to the V-cut groove cut into his abdomen and let her fingers find the dips and valleys of his musculature as they arrowed down to his heavy cock.

His body shuddered under the assault of her fingers.

"You know," she said. "There are other things we can do."

"Other things?" His throaty chuckle did things to her insides. Good things. Wonderful things she wanted to explore.

"Fun things."

She stared at her hand, resting against his hip. Did she dare? Scott had always been particular about putting her hands or mouth on that part of him. Making love to his wife didn't involve hand jobs or blow jobs. He saved those for the girls he fucked and then killed.

What would CJ think of her lack of oral skills?

She felt different with CJ. Bolder? Perhaps. More willing? Definitely. Things had never been like this with Scott. Ugh, she shouldn't be thinking about her ex-husband when she was in bed with CJ.

"I don't want you to think I'm an ungrateful lover." She cupped his balls, and he rewarded her with a lusty groan.

"Your hands are magical things, darling."

She turned her attention to his cock, stroking the long length of him. Her hand barely closed around his girth, which made her worry about what would happen when, or if, they ever had sex. How much would it hurt? Would he even fit inside?

"Don't over-think it." He wrapped his hand around hers. "Let me show you what I like." The warmth of his hand folded around hers, his fingers overlapping hers as he showed how he liked to stroke himself.

The motion began as a gentle glide, then he fisted his hand around hers, forcing their combined grip harder. Slow turned needful and became relentless as he chased his orgasm and guided her efforts.

This was easily the most sensual moment in her life. A handjob turned into an erotic coupling of two souls.

She wanted to give him more.

"CJ," she said, "I want to—"

The strain of his breathing surprised her, even as his hips rocked against her hand.

"So close," he said. "Don't you dare stop. Your hand feels fucking amazing." A low groan escaped him as his hips bucked.

Her breathing hitched, and the tingle between her legs turned to a needy pulsation. CJ controlled her, showing her how to hold him, stroke him, and draw forth his pleasure. His openness to sex captivated her every breath. Her nipples tightened, his need infectious and overwhelming. But this was his moment. She had her orgasm.

Should she hide her reaction? The ache between her legs demanded release. She should straddle his lap and ride him until they were both exhausted. Nope, not until they had a condom. Would CJ allow such a thing? Scott never did.

She'd probably fumble and look ridiculous, but this, stroking CJ's cock, she could do. And while Scott never allowed her to go down on him, she understood the mechanics of a blowjob.

CJ's eyes pinched shut with his pleasure, breaths billowing out of his lungs with sharp exhalations.

She wriggled into a better position, never once letting go of his cock. Not that she could with his fingers fisted around hers. But she leaned over and took the head of his cock in her mouth. The salty tang of him hit the tip of her tongue.

"Holy fuck!" CJ stilled. "You should warn a guy."

"Does that mean you don't want me to…"

"Baby, if you're going to put me in that mouth of yours…holy fuck." He released the death grip on her hand, and with a sly smile, he laced his fingers behind his head. "I'm officially at your mercy."

"My mercy?"

He closed his eyes. When she didn't move, he opened one eye and peeked at her. "Are you going to make me beg?"

"I should," she said with a half-hearted laugh, but she had no intention of making him beg. This was a gift she intended to give. "But since you saved my life, I'll spare you the begging."

"Good," he said with relief, "but damn it, woman, a man can only take so much."

Melissa bent again and stared at his cock. It was a natural reaction to kiss the crown and lick the slit. CJ groaned, and his body shivered. She opened her mouth and curled her lips over her teeth. Very few men enjoyed the scrape, or so she'd heard, but he was so big. Hopefully, he'd forgive a little teeth.

Instead of taking him in her mouth, she took him from the side, sliding her tongue over his ropy veins and tracing their path with short flicks of her tongue. CJ squirmed beneath her, his moans deepening, becoming guttural and needful. She lost herself in the joy of pleasing him and went to work.

There was no way she'd fit all of him in her mouth. She fisted the base of his shaft, applying the same amount of pressure he'd shown her during the handjob, and then she slid her mouth over the tip of his cock. His moans and sighs told her she wasn't doing a bad job, but whether she was doing a good job remained to be seen. Each lick, and sweep of her tongue, brought forth more moans.

She had a man's cock in her mouth, and as far as she could tell, he loved it. Now, how to bring this home? She did her best to take him, fighting against her gag reflex.

It took time to find a rhythm, but she learned how to coordinate her hand and mouth. The corners of her mouth hurt from stretching around his girth, and the muscles of her jaw ached. Dear Lord! Was she going to get a cramp in her jaw?

That thought had her giggling.

"Holy fuck, what was that?"

Oh, shit.

"Do that again." The husky drawl of his voice surprised her. His accent was sexy, but with his need laced through it, his voice turned combustible. Her clit throbbed in response, needing something, anything.

Wanting him.

The head of his cock pulsed with each flick of her tongue. She couldn't wait to feel him stretching her wide and taking her fully—damn condom.

She hit a spot on CJ's cock and made him jerk.

A strangled cry erupted from his throat, and his fingers dug into her hair. Guess he was done being hands-off. She stroked that same spot again. His hips bucked, and his fingers dug into her scalp. No longer in control, he set the pace. It was all she could do to keep her mouth open, and her hand clamped around his shaft. If it weren't for her hand, he'd be choking her with every thrust.

"More," he growled. "Deeper."

His command had her somehow taking him deeper while he guided her head. She squeezed her eyes shut and fought her gag reflex, desperate to make this as good for him as she could. He dug his fingernails into her scalp and moved her head according to his demanding rhythm.

And then he cried out. His hips thrust upward, and he pushed her head down, burying himself as deep as possible. The tip of his cock hit the back of her throat, and then she felt his orgasm roll through his body, unstoppable and full of potent fury.

His hips bucked as she fought for air. His moans filled the darkness as he spent his need and then stilled. Then, he removed his hands from her hair as she licked his shaft. Melissa collapsed beside him and snuggled into the crook of his arm. She liked this spot.

"Was that as good for you as it was for me?" She couldn't help the snarky comment.

His deep throaty laughter filled the room. "I'd say we're even. Just wait until I buy that box of condoms."

"What if I'm not interested?"

"Darling, you and I both know you're dying to find out what happens next." A rumble of laughter swept through his chest; the deep vibrations fluttered against her cheek.

She stilled at those words and then gasped when CJ rolled her to her back and spread her legs.

He grinned. "Time for round two."

Her back arched, and her eyes rolled as the tip of his tongue stroked her clit.

TWENTY-NINE

A Prince's Work

PIERCE

MY PRINCESSES WHIMPERED IN THEIR CAGES. EVEN OUR FAIRY Godmother gaped, her eyes wide with unasked questions, as I dragged the unconscious man across the floor.

Her training, while slow, continued in the proper direction. Compliance was a skill she learned quickly, and she was keen to please me now that the others would suffer for her indiscretions. She had finally found her maternal instinct.

The nurse was an armful—a bastard with a mean left hook. My left eye had swollen shut until I could barely see out of it, and I couldn't wait to get upstairs to ice it down.

I had given considerable thought to my preparations, but getting him home had been even more difficult than I'd expected.

He headed straight to a bar after his shift. I wandered in a few moments later and slipped something into his drink. He could barely walk to my van but was aware enough to haul off and punch me when he saw what waited for him inside.

The leather, chains, and the duct tape were dead giveaways, and although he'd fought, he'd been in no condition to win. My eye was an unfortunate casualty, something I would take out on him at a later date. I pressed a rag saturated in chloroform over his face, and that had been the end of his fight. The rope and duct tape secured him and took his fists out of the picture. It nearly broke my back, half carrying, half dragging him downstairs and through the tunnel to my dungeon.

My attention shifted to Gretel, and I bit my lower lip with worry. Blood soaked through her bandages again. When I called her, she didn't answer. Not because she was disrespectful, but because she was unconscious.

Had she lost too much blood?

Once I had Dickwad secured, I would check on her. If she were seriously hurt, I'd never forgive myself.

Dickwad was bigger than I remembered, and I was concerned the chloroform would wear off before I had him secured. I struggled to work quickly.

"Cinderella, how's my girl?"

"My Prince, I am well." Her sultry voice echoed from her cage, but she didn't come forward to greet me. I sensed fear in her voice, and I was not pleased.

"Come into the light, so I can see you," I ordered.

She shuffled forward, and I glanced at the bandages over the X I cut between her breasts. Red saturated the material. Her bandages needed to be changed, as well.

"Good girl," I said. "Tell me about Gretel."

Cinderella hung her head in a proper submissive pose. She clasped her hands in front of her, making sure they didn't obscure my view of the triangle of blonde hair between her legs.

"My Prince, Gretel has not spoken for some time."

I dragged my unconscious helper to the wall and chained him there. A steady pulse thumped under my finger when I held it to his neck. Slow, rhythmic breathing told me he was still out, but I didn't trust him. I leaned my elbow against his sternum and gave a deep rub sufficient to wake the dead. He responded with a moan.

Satisfied he wouldn't revive anytime too soon, I left him against the wall to check on Gretel. She looked so pale, but her breathing was steady. Her pulse fluttered in her throat—at least she had a pulse—but it was way too fast.

Looking at the amount of blood she lost, it wouldn't be long before her pulse turned thready and weak, or stopped altogether. I had at most a few hours left, and I needed Dickwad to get her bleeding under control.

I slapped her face but got no response. I hit again, and her head flopped. When I nudged her with the toe of my boot, she gave me nothing. Satisfied she wasn't ignoring me on purpose, I squatted down to get eye-to-eye with her. She breathed with a gentle rise and fall of her chest. Blood soaked through the bandage, covering the large X carved between her breasts. I yanked it off to examine the cut beneath.

The gaping wound entranced me. The congealed blood accentuated the sharp surgical cuts. I couldn't wait to see the scar left behind after she healed.

Dickwad groaned against the wall and startled me. That pissed me off. My reaction revealed weakness and hinted at the tiniest thread of fear lodged deep within me. This was the first time I had another male in my dungeon. Drugged or not, he posed a threat until I disposed of him.

Gathering the supplies needed, I wrapped the man in thick leather belts and bound him with chains. Every restraint was tripled for redundancy, and I placed locks on each chain.

The biggest problem I faced was how to handle his hands. He needed to tend to Gretel, but how much slack should I allow? If he got loose, I wasn't afraid he'd escape my dungeon. I was worried about what would happen if I had to fight him down here.

Best case, I killed him, but he'd been hard to take down while drugged, thus the black eye. And that was after I'd drugged him. If we got into it down here, he wouldn't be under the influence of a drug, and any fight would put my princesses in danger. I couldn't have that.

Locked in their cages, the chances of them getting injured would be small, but I didn't like the thought of violence around them.

Worst case, he overwhelmed me. Things would turn bad for everyone because the mother fucker would have to kill me. They'd all die because there was no way any of them were getting past the locks, and none of my girls knew about the backdoor I'd built down here. Even if they found it, they'd have to contend with the locks.

After much fiddling, I finally had him how I wanted. The belts and chains crisscrossed his chest, and pulleys strung him up like a puppet. Leather encased his legs, and a web of chains and ropes secured him to the wall and the support beams overhead. Locks glittered in the light, tying everything in place.

When he tended to Gretel, I would bring her to him with whatever supplies he required and lay them all out. Then I would step a safe distance away and release the chains holding his arms with the pulleys overhead. He'd be free to move hands and arms, nothing else, and when he was done, I would string him back up.

I watched Dickwad with a wary eye. Sharing had never been one of my strengths, and I hated to share even this little bit of my private world with him.

I despised him for the intrusion.

Less than half an hour later, his moans turned more purposeful. Soon he would wake. I went to the closet and pulled out gowns for my princesses, folding them with care over my arm. My princesses looked lovely in their garments, and while he was here, they would be covered. All, except Gretel and Cinderella. That could not be avoided.

As I passed out the dresses, I stopped by each of the cages to reassure them.

Red Riding Hood crawled to me. She dared not look at me. We'd had to repeat a lesson last week, and she still bore the marks from her punishment.

I reached through the bar and tangled my fingers in her raven locks. "How is my princess?"

"I am well, my Prince. May I serve you?"

The change in her attitude had been a pleasure to behold since her punishment. My dick twitched with arousal, but I was too wary of my unwanted guest tied to the wall. I handed her the dress.

"Put on your dress, Red. You can please me another day."

She bowed her head and took the gown.

Next, Sleeping Beauty crawled to the front of her cage. Perhaps the most intelligent of my princesses, she rarely required punishment. Gracefully, she knelt with her head on her hands in supplication. She never spoke unless I addressed her directly. I loved that about her.

I handed over her dress. "Get dressed, Beauty."

"Yes, My Prince."

Red welts crisscrossed her back. I'd had fun with the whip this morning. The deep bruise over her kidney had yet to fade, though. I twisted my lips and wondered if I shouldn't have Dickwad take a look at that.

Goldilocks greeted me much the same as the others and stretched out her hand to retrieve her dress. I moved to Cinderella's cage. She watched me warily with wide, expressionless eyes. She endured such pain for me, which made me proud.

I knelt in front of her cage, and she shuffled forward to press her forehead against the bars. "You do not get a dress. I want him to check your cuts."

Belle, my beautiful Belle, my first, and the only one I ever allowed unchained while out of her cage, waited for me. She didn't kneel like the others but rather prostrated herself on the floor.

I smiled at her display. "Belle, what do you want?"

"Whatever pleases you, Master." She was the only one who ever called me Master.

I would die for Belle.

"It would please me if you got up."

She jumped to her feet and gave a smile as her eyes flicked to mine. She wasn't permitted to look me in the eye. It would earn her a caning. That was the stated price when any of the princesses dared to look upon me without permission. I shook my head, playing her game, relishing the thought of welting her perfect ass and then fucking it until I passed out.

I wagged my finger and clucked my tongue. "Belle, you are a naughty princess."

Her look of contrition was anything but repentant. My dick swelled with arousal. I could not ignore my need much longer.

Her eyes cut to my crotch, and she swept her tongue over her lower lip. I was tempted to let her bring me relief, but I had a much better idea.

"Put on your dress, Belle. I'll cane you later. For now, your punishment is to watch your Fairy Godmother please me."

Belle snatched her dress out of my hands. "She doesn't know what you like, Master."

"No, she does not, which is why she must learn." I would never tell Belle our Fairy Godmother surpassed Belle's oral skills.

In the corner cage, our Fairy Godmother hunched her shoulders. She learned her lesson and would do whatever I wanted. I released the button on my jeans, loving the wide-eyed expression on her face. I gestured for her to take to her knees.

There was a look of utter disgust on her face as she approached the front of her cage. I would attend to that bad habit soon. Reaching through the bars, I secured a chain to her collar, and then I tugged her close.

It took but a second to free my cock. I stood outside the bars, shoving my cock through the gap and into the heat of her mouth. Her velvety soft lips wrapped around me. I had a momentary hesitation about her teeth. Still, I was confident she understood the price of failure after watching me with the knives.

A deep voice, groggy from the after-effects of the drugs, cried out. "What the fuck!"

I rocked my hips into Henrietta's face, enjoying the sensations she pulled from my body.

"You! You mother fucking bastard!" Chains rattled, and held firm, as Dickwad tested the strength of his bonds.

I had no concerns about him getting free. I had been careful and checked everything six times.

"You sick fuck! What the fuck have you done?"

His words rang in my ears, speeding me toward release. The rising panic in his voice added a delicious counterpoint to the soft pulls of Henrietta's mouth.

Her dead husband trained her well.

THIRTY

Good Morning

MELISSA

Melissa woke to sunlight streaming through the windows of the hotel room. Dust motes danced in the room, drifting on the lazy currents of air. The bedcovers twisted around her legs, trapping her in their tangled web. Her side ached. The healing muscles complained each time she moved.

It had taken every ounce of self-control not to flinch when CJ's hands had roamed her bruises, but every other inch had been pure pleasure. She stretched out, disappointed to feel the other side of the bed empty.

No CJ.

She rose to her elbows, her mind not thinking so much about CJ, but what the rest of the day would bring. Detectives would come. Questions would be asked. She'd be forced to deal with the reality Scott was out there. He'd keep killing until she came to him, or until he took her back—either option sent shudders trembling down her spine.

A soft knock pulled her from her morbid thoughts.

"Melissa, are you awake?"

She loved the rough timbre of CJ's voice. He had one of those deep male voices that captured attention, but then there were moments, such as now when the tenderness within him shone through. Her heart softened, listening to that voice.

Brushing back the hair from her face, she scooted to a sitting position, pleased to find she didn't hurt as much as she had the night before.

She cleared her throat. "I'm awake."

He pushed open the door to her room. The white terrycloth robe clung to his amazing frame, and he held a bundle of clothing in his hand. Her mouth watered at the sight of him, and her eyes dipped down to the belt of his robe.

"Do you mind if I use the bathroom?" Fine lines marred his face.

She waved him through. "No, please, go ahead."

He headed to the bathroom without another word, giving the bed a wide berth. He was out in less than five minutes, dressed in the clothes he'd worn the night before.

"Bathroom's yours." He gave a wink, and her belly flip-flopped.

"How did you sleep? You look horrible."

His eyes narrowed. "For someone who claims to be upset by my compliments, you don't hand them out very well yourself."

Melissa couldn't help but roll her eyes. "Sorry, but you look like hell."

"I didn't sleep well."

"Why didn't you sleep in the bed?"

He took a step toward her, heat smoldering in his gaze.

"I considered it."

"You should have joined me. Maybe then you would've slept better." As bold as her words were, she still pulled the covers high on her chest.

He snickered. "The thought crossed my mind. Several times."

She bit her lower lip. "Then, why didn't you?"

"I tried."

"No, you didn't."

"Yes, I did."

"I waited…"

"You fell asleep."

The second orgasm had been more intense than the first. Heat bloomed in her cheeks, and she was helpless to stop the flush she was certain betrayed her embarrassment.

The smirk on his face told her how much he enjoyed making her blush.

CJ sat at the edge of the bed. They stared at each other across the distance. He touched her leg, and burning contact was reestablished. Her chest did that flutter thing when the desire in his eyes couldn't be ignored. She wanted him to kiss her, but he didn't, and she was too hesitant to take the initiative.

Instead, he spoke in a teasing tone. "I left to make a few calls when I returned you were snoring…"

"Snoring! I don't snore."

A smile lit his face, erasing the lines of fatigue she had seen earlier. The sunlight streaming through the windows twinkled in his eyes.

"Snoring…and drooling." He winked.

She threw a pillow at him, but he blocked it, sending it tumbling to the ground.

He scooted closer, close enough for a kiss, but only stared in her eyes.

"Did you go shopping last night?" She couldn't come straight out and ask if he'd bought condoms. While eager to explore more with him, she didn't want to appear desperate.

"We'll get there, darling, There's no rush."

He leaned in, and their lips collided. Soft and gentle, he brushed his lips against hers, his tongue teasing her mouth open before he delved inside to tangle tongues. He ended the kiss long before she was ready.

"I'm sorry," he said, "but, I have to leave for a bit."

She placed a hand on his arm. "Why? What happened?"

He shook his head. "Nothing happened. I asked Mac to pick up my things from my hotel, but he's busy with Jenny. I need to check out of my hotel and bring my things here, maybe buy those condoms while I'm out." He winked and pressed her nose with the pad of his thumb. "I'll be back in less than an hour."

"Okay."

"This is important, your security detail isn't here yet, but hotel security knows what's up. They're watching through the security cameras, but there's no one posted outside the door. Lock the door behind me. Let no one in. You understand?"

She nodded. "Lock the door and let no one inside. Don't worry. I know what to do." She'd feel safer if he wasn't leaving, but the hotel had decent security.

He pointed to the bathroom. "No showers until I get back."

"I feel a thousand times better. I can manage a shower by myself. Although if you'd like to redeem your nun-ish ways…"

"I'd love nothing better." He breathed out a sigh. "But, I have to go. I'd feel better if you didn't shower while I'm gone. I don't want to worry about you falling."

"Fine," she said. "No showers."

CJ rose and tugged at the bottom of his shirt, straightening it. "If anyone, and I mean anyone but me, Mac, or Jenny tries to get in, you call 9-1-1, then you get inside the bathroom and prop a chair under the doorknob."

"He's not going to come after me here. Scott's too smart for that."

"Better to be cautious." CJ kissed her again but broke it off before the kiss became too intimate. He showed her how to brace the door with a chair.

His caution made her wonder what he did for a living. Still, a little paranoia was probably a good thing when a person had a serial killer ex-husband out to get them.

She kissed him goodbye, a much more affectionate and satisfying embrace than their first kiss. He copped a feel of her breasts, and his smirk promised more later. She locked the room after he left, but she wasn't going to listen to all his rules.

She was dying for a shower.

THIRTY-ONE

Stitches

PIERCE

I WAS A LITTLE CONCERNED ABOUT GETTING DICKWAD TO HELP Gretel, but I hoped his desire to heal would prevail.

After I finished with Henrietta, I stalked over to him, making sure to stay well out of range.

He strained against the chains as we eyed each other. Oh, how his hatred rolled toward me in that heated gaze. His attention kept dipping down to my crotch. Eww! I tucked my satiated member inside my pants and zipped it away from his homosexual eyes.

That was the last time that prick would get a look at my junk.

Crossing my arms, I glared back, taunting him. "Like what you see?"

"Fuck off, you crazy bastard. I'm going to kick your ass, you wimp-assed prick."

I shook my head and gestured to the chains. "Not likely."

Already this conversation bored me. I pointed to Gretel. "You will take a look at Gretel."

He glanced at where Gretel lay in her cage, his eyes widening as if seeing her for the first time. Then, his attention cut to the three cages beside hers, no doubt taking in the beauty of Cinderella, Red, and Beauty. Shifting left, his terrified eyes widened when Belle waved to him with a smile. Goldilocks knelt at the door of her cage, head bowed and impassive. The other two cages were empty. One waited for my Queen; the other would hold our Fairy Godmother after I was through with her training.

No wonder he'd been such an easy target. The man wasn't very observant.

Casting his gaze to the right again, he stared at Gretel. "What did you do?" His words came out as a growl, directed toward me, but there was that undercurrent of compassion I was counting on.

"Just a little knife play. Some of the cuts went deeper than I planned. You're here to sew her up."

"She's bleeding out!" His breathing changed. No longer angry, fear sawed in and out of his lungs.

Seeing him come apart wasn't as satisfying as when fear took hold of a woman. Women were fragile. Smaller than men, they lived daily with fear. It affected them on a primal level men didn't understand. Women's instincts were to nurture and serve. Men sought to defend and own.

"The bleeding is why I brought you here." I gestured to the stack of supplies. "I should have everything you need to stitch her up."

"She needs a doctor, asshole. You need to call 9-1-1."

I shook my head. "Not going to happen."

His strength returned with his anger. I didn't like that. Fear would make him more dangerous. I hoisted his arms above his head and locked them in place with a tug on the pulley mechanism. I gave the chains on his legs the same attention, fastening him tight against the wall. He grunted and jerked against his bonds.

I was safe, but he wasn't safe from me.

We were good.

I checked the supplies and laid them out in neat lines. Then, I unchained Gretel and carried her to the table I'd set up. As expected, Dickwad tried to lunge for me, but he couldn't move.

Poor Gretel. More blood had saturated the second layer of bandages.

Punching him in the face crossed my mind. He deserved a black eye to match the one he'd given me, but he would need his vision to care for my princess.

I pointed to the supplies, making sure he listened. "Is there anything else you need?" There shouldn't be. Bandages, antiseptic solution, alcohol, antibiotics, needles, and suture material were all present.

"How about a doctor?"

With a shrug, I looked him in the eye. "If she bleeds out, I'll kill you."

His eyes flared, the lids pulling back. I'd injected no emotion into my voice. I had none for him. Gretel, on the other hand, I cared for quite a bit.

"And if I do this?"

Another shrug. "Then, I'm happy."

"What happens to me?"

"I won't need you anymore." He needed to think he was getting out of here. Without it, he might make the wrong choice. "I'll drug you. Take you out of here, and that's the end of it."

"And the girl?"

I laughed. "She stays."

I motioned for Belle to come to the front of her cage. "Tell him, Belle. Tell him how this is our little thing." My arms swept around the room, encompassing all my princesses, even Henrietta. "They're here because they want to be. You're a bright guy. You've heard about these things."

I pointed to Gretel. "We got a little carried away with the knife. This isn't something hospitals understand."

"So you kidnapped me?"

"You have a certain skill set."

His gaze hardened, then swept to Belle.

My beautiful Belle went to her knees. "Please, kind Sir, help Gretel."

"You're here by choice?" Disbelief saturated his voice, but he didn't understand my kingdom, what I had worked to build. I turned my attention to Henrietta. Now would be the time to see if she had learned her lesson. Her eyes flicked to mine, wide-eyed and terrified, then skittered away, cowed into submission.

All was as it should be in my realm.

"Yes, Sir." Belle, beautiful words dripped like honey from her tongue, but then she had always had a sultry way about her. It was one of the things I enjoyed about my most favored princess. "Please help our sister."

"In chains?"

"The chains are for our Master's safety, Sir."

I walked to Belle and reached through the bars to stroke her hair. I loved her so much.

Dickwad did another sweep of my dungeon. His gaze moved over the cages and beyond to the king-sized poster bed where Henrietta was chained. Beyond the bed, the squat door locked all of us inside together.

He might kill me if he broke his chains, but he wouldn't be getting out of this room. If the bastard killed me, this room would become his grave. My princesses would suffer if that happened. Good thing I always thought things through.

When his survey of the room ended on Gretel, I knew he would do what I required.

Her eyes fluttered, the first sign of life in the past hour, but she still didn't move. I went to the pulley mechanism and slackened his chains. Dickwad's arms lowered.

I drew up a chair, far out of his reach. I would be with Gretel every step of the way.

A grimace stretched across his face. "She needs stitches."

I pointed to the sutures. "Then stitch her up."

"I'm a nurse, not a doctor. I don't do this kind of thing."

"You seem like a smart guy. I'm sure you've watched doctors do this a thousand times. How hard could it be?" I gestured for him to get started.

While he began, I pondered how I would find my Queen. Protective custody posed many problems, and I didn't know where to look.

The biggest news of all was why she'd been placed in custody.

My mentor was free.

I wasn't sure how this would affect my plans.

THIRTY-TWO

Diner

CJ

CJ MET MAC AND JENNY AT A DINER AFTER HE CHECKED OUT OF HIS hotel room.

Mac ran a finger around the water ring left by his glass. In the five years, they'd worked together, CJ couldn't remember Mac drinking anything other than water. Perhaps he should ask why someday.

Jenny ordered a complex concoction of coffee, milk, sugar, and cream. She clutched the warm brew and held it below her nose, sniffing it like a lover. Their waitress deserved a double tip for being a good sport about Jenny's insane order.

He tapped his foot against the bench seat, nervous about leaving Melissa alone. But Mac and Jenny requested a sit-down session to strategize on the kidnapping case. Hotel security had eyes on Melissa's room.

She was safe.

"It makes little sense with Henrietta Jones." Mac updated him on what little they'd discovered.

CJ looked across the table at the design Mac created from the water ring, an elephant, or a rhino. It was hard to be sure.

"What doesn't make sense?"

Mac stopped his water doodling. "I don't see someone snatching her off the street in between shopping runs in this town."

"She could've been targeted," Jenny said.

CJ shook his head. "As a kidnapping victim, she doesn't have much to offer. Not much money, and no real family to pay a ransom."

Jenny blew on her coffee. She had yet to sip the foamy mess but seemed content to inhale its aroma. "We were thinking about a sex crime, but you're right. She falls out of the usual age range for that. Not that it doesn't happen, but…I'm grasping at straws here."

CJ leaned back and stared out the window of the small diner. "Something new must have happened. We need to trace every detail in the days leading to her disappearance. I want every second accounted for. Who she spoke to. What she was doing. Where she shopped. What she wore. Everything."

Mac looked up from his newest creation, a stick figure of a Jedi Knight. He frowned. "That will be hard. Most of her days were spent with her girls. And from what everyone says, not only wouldn't she let anyone near her daughters, but the woman didn't date."

CJ shook his head. "That may be. But don't you think little Miss Perfect might have gotten lonely over the years? Maybe someone talked to her? It doesn't have to be a date or a lover. We've solved cases with much less to go on than this. Talk to the girls."

Jenny and Mac exchanged glances.

"They won't speak to me." Mac used air quotes. "I'm scary."

Jenny rolled her eyes. "I hate kids, and little girls are obnoxious. They were kind of skittish with me too. I don't think they've ever talked to a Black woman."

"They're kids." CJ had never met a woman less in touch with her feminine side than Jenny. "They'll talk to you."

Her eyes narrowed. "You think because I'm a woman, I'll relate to them?" Her shoulders twitched. "Kids annoy me."

CJ took a long pull from his coffee, needing a moment to compose his next few words. Jenny could get touchy. The more conversation centered on her femininity, the jumpier she got, and the more likely he'd wind up with a black eye. Frankly, he didn't understand. He'd never met a more stunning woman, except maybe for Melissa.

The waitress arrived with their meals. Jenny poured half a bottle of syrup over her pancakes and shoveled a large bite into her mouth. CJ sprinkled pepper on his eggs and toyed with them, while he considered the plight of their investigation.

It had been too many days since Henrietta Jones' disappearance. Chances of them recovering her alive had taken a sharp nosedive south, and with each passing day, those odds worsened. The best they could hope for was a rapist. A rapist would play with her first, giving them more time. Murderers tended to be more impulsive and dispose of their victims quickly.

Briefly, he considered the possibility Scott Patterson abducted Henrietta Jones. Still, the timeline didn't fit, and the Fairytale Killer had a particular type—the promiscuous college coed. He ground his teeth.

If only his sister had listened. If only she hadn't trusted too easily. His sister couldn't have fit Patterson's mold any better. Scott Patterson never deviated from his set type: young, blonde, and the girl next door. How had Melissa ever wound up with that freak?

Jenny demolished her pancakes while Mac stirred the food around on his plate, mixing grits, pancakes, and eggs into one disgusting mess.

She angled her fork at CJ, dripping syrup on the table. "You should talk to her daughters. You've got a kid vibe. Kids love you."

"I will, but let me get back to the hotel. I told Melissa I'd be gone for an hour, and it's already been at least that long. Then I'll speak to the girls."

Mac shoveled some of the disgusting mess on his plate into his mouth and spoke with his mouth full. "The kids are meeting with a potential foster family for placement. They should be free by noon."

"Perfect. I can take them out for lunch, build up a rapport." He ran a hand over his head. "Hmm, have you heard from the rest of our team?"

Mac nodded. "They'll be here around noon."

"That'll be perfect. I can stay until they arrive, then meet with the girls. Let me tell Melissa." He fished out his phone and dialed Melissa's number.

No answer.

With concern, he dialed again.

Nothing.

"Goddamnit."

He dialed the direct number to the room, but it rang and rang. Had she not listened to a word he'd said? Surely Melissa wasn't stupid enough to walk down to the lobby and grab a coffee, or worse, the local drug store for condoms.

No. She would've brought her phone. He rubbed at his jaw. Maybe she was in the shower, exactly where he told her not to be.

Damn. He refused to consider the other possibility, but Scott was out there.

He bolted out of the booth, laying two twenties on the table.

"What the hell?" Jenny looked up to him, confused.

"She's not answering."

"Fuck," Mac said with a growl.

Mac and Jenny knew the drill. They hopped into Mac's SUV and hauled ass back to the hotel.

THIRTY-THREE

Plans

PIERCE

STALKING THE ASSHOLE HERO DUDE TOOK TIME I DIDN'T HAVE. MY princesses had been left alone with Dickwad. I didn't like that one bit, but I had no choice if I was going to claim my Queen.

All my princesses had been gagged, even poor Gretel. I hated doing that when I wasn't there to watch over them, but I couldn't trust our Fairy Godmother to behave, or Dickwad to shut up. Chains secured him to the wall, but nothing stopped him running at the mouth. Wait...the ball gag was doing that right now.

He was a strong motherfucker. It took some effort, but I worked a gag into him. I hooded him first, chained his head back so he couldn't move, and then forced the gag into his mouth. I hated the risk posed by getting that close. He'd already head-butted me once, but I couldn't risk the nurse filling my princesses' heads with lies about me.

I had thought of killing him right then but decided against it. If Gretel didn't get better, I'd need him. There was plenty of time to dispose of him later.

The first part of my day had been slow and frustrating. I had no idea where to begin and spent the morning parked three down from my Queen's house watching cops and men in dark suits crawl all over her driveway.

Then I got an idea.

Flowers in hand, I approached the house. It was the perfect cover, and the police greeted me with smiles instead of scowls. They wouldn't answer my questions and eventually turned me away, but I'd been smart. The flowers had to be delivered, I'd argued. I handed the arrangement to one of the guys wearing a wedding ring, and while he took the bouquet, I lifted his radio.

People weren't very observant, and picking pockets came easily to me.

And so, I listened to their chatter all morning. You'd think they would have said something important by now. My irritation grew with each passing hour. Did none of them know where she'd been taken?

As I peered through my spotting scope, my thoughts turned to my mentor. To meet him in person made me apprehensive. We'd only exchanged letters, fabricating a code over the years to speak more plainly about life. He hadn't attempted to contact me yet. Part of me wanted to meet him, but another part knew it was too dangerous. Besides, we'd been pen pals for years. With him escaped, I was sure someone was looking into who might aid him on the outside. My name being high on that list was a risk, but I wasn't worried. The police were welcome into my home. I had nothing to hide, and they would never find the entrance to my dungeon.

But, I obsessed about meeting him. Was he out here too? Watching for his wife? Would he insist my Queen still belonged to him?

A dark blue SUV rolled into the driveway. An enormous Black man stepped out of the driver's side. He looked familiar, but I couldn't place where I'd seen him before. Then, I remembered. He was the fucking hero's sidekick. The door to the passenger side opened, and an African beauty exited.

My heart stuttered with the hitch in my breath. She was an exquisite display of ebony perfection, and her lithe frame moved like smoke on the wind. Small tits, but I could get past that. My cock twitched, demanding a taste, and ordered me to make her my African Queen.

Could I have two queens?

No one else jumped out of the car. Hero-boy wasn't with them. It would be fun to string hero-boy up in my dungeon instead of that pathetic nurse.

But, I'd found his friends.

Flowers.

Shit! I needed more flowers.

There weren't any more in the van, and my Queen deserved the best arrangement I could find.

The big man talked to the suits standing in the driveway while the woman disappeared inside. What little chatter squawked through the radio yielded zero information.

My thoughts wandered down the wrong path, and with it went my attention. I almost missed it when Goliath jumped into his car. The ebony beauty followed.

I determined then that she would have to join the ranks of my princesses.

Goliath backed down the drive and peeled off. I barely caught up as he turned the corner.

I struggled to keep the SUV in sight and prayed he didn't notice me following in my van. Goliath would lead me to the fucking hero, and Hero-boy would lead me to my Queen.

At some point, I'd have to get those flowers.

He pulled up to a greasy diner, and the two of them climbed out. I found a spot where I could watch the door and was happy to see them take a booth against the window. I had a clear view. Ten minutes later, a cab arrived, and Hero stepped out. Another man I would need to kill. He slid into the booth across them.

My scope wasn't powerful enough to see the screen of his phone, but I picked out three of the four numbers of his passcode. I would need that phone.

About twenty minutes later, something happened, because all of a sudden, they rushed out of the diner.

This time, I was ready and had no difficulty following them to an upscale hotel. They ran inside while I parked my van behind their car. I handed my keys to the valet, along with a fifty.

An atrium formed the core of the building. Four sets of glass elevators lifted from the lobby floor to scale the inner walls. Spotting my eager trio was easy. They stood at the bank of elevators.

I strolled into the middle of the lobby and took a seat in an overstuffed chair where I had the best view of the elevators and the balconies of every floor.

I swore they had guns drawn.

My heart leaped with worry over my Queen, praying nothing terrible happened to her.

Their elevator ascended to the eighteenth floor. When they rushed out, they headed left. Thankful for the open design, it was a simple matter to track them. All I needed now was a plan.

I walked to the bar and ordered a drink. My princesses could wait a little longer. I needed to think.

The bartender poured a beer and left me alone.

My Queen's hero intimidated me, as did the large Black man. They had the same look about them like they'd gone a round or two before. I didn't want to think about going toe-to-toe with Goliath; wait…I didn't like that name. I would call him Tank.

Even the Amazon frightened me a little, as ashamed as I was to admit being scared of a girl, it was the truth.

And I hated guns.

But, I would brave it all to get my Queen.

THIRTY-FOUR

Card Key

CJ

Ten agonizing minutes later, Mac pulled up to the hotel. CJ grabbed his duffle and launched out of his seat. From the corner of his eye, he spotted keys flying as Mac tossed them to a valet.

He'd never forgive himself if something happened to Melissa while he was gone. Jenny followed, easily keeping pace with him and Mac as they sprinted through the lobby.

Please God, let her be all right.

Jenny arrived at the elevators first and jabbed at the call bell. The wonder of wonders, the metal doors opened. He breathed a sigh of relief, but nothing could ease the lump of anguish sitting in his gut.

Prayers are for pussies. That was a saying his alcoholic father had beat into his young body until the message imprinted itself in his bones. Still, he wasn't beyond asking God for a favor this once.

"What floor?" Jenny's finger hovered over the columns of buttons.

He reached around her and pushed the button marked eighteen. Jenny took a step back, saying nothing, her placid expression conveyed much. She exchanged a glance with Mac, an entire conversation flowing between them in that one look. He'd never met operatives who moved with the same unified purpose as they did. Those two had an eerie connection.

As they neared their destination, Jenny pulled out her Glock. She gave Mac a questioning look, and he responded with a jerk of his chin to the left. CJ readied his gun then cursed, realizing he needed the room key buried in his wallet. He holstered his weapon, dropped the duffle, and dug the card key out from among his credit cards.

The doors to the elevator opened, agonizingly slow, and he squeezed through the widening crack the moment his shoulders fit through the opening. He was off at a sprint, card key in hand and weapon ready. Jenny and Mac jogged behind him. He pulled up to Melissa's room and slid the card through the reader.

The light flashed red. He cursed and reran it through the reader.

Red.

"Fuck!"

On the third try, the light blinked green and the lock disengaged. He rushed through the doorway, sweeping the room, gun level, and steady.

"Melissa?" He called her name in a steady, but low tone.

No answer.

Jenny and Mac had his back. Mac closed the door and gestured to the bedroom. He dropped CJ's duffle bag on the floor. Jenny stepped to the bedroom door and covered him while he turned the knob. He put his palm to the door and pushed it open, sweeping his weapon left then right.

Melissa's suitcase lay in the middle of the floor, zipper open and clothes strewn everywhere.

No Melissa.

His heart rate jumped as he took in the neatly made bed and the disaster on the floor. Had she been taken? Had she been foolish enough to let the maids in? After his strict instructions that no one was to enter?

The light patter of falling water hit his ears. He tilted his head back and cursed.

"What?" Jenny's whisper brought his attention back to business.

"She's taking a fucking shower."

Jenny lowered her gun. "And that's a problem why?"

He gritted his teeth and ground out the words. "Because I told her not to, that's why."

Behind them, Mac cleared his throat. "Might I remind you we have yet to confirm she is inside the bathroom? Are you going to chat all day long, or are we going to clear all the rooms?"

"I'll do it," CJ said.

Jenny shook her head. "Like hell you're walking in on a woman taking a shower. I've got this."

He put out a hand to stop Jenny.

The look she gave suggested he had a fight on his hands, but he would be the only one stepping through that door. What if Melissa had fallen again? His heart pinched, remembering her crumpled body sprawled on the shower floor.

"No way." Jenny made to step around him.

He pivoted and pinned her to the wall, holding her in place with his hand wrapped around her throat. "I said I'd deal with it."

"You think because you fucked her, she's yours? Get your head out of your ass." Jenny grasped his wrist. If he'd been anyone else, she would have incapacitated him by now. Instead, she allowed him to hold her against the wall.

"Jenny." Mac gave a warning.

"I didn't fuck her," CJ ground out. At least not yet. He had bought a pack of condoms. One was nestled within the leather folds of his wallet.

Jenny pulled his hand away from her throat. "Then what the hell is wrong with you?"

He had no answer.

Mac stepped around the two of them and entered the bathroom.

Before CJ could stop him, a high-pitched screech sounded against the tiled walls.

"What the hell! Get out! Get out!"

Mac backtracked out of the bathroom, his gun held up, and a grin splitting his face. "Lady's alive, and might I say—"

CJ leveled a finger at his friend. "Don't you dare say a word." He rushed around Mac's massive frame. "Melissa, it's okay. It's me."

"CJ?"

Steam saturated his shirt between one step and the next. The mirrors were fogged over. She sat on the shower enclosure floor, curled into a ball, hugging her knees to her chest. Worried she'd fallen again, he threw open the shower door and stepped inside. Water soaked his clothes for the second time in less than 24 hours.

He crouched down. "Are you okay? Did you fall?"

Melissa turned red-rimmed eyes on him. "I'm fine. I was just trying to relax."

It wasn't until he was pulled back by the scruff of his neck that he moved.

"Out, asshole," Jenny said. "Get the fuck out." She threw him into the bedroom and slammed the bathroom door on him and Mac.

Mac sat on the bed and wheezed with laughter. "That'll teach you to put Jenny in a chokehold. Shit, even I wouldn't do that."

Melissa's frustration sounded from behind the closed door. It was too muffled for him to make out the words, but her emotion carried well enough.

He started toward the door, but Mac's cautionary tone pulled him back. "I wouldn't do that. Your girl's safe. Let's wait in the other room."

He shook out his wet clothes. "I fucked that up."

"Pretty much."

"She didn't listen. She didn't follow my orders."

"She's not your team." Mac tugged CJ toward the living area of the suite. "You and I, we need to talk."

"I'm good."

"Are you? The way you went after Jenny? Do we have a problem?"

"I said I'm good."

"Really? Because from here, it looks as though your feelings are for the lady are becoming a liability." Mac shook his head. "Shit, did you have to pick the wife of the man who killed your sister?"

A gasp sounded from behind them. "What?"

CJ spun around and watched as all the color drained from Melissa's face. One of the white, fluffy robes wrapped her body, and now her complexion matched the robe.

"Is that true?" Her hand pressed against her mouth, and tears sprung from her eyes.

"Please, you don't understand." He took two staggering steps toward her, but she backed away, holding up her hands.

"Why didn't you tell me?"

"Shit, CJ," Jenny muttered. "You didn't tell her?"

Melissa slammed the door to the bedroom, and the lock turned into place.

Mac took several steps backward. "Sorry, I didn't see her standing there."

"Why haven't you told her?" The recrimination in Jenny's voice made CJ's stomach sour.

"I was going to; it just hadn't come up yet. Inserting 'your ex-husband murdered my baby sister' into a conversation isn't easy."

"Don't you think that might have been the first thing you should have mentioned before you slept with her?" Jenny lacked a few inches on him, and yet, with her arms crossed over her chest and head tilted back, she managed to look down her nose at him.

He felt like a five-year-old getting scolded by his mother.

He shrugged. "There was never a good time."

She stepped past him and tugged on Mac's shirtsleeve pulling him toward the door. "Because you were too busy shoving your tongue down her throat. Mac and I will be in the bar. Patch things up with your girlfriend, then meet us downstairs. I don't care about your personal love life, or how you made a mess of it in less than a day, but we have work to do and two cases to solve. Get your ass focused."

"Jenny, that's uncalled for—" Mac shut his mouth when Jenny pressed a finger to his chest.

"You stay out of it." Her finger lifted to point accusingly at CJ. "His personal love-fest has sidetracked our investigation."

"There's no love-fest, Jenny, and I've been on point. Besides, you're in charge of the investigation. And you just said it…we have two cases; recovering Henrietta Jones and protecting Melissa Evans.

Until the rest of Delta team arrives, Melissa is my responsibility. The Henrietta Jones' case is yours."

"We're getting the girls at noon." She pressed her fingertip against his sternum, grinding it into his breastbone.

"Agreed." He pinched her wrist until she backed down and then glanced at his watch. Just past nine, he had a few hours to fix this mess with Melissa.

Jenny and Mac exited the hotel suite, leaving him alone with his thoughts and the locked door to the bedroom.

He rummaged in his duffle and drew out a pair of jeans and an old shirt with a picture of Goofy on it. Not that he was a fan of the Magic Kingdom, but it would be perfect for the girls. The shirt was one of the few clean ones when he'd packed his bag. Upside? He'd appear less threatening to Henrietta's little girls when he talked to them.

After dressing, he rapped on the door to the bedroom. "Melissa, I'm sorry." Always best to begin with an apology.

Her soft cries stopped, which he took as a good sign.

"Mac and Jenny left. Can we talk?"

"Is it true?" The lock turned, and she opened the door. Her eyes carried so much pain. They made his heart ache. He reached out to touch her cheek but hesitated when she flinched. Avoiding him, she crossed the room and perched on the edge of the couch. "The execution brought you to town." She didn't phrase it as a question, but more as a statement.

He nodded.

Her eyes lowered. "I'm so sorry." Her cheeks flushed. "I…I didn't know what he was doing all those years."

He hated the guilt transforming her face into a mask of grief. She seemed so calm, almost resigned to believing the worst about herself when she'd done nothing wrong.

"Melissa, it isn't your fault. And as for you and me—"

"Why didn't you tell me?" She tried to meet his eyes, but her gaze skittered away as if she could no longer stand looking at him or have him look at her.

He needed to say something. He'd been quiet too long, and it wasn't safe to leave her questions unanswered. He closed the distance and took her hands in his, but she tugged out of his grip.

"Because I was more concerned about you. Jenny's right about one thing. My head's not in the game. I haven't stopped thinking about you since the day we met. It scares me. I've never felt like this before, but there's something between us, a connection I want to explore. As for my sister, what happened to her has nothing to do with you or my feelings for you." He scratched his head. "Hell, you stole my heart the moment I held you in my arms."

"How can you bear to look at me?" She pulled at her hair. "Let alone…" Her hand covered her mouth, and a sob choked in her throat.

"Stop," he demanded. "When I look at you, I can't help but smile. When I touch you, I can't help but pull you close to me. I can't get enough of you, and as for last night, I want more of that. I can't wait to slip inside of you. I don't see Patterson's wife when I look at you. I see an amazing, resilient, and beautiful woman I want to spend all my time with."

Her eyes widened.

He wasn't letting something she had no control over steal whatever had begun between them, not when he ached to fill her with happiness. He pulled her to her feet and gathered her into his arms, smoothing and straightening her wet hair.

"How can you not be disgusted by the thought of me?" Her hand came between them, and a sob wracked her body.

"As I said, whatever this is between us, it's real." He pointed to his chest. "I feel you in here. I'm not disgusted. I'm fucking entranced." The pain threading through her words appalled him. That one man could wreak so much havoc on so many lives made him sick to his stomach.

What to do? Holding her seemed to help, but the more her body pressed against his, the more aroused he became. And while he'd love nothing more than to take her to bed and finish what they'd started the night before, now did not seem like the best time.

He held her face in his hands and pressed his lips to her forehead.

"Everyone comes with a past. It doesn't mean we have to live there. I didn't know who you were when we met. I didn't know until the day I drove you home from the hospital. You'd already marked my heart. And I know two things with complete conviction."

Her teary eyes regarded him.

"I can never bring my sister back, and I believe you had nothing to do with your ex-husband's crimes. Maybe it's time you believe it, too."

The uncertainty and self-doubt in her expression softened. Between one breath and the next, she smiled. That one small act transformed her face into something achingly beautiful.

He cupped her chin to kiss her, running his fingers along the curve of her jaw until they tangled in the wet mess of her hair. Her lips were pink and begged for a kiss, and he couldn't get enough of her taste. Without rushing the moment, he let his focus drift and reveled in the glide of his lips over hers. A deep groan rumbled in his chest as a sharp ache settled in his balls.

"I want you, and I know you feel the same about me." He loved the way her body responded to his touch.

His pulse went ballistic as she dug her fingers into his waist. Her entire body trembled before him. He ended the kiss sooner than he would have liked and dipped his head to nuzzle at her throat. He glanced down at her robe. The soft fabric gaped, revealing the swell of her perfect breasts.

Lifting her chin, he forced her to look him in the eye. “Never doubt what we’ve shared is real. This thing between us belongs to us, not to anyone else, not to our pasts and definitely not to him.”

“But he—”

“Did terrible things to innocent women. I came to bury my anger and find peace for my sister. Never in a million years would I have thought I’d stumble across an amazing woman.”

“Nothing is amazing about me.”

“Do you need me to show you what I see when I look at you? How you make me feel? How my body comes alive with your smile or the light twinkling in your eyes?” He placed her palm against his chest. “Do you feel that?” His heart slammed against the cage of his chest, desperate to touch her.

She gave a small laugh and nudged her hip against the hardness of his erection straining behind the fabric of his jeans.

“I feel it, too.” She released the sash of her robe, letting the fabric fall in a puddle at her feet. His breathing hitched. The air disturbed by nothing other than the heat of her gaze and his determination not to fuck up. “Speaking of which.” She teased him with a smile. “I owe you something.”

He groaned with his need, wanting to sink into her lovely heat and make her scream his name. She swiveled her hips, the movement hardening his cock until it ached. Wrapping her arms around his neck, she leaned her head against his chest, breathing out a deep sigh. Without another word, she grabbed his hand and led him toward the bedroom.

He almost stopped her, his mind drifting to how much trouble he would be in with Jenny—hell, with Sam—but she drew him into the dimly lit bedroom, naked and determined.

And technically, he had a few hours to kill.

There was no way in hell he would stop whatever was happening next.

When she reached the bed, she turned to face him. Undoing the buckle of his belt, she lowered the zipper, reached in, and pulled out his cock. He moaned as her hand wrapped around him, then hitched a breath when she fisted the shaft. The slow, agonizing twist had him rising to the balls of his feet.

"Sweet Jesus." He kissed her, exploring her mouth and the angles of her perfect face. She kept her hand on his cock, moving from root to tip with tentative fingers becoming much more confident the longer he kissed her.

He ran a hand over her skin, tracing the satiny swell of her breasts, and used his thumb to draw circles around her nipple until the flesh pebbled into a tight bud.

It was time to slow things down.

She moaned when he flicked her nipple. He palmed her belly and then sought the heat between her legs, where he found her wet and ready.

Maybe slow had been a bad idea.

He pushed his jeans down. Kicking his shoes off, his socks joined his jeans in a pile on the floor. He stopped kissing her and took a moment to admire her nakedness.

"Is this what you want?"

"Yes." Her breathy reply sent blood surging to his cock.

He lowered his mouth to take hers in a long, lingering kiss, lifting her off her feet to lay her out on the bed.

She scooted up, and he crawled over her, their lips never once separating. She canted her hips upward, positioning herself so his cock met the hot, wet flesh of her pussy.

Her fingernails scraped his back, desperate for more contact, and when he shifted over her, his cock almost slipped in.

She froze and whispered. "Did you get any condoms?"

Thank fuck he had. He retrieved one from his wallet, sheathing himself with a rip of foil and slide of protection. Then he dragged himself back up the bed, stopping to inhale her intoxicating scent and taste her essence.

"I'm going to erase that bastard from your memories." He kissed down the length of her body.

"What man?" She cried out the moment his tongue found her clit.

He closed his mouth around the tender nub, drawing her deep into his mouth, flicking the sensitive tissue with his tongue in short bursts until she writhed beneath him and begged for more. Her fingers dug into his scalp, desperate and needy, and he gave her exactly what she needed. He didn't stop until she came apart on his face.

"I need to be inside of you." He shifted, moving back over her body. "Now."

While she quivered with the aftershocks of her orgasm, he fisted his cock and pressed just the tip against her folds. Their eyes met, and he held her with a fierce stare. The moment she gave the briefest of nods, he plunged deep into her with one long thrust, not content to move slowly anymore.

She gasped as he filled her. Her warmth clenched around his cock. This was Nirvana, wrapped in the heat of this amazingly beautiful woman. He never wanted to leave, but he needed to move. Hunger for her sweet heat propelled him.

His heart beat with a solid thump, and he tried not to crush her with his weight. Slow and steady, he pulled out. She matched him with a rock of her hips. The sensation went straight to his cock, the feeling so overwhelming he thought he'd lose control and embarrass himself right then. But he gritted his teeth, and balanced on the edge of consuming pleasure, determined she would come again before he was spent.

"You feel so fucking good," he said. "So fucking good."

Already, that telltale tingle began at the base of his spine and traveled to his balls. He held his pleasure back, never wanting this moment to end.

"Oh, my God." She arched her neck. "CJ, faster, please." She dug her fingers into his shoulder. "Oh, my fucking God!"

Her tits bounced with each thrust and shook every time he pulled out. She begged him to move. Faster! Harder! And he wanted to howl a primal yell to the world. This was him making her feel this way.

Making her beg for more and scream with pleasure.

He moved faster, gauging her response, afraid he might hurt her, but she urged him on. To go deeper. Push harder. Move faster.

He lifted, thrusting with his hips and using as much force as he could leverage, pounding in and out, dragging his cock against the velvety warmth of her walls.

The tingle at his spine grew, and his balls drew up. He bent his head down, sucking at the soft spot on the side of her throat. Her sweet, salty essence drove him wild, and he pulled hard at her skin, marking her as his.

Her body shuddered beneath him, her pussy clenching against his cock in long tight pulls with the sweep of another orgasm. She cried out his name. Over and over again, she screamed.

His name on her lips.

Heaven.

Her cries triggered his release, his balls tightening, clenching, then pumping his essence with the force of his orgasm.

His breaths came as ragged pants, and he collapsed on top of her, his arms giving out. He couldn't remember the last time he'd come so hard, or when sex had felt so damn good. In her arms, he felt content. He pressed a soft kiss against her ear.

"Fuck, that was amazing." Perhaps not the most romantic words, but they were true.

She wrapped her ankles around his hips, drawing his cock deep into her heat.

"I never want to leave this bed," she whispered.

He agreed. He'd never felt so good.

It had been too long since he'd felt anything close to what he experienced in Melissa's arms. It didn't matter who she had once been married to. At this moment, and every moment from here on out, she belonged to him.

The angry tone of his cell phone interrupted them.

"Damn!" He'd ignore it if he could, but he knew who was calling. He rolled off Melissa and found his pants on the floor. Reaching into the pocket, he retrieved his phone and glanced at the text.

Jenny: Change in plans. Need you now.

Melissa laughed. "I guess this means you can't stay?"

He growled.

She rolled onto her side while he swung his legs over the edge of the bed.

"What do you do for a living? You said you were a paramedic, but I'm sensing there's more to it."

He was done with not telling her the truth, and he was proud of his job. He got to save lives…most of the time. Not every job came with a happy ending. "I'm a Guardian."

"What does that mean?"

"The Guardians are hostage rescue specialists. We consult with the FBI when they have difficult cases, and we work for private clients when needed."

"What does that have to do with my husband?" She seemed confused.

"Nothing, actually. I came for his execution, but you know what happened with that. Then a woman was kidnapped. Her husband is well respected, and the Police Chief reached out to my boss to look into it." He understood her confusion and left the bed with great reluctance. Walking into the bathroom, he discarded the condom. "My company was hired to investigate the kidnapping of a woman named Henrietta Jones. Since I was already here on personal business when the case was assigned, it was assigned to my team."

"Do you think Scott kidnapped this woman?"

"Henrietta doesn't fit his type, but it did happen the day after his escape. We can't rule him out, but I think they're unrelated. He didn't have time to take her and…" He hesitated to bring up the poor girl killed in Melissa's house.

"Kill that other girl." She finished his thought and wiped at a tear.

He walked to the foot of the bed and retrieved his clothes, dressing slowly while savoring Melissa's still naked form. He'd never get enough of her beauty, or how she felt wrapped around his cock.

"Is that why Jenny was mad at you?" Her brows knitted into a pensive expression. "You should be working that case instead of protecting me?"

"Yes and no. Guardian HRS is protecting you, which means I'm protecting you. The local cops are spread too thin with the storm damage. Jenny is taking the lead on Henrietta's kidnapping, but I'm helping her out. And I have to go. I have a meeting at noon. In the meantime, the rest of Delta team is inbound to protect you." He lifted the phone. "Something happened, and Jenny needs me now."

"Delta team…sounds very military."

"Most of us are ex-military, in some form or another."

"Impressive. So I'm both work and pleasure?" Her impish grin made him smile.

"You most definitely are." He threaded his belt through the buckle and crawled on top of her. Staring down into her innocent eyes, he couldn't help but smile. "For the record," he kissed the tip of her nose. "You're worth it."

"I wish you didn't need to go." She rolled to her side, much of her stiffness seeming to be gone.

"Me too."

"We should talk when you get back."

"We will. Now, promise to lock the outer door. Use the swinging latch and stay in the bedroom with this door locked too. Prop a chair under the doorknob. Don't answer the door. Let no one inside. Your security detail will be here in less than an hour."

"When will you be back?" She tapped him on the nose with her finger.

"Later tonight." He would bring her flowers, order a romantic dinner, light some candles, and take his time to explore her body the way she deserved.

He kissed her, his heart solid and whole. "I can't wait to see you when I get back."

She stretched her hands over her head. "I'll be waiting for you right here."

"Dammit woman, you're going to be the death of me." He reached down to adjust his growing erection.

"Hopefully in the best possible way. Be safe out there, CJ."

"I will." And with that, he left a naked woman in bed who had somehow grabbed a hold of his heart. There was far more than sex going on between them, and he agreed. When he got back, they would talk. Melissa didn't know it yet, but he wasn't letting her go.

THIRTY-FIVE

More Plans

PIERCE

MANY MINUTES AFTER I SETTLED IN AT THE BAR, I WATCHED TANK, and my Amazon, walk into the elevator on the eighteenth floor. She stared out of the glass while he faced the doors. The difference in their sizes fascinated me. She was thin and tall, with musculature accentuating her curves. Towering above her, Tank was a monster.

If the two of them were coming down, what the hell was Hero-boy doing to my Queen?

If he touched her, I would rip his head off.

Moments later, Tank and Amazon took a small table not more than ten feet from where I perched. Terrified that Tank would recognize me from the hospital, I placed my back to him, keeping an eye on them through the mirror behind the bar. My position allowed me to admire my Amazon and her flawless perfection.

She ordered a glass of wine, and he asked for water. I shifted, straining to listen to their conversation, hopeful something could help my quest.

"You didn't have to be such a bitch." Tank stretched back in his seat while his cold eyes scanned the hotel lobby.

"Someone needed to say something."

Her sharp retort made me snicker. I couldn't wait to make her mine. I loved the light lilt of my Amazon's voice. What accent was that? Something exotic and raw. What would she sound like when she screamed?

She continued. "You weren't stepping up to the plate."

My hearing perked up, eager to exploit anything I could.

"CJ's cool."

So, Hero's name was CJ.

"He's distracted."

"No. CJ doesn't get distracted. Besides, you haven't given him anything to do."

"The girls…"

"He's going to talk to them at lunch."

It seemed like Hero-boy had lots of girls hanging around. Yet another reason to get my Queen out from under his influence. I struggled with my lack of a plan.

The big guy sipped his water and watched the woman over the rim of his glass. Tank traced a finger over the water rings left by his glass, doodling on the tabletop.

Her mouth entranced me. A darker coloring deepened her plump lips. Would they feel different wrapped around my dick than a white woman's lips? I shifted, trying to relieve the ache in my pants as they tightened with my need.

With great effort, I forced myself to focus on their conversation, but every time she licked her lips, my thoughts wandered to having them wrapped around my dick.

The bartender swapped out her empty wine glass with a new one. She took a sip, those entrancing lips of hers hugging the rim of the glass.

Tank pulled a phone out of his pocket, the vibrations buzzing as loud as a ringtone. "Yo!" A minute passed without him saying a word, then he answered. "Got it."

"What's wrong?" My Amazon tipped the glass and emptied its contents.

"That was Sam. Our team's delayed… weather. Won't be here at noon like we thought."

"Shit," she said. "When?"

"They're renting a car and driving down. Sam thinks no later than three."

"CJ won't be pleased." She tapped on her phone. "I'm letting him know. Besides, it's almost time to go."

A few minutes later, Hero-boy walked into the bar. I watched his approach through the reflection of the mirror. He scanned the room, and my heart thundered, but he looked through and past me like I didn't exist. Although he could only see the back of my head. I was safe.

And what was that? His cell phone poked out of his back pocket, an easy lift if I wanted it. And I would need his phone. My day just brightened.

They were pushing me to take risks because I would have to get close to him to snatch that phone. I didn't like that. I didn't like him. His walk irritated me, all confident like he owned the place. His deep voice carried that soothing edge women flocked toward, and I had no doubt he'd been using it on my Queen. I hated the expanse of muscle spreading beneath his t-shirt. I hated everything about him because I knew he desired my Queen.

An image of him chained and bleeding flashed in my eyes. I'd love to slice his pretty face. Speaking of, I needed something to hide my face. Fortunately, the dude beside me left his ball cap on the bar. It would do.

"I won't be pleased about what?" Hero-boy grabbed a nearby chair from another table, raising a hand, he flagged over the bartender.

Tank tossed a couple of twenties on the table and stood. "Security detail won't be here until three."

"Three!" Hero-boy's face turned cherry blossom red. For a moment, I hoped his head would explode. That would save me a lot of trouble. "What happened to noon?"

His gaze surveyed the room and settled on my reflection. A flicker of recognition flashed in his face, but he didn't do anything. But then why would he? I was just a guy sitting at a bar. But damn! The intensity of his stare had me practically pissing myself.

"Weather delays." Tank breathed in, and his barrel chest widened even further.

The bartender made his way over to their table, but instead of Hero-boy ordering a drink, he waved him away. They got up to leave, and the roundness of my Amazon's hips snagged my attention. Shit, I needed to focus. I needed that phone. And then the universe answered my prayers.

An elderly couple sitting a table away stood. Their ponderous movements, unsteady and frail, provided the perfect opportunity. I snagged the ball cap and set it low to shield as much of my face as possible and then positioned myself to provide a distraction. A collision of the old and the overly-rushed would be perfect.

Tank put a hand on Hero-boy's shoulder. "Melissa will be safe. Hotel security is aware."

It took little to make the old woman stumble as I pitched her toward Hero-boy.

Her shaky voice trembled with surprise. "I'm so sorry." She placed a hand on Hero-boy's arm. "I'm so clumsy."

While she gave her apologies, Hero-boy steadied her on her feet. I took advantage of his distraction to lift his phone out of his back pocket. With a polished flick of my wrist, I tucked it into the waistband of my jeans.

Hero-boy's gaze lifted to the atrium, his eyes sweeping left. Mine followed the direction of his gaze, but for a different purpose. He was thinking about what he was leaving behind. I was thinking about what was soon to be mine.

THIRTY-SIX

A Hundred Roses

MELISSA

MELISSA CHECKED THE, DOUBLE-CHECKED THE SAFETY BOLT, AND triple-checked the chair shoved beneath the doorknob.

Her phone buzzed with an incoming text.

> *CJ: Hey, beautiful.*
> *Melissa: Hi. Miss U.*
> *CJ: Miss U2. I sent you something special.*

He knew about her past but still wanted to be with her. Her heart felt as if it would burst.

If only Scott wasn't in the picture.

She closed her eyes and breathed. It took all her focus not to think.

Breathe in. Hold. Count to three. Breathe out. Breathe in. One. Two. Three.

The repetition soothed her nerves. Soon the fluttering in her chest eased as well.

Breathe in. Breathe out. Do not think.

But her thoughts jumped from Scott to CJ, and back to Scott. She yanked her mind's wandering back to the simple act of breathing.

Had it been less than a week since she'd met CJ? It seemed like a lifetime.

Scott's ugly presence festered. Like a cancer, she couldn't cut him out. In killing that woman, he'd made a statement. He wasn't finished, and he intended to take her back.

There was nowhere to go—no one to go home too. As much as this town had turned its back on her, it was her home. Her parents were buried here. If she moved, who would tend to their graves?

Even when love, or a second chance for love, had dared to poke its shy head back into her life, Scott's taint ruined it. Of all the men—all the strange coincidences—how had she fallen for one so intimately connected to her husband's past?

So much for not thinking. Melissa focused back on breathing.

Perhaps she was one of those women unlucky in love? The first love of her life turned out to be a sadistic killer. The second…well, she didn't even know how they would ever straighten out the tangled threads of their pasts.

CJ's caution about locking herself inside the bedroom seemed overkill, and the television was out in the main living area. He'd be upset, but she was bored. After she found the remote, she flipped through the regular channels. Nothing interested her until she found the pay-per-view menu. She accepted the charges and curled up with a pillow to watch a chick-flick with nothing else to do.

This time the flow of tears had nothing to do with her complicated mess of a life. A good, ugly cry had been exactly what she needed as the romantic movie scrolled its credits. She wiped the tears off her cheeks and jumped as a knock sounded at the door.

Her heart leaped into her throat. Was it Scott? She calmed herself down. Scott would never be that stupid. It had to be the security detail CJ mentioned.

She almost opened the door, but then CJ's orders echoed in her head. Making sure the security chain was in place, she looked through the peephole.

"Hello?"

She squinted through the distorted glass, seeing a single figure. Her brows pinched in confusion. CJ had said a team was arriving, but that was a single man.

The man's head lifted. He seemed vaguely familiar, although she couldn't say why. "Delivery for a Melissa Evans?" The man held a clipboard in his hands, and a large cart sat beside him.

"Just leave it by the door." The security team would bring it inside.

"Are you Melissa Evans?"

"Yes, but I didn't order anything."

His easy laughter traveled through the door and relaxed her with the complexity of its tones.

"Trust me, the delivery is for you."

She liked his voice. Rich and full of warmth, a hypnotic quality oddly soothed her.

"I'm sorry, but I can't accept any deliveries. Can you please leave it with the front desk?"

"You sure you want me to leave them at the front desk? The flowers are from someone named CJ."

"CJ?" Why would he deliver flowers after telling her not to open the door? Wait, he'd said he'd gotten her something.

"Yes, ma'am." The man turned to the clipboard as if reading a note. "There's a card…" He leaned close to the peephole. "Miss Evans?"

She gripped her phone and shot a text to CJ.

Melissa: There's a man outside my door.

CJ: It's okay. I sent you something.

Melissa: You said don't open the door.

CJ: I wanted to surprise you. Don't worry. It's safe.

A hell of a surprise considering she was scared to death about Scott, but she trusted CJ. She peeked through the keyhole and recognized the deliveryman from the hospital.

"I know you."

"Excuse me?"

"You delivered flowers to me before. Tulips." Her stomach knotted, thinking about that bouquet.

"I did?"

"Yes," she said.

"Oh, I remember now. My boss had me come back the next day with a different bouquet. That was you?"

"Yes, you brought roses."

He smiled. "I thought the name on the delivery slip sounded familiar, but I deliver so many flowers. It's hard to remember them all."

An awkward pause followed, then he cleared his throat. "Um, what do you want me to do with the flowers?"

Melissa bit her lower lip, considering what to do. He deserved a tip for these flowers and the previous two deliveries at the hospital.

CJ's rules were in place to keep her safe from Scott, not an innocent delivery man, but she wanted to be sure. She turned back to her phone and sent another text.

Melissa: Is it okay to open the door?

CJ: If they're flowers. I hope you like them.

She felt bad for keeping the deliveryman waiting. "Let me find my purse. I need to get a tip."

"Oh, no need to tip."

"I know, but I need to…hang on."

After grabbing a twenty, she undid the chain and turned the deadbolt on the door. When she opened the door, the smile on his face spread ear to ear.

He rocked back on his heels, gave a half-bow and a grand flourish toward an amazing display of what had to be a hundred roses. Odd that they weren't daisies.

Her hands flew to her cheeks as she stepped back. "Oh my!"

CJ had done that?

The deliveryman pushed the cart inside the room. "One hundred long-stem red roses." The door clicked shut behind him.

A blackish discoloration around his eye drew her attention. "What happened to your eye?" She remembered him saying something about boxing.

He grinned. "I was in the wrong place at the wrong time."

"It looks like it hurts." She stared at his black eye. He had a handsome face, and it was a shame someone had tried to mess it up.

"It's nothing."

She bent to breathe in the rich aroma of the roses. "They smell amazing."

"I thought you'd like them."

"Is there a receipt I need to sign?" She couldn't keep her eyes off the roses. The blooms filled the room with a heavenly perfume. "I can't believe he did this." She was smiling so hard, her cheeks hurt.

The timbre of his voice changed, turning sour. "The roses are from me, my Queen."

The smile fell from her face at the hardness in his gaze. She took a step back but wasn't fast enough. He lunged, placing her in an armbar, and pressed a cloth over her nose and mouth. Pungent fumes irritated her sensitive nasal passages and coated the roof of her mouth as she took in a breath to scream. Her strength faded with that first inhale and disappeared with the next. Her body went limp, and her vision faded black.

THIRTY-SEVEN

Sugar And Spice

CJ

Mac and Jenny dropped CJ at the shelter where Child Protective Services had placed Anna and Angela Jones pending foster care assignment.

He climbed out of the car. "Okay, I'm going to convince these girls to take me through the last couple of days before their mother disappeared."

"When do you want to meet up?" Mac tapped the steering wheel. "Shouldn't take us long."

Mac and Jenny were meeting with the Chief of Police and providing consultation services to help coordinate the efforts to track down Scott Patterson.

"It'll take me a few hours. Once you're finished at the Police Station, get back to the hotel. I hate leaving Melissa unguarded for too long. Call me when you get there."

He felt for his phone in his back pocket. "Ah, fuck it."

"What's wrong?" Jenny asked.

"My fucking phone. I must have left it at the hotel." Except he didn't remember leaving it in the room with Melissa.

"You left your phone?" The recrimination in Jenny's expression didn't go unnoticed.

It wasn't normal for him to be so forgetful.

"Can I borrow yours?" He stretched out his hand, palm up.

"You going to lose mine, too?" she quipped.

Wise-ass. "I will guard it with my life." Like he should be guarding Melissa. Instead, he had two little girls to entertain and a mother to find.

Jenny handed over the phone. "We'll be in touch."

As they drove off, CJ glanced at his watch. He didn't have much time.

A few minutes later, he sat with Anna Jones, and her older sister, Angela, in the playroom, his butt pinched by the hard plastic of a kiddie chair.

"How old are you, Anna?"

Angela answered his question. "Anna's seven. I'm eleven-and-a-half."

Anna frowned and stuck out her tongue.

Angela crossed her arms and turned away.

He gave Anna a wink, which she returned with a brilliant smile. "Yes, you most certainly are seven. What grade are you in?"

She scrunched her chubby face, thinking hard. Then her eyes brightened. "I'm in first grade. Mrs. Malone is my teacher."

Women loved compliments, as did little girls, and every little girl wanted to be older. He turned back to Angela.

"You're a wonderful big sister."

The bin full of toys kept drawing little Anna's gaze. She squirmed off her tiny seat. "I'm gonna go play. Angela answers all the questions, anyways." She flounced over to the corner and dug through the toys.

Angela looked to the corner, her finger twirled a long blonde curl. A big sigh escaped her tiny body.

He rocked back in the kid-sized chair. His knees nearly met his chin. "I can see you're taking fantastic care of Anna. Your mother would be proud."

Angela looked sad at the mention of her missing mother. She was trying hard to be brave, but there was a sense of hopelessness in her gentle gaze and fear.

He had to remember these kids had gone from two parents to one, and now to none.

She twisted in her seat to watch her sister.

Anna had dolls lined up in a row, a beauty pageant of epic proportions underway.

Angela shifted again, leaning forward, interrogating him with eyes full of suspicion and distrust. CJ kept his smile relaxed.

"It must be very hard on Anna," he soothed. "She's lucky to have such a brave big sister to lean on."

Angela's lower lip trembled. "You don't look like a cop. They asked me bunches of questions." She gave him a flat stare.

"I'm not a cop, and I'm sure you did a great job answering their questions."

Her brows lifted. "Then why are you here?"

"I'm working with them. I hope to help them find your mother."

Her brows pinched, and her eyes squeezed shut.

He grabbed a coloring book on the table, and drew an octopus, ignoring the tears building behind her eyes. When he was done with his drawing, Angela had wiped her eyes. He tapped the tabletop with the crayon.

"Did you know the Police Chief knew your dad?"

She straightened in her chair. "My daddy?"

CJ nodded. "Yes! And the Police Chief knows my boss. I learned all about your dad. He was a hero. No wonder he has a daughter who is so brave."

She nodded, but she still wasn't talking.

He continued. "Did you know the whole police department has been watching over your family because of your dad?"

Her eyes widened. "They are?"

"Oh, yes," he said, coloring in the arms of the octopus. "When your mom didn't come to pick you up from school, a lot of people got really worried. They called my boss right away to get extra help. That's why I'm here, but I'm not a cop." He lowered his voice to a whisper as if sharing a deep secret with her. "I don't work like a cop."

She paused as if considering the last thing he said. "They asked lots of questions. But I didn't know any answers." Her head tilted as she examined his octopus. She pointed to his picture. "That's not right."

He twisted the drawing. "Looks right to me."

She giggled. "You missed one."

"One what?"

"Octopuses have eight legs." She counted out each one. "See, you missed one."

He brought his hands to his cheeks and gave an exaggerated gasp. "Oh, no! You're right." He pulled out a blank sheet of paper. "Maybe you should help me this time?"

He spent the next ten minutes drawing an octopus, a whale, a shark, and various kinds of seaweed for them to swim through.

"Cops ask a lot of questions," he said with a sigh. "It's hard when you don't have any answers."

Her head shot up, and she looked at him with knowing eyes.

"I have a secret. Do you want to hear it?"

Her head bobbed.

He leaned in, and she moved a little closer.

Keeping his voice to a whisper, he said, "Many times, when we think we know nothing, we know quite a bit."

"We do?"

"Oh, yes." He shaded in the shark. "But you have to know how to look for the clues. They're there, begging to be found, but you have to know the secret to discovering them."

"Do you know the secret?"

"Definitely." He placed his hand on her shoulder and gave it a quick squeeze. "I'm an expert clue finder."

Her eyes widened at his words. "A clue finder?"

"Yes. Do you want to help me find clues?"

He got another nod.

"Okay, the trick is to try really, really hard not to think about them."

Her brows scrunched up. "How can you find them if you don't think about them?"

"Well, the cops are awesome, but they weren't asking the right things. No wonder you didn't have answers. Their questions were the wrong ones."

"You know the right questions?" Awe filled her voice. She tucked her hands beneath her legs.

"They're not questions. They're more like fact-finding tasks, but we have to get out of here to do it right." He pointed to Anna. "I want to bring your sister, but I need you to help me watch over her. Do you think you can do that?"

Another nod.

"Good. Now, have you ever seen one of those shows where people go back in time?"

"People can't go back in time."

"We're not really going back in time, but we're going to ride around and pretend it was a couple of days ago. You and Anna can tell me what it was like then. You know, where you went, and what you did with your mom."

"And that's going to find clues?"

He smiled. "It's worked in the past, but only if you believe. If you and Anna pretend with me, we may find the answers we need."

Anna brought over one of the dolls. "I want ice cream. We don't get ice cream here. Mommy always let us get ice cream."

Angela rolled her eyes. "Not always."

"Yes, she did. Every day after the park, we got ice cream." Anna's little eyes misted over.

Sometimes he hated his job. He would spend the entire day, reminding them of everything they used to do with a mother who was by now likely dead.

"Oh, I think we can do that. Angela says it's okay if we all get out of this place." He turned to Angela, hoping she would give another of her precious nods. When she did, he continued. "We can get ice cream, but we have a mission first."

"A mission?" Anna's expression brightened. "What mission?"

"Mr. CJ is going to help us find mommy," pronounced Angela with the surety of a child.

Anna turned to CJ. "Really, Mr. CJ?"

He hid his wince by reaching out and scrubbing Anna's curls. "We're going to try."

Her sister stood, surprising him with her eagerness. It should've taken a lot more to win her over.

"Can we go now?"

"If you're ready." He put down the crayons and straightened the stack of drawings. He struggled to get out of the small chair built for bottoms much tinier than a grown man's butt.

"We're ready." Angela squared her shoulders and jutted out her chin.

"Let's get you checked out then."

Anna bounced on her feet. "We're getting ice cream."

"Yes, we are Miss Anna, but only after our mission is complete. If you do a great job, I'll make it a double scoop."

She squealed, gripping her hands together. "Two scoops?" She pivoted and yanked on her sister's sleeve. "Did you hear that? Mr. CJ said I could get two scoops."

"Only if you behave," Angela said.

CJ pointed to the corner. "Anna, why don't you grab one of those dolls to bring with you. Angela and I will meet you at the check-out desk."

He crouched, getting eye-to-eye with Angela. "Are you all right?"

Her entire body trembled. He wanted to hug her but refrained from too much contact.

"Don't worry," he reassured. "We'll do our best."

She sniffed. "I heard one of the cops." She lifted her face to him, eyes pleading. "They asked me all kinds of questions, but they never answered mine."

CJ sighed. "I won't lie. I don't know if we'll find your mother, but I promise to do my very best. That's why you and your sister must come with me. Some of what we do may seem silly, or stupid, and some things might not even make sense, but it does to me. I need you to trust me. Do you understand?"

She sniffed and bit her lower lip. "Do you think she's d-dead?"

He placed his hand on her shoulder and told the truth. "I don't know, but I hope not."

THIRTY-EIGHT

Dolls

CJ

ANNA RETURNED WITH A DOLL CLUTCHED IN HER ARMS. SHE TUGGED at CJ's sleeve.

"I'm ready."

He loved kids. They reminded him not all the world was tainted with evil. He held out his hand, which Anna eagerly took and headed to the door. When Angela didn't move, he stretched out his other hand, coaxing her to join them. She looked at her sister, then tentatively reached out. He gave her hand a little squeeze and a special nod. She returned both.

He signed the girls out and loaded them into his new rental car, using the child seats he provided.

"Now, what did you do Friday after school?"

Anna told her life story while Angela remained silent in the passenger seat beside him. Angela concerned him, but he gave her the time she needed to shore up her defenses after their little talk. She had come dangerously close to falling apart.

By the time they pulled up to the girl's school, Angela had added to her sister's monologue. Slowly, he was able to piece together the last few days of Henrietta Jones' life.

He walked through their home; the girls showed him everything. He asked Angela to play with her sister in her room while he looked through Henrietta's bedroom. Their mother kept an immaculate house, a shrine to her dead husband, and filled every wall with pictures of him and their little girls.

He remembered Mac saying she didn't have an extended family.

Boxes and boxes of Girl Scout cookies were stacked in the study. Anna walked in, carrying a cup filled to the rim with milk. She thrust it out at him.

"Whoa," CJ said as he rescued the cup from her hands.

"For you," the little girl said. "Momma always said you're supposed to offer a drink to guests."

"Ah, well, I thank you then." He sat on the floor of the study in between stacks of cookie boxes. "You're a Girl Scout?"

"I'm a Brownie. Angela's a Junior."

"I was a Boy Scout."

"You were?"

"Yes, Eagle Scout." He pointed to the stacked boxes. "Cookie time, I see."

Her eyes lit up. "Yes. We were selling cookies before the storm hit. We were supposed to go out on Sunday too, but Mama took us to the park instead. Then we got ice cream. Mama was real happy."

"Really," CJ cooed, trying to keep her talking about her memory. He drank from his cup, getting a milk mustache on his upper lip. He pretended like he didn't know.

Anna giggled and pointed at his lips.

"What?"

"You're messy."

He made a show of wiping his mouth, dragging his sleeve across his lips, and rubbing the milk mustache off his face. Her laughter filled the room, and he was pleased to bring this tiny moment of happiness into her life. Angela wandered in and sat beside him.

He pointed to Anna. "Your sister was telling me she's a Brownie and you're a Junior. She said you were selling cookies on Saturday."

Angela's gaze bounced across the stacks of cookie boxes and crash-landed on the carpet. She sighed. "We did."

"I'd like to see where your mom sold the cookies."

Angela lifted her eyes and met his. "We sold the cookies. Mama just stood on the curb. She didn't talk to anyone." He could see the pride in the firm set of her chin.

CJ sipped from his cup. This time he licked off his milk mustache. Anna giggled. "Remember what we talked about? Any little thing can be important."

He wasn't sure, but he thought she gave a nod of agreement, or maybe she thought he was the stupidest adult on the planet.

"Come. It's almost noon. Let's grab a bite to eat, and then you can show me where you sold cookies."

"Are we going to sell some more?" Anna gazed up at CJ with innocent eyes.

"No, I—" He tried to explain the plan for the day, but Angela took over. Typical bossy older sister.

"We're just gonna drive by the houses. Mr. CJ wants to see where we went with Mama. Get your dolly. We have to bring her back with us."

"I don't want to go back," Anna whined. "Can't we sleep at home? Mama will be back soon, won't she?"

"Maybe," Angela said. "Now get the doll. We need to go."

He drove the neighborhoods while they guided him, arguing more often than not on where they had or hadn't been. Angela's memory surprised him. She knew each street they had visited.

Anna chimed in with their sales. He learned all about Mrs. Cleary with her three black cats who bought two boxes of Tagalongs. Sergeant Mallory didn't like cookies, but he liked Girl Scouts. He bought a case for his work. Anna remembered because her mom didn't have a case of cookies, and they had to come back.

Mr. Blackstone, with the black dog, ordered Thin Mints. Anna proudly informed CJ that Thin Mints were everybody's most 'favorite-ist' cookie. Timothy, a high schooler, bought five boxes of Samoas. Anna scrunched up her nose at that because those were the yucky ones.

"Wow, you two really know a lot about the people you sold cookies to," he said, after listening to an in-depth conversation about Mr. Willy and his pet monkey.

"Mama didn't like us going to stranger's houses," Angela said. "She knows lots of people, so we go to their houses."

"Sounds like a good plan. How does your mother know so many people?"

Angela shrugged. "She's a volunteer."

Anna tapped Angela's headrest. "Mama didn't know everyone, 'member? We went to that other neighborhood." Her voice rose with excitement. "They didn't have Girl Scouts of their own. We sold lots of boxes there."

CJ's ears perked up. "Really? Where is that?"

Angela's mouth twisted as she tried to remember. They were looking for something out of the ordinary in Henrietta's routine. "I'm not sure, Mr. CJ." Tears pooled in the corners of her eyes.

Damn.

He reached over to pat her knee. "It's okay. It's hard to remember things. Did you get on a highway?"

"No," Anna piped up from the backseat. "We drove through the fields, you remember? We went past the farm with the rabbits and the goats? It was all farms, except that neighborhood. It's pretty and next to a forest. Mama pulled in there because the houses were close, and we wouldn't have to walk far. Remember, Angie?"

Beside him, Angela nodded.

He breathed a sigh of relief. "Anna, your memory is super awesome. Now, how do I find this farm with the rabbits and goats?"

Between the two of them, they were able to direct him through town. The small development they took him too was on the edge of the city they lived in. He drove around that neighborhood, but they had little to tell him about the inhabitants. No stories of dogs, cats, birds, or monkeys. They didn't even remember who bought what kind of cookies, or how many boxes. As they were driving out of the development, they passed a house nestled back against the trees. It looked out of place until CJ realized it took up two lots.

Anna bounced in her seat. "Angie! Angie! Remember him. He bought ten boxes. And gave us a fifty."

Angela crossed her arms. "Yeah, I remember him."

"What's wrong, Angela?" CJ asked.

"I didn't like him."

"You were being a poop-face." Anna stuck her tongue out. "He was nice, and he gave us extra."

Angela shrugged.

CJ slowed down in front of the house. It was a nondescript cookie-cutter, builder's home. The only thing distinctive about it was how it was set apart from its neighbors by the double lot. The lawn was cut and edged with meticulous precision. The bushes were well-groomed. Flower boxes sat in front of all the windows, and they overflowed with blooms. It looked quaint and inviting, more like an old lady lived there than a man who bought Girl Scout cookies.

It made his skin itch.

"Did your mother talk to him?"

"No, she watched from the curb like she always does," Angela said.

"That's not true," Anna quipped from the backseat.

"Shut up," Angela said. "He waved, and she waved back."

"Mama did so talk to him." Anna stuck out her tongue again.

"Shut up, Anna. You don't even know what you're talking about. You're such a baby."

"Girls," CJ said. "Let's not argue."

The two fell silent. He pulled forward but stopped to let a white florist's van turn into the driveway of the house. On the way out of the housing development, he searched for an ice cream shop to satisfy the argumentative little girls.

THIRTY-NINE

Mine!

PIERCE

MINE!

I wanted to dance in the streets and yell it out to the world. My Queen, my beautiful Queen, was home!

My plan had worked without a hitch.

It was brilliant!

I was brilliant.

Of course, I had been brilliant.

For a moment, I worried she wouldn't open the door. Everything hinged on that one thing.

I'd hoped.

I'd prayed.

Can you believe the whole tulip and roses thing? Bless her royal heart. My Queen remembered me!

I wanted to look my very best for her too, but thanks to Dickwad, deep bruising circled my eye. Odd how things work out, though. I couldn't have planned for a better reaction. Her sympathy had made my heart flip.

When she told me to leave the flowers, I nearly panicked. Thank goodness I had Hero-boy's phone. A few quick texts, and she did exactly as I'd wanted.

My window of opportunity had been tiny. My chances slim. But I prevailed!

Honestly, today felt like divine intervention. As if God himself smiled down on me.

I wanted to linger in that hotel room, but security could have shown any time. Hero-boy could have come back. That freak of a man, Tank, could have been with him. My Queen could have roused from the chloroform.

Now that I had her, I realized her body did not have the curves I preferred, but her sleek athletic frame would prove resilient for what she must endure.

Once she opened the door, she'd been easy to subdue. I liked the way she fought, as pathetic as it had been. The fear rimming her eyes had my dick weeping for more. After the chloroform worked its magic, she crumpled to the floor.

Her resistance promised delicious training in the days to come. With my other girls, I used zip-ties and duct tape, but this was my Queen. She deserved my best. I used two sets of fleece-lined leather cuffs, one for her wrists, the other for her ankles. The locks that came with the cuffs were meant for casual play. I replaced them with the sturdy combination locks I preferred.

One. Two. Three.

Four. Five. Six.

I always checked my locks.

The cart I found downstairs couldn't have been more perfect. There had been a shelf inside, but I discarded that and left it in the hotel kitchen.

She'd been so small and light. I tucked her knees to her chest and wrapped her arms around her legs. Chains bound her in position. I even fastened a leather collar around her neck to run the chains through.

My heart thudded in my chest. Adrenaline surged. I could feel my excitement in the trembling of my hands, and in the shakiness in my gut. In fact, I had the sudden urge to take a crap. You probably don't care about that.

That had been the longest drive home ever. I drove five miles below the speed limit. No way was I going to risk a ticket. How would I explain the woman cuffed and bound in the back of my van?

I held my breath as I pulled into my driveway and closed my eyes when the garage door opened. I breathed out when the door lowered. Only then did I relax.

We were home, and she would never leave.

She moaned and tried to move her hands, but her muscles didn't cooperate.

"Shush, don't fight. I have you."

"What? What are you doing?"

"Everything is going to be all right."

Everything would be perfect.

FORTY

Swing

CJ

Lunch and ice cream pacified the cranky girls. CJ had them talk him through the rest of their last Saturday with their mother and found nothing much happened. Henrietta Jones took her daughters home after selling cookies. She mixed homemade cookies after a dinner of chicken and rice—yuk on the rice, according to Anna, and gross on the chicken, according to Angela. As a pair, the kids were crushingly adorable.

Despite the yuk and gross, he was informed the cookies had been yummy.

He walked them through their bedtime routine and finally made it to the morning, where an argument ensued as to who had been the sleepy head. Once they sorted that out, Henrietta took her daughters to their favorite playground. Anna showed him all the slides and then headed to the swings.

Pushing her high enough to get an excited squeal, he scrutinized the playground. "So, Anna, where did your mother sit when you girls played?"

Angela pumped her swing beside them, declining any adult help, and flew as high as her sister.

Anna kicked her foot out toward a park bench across the way. "She always sits there."

"Ah," CJ said. "Did she sit with friends? Other parents? Mothers? Fathers?" Romantic interests who might have stolen her from you?

"No," Angela said. "She read her book."

The constant laughter of other kids filled the air. The squealing and occasional screams made his ears hurt. He pushed Anna higher.

"There are a lot of kids here." Interspersed here and there, when necessary, the calming tones of adult voices encouraged children to be nice. "Do you play with any of them?"

"We do." Angela gave a vigorous nod.

"Who did you play with last week?" His eyes roamed the playground looking for anything out of sorts, finding nothing. The whole day had been like this, frustratingly normal.

"I don't remember," Angela said.

"We played tag." Anna chimed.

"Did your mother play, or did she just watch from the bench?"

"She watches," Angela confirmed. "I told you, she always sits alone." Irritation rimmed her tone, and her little legs pumped in the air, trying hard to match Anna's height on the upward arc of the swing.

"Nuh-uh," Anna said. "Remember?"

He slowed her swing, interested in this bit of news.

"You were playing hopscotch with that boy. I told you Mama was talking to that man. The one with the fifties who bought ten boxes."

"What boxes?" he asked.

Anna continued, excited to be the center of his attention. Her eyes were bright with the knowledge she knew something her sister did not.

"Angie said I was being a baby, but Tommy was chasing me. The man told Tommy I was a lady and to stop hitting. He's nice. I like him. I think Mommy liked him too."

CJ pulled out Jenny's phone and sent a text message to Mac.

CJ: Sketch artist ASAP. Lead on case.

"Wow, you have an amazing memory, Anna."

CJ glanced at her sister only to find Angela's hands fisted on the chain of the swing and a scowl planted on her face. He intercepted the outburst.

"Remember what we talked about? Any detail is important, no matter how small."

Angela's gaze flicked to his, and the anger she had been about to direct at her sister melted from her expression. A glimmer replaced it. Not hope. Something else. The deepest trust.

Angela had said the man had rubbed her the wrong way. She might provide a better sketch than her sister.

Angela chewed at her lower lip. "Mr. CJ, I need to use the bathroom."

He cocked his head. "Sure. I'll take you."

Her head shook. "I'm old enough to go on my own. I'm not like Anna."

"Okay. Please don't be too long."

"I won't." The beginnings of tears pooled in the corners of Angela's eyes.

He pretended not to notice and scooped Anna into his arms to carry her to the bench where her mother had sat with the unknown man. He swung Anna in the air and had her laughing and squealing by the time they made it to the bench.

"Now Anna, tell me everything about your mom's new friend."

"Oh, he's nice. Tommy was chasing me, but I ran to Mommy. I was safe, but he tried to tag me. Then, he pinched me!"

"He pinched you!" CJ put his hands on his cheeks and pulled a face.

Anna giggled. "Yes, but he told him that wasn't nice."

"Tommy?" Anna's use of pronouns confused CJ.

"No, not Tommy, the cookie's man?"

"Cookie's man?"

Anna rolled her eyes. "Yes, the man who bought the cookies."

"From the neighborhood?"

"Yes."

The problem with interrogating seven-year-old girls was they were seven years old. It was virtually impossible to get a cogent thought out of them.

"So the Cookie's man told Tommy to stop pinching you?"

"Yes!" She clapped her hands together. "He was real nice."

"And your mother liked him?"

Anna leaned in and whispered. "She was all googly-eyes."

"Ah. I see."

"Mama didn't remember him, but I did." She leaned in and whispered again. "I gave him a big hug. He told me he ate all the cookies." Anna leaned back and gave me a wide-eyed look. "I told him that was bad. You're not supposed to eat that many cookies. His mommy would get mad at him. He said he was never good at following rules."

No doubt. "What else did he say?"

Anna shrugged. "Don't know."

"Where was Angela?"

"Angie was playing hopscotch with her friend."

"Hm. Do you remember how long your mother talked with this man?"

"Nope."

CJ's phone buzzed.

Mac: Sketch artist will be there in five.

"Hey, Anna, I need you to do something for me."

"Sure." Her eager eyes lit up, ready to please.

"I have someone coming, and they're going to draw a picture of this man using your description. Have you ever had anyone pull a picture out of your mind before?"

Her mouth dropped. "They can do that?"

"With your help."

Angela trudged back from the bathrooms. He lifted Anna off the bench and gave her a slight push toward the playground.

"They'll be here in a few minutes. Why don't you go play while we wait?"

"Cool." Anna took off at a run.

Angela scuffed her heels against the ground. CJ patted the seat next to him.

She plopped down. "I didn't even notice Mama talking to anyone."

CJ leaned back on the bench and stretched his arms out wide. "You notice more than you realize."

"Do you think my mom is with him?"

He noticed the change from 'Mama' to 'my mom' and sighed. "No. Is that what you think happened?"

The eleven-year-old heaved a deep sigh, appearing much older and wiser than her years. "She's been so sad since Daddy died. I saw a note he wrote. He said if anything ever happened, he wanted her to find someone else. Someone to take care of her. I thought if she ever did, she would leave us. I figured that's why she never looked. Then she talks to this man…and now she's gone."

CJ put his hand on Angela's head and stroked her hair. "Angela, it doesn't work that way with grown-ups. It takes time."

"So you don't think…"

"I don't think your mother left. Whatever happened, I'm certain she's trying her hardest to get back to you. I'm here to help her do that. You're going to help me. You and your sister."

He told Angela about the sketch artist and what he wanted from each of them. Explaining things helped the pre-teen maintain the sense of control she needed in her life.

CJ was all about fostering that in this young girl who had a lot of growing up to do real fast. Anna was so much easier. She didn't understand what trouble her mother was in.

The sketch artist arrived a few minutes later. She was in her late forties, wearing a pencil skirt and silk blouse, sketch pad tucked under her arm. They shook hands and exchanged greetings.

"Sandra Collins."

"CJ," he replied.

She arched a brow, perhaps expecting more, but CJ liked to keep things simple.

"Angela, this is Ms. Collins, and she's an artist. She's going to ask you to describe the man you sold the cookies to. Do you think you can do that?"

A shrug. "I can try."

FORTY-ONE

Van

MELISSA

MELLISSA WOKE TO A SUDDEN LURCHING SENSATION. SHE TRIED putting a hand out to steady herself only to find her wrists connected to her ankles by a chain running through something strapped around her neck. Her body was bent over double.

Was that a collar around her neck? Terror welled up inside her, and she suppressed the horrible mewling sound, desperately crawling out of her throat.

Kidnapped.

She remembered everything, but couldn't wrap her mind around what was happening. Why had the deliveryman kidnapped her? Had Scott orchestrated this?

Her hip protested being pressed against the hard metal floor, and her bruised ribs complained. Thick leather wrapped around her wrists and ankles. She could work the buckles with her teeth, but locks stopped her cold.

Something smooth wrapped around her neck, and a chain from her wrists went right to it.

A quick inspection revealed she was in the back of a van. The windows had been blacked out. She was alone, except for hundreds of roses tossed toward the front.

She gagged against the overwhelming rose perfume.

CJ had warned her to be careful. He told her not to trust anyone. Why had she been so stupid? But he'd texted her.

Fear filled her, but she refused to let it rule her emotions. If CJ and his friends were a tenth as good as she hoped, she needed to hold it together until they arrived.

Shivers went down her spine when a garage door rattled in its tracks. The van moved forward, and then the door lowered with a crash. A few minutes later, the door latch to the back of the van clicked.

She squeezed her eyes shut and prayed for strength.

Bright light filtered through her eyelids. She opened them a crack, craned her neck and squinted at her captor.

"Good, I'm glad you're awake," he said. "I tried to make the ride as smooth as possible. How do you feel?"

She remained silent. Maybe she should scream? But, who would hear?

"You'll have to forgive the bindings, but it's for your safety."

Her safety? There were so many things she wanted to say. Bastard. Freak. What the hell are you doing? Don't touch me. Instead, she remained quiet, afraid he'd hurt her if she screamed.

"I've waited for this moment for so long." His eyes glistened.

She couldn't bear to look at him and squeezed her eyes shut.

"I've tried to get you to join me so many times, and it seemed like it would never work out, but you're with me now. You have no idea how special this day is."

Hypnotic didn't even begin to describe his tone. His words wrapped around her seeped into her, made her want to believe every foul thing he said. She shook her head to clear it from his spell.

He leaned forward, and she flinched when he touched her. "Tsk. It would be best if you learned not to do that, my Queen. It makes me mad, and we don't want that."

What would he do when he got mad? His face hovered mere inches away. And why did he keep calling her his queen? What did that mean? Scott had had princesses. Was there a connection between her husband and this man?

His smile unnerved her, sending her stomach into a terrifying free fall. Okay, there was a little bit of crazy going on here, which didn't bode well for her chances.

Please, CJ! Please find me. Save me!

The deliveryman pulled her into his arms, lifting her with little effort and snuggled her close to his chest. He breathed deeply as if inhaling her essence and savoring a moment he had anticipated for far too long.

"Don't be afraid, my Queen. I am yours, just as surely as you are mine. I will take care of you."

His words made her skin crawl. She tried to head-butt him, but the chain attached to her neck kept her immobile.

"Let me go." The words rushed from her lips, pushed out by her subconscious.

He shook his head. "My Queen, you are destined to be mine. Fated to serve. I've waited years, and now you're finally here."

She scrunched her forehead, trying to make sense of his insanity.

"I'll take care of you, for now, and for always. Come, I will carry you across the threshold, just like in the stories of old. You will be my Queen and I, your King. I am so excited to have you join us."

"Us?"

"Yes, my Queen. Your court awaits."

A roaring sound filled her head. She could hear nothing except for the blood pounding past her ears, giving her an instant, nearly incapacitating headache. This was Scott all over again. Only this time, she wasn't an oblivious wife. She had become a victim.

She struggled but bound as she was, her movements amounted to nothing.

He carried her through a mudroom and into a kitchen, then jerked to a stop. "What the hell are you doing here?"

"Hello, Sissy." Scott stood in her abductor's kitchen, his face full of a triumphant smile.

Melissa screamed.

FORTY-TWO

Evil

MELISSA

An unrelenting drumbeat banged away inside Melissa's chest. Combined with the electric charge running over her skin, her entire body vibrated with the need to run. To fight. To do something. But she couldn't move. Melissa was trapped by chains, and cuffs, and the prison of her captor's arms. She tried chasing away her fear, but the man standing before her made her blood run cold.

Scott had found her.

Breathing became a struggle, one she was losing, and she couldn't pull enough air. The hammering of her pulse deafened her and raced past her ears in one terrifying roar. With a blink, she tried to force the blackness shrouding her vision away, but the smothering weight of Scott's presence made that impossible.

She kicked against her bonds, a futile effort. Pierce had her trussed up so well she could barely move.

"My, my, Pierce Channing," Scott said with a taunting smile, "as I live and breathe, you have brought me the perfect get-out-of-jail gift."

She squeezed her legs together and drew inward, trying to hide from Scott's view. Panic had a hold of her, setting her stomach to churning and bringing whimpers to her throat. Her heartbeat wavered, a weak fluttering thing and a scream struggled to be free. But she smothered the sound.

Why hadn't she listened to CJ and kept that damn door shut?

Scott crossed his arms and gave one of his cruel smiles. His gaze drifted over her body, moving with measured purpose and traveling at a languid pace from her feet to her breasts, finally to settle on her face.

She met his stare with as much strength as she could muster, but her determination to meet him head-on skittered away.

Pierce adjusted his grip, hefting her in his arms, and shifting her ever so slightly away from Scott. Such an odd embrace. She should be frightened by her kidnapper but found herself burrowing against his chest—anything to get away from her ex-husband.

A deep groan rumbled outward from Scott, needful, raw, possessive, and terrifying. His masculine jaw was set with purpose, and there was no confusion about what he wanted.

There had once been a time when she had believed him to be a handsome man. Power, wealth, and a raw beauty had drawn her to him. In many ways, he had been her Prince Charming.

Until he became a brutal killer.

Now, she cringed, desperate to flee. All she could see was the hardness of his eyes and the depravity of the psychopath he'd become.

A sharp tick-tick-tock grated on her nerves. A grandfather clock sat in the hall and announced the time with three long peals of its bells. She twitched with the noise, jumping with each beat.

Pierce shifted, taking another step back. "Should I be surprised you're in my home?" Her captor's voice wavered between anger and awe.

"In the flesh." Scott spread his arms. Light glinted off his thousand-dollar smile.

"Risky coming here." Recrimination floated in the unusual timbre of his tone.

Held by Pierce, Melissa couldn't move. Even if he put her down, she was bound in chains. Her gaze cut from Pierce to Scott and back again, feeling every bit trapped.

"I needed a place to stay, and I couldn't think of a better person who understood me." A devilish smile spread across his lips.

Melissa's muscles ached from her contorted position. The pain settled into an unrelenting throb.

Scott closed the distance, the ticking of the clock, the strike of his heels against the floor, her ragged breathing, they all combined into one thunderous roar. She'd never forget the sound of his distinctive walk. Seeking protection in her kidnapper's arms made no sense, but she tucked her head against Pierce's chest and felt his ribcage expand with a sharp pull of his breath. He held it for a beat, then expelled it in a rush.

Seeking protection from her kidnapper? She had gone mad.

Scott approached and brushed her chin, his fingers rough and calloused, nothing like the smooth manicure he'd once sported.

Their gazes locked. His stare promised retribution, and she wanted nothing more than to disappear.

Pierce stood rock steady when all she wanted was for him to yank her away from her ex-husband. The two men exchanged a glance, more of a glare: two predators and only one prey.

She jerked her chin out of Scott's grasp, turning again toward Pierce. She didn't know his brand of crazy, but Scott's was undeniable.

Scott reached out and pinched her chin, increasing the pressure until she had no choice but to turn and face him.

Pierce still hadn't moved, and he let Scott paw at her. The depth of her kidnapper's breathing intensified, and the beat of his heart pounded against her chest. He didn't appear happy having a serial killer in his home, but he wasn't making a move to get rid of Scott.

"My beautiful bride, how I have missed you." Scott kissed her with a light brush of his lips.

Melissa bucked, thrashing in her captor's arms.

"Be still." Pierce's grip tightened.

Why didn't he step back and pull her away? Her mind screamed, one long piercing wail confined to the inside of her skull. She was going to die. She didn't want to die. Not when she'd found CJ.

CJ! Please. Find me. Save me. Don't let him hurt me.

A growl sounded low in Scott's throat, then he leaned forward, invading her space to give one of his punishing kisses, the ones he saved when he wanted her to feel pain. He pulled back, leaving her lower lip bruised and pulsing.

"Have you missed me?" He sneered.

Her lower lip quivered, and her limbs trembled. Nothing of the man she had once loved remained in the person standing before her now.

Scott believed in a wife's duty to love, honor, and obey. Even more than her duty, he believed in his right to ensure her obedience by any means he saw fit, by the cruelty of his words, by the absence of his affection, but more often by his hand or belt.

She sucked in a deep lungful of air. He always made her feel small.

He turned his attention to Pierce. "You did extend an invitation."

Pierce had the strength of steel because he showed no signs of tiring, holding her in his arms. He brushed her temple with a kiss of his own. The tenderness in his lips sent a shiver down her spine because it had been protective, possessive, and terrifying.

Scott's eyes narrowed.

"My invitation was for if you were ever released. You weren't released. You escaped." Pierce measured his words. "I'm not interested in helping a fugitive."

Scott's eyes flared. "An act of God set me free. Besides, I knew you'd be collecting my bride. I couldn't imagine leaving town without seeing my Sissy one last time."

Melissa's breath caught in her throat. His nickname had never been one she liked. It used to grate on her nerves, but now? Now, it portended her death. One last time?

"She belongs to me now." Pierce ground out. "You gave her to me."

The warning in Pierce's tone was unmistakable. The possession undeniable.

Melissa stilled in Pierce's arms. He was the only thing keeping her away from Scott and his twisted desires. She pressed her cheek against Pierce's chest and felt his breathing hitch.

Scott shrugged and gave a dismissive wave. "Of course, she's yours now." He tried to appear nonchalant, but Melissa knew he'd never give her away, at least not while he still pulled breath.

Had that been it? How long had these two been in communication, and how horrible for Scott to have seen to her future after his death? The twisted bastard would've done something like this.

"Do I need to remind you she's still my wife?"

"You gave her to me." The confidence in Pierce's voice faded.

"Technically, I had no choice." A slick smile spread across Scott's face. He held his hands out. "Look, we need not argue." A snicker filled Scott's voice, "She'll be your Queen. I don't want her anymore. I only ask for one last night, and I'm sure you won't mind."

If Scott was done with her…a shiver worked down her spine and shot to her fingertips.

"She's no good dead," Pierce ground out. The air crackled with the intensity of these two men squaring off against each other.

Melissa cringed. If Pierce gave her to Scott, she wouldn't survive the night. As much as the idea made her gut churn, she had to play Pierce against Scott. But how?

"I have no intention of killing her, but she needs to pay." There was a hitch in Scott's voice that turned her stomach.

"I'm serious. I want her alive."

Scott took a few steps back. "After everything I taught you, you owe me this much!"

Melissa struggled to breathe. She lifted her bound hands as best she could and clutched at the fabric of Pierce's shirt. He was her only hope. A whimper escaped her throat.

Pierce hugged her tight and kissed the top of her head. She found the act oddly comforting.

Pierce whispered into her ear. "I'll keep you safe, my Queen. I promise."

"Please," she whispered. "Don't let him have me."

Scott pointed an accusatory finger at Pierce. "After everything I taught you, after helping you build your collection, you owe me. It takes one phone call to bring this all down."

Pierce's voice dropped an octave, ice coating his words, turning them hard and brittle. "Exactly. Only one phone call to end it all."

A phone! That's what she needed. If she could only find a phone, get out of Pierce's arms, and do what? Crawl?

She wouldn't be able to reach a phone. Hers had been left in the hotel. She prayed CJ found it. Until then, she needed to stall for time and give CJ a chance.

She pressed her cheek against Pierce's chest. "P-please. Don't let him touch me."

He pressed his lips to the top of her head. His low murmur made her skin crawl. "My dearest Queen, have faith in your King."

Hope chased the fear flowing in her veins. He would save her, but for what fate?

"Then we understand each other?" There was a tremor in Scott's voice.

He'd been a successful lawyer once, a theatric player who ruled the courtroom. She used to love watching him argue his cases. Even in the most heated cases, Scott never lost his cool. It had made him seem powerful, sexy even. He never backed down, and she'd never seen another man dominate him.

Until now.

That quaver in his voice was the first time she'd heard a thread of uncertainty from him. Any man who could off-balance Scott was someone to fear, but in choosing one evil over another, was she making an even worse mistake?

"Tell me what you want." Pierce readjusted his hold.

"I want to punish her for turning me in to the cops. I want to hear her scream. Give me that, and I'll leave."

"That's all? And you'll go?"

"Not all. Share one of your princesses. Prison makes for quite a dry spell. I'm itching to fuck a real woman."

Wait? There were other women trapped here? Pierce had mentioned a court awaited.

"Share?" There was that pause again, a hitch in Pierce's words.

"I'm certain we can come to some arrangement."

"We differ in our definition of what it means to have a woman," Pierce warned.

"And I've told you that soft spot in your heart will be your undoing. If one of them ever gets out—"

"They're never getting out."

Melissa twitched in the steel embrace of Pierce's arms. Confidence oozed from his pores, and if none of them could get out, what would happen to her?

"No killing. You can fuck one, but that's it."

"Well, not just fuck. I know what toys you keep in that dungeon of yours. Tell me it hasn't been your fantasy to watch me in action? We could take them together. The master and the student?"

"Our idea of fun is different."

"Don't worry. I'm not here to take over your little kingdom. All I want is a moment with my wife and something to fuck instead of my hand."

She clawed at Pierce, desperate for his protection.

Pierce's eyes narrowed.

Melissa prayed he would refuse. If he didn't, they were both dead. Hopefully, Pierce was smart enough to figure that out.

Another brush of his lips had her skin crawling.

"Forgive me, but I must allow this," Pierce whispered. He met Scott's stare and firmed his voice with the power of command, one psycho attempting to dominate another. "You stop when I say stop."

Her hopes faded with those words.

"Then what are we waiting for?" Scott rubbed his hands together, anticipation lighting his eyes.

He wanted her pain. No matter what he did, no matter how much it hurt, she would not cry. Her fear would feed the beast inside of him.

God help her if she screamed.

Melissa's insides churned in a tight knot. Her mind screamed to flee, to fight, to get the hell out of there, but Pierce's cuffs and chains, and the prison of his arms trapped her with no way out.

There had to be neighbors, but she kept silent. Any foolish attempt would be her last. She needed to be smart, not stupid.

Scott turned and paced the long length of the kitchen, scrubbing at his sandy blond hair. He opened the refrigerator and pulled out a cold beer.

Each time he drew near, her heart fluttered with renewed panic. As long as Pierce held her, Scott couldn't touch her.

"Want one?" Scott acted as if he owned the place, playing host to the man whose home he'd invaded.

The bottle hissed as Scott popped the cap. The noise had Melissa cringing. He tipped the longneck back and took a pull.

"No, I'm good." Pierce's teeth made a grinding sound.

Scott wiped his mouth with the back of his hand. "God, I've missed beer." He pointed the bottle at Melissa. "What are we waiting for?"

This time, she couldn't hold back the whimper and turned her cheek to Pierce. The move had been instinctual. She coiled inward, preparing to defend against Scott's sadistic pleasure.

"I want to make sure we understand each other." Pierce's hands gripped painfully against her bruised ribs.

Melissa bit back a cry but didn't know why she bothered. Scott meant her to pay, and she would drown in screams.

"Damn, this is good." Scott slammed his half-empty beer on the granite counter.

Pierce Channing was a mystery she needed to crack. He kidnapped her, bound her, and there was no doubt he planned horrible things. But, he seemed protective, and she sensed he didn't relish handing her over to Scott. There had to be a way to use that to her advantage.

She snuggled into his chest and whispered. "Please, don't let him hurt me."

Pierce kissed her forehead. "I can't say no. Not to him. You must understand…"

"Understand what?" Scott asked. "What did she say?" He tipped the bottle and drained it. The refrigerator door opened again, and he pulled out a second bottle.

She placed her cheek against Pierce's chest. "Please?"

"Don't worry, my Queen. I will stop him if he goes too far."

No. She needed him not to allow it at all.

She needed an ally, and right now, her kidnapper was her best bet for making it through this alive. There was no doubt in her mind what would happen if Pierce left her alone with Scott.

"Beer and sex," Scott said. "Two things you don't get in prison. I'm ready to see this dungeon of yours. I want to see how you improved on my design. Show me your kingdom."

Melissa startled. How close did the similarities go between these two? Had Scott been coaching Pierce from prison?

Bile rose in her throat, but she swallowed it down.

Pierce gestured to the second beer. "If you're going to punish my Queen, you'll do it with a clear head."

He spoke about her impending torture with a calmness she found chilling, reminding her that he too was a predator—a man she should fear, not an ally against her ex-husband.

"She's lousy in bed. I'm just warning you. Lays there like a limp fish. Why do you think I had to find my princesses? I know why you want her, and as honored as I am by that, I have to wonder why?"

Lousy? He'd been the one who relegated her to one sexual position, who refused to let her touch him with her hands or mouth. Ugh, the thought of anything sexual regarding Scott brought a vile taste to her mouth.

He'd been her first, and until recently, her only sexual experience. He'd been the one who had stunted her sexual awakening.

Lousy? Scott had been the most selfish of lovers.

Pierce's jaw clenched again. "I enjoy the challenge of breaking them and training them. She'll serve me well when I'm done."

Pierce would never have a chance because Scott would kill her first. She wasn't sure which of them was the most repugnant, the kidnapper or the killer.

Scott tilted his head. "Never understood why you keep them around. Huge liability. I say have your fun and get rid of them. Make it clean and neat."

Pierce chuckled. "Look where that got you."

Scott's eyes flickered with an unsettled emotion. He finished his beer and tossed it in the trash.

"Are we going to chitchat all day? I'm horny as hell and tired of doing all the work." He fisted his hand and jerked it over his crotch, pumping in and out.

He'd never been so crude. Prison had changed him.

His actions nearly had her vomiting in her mouth. Would he want to have sex with her? But he hadn't asked Pierce's permission for that.

A shudder rolled through her body.

"I get the picture." Pierce smiled, not a kind smile, but something much darker. "And you only cane this one ten times."

"She deserves a hundred!"

"Ten."

"Fifty."

"Ten." Pierce insisted.

Scott's eyes narrowed.

Like a piece of meat at an auction house, her fate was being argued by the insane. She may not have long to live, but she'd be damned if she'd die like a piece of cattle.

"You don't deserve to touch me." A bold and stupid thing to say, but she couldn't remain silent.

"Twenty," her husband said with a glower. "And you'll feel every strike, my dear."

Pierce shook his head. "I've seen what you can do with a cane. Ten strikes."

Testosterone surged in the air, swirling with festering depravity as two psychopaths puffed out their chests.

She expected Scott to win. He always did.

"Please." She turned to Pierce. "He doesn't deserve me."

"I've earned this," her husband screamed. His face turned beet-red, and he advanced with his arm upraised.

Pierce turned, shifting her away. "Be careful. My terms are non-negotiable. She's no good to me a cripple." He angled his face down to look at her. “I would suggest silence, my Queen.” His muscles tensed.

A sharp ache knifed in her chest. Caught between Crazy and Crazier, she gave a slight nod and acquiesced.

“As you wish. Ten, but I can use my hand as much as I want.” Scott gave a grunt of displeasure, but he had caved to Pierce’s demands.

Melissa breathed a sigh of relief. As crazy as it seemed, she had an ally in Pierce.

She was lifted a few inches as Pierce shrugged. “Stay away from her face.”

Scott came close once again. Exhaling a fume of hops, his fetid breath overwhelmed her. He yanked on the collar around her throat, forcing her head off Pierce’s shoulder.

“You have been disobedient, Sissy. You should have protected your husband as I protected you.”

“You never protected me.” The urge to add ‘you crazy bastard’ had been hard to suppress, but Melissa wasn’t a complete fool.

He placed a finger over her lips. “Don’t speak. It’s just a waste of breath. You’re not going to change what happens next.” He took a step back. “Show me your dungeon, my padawan.”

Pierce headed for a door off the kitchen.

FORTY-THREE

Sketch Artist

CJ

When the FBI profiler finished with Angela, CJ tried to get Anna out of the swing. She didn't want to let go of the chains, insisting he push 'just one more time.' He gave her three more pushes, sending her high into the air. Then he pulled her swing to a halt and coaxed the little girl off the playground.

Leaving Anna in the capable hands of Mrs. Collins, he tried to engage Angela in a contest of who could swing the highest. Angela didn't want to play and walked off the playground to stand beside a bench. CJ followed, taking a seat on the far end. Angela pretended a deep interest in the grass at her feet, then bent to pick up a stick. She hit the back of the bench, jarring his teeth with each strike.

He brushed off his trousers and stood, giving her the space she needed. Anna might be young enough to really not understand, but Angela held the wisdom of an older soul. He remembered what that knowledge felt like. He'd been older, fifteen-years-young, and his circumstances had been much different, although no less challenging.

His father killed his mother while he watched. The memory haunted him and had been improved only slightly by what happened next. Rage powered the adolescent jangle of his limbs and developing muscles to action. Fury fueled the need to stop his father, but what he remembered was feeling cheated because his fists hadn't killed the old man. He'd been smaller, weaker, and knew he wouldn't last in an all-out brawl, but he'd been smart and gone for the gun. The shot rang out before it registered that he pulled the trigger. His arm jerked, then he blinked. Half his father's face disappeared, and the ringing in his ears lasted until the police came.

His moment of retribution had been stolen in that one shot. All his anger bubbled to the surface and struggled for an outlet. He wanted to beat his father into submission, but the focus of his hatred lay dead on the floor. There'd been no satisfaction because his father hadn't suffered.

Angela faced a different grief, but no less powerful. She'd seen the face of her mother's potential killer. Growing up in foster care wasn't easy, and he didn't envy Angela the trials that might bring. He'd like to think Henrietta Jones was still alive, but he knew how these things usually ended.

Angela lifted her face and blinked against the sun. "My mom isn't dead." She pointed the stick at him. "You think she is. Mrs. Collins and those cops do too, but she's not. My mom is strong, stronger than you know. She's going to come home." Wetness pooled at the corners of her eyes, but her cheeks remained dry, her upper lip was set with her conviction.

He held his hands up, unwilling to crush her hope. "I never said your mother wouldn't come home."

Her chin trembled.

"I see her in you; her strength is written in your eyes."

She threw the stick toward the playground. "Do you think that man had something to do with Mom going away?"

He knelt down, eye-level with the girl. "Angela, why don't you like this man?"

She shrugged. "I dunno."

He turned to keep an eye on Anna, who spoke with great enthusiasm to the sketch artist. His watch showed half-past three. The backup team should be at the hotel by now. Melissa was safe, and he didn't need to worry about leaving her alone anymore.

Jenny's cell phone buzzed, and he fished it out of his pocket. "Mac, what's up?"

"Where are you?" A terseness clipped Mac's words.

"Sitting at a park with two lovely little girls. The sketch artist is finishing with the younger one."

He pinched his brows together and placed a hand over the spot above the bridge of his nose. A headache coiled behind his eyes, building with strength. It had been a long unproductive day.

"You need to get back to the hotel."

"What happened?"

"Melissa's gone. The team arrived, and she wasn't in the room."

His stomach churned with fear for her safety and rage for whoever had taken her. He would kill the fucker if he hurt Melissa.

Keeping his voice even so as not to alarm Angela took every ounce of self-control. He paced, needing to move. To act. To do something other than babysit two little girls at a goddamn park.

First, he needed to calm down. He focused on Mac's deep voice.

"Did she leave, or was she taken?"

"Taken."

"Struggle?"

"Door's intact. She either knew the person, or they convinced her to let them in."

He understood the subtext but didn't think Scott Patterson would be stupid enough to brave a public hotel with video surveillance and security.

"You coming?"

"I'll be there."

Maybe he could pawn the girls off on the sketch artist and head straight to the hotel? He cut the connection and tried to appear as if his entire world hadn't been snatched from under his feet.

He held out a hand. "Angela, let's get your sister. It's been a long day."

FORTY-FOUR

A Lead

CJ

"Mrs. Collins, do you think you could take the girls back to the shelter?" The Social Services shelter was on the opposite side of town. It would take an hour to take the girls and return to the hotel.

She shushed CJ, a look of intense concentration scrawled across her face. "I'm almost done."

"You'd be doing me a huge favor."

Time! He'd lost too much time. He would have left already if it weren't for Henrietta Jones. This sketch was the closest thing to a lead they had, and he couldn't abandon the girls' hopes of finding their mother.

But damn, he hated wasting time.

Anna, bless her talkative little mouth, would not shut up. Her inherent cuteness saved her hide, and he couldn't help but smile when she peeked at the drawing. Her actions were slowing the ponderous Mrs. Collins down.

There was no choice but to wait. Angela stood beside him, displaying greater patience than him.

His pacing drew stares from Mrs. Collins.

Anything could be happening to Melissa. He hated this inaction. His pulse strummed with the need to do something.

But, he trusted Mac. Mac would coordinate the action at the hotel, gather witnesses, and scour surveillance tapes. Mac had probably assigned Jenny to the police detail, making sure they didn't foul the crime scene. And the rest of Delta team was there too. Their help would be invaluable.

He trusted them, but he wanted to be there.

Mrs. Collins scratched at the drawing tablet. What was he to do with the girls? No way was he making the hour-long round-trip to the shelter. With a flourish, she drew her last line. "It's done, Anna. Do you want to see?"

Not a moment later, Anna was on her feet, peering over the sketchpad. She waved her hand, beckoning him forward.

"Mr. CJ. Mr. CJ!" Her voice squeaked, demanding his immediate attention.

He forced a smile. "How does it look?"

Despite his worry over Melissa, he had this case to solve.

"She did it! She did what you said." Anna turned to him, eyes wide. Her voice dropped to a whisper. A look of wonder filled her face. "She pulled him outta my head." She jumped on the park bench, pointing at the sketch pad.

Angela twisted her mouth and stomped around to look. She tilted her head and squinted. With a clucking sound, she said. "Anna, you made him look too nice."

CJ glanced at the drawing. An unremarkable man with a long face and narrow-set eyes stared out from the page. He looked vaguely familiar. Where had he seen that man before? Because he'd definitely seen him and recently, too.

He took another look at the two sketches, comparing them side by side. Angela's portrayed a much harder man than Anna's image. *A skinny man jogging toward him.* Where had that been, and why would a man be bringing him roses?

Not him.

CJ pinched his eyes, willing the memory to surface. *The man had been running toward…Melissa!* He jerked as the memory unfolded. *Red roses were bouncing in the grip of a skinny ass guy. He had reacted, placing himself between Melissa and what he'd perceived was a threat. The look on the guy's face had seemed possessive, predatory even. CJ had adjusted his stance, balancing on the balls of his feet, getting ready to fight. Melissa had stepped around him. She'd placed a hand on his arm and pushed him to the side. "It's okay, CJ."*

What did this man have to do with Henrietta Jones?

He needed to get to his team.

Mrs. Collins packed up and turned to Angela. "Do you want to see what I drew from your description?"

Angela shook her head. "No." She pointed at the pad of paper. "He looks like that, but weirder." Every now and then, her eyes lifted to the sketchpad and fell back to the ground.

Time to leave.

His words cut sharper than intended. "Listen, something's come up if you could take the girls…"

"I'd love to take them."

"Girls," he called out, "it's time to go."

"We're leaving Mr. CJ?" Anna asked, skipping with her endless energy.

He put a hand on Anna's head. "Yes, Mrs. Collins is going to take you back to the ladies at the shelter."

Angela hugged herself. "Did the pictures help?"

He squatted down and drew Angela into a hug. "The pictures helped more than you know. Thank you for being so brave."

She lunged at him, wrapping her tiny arms around his neck. "You mean we did it? You're going to bring Mommy home?" Hope and despair warred with each other in Angela's expression, and a tear pooled at the corner of her eye.

He wrapped her in a hug, pulling her close. "I hope so." He prayed he wasn't lying and would find Henrietta Jones alive.

"Mr. CJ," Angela said with a whisper. "I didn't like the man because he smelled funny. Does that help?"

It didn't help at all, but he wanted her to think she was helping. "Yes, that helps. Men can be stinky sometimes."

Angela shook her head. "Not stinky!" She wrinkled her nose, "He smelled like dirt and had lipstick smeared on his face. The bright red kind Mom doesn't like. He made me feel funny too." She pulled her shoulders inward. Her voice dropped so low he had to lean forward to hear her whisper. "He looked at my…my…" From the way she crossed her arms over her pre-pubescent chest, CJ had no difficulty finishing that thought.

"You did very well today, Angela."

"Will the pictures help find my mom?"

He shouldn't be nodding because there was no reason to give her false hope, but his head moved.

"Thank you," she said in her soft whisper.

Anna launched herself at him, joining her sister in the hug. "Mr. CJ!" Her squeal aggravated his headache, but he pulled her close and gave them a combined hug.

"Come girls, we need to get moving." He herded them to Mrs. Collin's car, transferred the child seats, and ensured they were buckled in. With a nod, he gave his thanks to Mrs. Collins and waved goodbye to the girls. Then he headed to the hotel.

On the way, he phoned Mac.

Jenny answered. "Hey, CJ."

"Status update."

"Mac wanted to wait until you got here to go in, but I told him we needed to get started."

CJ agreed. There was no reason to wait.

"I'll be there in a few minutes. What have you found so far?"

"The room's clean," Jenny said. "Whoever did this planned well."

"There has to be something. Surveillance? Cleaning and room service staff?"

"Brett and Jon are talking with the staff, and Charlie is with hotel security to see if anyone saw anything."

Brett Parmley and Jon Knutt were top notch. Charlie Moudin was a relatively new addition to the team, recruited, not from the military, but from Forest Summers' Facility. The Facility was something like a halfway house for people Forest rescued. They received counseling along with intense self-defense training. He liked what he'd seen so far in Charlie's skills, enthusiasm, and a unique outlook.

"Police?" He was curious how involved they might be given how stretched thin they were.

"They're sending a detective, and the Feds are coming online since Patterson is likely involved."

The man with the roses was connected to Henrietta's disappearance and tied to Melissa's as well. He didn't like what that might mean.

"I have a lead on the Henrietta Jones' case."

FORTY-FIVE

Video

CJ

CJ crowded into an elevator along with a family of four, an elderly couple, and two teenage lovebirds. By the time he reached the eighteenth floor, he was alone.

A small crowd had gathered, and police tape blocked the way to Melissa's room. Down the hall, he spied Mac speaking to a cop. His friend waved and came toward him.

"How are you holding up?"

"Give me an update, and I'll be doing much better." He released a pent-up sigh.

"We found something."

"What?"

"You need to see this." Mac led him to the hotel room, holding the ribbon of yellow tape out of the way. A local cop stood outside the door and gave them a nod.

"And no sign of a struggle?" CJ rubbed his jaw.

"None. Looks like she let whoever it was in, so I figure she knew him."

"Do you think it was her ex-husband?"

"We don't think so." Jenny turned as they entered the suite. The look on her face telegraphed her concern. "Charlie is downstairs with security. We're checking to see if Patterson was anywhere in the building. She's getting the tapes as we speak; the problem is they don't monitor the halls."

"Shit." He rubbed his hand over his head. "Show me what you found?"

"Your little lovebird is a smart cookie; she left us a crumb. I have to say I'm impressed, but you're not going to like it."

"What did you find?" Breath tugged into his lungs. Had she been hurt?

"I found her phone."

His pulse jackhammered. They wouldn't be able to GPS her phone.

"She set the video to record, then shoved it under the bed," Jenny said. "Good thing, because this guy did some clean-up work, but missed her phone." Jenny sat him down on the couch. "You ready to see this?"

No.

He took in a measured breath and used it to calm the tension wound in his body.

Focus on the clues. Don't worry about the unknown.

Sage advice he'd given to those he'd trained, but hard as hell to accomplish when the victim was someone he cared about.

"Yes," he said.

His palms were a nervous mess, cool and clammy; he wiped them on his pants. His normally slow and steady heart chugged along like a freight train, and breathing deep wasn't helping.

She pulled out Melissa's phone and queued up a video. The footage jerked all around, but Melissa was lying on the floor. A flash of brown wrapped around her wrists, and what looked to be a chain lead ran down her legs where there were more cuffs.

He leaned forward, pulse-pounding with the need to punish whoever had done this to Melissa.

"Just wait," Jenny soothed. "Watch."

All he could see was Melissa's ragged gasps, but he forced himself to remain professional and focus on the details.

His mouth went dry as a pair of men's shoes moved into the frame. It was hard to tell because the lighting was terrible.

Melissa moaned, struggling to free herself.

Then a man's voice sounded. "Shh, don't fight. Don't worry. I have you."

"What? What are you doing?" Melissa's voice sounded slurred, drugged perhaps.

"It's all going to be all right."

The man knelt. Impossible to tell what he was doing, except Melissa struggled before going still. And fuck it, but there wasn't a clear view of his face. All they had were his damned shoes.

"He drugged her," Jenny said. "Easier to get her out of the room."

CJ nodded. It made sense.

The man moved around the room. Something big and white flapped, then a door opened and shut.

"That's how he got her out," he said.

"Exactly. It looks like a laundry or valet cart. It's the only thing large enough to put her in."

"And no one saw anything? You said the security cameras don't monitor the guest hallways?"

"That's what they told us. But they monitor the exit points and common areas. Charlie is working on getting us copies."

"We need to look at their delivery docks, and canvas the cleaning staff about anyone pushing a cart who didn't belong. Someone must have seen something."

"Already on it." Jenny pulled out her cell phone.

"And we need to show these around."

CJ handed her the sketches. The video wasn't much, but the strength of foresight Melissa showed in setting the phone to record amazed the hell out of him.

Jenny examined the sketches. "Charlie has the security folks wrapped around her finger. They're cooperating. Who is this?"

"A man the girls' mother was talking to at the park. And I've seen him before. He was at the hospital when I picked up Melissa."

Jenny tapped her finger over the paper. "I've seen him too." She squinted. "Now, where have I seen this guy?" She glanced at the ceiling, frustration edging her tone. "I hate it when this happens."

FORTY-SIX

Petals

CJ

"You've seen him, too?" CJ's interest perked up. Jenny hadn't been with him and Mac at the hospital. "Where?"

"Damn, I don't know." She played with her long braids and pursed her lips. "Recently, though."

"Shit." Another coincidence? "I need to know where you saw him."

"I'm thinking." Jenny lifted her hands in the air. "Stop pestering, or it'll never come to me."

Gripping Melissa's phone, he couldn't help hitting the replay button. The video's poor resolution and low lighting made it difficult to ascertain details. There was the flapping of something white and a man with black shoes.

He pressed the pause button, backed up the recording, and started it forward again. Immediately after the flapping fabric, a blur of red fluttered.

He waved Jenny over. "Look at this." He queued the video and slowed down the rate to watch frame by frame. A blur of red materialized on the screen.

His heart thumped. Seeing Melissa's kidnapping play out in front of him had him in anguish. This was all his fault.

Jenny pointed at the flash of red. "Back it up."

He shoved the phone in her hand and got to his knees, looking at the carpet, under the couch, and even under the bed. He crawled all over the room.

"What are you looking for?"

"I think it was a rose petal." But there were no signs of roses in the room, not even the lingering perfume of them.

Mac wandered into the hotel room. "What are you doing?"

"CJ found something in the video."

"It's not much," CJ said with a pained sigh.

The couch groaned under the weight of Mac's massive frame. Mac and Jenny pressed their heads together as she showed him the part of the video under question.

"CJ thinks it's a rose," Jenny said.

"It was. Hundreds of red roses!" A lilting voice proclaimed.

Framed by the doorway, a walking cliché struck a pose. From her platinum locks to her double-D's, the striking beauty screamed college cheerleader, every man's wet dream brought to life. Still, it was the holster strapped to her hip with the sweet .45 revolver tucked into it, which snatched his attention and garnered CJ's respect.

"Good to see you, Charlie. What did you find out?"

Her smile sported signature dimples and perfectly straight, white teeth. She rocked back and buried her hands in the back pockets of her hip-hugging jeans. Charlie was walking male kryptonite and a wiseass too

They had confirmation now, and he had too many coincidences lining up. His gut churned, and his mind picked at the pieces of how Melissa and Henrietta Jones might be connected.

"Security didn't want to share, but I sweet-talked them into giving me access to their tapes. Wanna see?" Charlie winked. "The guy who took your girl was delivering roses."

He had a good idea who that might have been. Fuck! Where was Scott Patterson in all this mess? Not for a minute did he believe Scott didn't have his fingers embroiled in Melissa's disappearance.

They needed to find a connection.

"I need to know who Scott Patterson communicated with while in prison." If the man with the roses and Patterson knew each other, they were running out of time.

"On it." Jenny tapped her phone.

Two men filled the doorway behind Charlie. The tall, muscular man standing to Charlie's left had a scar on his cheek. Brett Parmly frowned. "We got confirmation on the roses from the cleaning staff."

Jon Knutt was similar in build to CJ, tall and broad, sported deep-set, penetrating eyes. Jon stepped around Charlie and stretched out his hand. "Sorry, your leave got fucked up."

"Same here," he replied.

"Hope we can help." Brett extended his hand, completing the meet-and-greet.

"Nice to have the team together again." He couldn't ask for a better team.

"Tell me what you found," CJ demanded.

Jon leaned against the doorframe, kicking one heel over the other foot. "Cleaning lady said a man came by with an impressive display of roses, stopped here, chatted with the guest in this room, wheeled the cart inside, and then wheeled it out a few minutes later. Took the freight elevator down to the loading dock."

"The fucker cleaned up after himself." CJ scrubbed his jaw. There wasn't a trace of a rose in the room.

At least they hadn't been tulips. Scott Patterson had an obsession with tulips.

Charlie nodded. "Video footage confirms. A guy with a cart and a boatload of red roses came to this floor and left not fifteen minutes later. He was in and out."

Fucker hid Melissa in the cart and shoved the roses in there with her. His fists clenched.

"You have a picture of his face?" He didn't need a picture, he knew who took Melissa, but he needed confirmation. Adrenaline surged through his veins and raced around until it gathered in his heart and slammed against his chest.

With a photo of his face and the plates off his van, they wouldn't have to wait for a database match to figure out where he lived. The girls had provided that bit of information. CJ felt a thousand times better, knowing the kidnapper had made such a juvenile mistake.

Charlie looked down. "Only a partial on his face. He knew where all the cameras were located and shielded his face from the lens. There's footage in the loading dock with a cart, but same problem. No clear shot of his face."

That was okay. With the sketches, CJ didn't need a clear shot. It wasn't enough for a warrant, but he and his team didn't necessarily bother with warrants.

"What about plates?"

"Obscured," she said. "He probably muddied them up for the job."

"One of the cleaning ladies got a good look at him," Brett said.

CJ grabbed Anna's and Angela's sketches off the couch. "Have her look at these. I need a positive ID."

Charlie glanced at the sketches. "Odd. Looks like a Jekyll and Hyde rendition of the same man."

Mac peered over Charlie's shoulder. "That guy was in the bar."

Jenny snatched the sketches.

"Holy fuck! I knew he looked familiar. He helped that old lady, the one that tripped."

"This might be the guy from the security tapes," Charlie added, "but I need to see the footage again."

CJ's blood chilled. "I know him." Had the fucker lifted his phone? Because he was sure as shit didn't see it in the hotel room. He wasn't one to leave things lying around and assumed he'd been careless when his phone had gone missing. Is that how the man had gained access to the room?

"The hospital," Mac said. He thumped CJ in the arm. "We saw him at the hospital, too." Mac had a great memory.

"Melissa knew him. He delivered flowers to her at the hospital. She may have even trusted him enough to open the door." Even more so if the guy had lifted CJ's phone and had been using it to reassure her.

Fuck!

"We need to trace my phone's location." It was possible the man still had it.

Jekyll and Hyde was a good description of the two images provided by Angela and Anna. *"He looked at my..."* Poor Angela was too young, too embarrassed to say what she wanted to say, but old enough for the blossom of youth to change her body and wise enough to know a man looking at her chest was wrong.

Melissa had taken the flower arrangement…He'd shoved a hand wrapped in bloody bandages toward her. "It's Pierce. Pierce Channing."

CJ ground his teeth, and his stomach knotted with the memory. "The fucker's name is Pierce Channing." He turned to Charlie. "Please, tell me the van at the docks was a white florist's van, black windows, with a big scratch down the left side?"

Charlie's jaw gaped. "How did you know?"

Jenny thumbed her phone to life. "I'll find an address."

"Don't bother." He headed for the door, pitching his words over his shoulder as he raced out the hall. "I know where the bastard lives." He cut his gaze to Mac. "Fuck it all to hell. Not only have we found Melissa, we may have just found the man who took Henrietta Jones."

FORTY-SEVEN

Locks

MELISSA

Pierce and Scott talked about dungeons and abductions like it was the weather. Pierce held Melissa, cuffed and chained, with the hammer of her heart rattling her teeth while he droned on about the dungeon downstairs.

Scott cocked his head. "I'm interested to see how you improved my design." His gaze roamed her body, lingering on her breasts, and sent a chill up her spine. The tortured screams of his victims reflected in the depths of those eyes and echoed their never-ending torment in her mind.

And was that the smell of dead animals creeping up from the basement?

She tugged on her chains, caged more by Pierce's unwavering grip than by her bonds.

Scott pumped Pierce for information about the dungeon. Didn't Pierce realize why that might be? His body would be left down there with hers, and others, if she understood about these princesses. Dear God, this was worse than her most terrifying nightmare.

Her vision zoomed in on Scott's twitchy hands. All she could see were fingernails caked in more blood than she ever wanted to think about. The bead of sweat forming at his hairline betrayed his unease, and his eyes shifted to the knife block behind Pierce. Melissa took a quick inventory, and the knot in her stomach eased, seeing all the spots still sported knives.

Scott would need an alternate weapon, but he would find one.

Pierce shifted back, and the creak of the floorboard beneath his foot had her jerking against her restraints. The wind howled outside and rattled the window panes. Her heart pounded, and her breathing deepened when Pierce gestured for Scott to head to the basement. Pierce followed, carrying her in his arms.

Her opportunity to escape had come and gone. And she'd done… nothing! Nothing but sit like a sack of potatoes in Pierce's arms. Why hadn't she tried to scream?

Scott would be allowed ten strikes, and although she'd vowed not to give him the satisfaction of her screams, he would drag agony from her body until he satiated his sadistic needs.

Putting up a brave front would only intensify the beating to come.

Pierce stepped between rows of shelving filled with crates of supplies that extended into the gloom of the dark basement. A single incandescent bulb lit their way.

Scott turned in a slow circle, admiring the ordered boxes. "Where's the entrance to the dungeon?"

Melissa twisted her wrists. Locks bound the cuffs, and more locks attached the chains connecting her hands to her feet. She'd been trussed up and immobilized.

"This way." Pierce headed to the back wall.

There were enough supplies to last for years. Pallets of bottled water formed a wall to the left, stacked beside them were filters of various types. More shelves stood to the right. There was barely enough room for Pierce to carry her between the shelving units. Her toes brushed stacks of water, crates of canned goods, and vacuum-packed food. The basement ended at an impressive wine rack. Hundreds of bottles lay on their sides.

Pierce jostled for position in the narrow confines and snagged his toe under the wooden wine rack. He activated a lever of some sort. The wall of wine slid to the side and revealed a heavy wooden door hidden behind. A combination lock barred further progress.

He jostled her, freeing one hand to spin the combination. The lock released with a snick, and he pushed open the door. Carrying her further underground, the concrete floor of the basement gave way to hard-packed dirt. Behind them, the wine-wall slid back in place with a churning of gears.

Cops might come, but they'd never find this entrance. Fear pulled a whimper from her throat, and she curled inward, pressing her eyes closed. But she wouldn't face her fate afraid or blind. Melissa blinked and forced herself to take in her surroundings.

Poured concrete of the basement no longer held back the dirt or stabilized the ceiling. Instead, a mixture of soil and rock, shored up with timber, formed the passage, making her think of a mining tunnel. A string of incandescent lightbulbs marched off down a tunnel longer than she imagined capable of lying beneath a home. A yellow glow lit their way. Pierce's breathing changed, becoming deeper with each pull of his breath until the tunnel ended abruptly around a sharp bend. A rough wooden door covered in locks waited.

"Take her," he said, spinning to Scott and thrusting her into her ex-husband's arms. "I have to open the next lock, and I can't do it while holding her." His lips twisted as if he didn't appreciate having to relinquish control to Scott.

She cried out when Scott's fingers dug into the bruising down her side. He held her with much less assurance than Pierce had, and, within moments, Scott's hold slipped. He hefted her weight and readjusted his grip. Prison must have weakened him more than she thought.

The feel of Scott's arms wrapping around her had her heart leaping to her throat. He smelled different from what she remembered; stale, like a cold prison cell. He placed more pressure on her bruised ribs, causing her to wince in pain. Pierce worked at the lock to an ominous door.

"Did you miss me?" His sour stench infiltrated her nostrils.

She clenched her teeth. "I mourned the loss of the man I fell in love with."

He tilted her and pressed his lips against her forehead. "Nonsense. I love you with every fiber of my being, just as you still love me. Why do you think I did those things to those girls instead of you?"

"You don't have to do this." Rationalizing made no sense, but she had to try.

Laughter bubbled in his chest, chilling her blood, and slowing the beat of her heart. His fetid breath had her cringing.

"Don't worry, love, I don't want to kill you. You belong to him now, my gift to my protégé. He treasures his princesses. That's what he calls his little whores, and you'll become his majestic Queen. But you need to pay for what you did, and Pierce will make sure you suffer a very long time. Much more fitting than death for what you did."

His words chilled her soul.

"He's right about me hanging around. I can't stay. They're probably subpoenaing my mail as we speak. Pierce has been smart, but they'll follow his trail. The police will come to see if I've stopped by. He knows this, but Pierce has prepared. They'll never find this underground retreat. But one night among friends is a twist of fate I can't ignore. I'm honored to spend this day with him…and you."

Pierce returned from unlocking the door. He gestured for Scott to give her back.

Scott tightened his grip, the muscles of his jaw clenched.

"We spoke about you in our letters," Scott said. "I thought it fitting you belong to a man like him. He knows how to punish you for your betrayal."

"I never betrayed you."

"You took vows," Scott said with a growl. "To love, honor, and obey. You did not honor me or obey me when you handed over the keys to the shed. You shouldn't have done that."

"I had no choice."

"You should have protected me."

"They had a search warrant," she argued.

"You done chatting?" Pierce yanked her out of Scott's hold.

Melissa's stomach flipped as Scott released her back to Pierce, who cradled her in arms much stronger than Scott's.

Pierce handed Scott six locks. "Pull the door shut behind you. I lock the door from the inside." He ducked inside the next room.

Melissa gasped at the size of the place. A king bed dominated the room, two rows of what looked to be cages ran down the sides, and what was chained against the far wall? Her chest tightened, and she struggled to breathe. Not what, but who was chained against the far wall.

Scott grunted with the effort of pulling the thick door back into position. He slid the bolt into place and locked them inside.

"Check it," Pierce demanded.

He spun to face the door, taking away her vision of the horrible room.

"They're locked," Scott said. "All of them."

"Recheck them."

Scott pulled and tugged on the locks. "Satisfied?"

"Again," Pierce insisted.

"Seriously?" Her husband frowned.

"Again." Pierce's voice was low and flat, lacking all the overtones she had noticed before. It made him appear even more lethal than Scott.

Melissa peeked over Pierce's shoulder. She didn't pray for strength. She hoped for a quick death.

FORTY-EIGHT

Tunnel

PIERCE

THE MAN BEFORE ME PALED COMPARED TO THE LEGACY I HAD modeled my life after. Scott Patterson came desperate and needy, so much less than the man who had accomplished greatness in the past. The voice in the letters, the years of correspondence we had exchanged, I thought he stood at a fount of wisdom dispensing knowledge through the years.

How horribly wrong I had been.

And I didn't want to share my Queen.

Lines of power needed to be established. Fear poured off my Queen when she looked at him. That adoration belonged to me. Not to the shell of a man who had once been my mentor.

"I can't believe you dug this out yourself," Scott said with awe.

He wouldn't have the patience for something this scale, nor the strength to build it with his bare hands.

"It took time." My comment fell on a mind lacking vision.

"Where did you keep them while you were tunneling this out?"

"I only had Belle. She stayed in the basement."

"Ah, your Belle. I'm intrigued to meet her."

My shoulders stiffened, thinking of his filthy hands touching my Belle. "Belle won't be playing tonight," I announced with more bite than intended. Belle was—forever and always—mine.

Now, how to get rid of him? I couldn't turn him in. That was a one-way street for us both. He would head back to execution by lethal injection. I might be judged, but my actions wouldn't buy death. A lingering life in prison would be my fate, a decision made by those who didn't understand. I would die before going to jail.

He knew this as did I.

We were locked in a stalemate.

I couldn't deny his request. He didn't dare cross me. We were like the armed society of the old West, polite to the extreme because the damage we could cause with our weapons would be lethal to us both.

Allowing him this night of punishment, even if it meant letting him defile one of my princesses, would be worthwhile if it ensured his departure in the morning. Two men, such as us, did not belong together. We were two very different beasts.

I had waited for years to bring my Queen to her kingdom. I itched to stroke her skin, to feel every inch of her flawless body. Having to wait—being forced to let him have her first—filled me with rage. Jealousy burned my gut, and I swallowed against the rising bile every time he opened his mouth.

There were only two outcomes. We separated at dawn, or one of us died tonight.

I couldn't deny Scott's skill, vision, or unique perspective, but how dare he stick his nose in the middle of my business?

Prison had made him weak. He could barely hold the weight of his wife. I think his mind had weakened too.

"I'm impressed with your thoroughness," he said. "No one will ever find the tunnel the way you have it hidden behind the wine." He tipped his head, but his praise meant nothing.

Our eyes locked, and I measured the man I'd idolized for so many years. The study of his techniques had provided me long hours of practice. I had explored and accepted my dark urges under his tutelage. At the same time, he guided my hands, honed my skill, and kept me safe when I had been inexperienced. His advice saved me from prison many times, stupid mistakes I would have made had it not have been for his caution.

I owed him some small measure of gratitude for that, but a truth hung between us, unspoken and dangerous. The student had surpassed the master. Perhaps this was fated to be—the two of us sharing this night? A graduation of sorts.

"Welcome to my dungeon." The left side of my mouth crooked up.

Scott stepped forward in a rush. I whispered into my Queen's ear, trying to soothe her as I prepared her to endure. "I can protect you, but only if you obey. You won't suffer long at your husband's hand."

She refused to meet my eyes, but I didn't need her consent. All I required was she understood her place.

"This is your home now. You decide your fate, my Queen; every choice is yours to make. Every consequence is a result of the decisions you make."

"Holy fuck! You have a man chained to the wall."

I flinched at the recrimination in his tone, then straightened my spine. An extreme homophobe, I needed to make sure he didn't get the wrong idea. I lay my Queen on the four-poster bed's black silk sheets and unlocked the chain connecting her wrists and feet. Poor thing must be in agony, but now she could stretch out and relieve the kinks in her body. Her comfort was important to me.

I kept the chain attached to the collar around her throat, and her wrist cuffs locked together, but I freed her feet.

Our Fairy Godmother had been placed in her cage nearest the bed. Her eyes showed white all around as she clutched the bars.

Delicious to see such fear.

"You have a thing for guys?" Disgust ran thick in Scott's voice.

I clenched my jaw and forced a smile. Gretel lay in her cage covered in bandages. "I got carried away with some knife play. He's a nurse and stitched poor Gretel up."

Scott looked at me as if I were an idiot.

I didn't like his expression one bit.

He continued in a caustic tone. "You can always get another princess." He jerked a thumb toward my bound, hooded, and gagged, male nurse. "He has to die." Scott made the pronouncement into the silence of my dungeon like it was his place to decide. It was not his place at all.

I hated him. This was my kingdom, not his.

The nurse thrashed in his chains, pulling and tugging until I thought he would dislocate his shoulders. Blood dripped down his wrists from his previous attempts to free himself.

"That isn't our agreement." I shrugged. The nurse was a dead man walking, but I still needed him. "Once Gretel is better, I'm letting him go."

Scott rubbed his hands together. "That's a mistake. Let me take care of him."

More thrashing followed, bringing a smile to my lips. Now, this could be interesting, and a perfect way to keep my hands clean.

Scott Patterson was such an idiot.

FORTY-NINE

Dungeon

MELISSA

The world tilted as Pierce dropped Melissa onto the massive bed. She bounced on the spongy mattress and flopped to her side. A wave of nausea surged up and demanded an outlet, but she swallowed down the acid burn.

Her shoulders ached from her bindings, and her hips cramped against the forced flexion caused by the tight chains. Her knees fared no better. The linings of the ankle and wrist cuffs protected her skin. Her wrists and ankles weren't abraded and raw, but that was a small blessing considering she was now in Pierce's dungeon.

Much bigger than she imagined, the dungeon looked to be a converted storm shelter. How had he dug this out of the earth? How had he hidden it from the neighbors? The bed took up the front part of the room. The back of the shelter had been removed, and the space extended—dug out of the earth. Thick timbers shored up the roof. Poured concrete filled in the gaps between naturally occurring boulders to form the walls. The whole place was horrifically…cozy.

On the far wall, a man was in chains, his arms pulled brutally over his head. An iron bar at his ankles forced his legs far apart. A black hood covered his face with holes for eyes, nose, and mouth, and a gag had been stuffed in his mouth. Terrified eyes stared out of the hood as the man thrashed against his bonds.

As if that wasn't scary enough, eight cages lined the space between her and the man on the wall. Every cell held a woman, except the one to the left of the bed, which remained empty. Her stomach twisted, wondering if that one was meant for her.

The women made no sounds, except for the slight rustle of movement. Soiled princess gowns adorned them. Scott paced the length of the cages, his gaze cutting left and right with a predatory intensity and a pang of desperate hunger.

What sort of mind created such a place?

"Ah." Scott's voice dropped an octave, turned husky, and sickening. "This must be Gretel?"

"Gretel," Pierce commanded. "Present yourself to our guest."

The woman knelt, hands on her thighs, head bowed. The poor thing could barely hold herself steady.

"I thought you kept them naked? Why are they dressed?"

Pierce pointed at the man chained against the wall. "Because of him."

"Does it even matter?" Scott already dismissed the man on the wall.

Beneath the black hood, the whites of the man's eyes grew even wider. Her heart went out to him. She didn't know how to help him but prayed for a miracle.

"I suppose it doesn't." Pierce clapped his hands, making Melissa jump. "Princesses, line up for our guest. Kneel before a great man."

Rustling sounded all around. The women positioned themselves at the front of the cages.

Without a break in his step, Scott called out their names. "Gretel, Cinderella, Red Riding Hood, Sleeping Beauty, Goldilocks, and this must be your Belle." He stopped at the cage closest to the bed and pointed to the last woman. "I don't recognize this one? You've added to the collection?"

Pierce stepped away from the bed, and Melissa craned her neck to get a better view of the room. Opposite from the cages, beside the chained man, a sight out of a medieval torture chamber revealed itself. Wood benches, padded with leather, sat beneath rows of whips, chains, and devices she'd only ever read about. They looked well used.

"This is our Fairy Godmother," Pierce said with pride. "She's in training, one week in, and she's learning how to please me, aren't you Henrietta?"

"Yes, my Prince." The woman issued a weak whisper.

It couldn't be?

"Too old for my tastes," Scott said with a sour tone.

"You'd be surprised," Pierce crowed. "Her oral skills are pleasing."

"I'm not interested in someone so old."

"She's not much older than your wife."

Scott turned, and she shrunk away from the brutality in her ex-husband's eyes. "I don't want to fuck my wife either." He pointed to the two blondes in the middle. "Can I have them? Beauty and Goldie?"

"You don't need two," Pierce said.

"I'll start with one and see where the night leads us." Scott rubbed his hands together. He turned, and his attention focused on the wall of torture. "What can I use?"

"I thought you wanted to deal with your wife's punishment first?"

Scott glanced back, and Melissa dropped her gaze. "I haven't had a woman in three years. I'm hard as a rock and ready to fuck. I'll deal with her later."

"Beauty is good with her mouth," Pierce suggested. "I don't allow them out of the cages more than one at a time." He snapped his fingers, and the woman moved. "On your knees, Beauty." He turned to Scott. "She stays in the cage. You don't need her out for this."

"A blow job?" Scott sounded disappointed, but he unfastened his pants. His eyes flicked toward Melissa, and she dropped her gaze, not wanting to incite her husband any more than necessary. "What about teeth and biting?"

"Beauty won't bite, and she knows better than to scrape with her teeth, don't you Beauty?"

"Yes, my Prince," came a soft reply.

Pierce placed a hand on Melissa's head, gripping her hair. He lifted her face to him. "Don't worry, my Queen, you'll have plenty of opportunity to perfect your skills, too." He tapped her lips with his free hand and then released her hair.

Melissa's head swam with horrifying images of her future if she didn't find a way to get free.

Scott dropped his pants and pressed against the bars, wiggling his hips as he did. His guttural sigh told her everything she didn't want to know.

"Holy fuck, that's amazing," Scott said with a groan.

Pierce shifted his attention to Melissa, giving the strangest look. It was at once compassionate and cruel. His fingers snapped, and he stepped to the cage holding the woman he'd called Belle. He unfastened his pants and freed himself. He rested his head against the bars and sighed as Belle pressed her lips to his cock.

"Serve your Prince, my beautiful Belle."

The men's low sounds of pleasure filled the room.

Melissa fought her bindings, coming no closer to unfastening the locks.

She propped herself on her elbows, determined to get a better view of her surroundings. The manacled man stared back, blinking behind his hood. She turned away, knowing his fate, and helpless to do anything about it. Her gaze landed on the cage closest to the bed.

The woman inside mouthed. *Are you okay?*

FIFTY

Suburbia

CJ

CJ let Mac drive, or maybe Mac insisted. He didn't argue because the decision seemed a wise choice considering how his heart banged around inside his chest and how his palms were slicked with sweat. This wasn't his usual calm self.

Jenny called shotgun, but one look from him, and she took the backseat. The rest of Delta team, Jon Knutt, Brett Parmley, the bubbly Charlene Moudin, followed in a separate car.

"You gonna explain how you know where this guy lives?" Mac's throaty growl bounced around the inside of the car. He blew through a stop sign.

"I was with the girls…" He recounted the girl's cookie expedition. "I stopped while the girls talked, and a van pulled into the driveway." He punched the dash. "I saw him. The fucking van. I saw it and the timing…" The timing fit with Melissa's abduction.

The late afternoon sun was fading. Clouds had blown in, a storm brewing perhaps, and the wind was picking up.

"How could you have known?" Jenny's warm hand touched his shoulder, rubbing at the tension in his muscles."Anna's sister knew." He rubbed the top of his head.

"What do you mean?" she asked.

"Angela got a weird vibe from him. Anna never picked up on it."

"Sounds like a perv," Mac said.

CJ looked in the side mirror. Brett Parmley blew through a red light, trying to keep up with Mac's driving.

"Do we have a plan?" Jenny asked. "Or, are we just going to knock on the door and say, 'Hey give me my girl back?'"

CJ ground his teeth. "Something like that."

Mac's tone turned serious. "Did anyone phone Sam? He's going to flip when he finds out we've gone all Rambo and didn't tell him."

CJ kept silent. He'd raced out of the hotel suite without a word. His team had followed after him, catching up at the elevators. The explanation about Pierce Channing left grim expressions on everyone's faces by the time they'd reached the lobby.

He'd kept moving, not wanting to wait on the Feds. They were busy following leads on Scott Patterson's disappearance, and convincing them that this was their best lead would take time he refused to waste.

"I'll call," Jenny said.

CJ fixed his eyes forward, thinking they couldn't get there fast enough.

They had no plan. Other than storming the place, all they could do was ring the doorbell. He needed eyes inside before charging in and making a fatal mistake. He chewed at his cheek, trying to strategize, failing miserably because all he could think about was the video on Melissa's cell phone.

Jenny spoke with Sam, her voice even and smooth. "Hey, we have a lead on the kidnapper. CJ's confident it's the same person who took Henrietta Jones."

She paused as Sam responded. Only the growl of his voice could be heard.

"The name is Pierce Channing," she continued. "Hey, did you get a copy of the sketch artist's drawings?"

More silence while she listened.

"The girls sold cookies at his house, and the younger girl remembers him sitting next to her mother at the park the following day. There's more." Jenny told Sam about the sketches and the surveillance tapes. She paused, listening to Sam's questions, and then answered. "So far, it appears the guy is working alone. No connection to Scott Patterson."

Silence again, this time longer.

Jenny tapped him on the shoulder. "Hey, CJ?"

"What?"

She handed him the phone. "Sam wants to talk to you."

He grimaced as he took the phone. "Yeah, boss."

"What the fuck is going on?" The sharp tone of Sam's voice spoke volumes.

"Jenny told you what's going on." He directed Mac as they headed out of town.

"You're headed to this guy's house?"

"We are."

A long pause followed.

"I want you to listen," Sam spoke slow and easy, a calming influence not generally present when his boss tried to get the point across. "You listening?"

"Yes."

"Under no circumstances are you to enter. I'm almost there, and I'm coming with backup."

"I've got my whole team, we're good." Brett and Jon were terrific. He trusted his life to them. Charlie never ceased to prove her skills.

"You're not listening."

"Because you're not making sense. We've got this."

"No, you don't."

Sam's sigh wasn't lost through the phone connection. CJ could imagine the shake of Sam's head as he prepared to break the bad news.

"Pierce Channing's name has come to my attention."

"Well, of course," CJ said with irritation. "We just reported it."

"Shut the fuck up and listen."

CJ snapped his mouth shut, grinding his teeth together.

"You listening?"

When he said nothing, Sam asked again. "CJ?"

"You told me to shut the fuck up," he said through gritted teeth.

"Pierce Channing is the name of Scott Patterson's most prolific pen pal. Does that paint the picture for you?"

Aw shit.

"Do not go inside that house," Sam ordered. "If this guy is working for Patterson, there's a good chance he knows where Patterson is hiding or has Patterson there. I'll be there in…an hour and a half. I have two teams with me and SWAT on the way."

An hour and a half? No fucking way would he wait that long.

"She could be dead by then."

"If you blow in there with a half-cocked plan, she will be. Trust me."

Trust wasn't the issue. Time was their enemy.

Mac pulled into the housing development. CJ had him stop several houses down from Patterson's home.

"I'll take that under advisement," he said to Sam with a growl.

"You'd better."

He ended the call and debriefed Mac and Jenny.

"So," Mac said, "we're going to sit and wait?"

"I have no intention of sitting around," CJ said. "Besides, I have a plan."

FIFTY-ONE

Dungeon Take Two

MELISSA

Melissa squeezed her eyes shut as Scott's roar of animalistic lust filled the air. But closing her eyes did nothing to keep the image of his bucking hips from her mind. While Pierce finished, Scott zipped his pants and then paced up and down the row of cages, reaching inside to touch the kneeling women, petting their heads and cupping their chins.

She could only imagine what horrors he envisioned when he looked at them and was thankful sturdy metal separated the women from the killer on the outside.

Pierce groaned. His hands gripped the iron so hard his knuckles turned white. His head pressed against the bars as he huffed and seemed to sag.

Silence descended for a time, except for heavy breathing coming from Pierce, but soon that evened out as he regained his composure. His body straightened. His fingers released their death grip on the bars and then moved to zip his fly.

Pierce faced Scott, who knelt before one of the cages.

"You like Cinderella?" Pierce's voice hitched. "I thought you wanted Goldilocks?"

"I like them all," Scott said with fascination. "How do you manage them?" Wonder filled Scott's expression as his gaze swept down the row of cages.

Pierce's laugh filled the silence. It should have made her shiver or brought on any string of nasty reactions, but the opposite occurred. Pierce's laughter was out of place, it was confident, sure, and slowed the drumbeat of her heart. He walked toward Scott, dragging his hand over the bars of the cages as he neared.

"I just do. Are you ready for Goldilocks, or do you need a break? Or maybe you want to take care of your wife's punishment?"

Ex-wife. She was Scott's ex-wife. Melissa's stomach clenched.

Scott's gaze darted across the dungeon and locked on hers. Blackness darker than coal, measured, judged, and reduced her to insignificance.

He waved a dismissive hand. "I'll get to her later." He licked his lips. "I, uh…"

Pierce unlocked a cage and pulled out a woman. He stripped her of her clothing with an economy of effort which stunned Melissa, then led her to the wall beside the chained man. The woman shook but didn't resist. She even assisted the process and lifted her arms to be cuffed. He secured her wrists with handcuffs attached to eye-bolts.

Pierce stepped to the far end of the wall. Implements of torture hung in ordered rows, causing a shiver to work its way down her spine as she took in paddles, crops, floggers, whips, and worse. She clamped her teeth together, fighting against a whimper rising in the back of her throat.

In stark contrast, the woman secured to the wall remained perfectly still and silent, resigned perhaps to what would happen next.

Pierce selected a flogger. He swung it, testing its weight.

"Nice," Scott murmured. "But I thought you were going to fuck her?"

"Oh, I am," Pierce said, "but I enjoy it so much better when they scream." Pierce pointed to the padded bench. "Why don't you have a seat? Watch for a bit, and when you're ready, let me know."

A twisted expression flashed across Scott's face.

The throws of the flogger flying through the air filled the dungeon with a hiss. Its many tails swished as they went, then collided on flesh with a crack and a very definite scream. Tears slicked Melissa's face as the bound woman's cries reverberated in the air with a long ear-piercing shriek.

"Hey," Scott pointed to the chained man. "You said no whips or canes for your girls, but what about him? I can do whatever I want to him, right?"

Pierce glanced at the bound man. He had fallen silent while Scott and Pierce had pleasured themselves, but he struggled anew once the men's attention turned back to him.

"I'm not willing to kill him." Pierce drew back his arm and landed a nasty strike on the back of the woman's thighs. She screamed, her head thrown back, eyes staring at the ceiling, lungs emptying of air, and filling the room with her pain.

Melissa curled into a ball, seeking solace the only way she could.

"Like it matters," Scott grumbled.

"I thought you didn't like men," Pierce said with a tease in his voice.

"I don't want to fuck him." Scott's lips twisted. "But why can't I toy with him for a bit?"

Pierce's eyes narrowed. He walked to the rows of implements and grabbed a flogger, thrusting it toward Scott. "Use this."

Scott looked at it, turning it over in his hands. "Heavy. I like it."

Silence.

The terrific weight of the room was suffocating.

Melissa hugged her knees to her chest, holding herself as tightly as she could. She couldn't bear watching the poor girl tortured. Hearing it was bad enough. The sound of a flogger whistled through the air, generating another scream, this one deep, masculine, and full of agony.

Her eyes flew open, and she silenced her cries, unwilling to draw unnecessary attention to herself. From the nearest cage, the woman motioned her to come to the edge of the bed. The cries of the bound woman masked the noise of her chains, as did the deeper timbre of the man's screams.

The woman in the cage whispered so low that Melissa had to read her lips to make out what she was saying. "What is your name?"

"Melissa." Her insides quivered.

"We're not allowed to speak," she explained, "we'll be punished, but…"

Melissa nodded, understanding the need to reach out in the face of this craziness. "Is your name Henrietta?"

The woman's eyes widened. "How did you know?" She wiped away a tear.

"People are looking for you."

A light of hope shone in the woman's eyes. Melissa prayed her faith in CJ held out.

"How long have you been here?"

Henrietta blinked. "I don't know. A few days, maybe a week? It's hard to keep track of time down here." Her voice broke, and a choked sob escaped her lips. "Obey him. Do whatever he asks. If you don't, you're not the only one who will suffer."

"How do we get out of here?"

Henrietta shook her head. "We don't. Some of these girls have been here for years."

Melissa flinched each time a scream pierced the air, but it provided cover for their conversation.

"I did this to myself." Henrietta's chin dropped to rest on her chin. She choked back a sob.

"We're going to get out of here."

CJ was out there, which meant there was hope.

Male and female cries filled the dungeon, promising her a future of similar pain if CJ didn't hurry up with the hero business. But maybe she needed to figure something out on her own, in case CJ didn't make it in time.

FIFTY-TWO

The Calvary

CJ

CJ GATHERED EVERYONE AND EXPLAINED HIS CONVERSATION with Sam.

"Are we really going to do nothing?" Jon asked.

"Fuck that," Brett said, slapping Jon's back. "What's the plan, CJ?"

He glanced at Mac, who gave a nod. Mac would support him.

Jenny stood with Charlie, the two women looking diminutive next to the men. Appearances were deceiving, however. He sparred against Jenny, and while he was still getting to know Charlie, he bet the pretty blonde held a few surprises. Everyone seemed eager to do something, but what? Sam's directive had been clear. He wasn't to enter the house.

He clapped his hands together. "All right…Brett and Jon, you're on recon. We need to know access points. Vulnerabilities. Water. Power." He didn't have to go into excessive detail. Brett and Jon knew what kind of intelligence was required.

"Mac and Charlie, you take the yard and garage, make sure there aren't any other entrances. Look for storm doors and basement entrances leading to the outside."

"What does that leave for me?" Jenny turned to him, confused.

"You and I will explore the vacant lot next door." He wanted to be at the house, doing recon himself, but he was too vested in this operation. It was best to keep a bird' s-eye view, stay away, and he needed Jenny to stop him if he did anything stupid.

"Fine." She twisted her face into a dissatisfied scowl.

"That lot makes my skin itch," he said in a flat tone. "Only house in this entire development on a double lot? If he wanted privacy, his yard already butts up next to the forest. Why buy the lot next to him? It sticks out."

He rubbed the back of his neck, thinking out loud. "We'll be spread thin. I'm okay with that, but we need to regroup in ten. We don't even know if Melissa's in there, or Henrietta for that matter. I need someone to get inside."

"I'll do it." Charlie flipped her bleach-blond hair. "If he's into kidnapping girls…" She made a suggestive gesture with her hands, emphasizing her curves, "let's give him someone he wants to bring inside."

Jon pulled Charlie to him, wrapping an arm around her waist and tugging her close. "No way in hell are you going in as bait."

Brett stepped close, sandwiching her between him and Jon. "Ditto."

Charlie pressed her palm to Jon's chest and gazed into his eyes. "It's the best way to see what's inside, and we have tactical gear in the car. It'll be easy enough to get past the door, and I don't mind being bait."

"I don't like it," Jon huffed.

Brett twisted his lips, considering her proposal. "Let's send Jenny in with her."

CJ shook his head. "Can't risk it. Jenny saw him at the bar, so we have to assume he's seen her. Charlie goes in alone."

Charlie beamed. She rose to her toes and kissed Brett on the cheek. "I'll be fine." She turned to CJ and put her hands on her hips. "We're doing this then?"

"Recon first," CJ insisted. "Brett and Jon, you're on the exterior with Mac and Charlie." He shook his head. Sam was going to be pissed. "I'll check out the empty field with Jenny. We meet back in ten minutes, and if everything looks okay, Charlie goes in."

"I don't like it," Jon said, but he didn't argue against the plan.

CJ didn't like it either, but if they could get Charlie inside for even a moment, it would make breaching the home that much more successful. "It's up to you," he said, giving Charlie a chance to back out.

She batted her eyelashes, doing a wonderful impression of a flirty co-ed. Then she unbuttoned the top two buttons of her blouse, showing even more of her voluptuous cleavage.

"I'm in," she pronounced.

"Okay," he said. "Let's do this."

Brett and Jon jogged ahead of Mac and Charlie, leaving Jenny and CJ strolling on the sidewalk.

"Sam confirmed Channing was a pen pal of Patterson?" Jenny asked.

"Yeah."

She turned to face him, placing both hands on his shoulders. "Are you ready to face what we might find in there?"

"No."

It wasn't the answer Jenny wanted to hear, but it was the truth. She wanted to know he'd established emotional distance, and that she could count on him, but that wasn't true. His insides screamed at him to rush inside that house, guns blazing, and save Melissa. It would be precisely the wrong thing to do, and more likely to get her killed. He knew this. Jenny knew this. Hell, Sam knew it, too.

"If this goes south, you can't kill him. I need you to promise you'll keep your cool."

He nodded, but he couldn't promise Jenny anything. He just found Melissa, and if he lost her before he explored whatever was happening between them, he'd be gutted for life. And, if Scott Patterson was inside that house, little could stop him from putting the motherfucker down for good.

He leveled a flat stare at Jenny. "Let's hope it doesn't come to that."

"You scare the living shit out of me sometimes."

As they skirted the outer edge of the property, his gaze cut to Brett and Jon ghosting around the outside of the house. Their movements were a study in economy of motion. In broad daylight, he wouldn't have seen them except he knew to look for them. Mac and Charlie had stationed themselves outside one of the windows of the garage. Something had captured their attention. He veered toward them, only to be pulled away by a tug on his arm.

"Keep to the plan," she said.

Their exploration of the vacant lot turned up nothing more than a manicured lawn, boulders too big to move, a culvert leading out the rear of the property toward the tree line, a dirt road, and a large storm drain. A glance at his watch told him it was time to regroup with the others. Sam would arrive in less than an hour.

CJ planned to be inside before then.

FIFTY-THREE

Her Turn

MELISSA

Melissa stopped flinching in response to the screams coming from the other end of the dungeon. When Scott grew bored whipping the hooded man, the poor man sagged against the metal cuffs. Blood seeped down his wrists. His back—his poor, tortured flesh—was a mass of raised welts and angry red lines. In contrast, Scott bounced on the balls of his feet as if the whipping invigorated him.

Pierce stepped away from the woman sobbing against the wall. Her back mirrored that of the man, raised welts, red and angry, laced her skin. He guided her back to her cage, whispering praise.

Melissa would have shed more tears if not for her ex-husband's coal dark eyes staring at her.

"I'm ready for her," he said, pointing a finger.

Pierce glanced over his shoulder, his magnetic gaze stealing her attention from Scott. With a nod, he came toward her. He reached for her, and it took all of her self-control not to flinch at his touch. She was surprised at the warmth of his skin and the gentleness of his touch when he cupped her chin.

"Are you ready, my Queen?"

His throaty whisper made her breath hitch in her throat. She had to swallow before she could speak, dreading the words, but knowing she had to play a role. It might be the only thing that saved her from Scott.

"Is this what you want…m-my King?"

His brow quirked at the use of his self-proclaimed title. She was hoping for a reaction, uncertain what she needed. She was figuring everything out as she went.

"It's what must be done," he said with remorse. "Only then can you be forgiven."

Melissa licked her lips. Her mouth had gone dry, and her lips seemed to want to stick together. She forced her gaze to drop, just barely submissive, but not surrendered, at least not yet.

"I'm terrified." The words cracked in her throat.

His forehead furrowed as he leaned down. "It will be painful, but you will endure this punishment. Do you understand?"

She took in a deep breath and let it out. Slowly, she allowed her gaze to travel up to meet his once again. "I don't know if I'm strong enough."

"I will be by your side, my Queen." He ran his thumb along her cheek, traced the angle of her jaw, and brought his finger to her lips.

"Hey, you going to talk all night, or what?" Scott's harsh words intruded on her moment with Pierce.

She lost what little ground she had gained when Pierce started at Scott's irritating words.

Pierce shook his head. He pointed to the wall with the implements. "Use the light cane on the far left. I'll move her into position."

Her ability to keep still failed as a shiver worked its way down her spine and nervous sweat made her hands clammy and cold. Her hips and knees ached from the prolonged flexion in the bindings, but that was nothing compared to the flare of agony in her shoulders.

Pierce swept her into his arms and carried her without strain, unlike her husband, who struggled to hold her.

"I will be with you the entire time, my Queen." His whispered words floated into her ears said so low she imagined she heard them until he continued. "I will protect you. You must endure ten strikes. Will you please me?"

She needed to draw out his protective instinct. So, she did the unthinkable. She gave him a nod. It was a calculated move, but what choice did she have? She could go with the evil she knew and die or see where this secondary evil took her.

Pierce was a collector of women and, unlike her husband, seemed to keep his playthings around. Years if she were to believe what Henrietta had said. If it took years, Melissa would find her way free. As long as she was alive, she would fight.

"Don't leave me alone with him," she whispered and pressed her cheek against his shirt. "Please? I can't do this alone."

His breathing hitched, paused for a beat. A deep breath followed, and she imagined his chest swelled with pride. He kissed her forehead, and she struggled not to pull back from the intimate touch.

"I will be with you, my Queen. I will never leave you."

"Thank you." She lifted her wrists, both hands rising together, bound as they were, and fluttered her fingertips against the buttons of his shirt.

The walk from the bed to the padded bench ended, and with it, their short conversation died. Pierce became businesslike, almost robotic in his motions. He draped her face down over the bench.

She flinched as pressure was put on her bruised ribs. He allowed her to reposition herself for comfort, an odd consideration in light of what was to come. Then, he released her ankles from their bindings, but only to strap them down again, securing each ankle to a leg of the bench. The same treatment followed with her hands.

Melissa's breathing turned ragged as fear overrode her instinct for survival.

"Do not fight, my Queen. It will only make it worse." Pierce placed a hand to her hip as he fastened a strap over her back.

"Aren't you going to strip her," Scott demanded.

She hoped he would not. Her jeans were her last defense against the long rattan cane Scott would use.

"I am not," Pierce said.

He came around to stand at her head, but she didn't lift to look at him. She couldn't. He knelt down, putting his head level with hers, forcing the issue with that movement.

Melissa wriggled her hands. Pierce had secured them to the legs of the bench. She had to develop his trust. "Please, release my hands."

"No."

She would not let that phase her. "Please…my King," she winced as the title passed her lips, but it was necessary. She flipped the hair out of her eyes and focused on his chin and the set of his mouth. The strength to look into his eyes was beyond her.

"I need you to hold my hands while…he does this."

Begging her tormentor to comfort her during this crazed beating made no sense, but there was nothing about the entire situation that made sense. His jaw clenched. It was a tiny gesture, but it was enough.

He spoke into her ear. "You must not flinch or jerk your hands from mine. You can injure yourself if you do. If you move your hands to protect yourself, you will be hurt."

She understood from personal experience and her one and only experience with Scott and a cane. Only then she'd been alone. Now she had Pierce, and she would be damned if he wasn't going to help her survive this.

"Thank you." She also wasn't above begging. Melissa brought her gaze up to meet his and met smoky darkness in their depths. It chilled her to her core to look upon such madness.

He released her wrists and lifted her hands to his lips. One kiss to each knuckle. She held still the entire time. Behind them, Scott whipped the cane through the air, as if testing its weight. She flinched with each swish, not knowing when the first blow would strike.

"Whenever you are ready." Pierce grabbed her hands, lacing his fingers with hers. The disdain in his voice was thinly veiled by the very real threat overlying it. "Ten strikes."

"I got it," Scott said. "Ten isn't even a drop in the bucket for what she deserves, but knowing she'll never see the light of day again is punishment enough."

The cane whistled through the air, struck her flesh, and cut right to the bone. Screams flew from her mouth, and her hands clenched around Pierce's grip.

He whispered into her ear, telling her to breathe, to take the pain, and coached her through that first strike.

"Oh, that was perfect, my love," Scott said.

If she was to be free of this place, she needed Pierce to trust her and keep her unchained. Melissa gripped his hands tighter, moaned against the searing pain in her backside as she prepared for the second strike.

It came sooner than she expected and before she could brace herself. Another scream ripped from her throat.

All the while, Pierce told her to absorb the pain, breathe it in. She locked eyes with him and did as he commanded. Somehow the pain flowed through her to him, and she breathed past it. There was power in his gaze, and crazy energy flowed between them. He took her pain. Without him, she never would have survived ten strikes from the cane, but she did survive, and that was all that mattered.

When Pierce released her from the bench, he carried her back to the massive bed. He reached up and tugged on a chain hanging from the canopy above the bed. He kissed her lightly on the lips. "I am so proud of you, My Queen."

He turned to Scott. "Let's head upstairs and refresh ourselves."

Scott sneered as he passed the bed. "She's a fucking bitch. Useless in bed, and you're welcome to her."

"I will claim her when we return, but we need to discuss your plans for leaving. Besides, it's dinner time, and I'm hungry."

Scott's eyes widened. "I'm not done. I want to fuck some more."

"You have all night. No reason to rush. Besides, you'll be stronger after a meal, and I'm curious how you intend to leave town."

Pierce led Scott toward the dungeon door. He stooped over to unlock the set of six locks that secured them all inside.

Six locks. Melissa groaned as the door closed behind her kidnapper and ex-husband. Then she looked down and gasped.

He'd left her hands unbound.

FIFTY-FOUR

Into The Lion's Den

CJ

Movement at the house caught CJ's attention. Mac and Charlie ran away from the garage, heading toward the backyard. Jon vaulted over a bush into the neighbor's yard, followed by Brett. CJ grabbed Jenny, pulling her into a crouch.

"Something's up," he said.

It would be much easier to walk back to the car along the sidewalk, but that would put them in view of the house and whoever was inside. The only reason his team would have bailed was if they had seen someone, which meant he and Jenny needed to take a detour to get back to the vehicles.

"At least we know someone's home," Jenny said.

"Yes, and that means Melissa is probably there, too."

"Let's wait to hear what the others found, then we'll go in."

CJ stopped, floored by Jenny's comment. "What about Sam?"

"Like you would ever wait? Let's just not be stupid about it."

They circled the back of the lot and skirted behind the neighbors' yards, weaving in, over, and around the fences. When they made it to the vehicles, they were the last to arrive.

"Report," CJ said.

Charlie, Jon, and Brett snapped to attention at the command in his voice. Mac's grin greeted him. CJ was probably only one in three people in the world who would think the look on his face was anything but terrifying, but he knew Mac well.

Charlie spoke first. "The white van is parked in the garage. The back doors were open, and there were red roses in the back and all over the floor."

"She's inside." Mac stared at CJ, not even trying to sugarcoat his words.

He'd already guessed as much but was glad to have it confirmed.

Jon leaned against the black SUV. "Not a sign of anyone at first. House looked empty. Three bedrooms, only one with a bed. Back door leads off the kitchen, and other than the front door and garage, the bedroom windows are the only other entry and exit points. Bedroom windows have security locks on the inside and are blocked with dowels."

"There were beer bottles on the counter in the kitchen," Brett added. "At least two. A door led down to a basement. I'm betting that's where he took her because we didn't see anyone in the house."

"Any sign of a second man?" They had to remain open to the possibility Pierce Channing sheltered Scott Patterson within his home.

Brett spoke. "I heard two voices but saw no one. I'm assuming they were headed up from the basement. We ditched before they could catch us, but definitely two male voices."

"Damn," CJ said.

Mac's lips pressed into a thin line. "Not good."

"Not good at all." CJ looked at Charlie. "Did you get a look at them?"

She shook her head. "No. When Jon whistled, Mac and I high-tailed it out of there."

"Anyone look at the yard? Any reason to think there's another entrance to that basement?" There'd been nothing in the vacant lot.

No one said anything. It would affect planning, not knowing. Everyone understood this.

CJ breathed out. "We're blind. It's risky."

Mac nodded.

Jenny's cell phone rang. She glanced at it. "It's Sam."

"Tell him we're waiting."

"You want me to lie?"

"I want you to follow orders," CJ said.

"Yours or his?"

He rolled his eyes. "Just answer the fucking phone."

She put the phone to her ear. "Sam?" Her gaze flicked to his. "Yes, we're around the corner, holding position. No, we haven't engaged…Yes, CJ's behaving." There was a bit of back and forth between Sam and Jenny before she hung up. "He believes me and says he's less than an hour out, …and under no circumstances are you to engage."

"Okay," CJ turned to his team. "Now who has suggestions for going in?"

They tossed around several ideas but settled on the only one that granted them access to the inside of the house. Charlie pulled a suitcase out of the back of Jon's car. She pulled her hair into a high ponytail, put on a pair of black running pants, and a tank top, which emphasized her cleavage.

Brett whispered in her ear, the sound too low to make out, but by his tone, Brett was not pleased.

In an uncharacteristic gesture, Charlie cupped Brett's cheek. She didn't kiss him, but there was definite tenderness in that touch.

"It'll be fine," she whispered. When she smiled, Brett's shoulders slumped. She twirled on the sidewalk. "How do I look?"

"You look hot," Brett said, "too hot."

Mac shook his head and rummaged around in the back of his car, searching. "Here."

He tossed earbuds and a small music player at Charlie, which she clipped on the inside of her bra.

"Don't lose them," he warned.

Jenny put a hand on his shoulder. "She'll be fine." She turned to Charlie. "If they invite you inside, tell us what you see. Stay only a couple minutes. Get in and get out."

Jon opened the back door of his car. He sat with a computer in his lap, typing away. A few minutes later, he pulled a piece of paper off the portable printer and handed it with a clipboard to Charlie.

"Your ticket in," he said. "You're asking for donations to a women's shelter. It's your sorority's charitable work this semester."

As capable as Charlie seemed, it would be two against one on the inside if things went down.

"We need to get a visual on the basement," he said. "See if you can get down there and give us a report. Mac and I will slip in the kitchen door and get in position."

Jenny shook her head. "Not a good plan." She pointed at him. "Channing knows what you and Mac look like. If he sees even a hint of you, it's all over." Her finger shifted to Bret and Jon. "Let them go. If they get caught, play it off as a fraternity prank."

"Sounds reasonable," CJ admitted, although he wanted closer to the action. Briefly, he wondered if this was how Sam felt, always sending in others to do the work.

"All right," he said as he clapped his hands together. "Charlie will work her magic and get inside." He turned to her, his tone turning serious. "You know who you're dealing with, and what these men are capable of. You need to be on guard."

"I got it, boss." She cupped her breasts and glanced down. "Let's see if these perky boobs are worth their weight in gold." She gave him a wink.

"Oh, honey," Jenny said with a laugh, "you're too much."

CJ motioned for Brett and Jon to follow Charlie at a discreet distance, while he, Mac, and Jenny hung back.

As Charlie walked away, Mac cycled through radio checks. To the men inside, it would look like she was listening to her music, but the sophisticated technology inside the player allowed full two-way communication.

Sam would skin CJ alive once he found out what he was doing, but he couldn't wait. He had a team of six skilled operatives who were well trained in hostage rescue and two women to save.

FIFTY-FIVE

Chains

MELISSA

THE DOOR SQUEAKED CLOSED, AND THE LAST MELISSA HEARD OF THE men were locks snapping into place and the low rumble of their conversation.

She was trapped.

Panic set in, claustrophobia hemming her in from all sides. She was in a tomb of stone, rock, and timber supports. Desperate for air, she clawed at her throat.

No way out!

No way to get to the locks.

Exploring her injuries kept her mind from the oppressiveness of the earth overhead. And despite her fears, she could breathe. There had to be a ventilation shaft. A grab for the bedpost had her jerking in surprise. Her arms and legs were free. Had it been intentional? An oversight?

She reached for the collar latched around her throat and felt for the lock. It seemed a simple keyhole and not one of the combinations Pierce seemed so fond of using everywhere else.

Melissa blew out a calming breath. The action distracted her from the room, from the locked door, and from the overwhelming sense of being buried alive. No ventilation shaft, but there was ductwork plumbed into the ceiling. What kind of perverted mind thought all this up?

A man who left women inside cages that's who.

Some wept, some slept, Gretel had yet to move. None spoke, and she wondered why, but then remembered Henrietta's warning.

Her gaze traveled to the woman in the nearest cage. Henrietta rocked back and forth, her lips mumbling something Melissa couldn't make out. She yearned to comfort her, as Henrietta had done for her, but a glance told her now was not the time.

The chain attached to the collar bound Melissa to the bedpost and limited her movement. Fortunately, Pierce had missed something. She pulled out a bobby pin from her hair. This wasn't something she had ever tried before, and it would be much harder than it looked in the movies, but she had to try.

She felt at the keyhole of the lock. Inserting the bobby pin was easy. Now what? She felt around. Something was inside, a latch or mechanism, but she couldn't get the bobby pin to grab it, push it, pull on it, or slide it to the side.

After several long minutes, what seemed like hours—she was afraid the men would be back any moment—tears of frustration streamed down her cheeks.

"What are you doing?" Henrietta whispered.

Melissa's head shot up, surprised by the sudden noise in the eerie silence of the dungeon.

Henrietta had moved to the front of her cage. Her fingers clutched at the metal bars.

"I'm trying to get this off."

"Do you know what you're doing?" Henrietta's eyes flicked to the dungeon door and back to Melissa.

"No. It seems so easy on TV." With a shake of her head, Melissa dropped her hands from the frustrating task.

Henrietta smiled. "Television makes things seem easy, but there's a trick to it."

"You know how to pick a lock?" Melissa widened her eyes, first with surprise and then with interest.

The woman nodded. "My husband taught me, God rest his soul, he was into picking locks."

"Do you think you could?" Hope bloomed in her chest.

Henrietta shrugged. "Why? When he comes back, he'll only punish you, and me for helping, and then the others while I watch. It's my job to watch over them."

"Watch over them?"

She shook her head. "Yes, in this crazy world, I'm the Fairy Godmother." She pointed to the other cages. "Everyone here is a princess for that demented jerk."

She pointed to each of the women, saying their names. "He punished Gretel because of me. I don't know if she'll make it. It's why he brought the nurse down. The others are Cinderella, Red Riding Hood, Sleeping Beauty, Goldilocks, and Belle." She pointed to Belle's cage, furthest from them both, and closest to the man. The woman was curled up on the floor, sleeping. "There's something not right with Belle. She adores Prince Charming."

"You mean Pierce Channing."

"No, Prince Charming. That's what we're supposed to call him except you. You're special. He was getting off when you called him King. Be very careful. You're not the only one who will get hurt when he gets mad." Henrietta's entire body shuddered.

Melissa firmed her lips into a determined line. "I know you've been down here a while, and I don't understand what he's put you through, but I'm not ready to give up. Besides, someone's looking for me."

CJ wouldn't stop until he found her. She believed that with every ounce of conviction she could muster.

"I'll do whatever I can to make it as easy on him to rescue me." Even if she had to save herself. Melissa had been tormented by Scott for six years; she wouldn't become a victim to Pierce.

Henrietta coughed. "I'm glad you have hope. I tried..." Her gaze traveled to the wall. "He's here because of me."

"The man?"

"He's a nurse. Our Prince," Henrietta's mouth twisted around the title with distaste, "your King brought that man to take care of Gretel."

"What happened to her?"

Henrietta explained the knives, and Melissa's stomach twisted with the horrific images. It was all she could do not to get violently ill.

"So, you see," Henrietta concluded, "I'm hesitant to do anything to make him mad. I don't know what else he's capable of, but now that other one is here." Her voice dropped to a whisper. "I'm scared. I think none of us are getting out of this alive."

Melissa wasn't ready to believe that, even if she feared it might be true.

"Which is why you need to help me," she insisted.

"No."

With great difficulty and no small amount of pain due to the recent caning, Melissa moved to the foot of the bed. The chain moved with her, tracking over one of the crossbeams of the four-poster bed.

"I think I can reach you," she said.

"I don't know." Henrietta worried her lower lip between her teeth.

"We have to try," Melissa insisted.

She scooted off the bed and stepped to the corner of Henrietta's cage. The chain tying her to the bed barely reached. Henrietta took the bobby pin from Melissa's hand, and Melissa feared she would toss it to the ground for a moment. The woman's hands shook, and her gaze kept cutting to the sleeping Belle.

"I haven't done this in years." A tremor of fear laced her voice, but she pulled open the bobby pin and fashioned it into a hook. "Lean close."

Melissa moved as far forward as she could, finding the limits of the chain when her neck came a few inches from the bars of Henrietta's cage. Henrietta reached through and grabbed hold of the collar in one hand. She inserted the bobby pin in the lock and fished around, poking and probing the inner mechanism.

Melissa kept her voice to a low whisper. "You warned me about Belle, but what about the others?"

"Oh, Belle is crazy. Don't trust her. She wants to be down here, and I wouldn't count on the others either. They've been here a long time from what little I can gather. He's great at instilling fear and turning it into an impulse to please. Trust me, I know." Henrietta's fingers rattled, scraping the bobby pin against the metal of the collar.

"What about the man?"

Henrietta pursed her lips. "He's a fighter. But, I'm afraid for him."

Melissa sighed. "You said there's no way out of here?"

"Only that door."

"There has to be another way. A man like Pierce seems too obsessive to leave himself only one way out. Have you noticed any drafts?"

"Drafts?" She bit her lower lip as she worked. Her brows furrowed with concentration.

"You know evidence of another exit? The tunnel coming down here was elaborate. I'm betting there's another way out."

"I don't know."

Snick.

"You did it!" Melissa gasped as the lock opened.

She unfastened the collar and threw it away with disgust. The leather swung in an arc dangling from its chain. She felt her throat and reached for Henrietta's hands. The contact of soft, warm flesh soothed her nerves, giving her strength.

"Now, how do I get you out of this cage?" She moved to the bars at the front and looked at the combination lock on the door. Her eyes lifted, widening with alarm to meet Henrietta's. "What do I do?"

Henrietta's breath stuttered out of her chest. "I know the first number is six. And the last is four or five, but I could never see the middle numbers."

It amazed her the woman had seen any of the numbers at all. Talk about paying attention to details.

"You're brilliant." She crouched down and set the first tumbler to six and the last to four. She moved the middle two dials around, moving from zero-zero to nine-nine, but nothing happened.

"It's not working," Henrietta said with a moan.

"Give me a chance."

Melissa turned the last dial to five and tried again. Nothing. She pressed her lips together, concentrating as she reset the tumblers and moved the dials again. The lock refused to budge. She leaned back and looked up at Henrietta. "Are you certain you saw the right numbers?"

"I thought so. I made myself pay attention, no matter how scared I was. He always unlocks the cage and leaves the lock hanging. It makes it easier for him to lock us back inside when he's …um… when he's through with us."

God, Melissa didn't even want to think about that.

"I'm certain."

"But not about the last number?"

"I only saw it once, and I think he bumped it when he dragged me out. I remember him having to turn it one turn."

"Maybe it was a three?" Melissa set to the task again, turning the last tumbler to three, but nothing budged. Her eyes glanced to the dungeon door. She didn't know how long the men would be gone. When she looked back at the locks, her eyes caught the numbers, and her breath hitched in her throat.

"Oh my," she said with rising excitement.

Her hands trembled as she turned the first tumbler.

"What are you doing? I know for sure that was a six."

She thumbed the dial to number nine. "I believe you, but Henrietta, you were looking at it from the top. The numbers were upside down to you." She turned the third tumbler back to four and then moved the dials. The lock opened with a solid clunk when she reached twenty-one.

"You did it," Henrietta exclaimed. Her hands flew to her chest. Her fingers entwined, and she kissed her knuckles as if giving thanks to a prayer answered. "Oh my." Wide, frightened eyes glanced at Melissa. "Now what?"

"We help him." Melissa pointed to the man chained to the wall. She glanced at the wall of implements and suppressed a shudder. "Then we arm ourselves. Three against two? Maybe we can get some of the others to help?"

Henrietta shook her head. "No. They won't help, or if they do, it won't be us they're helping. I'm telling you, he has them brainwashed."

Her attention turned to the rows of cages. Belle, the one who seemed most devoted to Pierce, slept quietly. Melissa had seen the crazed look in the woman's eyes and trusted Henrietta, but she wasn't sure about the others.

She removed the lock and opened the door to Henrietta's cage. The two women exchanged a hug.

"I'm terrified," Henrietta admitted.

"Me, too," Melissa said. "Come." She headed to the wall.

The man stilled as they approached. His head lifted. The gag in his mouth kept him silent. Melissa strode toward him, determined to remove the hood and the evil gag.

"My name is Melissa."

Henrietta moved to the side wall. Melissa cocked her head and gave Henrietta a questioning look.

"There's a mechanism in the wall that holds the chains. I've watched him use it." Henrietta opened a wooden panel and reached inside.

Henrietta struggled with something, but Melissa turned her attention back to the man and watched his deep, painful breaths.

She unfastened the gag, helping to guide it out of his mouth as he struggled. She could only imagine the strain the gag had placed on his jaw. The hood was wet from the saliva dripping out of his mouth, an effect of the gag. He said nothing, working his jaw in slow circles. She reached around the back of his head and undid the buckles securing the hood in place.

"I almost have it." Henrietta's voice pinched with strain. "Why is this so hard?"

Melissa pulled the hood off and stared.

"Charles? Oh my God, Charles!"

"I got it," Henrietta squealed in victory.

The thick chains rattled as whatever had held them in place released. The man crumpled to the floor, leaving Melissa holding a black hood.

Charles glanced up.

"What happened to you?" Melissa couldn't believe her eyes and dropped to wrap her arms around his tortured body. Tears streamed down her cheeks.

"Miss Evans," he croaked.

"Can you move?" So many questions flashed through her mind. She stroked his head, combing back his sweat-soaked hair.

He flexed his shoulders and groaned. "Give me a moment." His breath hissed between his teeth, cueing her into the tremendous pain he must be in.

"You know him?" Henrietta knelt beside him.

"He was my nurse."

"What are the odds?"

Charles struggled to move. "I can't feel my arms, and my legs are asleep."

"Let me rub them," Melissa said. "It will help with the circulation."

He shook his head. "No. Who knows when those two will be back. Go." His chin jerked toward the wall with the implements. "Grab something. Get ready for when they return."

"We can't take them alone." Melissa examined the cuffs around his right wrist and pulled on the straps. "We're in luck." She pointed. "I can pick these locks." After freeing him of the wrist cuffs, she turned her attention to his ankles.

They worked on unfastening the cuffs.

"You rest. Let the circulation return to your arms and legs." She tossed the cuffs to the side and placed a hand on his shoulder. "I'm so sorry."

He gave her an odd look. "For what? I did this to myself. I thought he was…" Charles hung his head. "Never mind. This isn't your fault."

She didn't believe him. What were the chances her nurse had been picked by the man who had been planning her kidnapping?

"I need…a moment," Charles said through a mask of pain. He might be free of his restraints, but she was afraid Henrietta was right. He wouldn't be much use when the men returned.

She hurried over to the wall and joined Henrietta before the rows of implements. Henrietta held a thick rod in one hand and a whip in the other.

She turned to Melissa. "I don't know which one is better."

"Take both," she said. "I'm going for a cane because I know I can use it. I've never used one of those whips before. I don't think I'd cause any damage with it."

Henrietta snapped the whip, and it cracked in the air. "I've seen him use it often enough." She held it out to Melissa. "Take both. We'll hit them with the canes, and if that doesn't work, we'll whip them." She pulled a third cane and a thick wooden paddle from the wall. "These are for Charles." Her voice dropped to a whisper. "Let's hope he recovers enough to use them. So what's our plan?"

Melissa waved her chosen cane in the air. It felt weird, almost too light to do any real damage, but she knew from experience how crippling it could be and how much it hurt.

She went to the door. "We wait. Ambush them when they come back. With all those locks, we should have plenty of notice."

FIFTY-SIX

Unexpected Guests

PIERCE

I OPENED THE CUPBOARDS IN MY KITCHEN AND THEN SLAMMED THEM shut, harder than necessary, not finding what I was looking for. Letting my irritation show with Scott was a bad idea, but I was mad, and maybe a little excited, too. I know it doesn't make sense to me either.

It was incredible down there. We were side-by-side, swinging our whips and soaking in delicious screams. I'd never had an experience like that. Not with him. Not with anyone ever again.

Fear sweat, the most delicious aroma in the world, still tickled my nose. And, thank God I hadn't passed out with that orgasm. It had been risky, but Belle knew how best to handle me. She protected me as much or more than I protected her.

Allowing him inside my most treasured space still had my skin crawling. Within one breath and the next, I both hated and admired him. But, he had the heart of a killer and was more than capable of bringing everything I'd worked to build crashing down around me.

My princesses depended on me for their lives. He needed to leave.

"I'm hungry," I called out. "I'm fixing a sandwich; do you want something?"

Scott walked around my kitchen island, dragging his hand over the marble surface. His dark eyes held mine with a wildness I couldn't match. At that moment, he measured and weighed me, leaving me to wonder what he found. Was I still his pupil, or had I become his equal? We were both sizing each other up, assessing strengths, weaknesses, liabilities, and threats.

"Yeah, sounds good. Do you mind if I use your bathroom?"

The man had used my princess for a blowjob, caned my Queen, and was bothering to ask permission to use my restroom? You see how crazy he is, right?

"Second door on the left." I pointed down the hall.

I busied myself, pulling out supplies to make sandwiches. Where was the mayonnaise? It was close to dinnertime, and I would've rather pulled out steak and grilled it the way I liked, but splitting a steak with Scott felt too much like sharing a meal. I didn't want him to get too comfortable. Holding the door to the fridge open with my shoulder, I poked my head inside and dug for condiments, thinking about getting rid of him.

The problem of him not having a car hadn't escaped me. His escape plan seemed poorly thought out and not at all what I expected from the man who taught me to plan for every contingency.

The doorbell rang.

Just what I didn't need. I continued my search for the mayonnaise and ignored the front door.

No one came to my house unless they were selling things. Whoever it was could move on to the next home and sell whatever it was to my neighbor. Not to mention, there was no way in hell I was answering the door with The Fairytale Serial Killer, a guest in my home.

I wasn't an idiot.

There it was, hiding behind the milk. I shut the door to the fridge with mayo in hand and heard the squeal of the front door hinges as it opened.

"Well, hello! Have I died and gone to heaven?"

What the hell was that idiot thinking?

Hastily, I put everything down and edged my way to where I could see the front room.

Bubbly female laughter floated through the house.

"We're organizing a charity event for our sorority, and we're hoping to get the neighborhood involved by sponsoring our event. We're taking donations of used clothing and other items."

Scott's low appreciative growl told me that conversation headed in a dangerous direction. I didn't know how to stop him, but I hurried to the living room, determined to get that girl to the house next door.

Unfortunately, he already invited her inside. My front door creaked closed, sealing her inside with him, a lethal predator, and me, the man now responsible for protecting her.

"Ah, Pierce," he said. "Look what landed on our doorstep."

My doorstep, you bastard, not ours.

"Good evening." I gave the girl my best smile.

Scott maneuvered her to the love seat, gesturing for her to take a seat. He gave the blonde a suggestive wink. Dear lord, her breasts were huge.

She soaked up Scott's attention, even wiggled her tits. A slow smile of anticipation stretched across Scott's face.

"My name's Charlie," she said.

"Nice to meet you," I replied.

Charlie's boobs bounced as she sat in the overstuffed love seat.

"My name's Scott," My unwanted houseguest sat opposite her in my favorite wing-backed chair. I took the empty one beside him.

"You said you were looking for sponsors for an event?"

"The run-walk is a charitable event for the local women's shelter, and we're looking for donations of clothing, women's and children's sizes, and soaps and shampoos. The best are those little hotel-sized bottles you get when you travel. We pack those up into gift packs for the women. You'd be amazed at how much these women have lost." She launched into her speech about battered women, her sorority's charity work, and the plans for the 5K walk/run.

Scott listened with avid attention; it focused on Charlie's tits, a fact Charlie seemed to capitalize on. Maybe she thought it would get her a more substantial donation. Little did she know, her breasts would lead to her death. Scott's eyes widened with each bounce and jiggle, and I knew what request he would soon make of me.

I don't enjoy killing and only did so when necessary. Take, for example, the nurse downstairs. Killing him was unavoidable, and nothing I would take pleasure in.

Scott, however, took perverse pleasure in death. Am I a bad person because there's a bit of me that hungered to see what that would be like? To stand beside him and watch him work?

It's not that I wanted to see the blonde die, but could I pass on this opportunity? Would it be a proper send-off to give him this one gift? It would keep him away from my princesses, that was certain.

"Well, I'm all for supporting a cause," Scott said with a laugh. "Anything I can do to help those in need is a worthwhile endeavor."

Charlie leaned toward him, pressing her ample breasts together to enhance her already astounding cleavage. She batted her lashes, and I coughed at how blatant she was acting. Didn't she know how foolish that was?

"Oh, that's wonderful! We could use all the donations we can get."

He moved to sit beside her, and to my surprise, she didn't back away. In fact, his move seemed to encourage her.

She put a hand on Scott's thigh, a bit too high, and it was clear her fingers were suggesting what sort of thank you would be delivered.

"Well, how nice." Scott's breath hitched. "Are you expected anywhere soon?" Scott nuzzled her ear with his nose.

"No."

Scott gave a low chuckle. "Darling, do you have any idea what you're getting yourself into?"

The girl pouted and drew back. "I think I have a good idea of what comes next." Her eyes shifted to the hall and to the bedrooms beyond.

Scott smiled. His straight white teeth glinted in the overhead light. His gaze caught mine, asking permission.

I nodded. Despite the risks, I desperately wanted to see him at work.

"Charlie, my friend, and I are a little…unconventional," he said. "How adventurous are you feeling?"

Her eyes widened. "I like unconventional."

"We have a playroom in the basement. Much more fun than the bedroom."

Charlie clapped her hands. "Oh, you're kinky!"

I loved college co-eds. They were curious and open to new experiences.

Just then, Scott's stomach growled. It was loud, unexpected, and broke the mood. It also reminded me of my hunger and the reason we had come upstairs.

Scott's booming laugh filled the room. "How about we grab a bite to eat? Pierce and I were just about to make sandwiches when you knocked on our door. Are you hungry?"

Charlie bit her lower lip, looking uncertain.

"Come," he said, leading her toward the kitchen. "I'll have much more fun if I'm not thinking about my stomach. We have all night to play."

She gave a slight smile. "Um, do you mind if I use your restroom?"

I gestured toward the hallway. "Second door on the left."

"Thank you," she said in a soft tone.

Scott and I moved to the kitchen, where I pulled out a third plate.

"I want her," he said in a lowered voice.

"I know."

He returned a surprised look.

"She's yours." Warmth surged in my chest to give him this gift.

"And I can—"

"Do whatever you want." I finished his sentence, giving him the affirmative he wanted to hear.

"And your rule about blood?"

I wrinkled my nose, thinking about the mess. "Just keep it contained."

Scott crossed his arms over his chest. "How are we going to get her down there?"

"You already told her the playroom was downstairs. We'll take her down. I keep my supplies down there. You finish up here while I go prep."

I headed to the back of my basement, past the long ordered rows of emergency supplies, and stopped short of my wine collection.

Opening a nondescript box, I pulled out a bottle of clear fluid and grabbed a couple dish rags. I saturated two cloths and placed them within easy reach beside the wine rack. The rags should stay moist enough until we brought the girl downstairs.

I grabbed a bottle of Merlot as a smile filled my face. Beer was good for a casual drink. Tonight deserved something special.

There were so many ways I could work this. My Queen waited for my attention. I wanted to take her tonight but felt awkward doing so in front of Scott. Did I claim my Queen? Or, did I fuck one of the others? I hated tough decisions. Belle would be fun. I could use her to show what I expected from my Queen.

When I came upstairs, the lilting laughter of the girl echoed through my home. Interspersed through her energetic chatter, Scott's more guttural tones grated on my ears. He had Charlie on the kitchen counter, feeding her a sandwich. Charlie giggled as he teased her with the food, pulling it away from her lips at the last second.

"A kiss for a bite, my pretty."

Didn't anyone teach this ravishing beauty to be wary of strangers? Her eyes kept darting down to the basement like she couldn't wait to get down there.

If she only knew she would never leave. I took my time with my food. There was no reason to rush, besides Scott was feeding Charlie her last meal.

I walked my plate over to the sink. "Last chance to back out," I called over my shoulder.

Charlie shrugged. "Oh, I'm good."

I turned on the water. "Go freshen up. Scott and I will clean the dishes." I waved her toward the living room, making it an order by the tone of my voice. I pointed to the dirty plates, indicating he should bring them over. She disappeared back into the living room and down the hall.

"You've got to be fucking kidding me?" Scott slammed the plates on the counter. "We're stopping to do the dishes?"

"Don't be an idiot."

His eyes widened, and he took half a step back. His fingers clenched into fists, and his arms flexed.

Seriously? I grabbed his shirt and pulled him close before his temper ran too far afield. Was he that stupid? "Do you want to know the plan or go in blind?"

My words mollified him. His shoulders relaxed, and his jaw unclenched. His head dipped.

I whispered. "I soaked rags in chloroform. They're sitting on the shelves just before the wine cellar. We take her down, subdue her there, then carry her to the dungeon. We'll tie her up once we're inside."

He rubbed his hands together with anticipation. He was a sick fuck.

But then I wondered, who was more messed up? The man who would torture, rape, and kill a young girl or the one who would watch?

What do you think?

FIFTY-SEVEN

Curtains

CJ

"There!" Movement in a window of the house caught CJ's eye. He waved to Mac to get his attention.

Mac squinted and stared at the suburban house.

"She's unlocking the windows."

A minute later, a curtain flapped in the second bedroom. The third bedroom faced opposite the street so they couldn't tell if she'd unlocked that one as well. Probably not, it would be too risky.

"She better not get caught," CJ said with concern. His skin itched to rush inside the house, take down the men, and save Melissa. Instead, he and Mac jogged up and crouched below the window.

"She knows what she's doing," Mac said, "Those assholes are cleaning up the lunch dishes before taking her downstairs. I'm sure she's in the clear."

"She'd better leave soon."

Part of him wanted Charlie to go with the men downstairs. That order had been one of her instructions, and he needed to know if Melissa was in the house. It was a dangerous gamble, and he prayed he didn't regret it later. He'd never risk Charlie's safety with such a bold move, but he trusted her ability to take care of herself. If he'd been able to send Jenny inside as well, he'd feel a lot better. He reminded himself Charlie was alone. No matter how well trained, she was outnumbered. Which meant they had to be ready to act.

He rapped on the glass, making sure he was concealed behind the bushes, damn things were filled with thorns.

Using Morse code, he sent her a message. If unsafe, outside now.

With a tap on the glass, she replied. GTG. Which meant she was good to go.

He blew out his breath. The final decision would be hers to make. He hated being so far removed from the action. Helpless. That's how he felt.

Mac's jaw was set. He'd sunk into attack mode. CJ felt the mood hit him, too. That moment before a mission when the world narrowed into crystalline focus and life balanced on a knife's edge.

There was a loud knock on the inner door. Charlie's squeak was followed by a deep masculine voice. "You going to stay in there all day, or do you want to play? Pierce and I are getting impatient."

"I'll be right out."

Damn. He hoped she could extricate herself without raising suspicion.

She tapped on the glass. Five. Then come.

Anything could happen in the next five minutes.

FIFTY-EIGHT

Light's Out!

PIERCE

I WAITED IN THE KITCHEN WHILE SCOTT FETCHED THE GIRL. HER lilting laughter sounded from the front room, letting me know it was time. Our guest walked into the kitchen. Scott had his arm around the blonde. He gave me a grin and arched a brow.

"Come." I stepped forward and extended a hand.

She did a little hop-step, the excited bounce broadcasting her eagerness to die. Her delicate fingers warmed my palm. Soon, they would be slick with fear, then cold as death.

"Let's head downstairs." I smiled, trying to do my best to make her feel comfortable, but my comment didn't return the eagerness I'd expected.

"Um," she said, "I don't know about this. I think maybe I should go."

"Oh?" I tried to hide the disappointment in my voice, "Stay and play awhile."

Her eyes shifted toward the living room and to the front door. I couldn't afford to lose her, not when we were so close. Her sacrifice would protect my princesses.

"I really think I should go."

No!

"We won't keep you, but you came for donations. I have boxes of supplies downstairs. You can have whatever you see."

She hesitated, but then seemed to remember why she'd stopped at my door—her need to make her charitable donation quota would be her end. Sorority girls were so dumb.

I led her down the steps, and Scott followed.

Keeping her close, I hoped Scott was smart enough to work with me. Timing was vital. I had to get the chloroform and smother her until I was sure she was out.

Charlie glanced at the rows of supplies. "Wow, you have tons down here. Are you one of those disaster prep guys?"

"Kind of. Come, the women's clothes are in the back." I draped my arm over her shoulder, tugging her close.

"Cool," she said. Her breathy voice annoyed me.

"Pierce was an Eagle Scout, Charlie," Scott chimed in. "He's always prepared."

I forgot I'd shared that with him. The guy was supposed to be dead, not wandering around my basement, messing up my life.

We finally made it to the wine cellar.

"Oh my," she said. "What a collection."

Yes, and behind the wine, a door led down a tunnel to my dungeon. For Charlie, it would be the last trip she ever made.

I grabbed the rag saturated in chloroform. She gave a look, then her eyes widened when I pressed the cloth to her nose and mouth, pinning her arms to her sides. She kicked at me, but she was no match for my strength. Oddly, she never screamed, but I was confident she breathed the foul substance in because her body went limp. Too much chloroform could be disastrous, so I removed the rag. She sagged like a sack of potatoes. A quick check of her pulse revealed her resting comfortably.

"How is she?" Scott's grin stretched tight across his face. He tried to lift her limp body into a fireman's carry, grunted with the effort, then looked for help.

Flabby bastard.

I helped him hoist her over his shoulder.

"How long before she comes around?"

I shrugged. "We have a few minutes. Don't worry."

The wine racks moved to the side, and I opened the locks. I had done this so many times I could do it in my sleep. Scott pressed himself beside me, too eager to get into the tunnel. I swallowed a curse as he bumped me, but I didn't have time to deal with his rudeness.

Charlie's arms hung limply down his back, hitting my butt as I turned to re-secure the door.

He was already at the far end of the tunnel, shifting back and forth with poorly concealed impatience for me to join him. I took my time because it would piss him off, and I had to check the locks.

One. Two. Three.

Four. Five. Six.

"Hurry." He waved me forward.

I didn't.

He pointed to the locks on the final door. “Open them.” He rubbed a hand over his face. There was a thin sheen of sweat on his forehead. “Hurry.”

I leveled a stare at him. “Relax, we have plenty of time before she comes to.” I lifted her arm and released it. Her arm flopped. No muscle tone, well, maybe a hint. She would be waking soon.

His eyes were wide and black. There was a fierceness in his expression, a hint of crazy that gave me a moment’s pause, but I continued with the locks.

We had an agreement.

Tonight only, then he would leave. If he didn’t, I had no problems killing him along with Dickwad inside.

His blood lust was too dangerous, and I had responsibilities. Finally, I pulled the last lock free and cranked on the door mechanism pushing the door inward.

Scott shouldered past me, Charlie’s limp body bouncing against his back. A new wave of irritation washed over me.

A loud *thwack!* sounded.

“Fuck!” Scott screamed.

Thwack! Whoosh! Snap!

A body thumped to the floor.

“You fucking bitch!”

Thwack! Thwack! Thwack!

I rushed inside—a bolt of pain connected with my shoulder.

“What the…”

The sting of a whip wrapped around my waist, taking my breath away as fire lit up my world.

Thwack! Thwack!

Swish!

Something solid connected with my ribs.

Whoosh! Snap!

A fucking cane!

Pain became my universe.

My ribs cracked under the pressure of the strike. A whip caught my cheek. Something smacked into my back, catapulting me forward onto the ground. I covered my face with my hands just in time to see my Fairy Godmother raise her arm and flick the whip.

FIFTY-NINE

Escape

MELISSA

THE CANE TWISTED IN MELISSA'S GRIP. HER HANDS WERE CRAMPED from holding it tight. The sound of metal rasping on the other side of the door had her stomach tangling in knots. Pierce was undoing the locks. A look of pure terror filled Henrietta's face. Melissa swallowed her fear. At least one of them needed to be strong.

It was now or never.

Dear God, she could die!

Charles lumbered over. Something wasn't right with the way he moved his legs. She waved him away, but he gave a determined glare like there was no way in hell she was keeping him from helping out. Not that she could fault him. Live or die, they would do it together.

Charles positioned himself behind the door and took the paddle Henrietta offered. His expression was nearly as fierce as the mother of two. Melissa's blood chilled.

Belle had been silenced. After Henrietta's concerns, they cuffed and gagged Pierce's first princess. Some sort of crazy lived in Belle's eyes. The others sat in their cages, fearful whimpers accompanied their tearful sobs, but they hadn't shouted a warning. Melissa and Henrietta had debated freeing them, but Henrietta didn't trust the brainwashing the girls had undergone. Not to mention, they didn't have the combinations to the locks.

"Now or never," Henrietta said. "They will kill us for this."

Melissa couldn't speak. She knew the evil beyond that door. The killing would only come after great pain.

When the locks released, she and Henrietta jumped. The door opened inward. Scott stepped through. The cane in Melissa's hand came up and then smacked down. Again and again, she struck, mindless, not with fury, but with suffocating fear.

Whack! Whack! Whack!

Scott dropped something from his shoulders. It landed with a solid thump.

A body? Had they brought another woman down?

There was no time to think.

The whip cracked. Her cane struck.

Scott cursed.

Melissa wielded the cane in one hand and the whip in the other, becoming something wild and altogether not sane.

Her ex-husband fell to his knees, giving her a much better target to aim at. She took advantage of his position and landed another volley of strikes.

Charles kicked Scott. His bare foot smacked Scott's stomach with a squelching sound. Charles brought down the paddle. That thick chunk of wood cracked her ex-husband on the head.

She took a step back, horrified—hell, she was a part of this madness.

A second figure shouldered through the doorway.

Henrietta fell upon Pierce with a ferocity Melissa had never seen before. The twisted expression on Henrietta's face didn't even look human.

And then, to confuse things even more, a blonde flurry of fists, arms, legs, and feet rose from the ground, spinning and kicking in a blur of motion. Melissa couldn't keep track of anything. The blonde concentrated her energy on Pierce, aiding Henrietta's efforts. Somehow, the girl kept out of range of Henrietta's cane.

Melissa staggered back, her hand moving from her mouth to her chest as if that would silence her heart's raging beat.

Charles beat Scott over the head with the paddle and kicked him in the ribs with legs and feet that didn't work quite right. Scott covered his face as he curled into a fetal ball. Charles's assault was relentless.

Henrietta screamed at the top of her lungs. The blonde furry of fists and feet landed blow upon blow on Pierce until he, too, was reduced to a pile of quivering flesh on the floor.

Melissa couldn't make out the words for all the screaming.

Wait! She was screaming, not Henrietta.

The blonde grunted as Pierce gripped her ankle and yanked her to the ground.

"Get a pair of goddamn handcuffs!" The woman yelled.

Melissa paused; this had CJ written all over it. He had to be close.

My Hero!

The woman kicked Pierce in the chin, both of them grappling on the ground.

Henrietta stood over them, looking unsure of what to do, perhaps worried one of her strikes might hurt the unexpected help.

"Get cuffs!" The woman barked again. She put Pierce in a headlock, and his face reddened.

Melissa looked to the wall and scanned for cuffs.

Henrietta shouted. "The bed! Get him to the bed!"

Pierce's face turned an unhealthy shade of purple.

The girl did some judo-flip move, which had her on her feet and Pierce's neck locked in a ninja elbow-hold. With Henrietta's help, she dragged Pierce to the four-poster bed. His mouth opened and closed, gulping for air.

Melissa reached for the collar and closed it around his neck with a satisfying clunk.

Pierce stared back, purple-faced, his eyes bulging with murderous intent.

Henrietta moved to the head of the bed and pulled out a set of metal wrist cuffs attached to long chains. She snapped these around Pierce's wrists before Melissa could blink. Seconds later, a set of ankle cuffs followed.

Melissa glanced toward the open door. Shadows raced toward them growing larger as booted feet echoed down the tunnel. She turned to stand in victory over her tormentor, but the look on the blonde's face made her pause.

A hand gripped Melissa's hair and yanked her head back.

Scott growled. "You fucking, bitch."

Something cold and sharp pressed against her throat.

Scott pulled her against his chest, spinning her toward the door. Pierce had been trussed up like an animal. The blonde stood behind him, holding the chains. Henrietta teetered by her side. Charles was on the ground, blood trickling from his temple, knocked out cold. And there, barreling through the doorway, CJ came to an abrupt stop.

"Come any closer, and I kill her." Scott pressed the knife to her throat.

SIXTY

Escape Take Two

CJ

A FLASH OF SILVER WAS THE FIRST THING CJ SAW, FOLLOWED BY THE whites of Melissa's terrified eyes. His mad dash ended between one step and the next, bringing him to a stuttering stop with his weapon aimed between Scott Patterson's eyes.

Take the shot!

Years of training kicked in. There was no way to assure Melissa's safety, not with the press of a knife against her throat.

Mac was two steps behind him. He gripped CJ's shoulder, but there was no need. It wasn't a clean shot. Jenny side-stepped Mac and swept the room with her gun drawn.

A man lay on the ground, horribly disfigured by whip and cane marks. He labored to breathe, and blood trickled from a gash in his head.

What the fuck was the nurse from the hospital doing here?

No way to know if he was a victim or a threat, but for now, he wasn't conscious.

There were too many fucking people to cover.

Trussed up between the uprights of a four-poster bed, Pierce-fucking-Channing yanked on the chains which bound him. The foulest expression of murder scrawled on his face.

Charlie stood behind him, chains taut in her hands, and beside Charlie, Henrietta Jones trembled, her face ghostly white. Terror shone in her eyes, and her hand covered her mouth, perhaps to stifle a scream.

His quick scan took less than a second. Two rows of cages, four to each side. All but two occupied. The farthest cage held a woman cuffed to the metal bars with a red ball-gag in her mouth.

"Release him," Scott Patterson demanded, "or I swear to God, I'll kill her."

CJ held his gun steady.

Scott jerked Melissa back, and the knife bit into the skin of her throat. A bead of red formed on her ivory skin and trickled down her neck. Melissa tensed.

Charlie stared at CJ, seeking his lead. Jenny edged into the room, her movements slow, deliberate, and meant to flank.

"There's nowhere to go," CJ said. "It's over."

Scott laughed. "As if." He jerked his chin toward Pierce. "I trained him well. I'm betting my life on another way out."

There was a look exchanged between the men, confirming CJ's fears.

"Your guns don't scare me," Scott said. "But I sure as hell bet my knife terrifies you. Release him, or I kill her." Scott jerked the knife against Melissa's throat.

So close. So fucking close.

He wouldn't lose her like this.

Henrietta backed away from the bed until she came up against the bars of one of the nearest cages.

He was glad to have her out of the way. It would make whatever came next easier. He tapped Mac's hand, which dug into his shoulder. "Check on him."

Mac bent down, placing a finger to the man's throat. "He's alive."

Brett and Jon were in the tunnel behind them but kept themselves out of sight. He could only imagine the fire burning in their bellies, knowing Charlie was inside, but they were well-trained and knew the mission came first.

Pierce's sharp command echoed in the dungeon. "Release me!"

CJ could kill Scott, but not before the lunatic put his knife to its intended use. There wasn't a clear shot that wouldn't place Melissa at unacceptable risk. With his gut-churning, CJ put his faith in his team.

"Release him," Scott growled.

Charlie removed the cuffs. Pierce ran his fingers around the metal band encircling his neck, pulled a key out of his pocket, and popped the lock.

The next few moments brought a bead of sweat to CJ's brow. He was playing a dangerous game of chess.

Scott pulled Melissa toward the back wall. A look of resignation filled her face and something else, undeniable trust.

He hoped he was worthy of that trust.

Pierce left Charlie at the bed and stormed over to the cage holding the woman with the ball gag in her mouth. She gazed at him, adoration filling her face. He petted the top of her head and worked the combination lock to the cell.

"Belle, will you serve me?" Pierce released the gag, easing it out from behind her teeth.

"Master," she said with a bow of her head. "How may I serve?"

"You must go upstairs."

Her head snapped up, a look of terror scrawled on her face.

"I know, Belle. You must leave your home, but only until we find another."

Her body trembled, but she agreed to his demand with a nod.

Pierce undid the cuffs binding her wrists.

"We don't have fucking time for this." Scott hissed.

"I won't leave Belle. Besides," Pierce said with a snort, "how the fuck do you think we're going to get away on foot?"

CJ glanced between the two men, feeling the tension spike between them.

Pierce made soothing sounds to the woman as he gave instructions. "Go upstairs. Get the keys to the van. Bring it around. You know where?"

Belle nodded.

CJ put a hand behind him and signaled Mac, knowing he would telegraph the message back to Brett and Jon, who hid in the tunnel. Mac took a step back to relay the code.

Upstairs. Girl. Van. Be inside.

He didn't hear Brett and Jon retreat, but he would have killed them if he had.

Belle fell to her knees. "Master," she said in a breathy whisper. "I'm so scared."

Her eyes flicked toward CJ, Mac, and Jenny. They blocked her exit from the dungeon with cold steel gripped in their hands.

"Be brave, my slave," Pierce said. He kissed the top of her head and then removed his shirt. "Put this on. Can't have you driving naked. The keys are on the kitchen counter. You remember where to go?"

She nodded.

"Good."

Pierce's eyes darkened when the sweep of his gaze landed on Jenny. He stepped back, wary of the three guns trained on his chest.

"No way in hell is that happening," Mac said with a rumble.

"The two of you will let Belle pass," Pierce spoke as if they would do as he commanded.

Mac leaned forward, his bulk intimidating Pierce into taking an involuntary step back.

"Put those down," Pierce demanded, "and kick them this way." He jerked his chin at Jenny. "You too, Princess."

CJ's mind worked the puzzle pieces in his head, moving his resources on a virtual board of chess. If there was another way out of this hellhole like Scott suggested, he needed to buy time for Brett and Jon. It was a risk, but one he was willing to take.

They were at a standoff with Melissa's life hanging by a thread. Losing the weapons was a gamble, but he believed in his team.

He lowered his weapon and placed it on the ground.

"CJ," Mac growled.

"Trust me."

He twisted the radio frequency ID ring on his finger. Their guns could only be activated in proximity to the rings worn on their trigger fingers. He kicked his weapon toward the middle of the room and prayed Pierce didn't attempt to take a shot. Glancing at the women in the cages, he made an assumption about the tension clogging the air between Pierce and Scott.

One was a killer. The other was not.

He gambled the lives of everyone on a hunch Pierce wouldn't kill.

Mac breathed out, then followed CJ's lead. His gun went skittering across the ground to join CJ's.

"Now yours," Pierce said to Jenny. "Kick your weapon over."

CJ didn't like having his entire team disarmed, but with Brett and Jon outside, the edge of surprise remained theirs. And Sam should arrive soon with even more reinforcements.

A triumphant grin filled Pierce's face when Jenny slid her weapon over to join the others. Pierce directed Belle to gather the guns. The woman scurried to the middle of the room and scooped up their pistols.

CJ's chest squeezed, then released when Belle handed his and Mac's weapons to Pierce and gave Jenny's to Patterson.

Pierce shoved Mac's weapon under his waistband and gripped CJ's gun. If Pierce tried to fire the weapon, he would discover the RFID lock.

Pierce's smile flashed greasy white. "Belle, you have always served me well."

"Thank you, Master," she said in a whisper.

"But you're not done yet."

She shuddered and glanced at the doorway leading out of the room.

"Lock the door on your way out."

Lock the door?

Melissa was too far away. While he and Mac could subdue Pierce, Jenny wouldn't have enough time to close in on and disarm Scott.

Melissa would die.

Pierce waved Belle toward the door. She scurried to obey, keeping as wide a berth from CJ and Mac as she could. She stepped over the unconscious man, then pulled the door shut. Metal rasped on metal, the sound of locks engaging.

CJ took in a deep breath. His team was unarmed and locked in. Time for the final move to play out, but he hadn't made it this far in his career by being a fool. Pierce didn't know it, but he'd made a juvenile mistake.

So far, everything was coming together, even if it didn't look like it. Pierce might discover the RFID locks on the triggers. If that happened, someone would die. But CJ had a feeling Pierce didn't enjoy killing. Scott was the wild card.

"You're going to rot down here," Pierce said with a snort.

"And what of them?" CJ waved to the rows of cages.

Pierce flinched. "Casualties I must accept." He breathed in and forced the breath out, looking resolute. He cocked his head.

CJ expected a reaction from the women, but only a soul-wrenching nothingness returned from the cages.

Pierce condemned these women to death, and not a single one reacted? What had he done to steal the life from them?

Pierce moved to a spot behind Belle's cage. He pried a panel off the wall, revealing a mechanism inside, and pulled on a lever. The wall behind Belle's cage slid to the side, revealing another tunnel.

Pierce gave instructions to Scott. "Go. I'm right behind you."

Scott forced Melissa into the tunnel, and Pierce followed. A few seconds later, the concrete slab slid back in place, leaving CJ, Mac, and Jenny trapped inside.

"I hope you know what you're doing," Mac growled.

Mac turned to the woman standing behind Charlie. "Where does he keep the keys?"

She rubbed her hands together and brought them to her mouth as if saying a prayer. "He carries them on him, and the cages are combination locks."

Mac went to the box on the far wall. "Fucking lever won't budge." He went to one of the cages and looked at the woman inside. "What's your name?"

The poor thing shook and buried her head in her hands.

"Shh," Mac cooed. "I promise we're going to get you out. This nightmare is over."

"Beauty, my name is Beauty."

Mac cocked his head. "No, sweetie. That isn't your name. It never was. Now, tell me who you are?"

"Is he gone?" She flinched when Mac rested his hand on one of the bars of her cage.

"He's gone."

"My name is Sarah, Sarah Mackenzie."

CJ called out. "Well, Sarah, you're getting out of here. Mac get over here. Jenny and Charlie find a way to break those locks."

A groan sounded from the floor. The unconscious man was coming around. He lifted himself to his elbow, and with great effort, struggled to a sitting position.

"What happened?" he asked.

"Do you think you can stand?" Mac reached down to help the man to his feet.

"Not just yet. I'm getting there, though." He shook his head, waving off Mac's help.

"Why do you look familiar?" Mac asked.

"We met at the hospital when Miss Evans was discharged."

Pierce had been there, too; the deliveryman with the rose. If he and Mac had arrived a few minutes later, Melissa might have disappeared from the world for good.

"How did you get here?" CJ asked.

Charles huffed a laugh. "Because I was stupid and didn't mind my drink. At least, I think that's how he got me. Nothing else makes sense. I went to a bar, talked to him, and things get fuzzy from there. Next I know, I'm strapped against that wall, and he demands that I take care of Gretel." He pointed to the one woman who had yet to move.

CJ turned to Henrietta. "Henrietta Jones?"

Her eyes widened with shock.

"Name is CJ. This is Mac. Charlie and Jenny are also on my team. I know two little girls who will be very happy to have their mother back. We've been looking for you."

"Are my girls okay?"

"They are."

Henrietta lifted her gaze to the ceiling, mouthing another prayer. "I wanted to believe. Melissa told me not to lose hope." A look of hopelessness crossed her face. "Oh dear God, what are they going to do to her?"

"Don't worry. Melissa will be fine."

He turned his attention to getting out and joining the rest of his team.

"Help me with the door," he said to Mac.

"How? It's locked from the other side."

He ran his hands around the edges and landed on the hinges. "This door might be locked, but it swings inward. It's a rookie mistake."

"So?" Mac's gaze traced the lines of the door.

CJ tapped the hinge holding the door in place

“We pull the pins, and the door comes off. Now, let’s get out of here.”

SIXTY-ONE

A Tunnel

MELISSA

Melissa's lunatic ex-husband had one hand wrapped around her waist. The other held a knife to her throat. The cold metal edge of the knife pressed against her fragile skin. She squeezed her eyes shut, not sure what scared her more, that he would slip and fall, killing her, or that he wouldn't, and this horrible moment would never end.

The door slid closed, taking the light with it. Dank, musty smells filled her nostrils, cloying in her mouth. The air reeked of death. Her death.

"There's a switch to your right," Pierce called out.

"Where?"

"Stretch your arm out; you'll feel it about waist high."

"Don't try anything stupid." Scott increased the pressure of the knife against her throat.

The rough sound of his fingers sliding against stone scratched in her ears. With the flick of a switch, light flooded her world with the steady illumination of yellow incandescence.

Pierce reached into a pocket and retrieved a set of handcuffs. "I'm going to cuff my Queen."

A trickle of blood pooled at the hollow of her neck, turning sticky as it dried. She had no idea how deep Scott had cut, but she was still breathing. Still alive. The pinch of pain across her throat helped focus her thoughts.

Pierce grabbed her hand, yanking her arm behind her back. Before she could think, he had both her hands cuffed. His breath heated her neck.

"You'll pay for your disobedience, my Queen. Don't think for a minute you won't." He punctuated each word with a short jerk on her wrist.

She swallowed against the cry struggling to get free. He didn't deserve her tears, but they flowed anyway. Nostrils flaring, he smelled her hair, then her neck. Her eyes widened, and a low whimper escaped her throat.

"So, what the hell are we doing?" Scott asked. "What's our plan?"

"Belle will meet us." Pierce gestured down the dirt tunnel. "This opens into a culvert at the back of my property where it backs up to the forest. She'll be there with the van."

"And then what?"

"Contingency plans."

"You put a lot of trust in a slave."

Pierce shouldered past Scott, pushing Melissa ahead of him. "You don't know Belle. Come! It's not far, but we need to hurry."

The faint yellow light cast dark shadows in front of them. The rough ground clawed at her feet, stubbing her toes, causing her to cry out. Pierce forced her forward, holding her when she stumbled and pushed to keep her moving.

Even though CJ was trapped in that horrible room, she had every faith he'd rescue her again. He wouldn't have let them take her if he didn't have a plan. Her eyes closed while she said a prayer.

Pierce's firm grip held her up. "Careful where you step," he cautioned.

A shiver worked its way down her spine at the concern laced in his voice. Pierce had a whole different crazy going on. Whereas Scott was a murdering psychopath, Pierce believed he was the good guy.

Darkness shrouded the tunnel as the light from the single bulb faded behind them. Melissa slowed, feeling her way forward with her toes. Pierce pressed against her back, his breath heavy on her neck, and his hand encouraging her forward with a gentle insistence.

"Just a little further, my Queen. We're almost there."

She squinted against the dimness. Up ahead, shadows became more distinct, and the ceiling dropped. The mustiness of the tunnel intensified, tickling her nose into a sneeze. Her foot splashed in a puddle of water. Slick, she lost her footing and slipped, but Pierce protected her from injury.

"Careful." He lifted and steadied her on her feet.

Behind them, Scott's ragged breathing rattled in the darkness.

"How fucking long is this tunnel. Is the roof caving in?" Her husband had never been fond of dark places.

"Not much further," Pierce said.

"Shit, I can't see a thing."

"The tunnel curves to the left." He guided her by applying pressure to her back.

Sure enough, the tunnel turned, and the ceiling dropped even lower until she hunched over and shuffled in the growing stream of water beneath her feet. Rock and slime turned to mud, which now squished beneath her feet. Thinking about what she was walking through was only slightly less nauseating than who followed her through the tunnel.

The only positive was the faint light at the end of the tunnel. The dim glow brightened with each step, providing a radiance that bounced off the tunnel's roughhewn rock. When she dared to look down, the muck at her feet glistened with a greenish cast.

They came upon a grate with a lock. Pierce handed her to Scott.

"There's a key I keep under a rock." Pierce stooped to move a pile of rocks, tossing stones to the side in his search.

Scott whispered in her ear. "I'm going to fuck you until you bleed. You'll watch as I kill him. Until death do us part, Melissa. Do you remember your vows?"

A shudder shot down to the base of her spine. Should she warn Pierce?

Pierce gave a grunt. "Found it." A thick metal key scraped against a rock.

"Your fucking slave had better be waiting outside." Scott nipped at her ear and whispered. "You're going to watch while I kill them both."

"Belle will be there," Pierce affirmed. His confidence seemed unflappable in the faith he placed in that crazy girl.

Melissa's heart slammed against her ribcage, and her pulse roared in her ears. She didn't want to die!

The lock clicked open, and after a lot of squealing of rusting metal, Pierce forced the grate open. He retrieved Melissa and then led her out into a concrete culvert.

Less than a hundred feet away, his white florist's van waited. Standing next to the van, Belle shifted foot-to-foot. She cast her gaze up and down a dirt road and glanced down the culvert. Belle fell to her knees when she saw them, pressing her head to the ground in supplication.

Pierce looked over his shoulder and caught Scott's eyes. "I told you she'd be there."

Scott sniffed.

Once they put Melissa inside that van, she'd never be free. Her feet dug in, refusing to move.

Pierce pushed against her back, but she fought him until he spun her around and lifted her onto his shoulders. He breathed easily, unconcerned with her weight.

"We're almost there."

"About fucking time," Scott said.

In less than a hundred feet, they would arrive at the van. Death waited for her there.

CJ, I really need a hero!

SIXTY-TWO

Devil's Dance

PIERCE

I WOULD KILL SCOTT PATTERSON. HE WAS A FOOL AND DESERVED A slow death—a cancer I needed cut out of my life. He brought a host of holy crap into my lap and cost me the perfect kingdom. In the blink of an eye, that bastard destroyed everything.

Didn't he get the hint when I tossed my Queen over my shoulders and shifted into a jog? I'd been learning from him for years; you'd think he'd follow my lead for once.

But no!

The bastard lumbered behind, no urgency to his step at all. The fool still had the damn knife out. I gave him a gun. Why wasn't he using it? But then, I shoved my gun down next to the blade when I lifted my Queen over my shoulder.

She didn't put up much of a fight. The only reason I carried her was that I didn't want her to think about running. Scott should pay better attention to what might happen and plan more than the next step ahead. We were so fucking vulnerable out here. Unlikely anyone would see us, but in a neighborhood like this, some bored housewife could be out for a jog. We would attract attention and be even more fucked than we were now.

My plan was to load my Queen in the back of the van. Drive. Kill Scott. Dump his worthless flesh the first moment possible. To think I'd ever thought to admire this lunatic.

Damn it. I couldn't kill him. Too messy. Too likely to be traced back to me.

I would tie him up at a filling station or rest stop, and call the cops. They'd take him back into custody where…he would spill every detail of what I've done.

Shit!

He may think he taught me everything I know, but Scott had a lot to learn.

The first would be how to die.

At least my Queen remained blissfully quiet. The shock of the past few moments had to be seeping into her head. She knew her punishment would be severe. It was good her mind turned to such things. Discipline wasn't something I could hold back, but I could reward her for silence. The sooner she learned this simple fact, the easier her life would be.

My heart broke with a glance toward my beautiful and obedient Belle. She did everything I'd asked and even kept the engine running, something I hadn't instructed her to do. God, I loved her perfection.

As we approached, she lifted her head. "Master."

That one word was a breath of beauty in my ears.

"Belle, you have pleased me."

She kept her gaze focused on my feet.

"Up," I said.

As she stood, I granted her my touch, placing my hand on her head so she could feel my mastery.

Behind me, Scott scrambled out of the culvert, his breathing labored with the exertion. I'd hiked out of there carrying my Queen and had barely broken a sweat.

"We going to stand here all day?" Scott looked down the road.

I turned away because I couldn't hide the disgust on my face. Soon I would be rid of him.

"Belle," I commanded, "open the back and climb inside."

"Yes, Master," came her soft-spoken reply.

My blood warmed at the sweet whisper of her words, and my cock twitched.

Belle walked around to the back of the van. Scott and I followed. Our heads were on swivels, scanning the streets.

We were in the clear.

Belle's scream had me twisting with surprise. A dark shape barreled into my shoulder, knocking me to the ground. My Queen landed with a thump underneath me. She screamed. Another blur moved to my right. Muscle smacked on flesh—more screams issued from Belle. Something rolled me. Moved me off my Queen.

"Son of a bitch!" Scott added his screech to this new threat.

My ears rang, and my head throbbed. Fists smacked something solid to my left. Cursing sounded over my shoulder.

Facedown, I struggled against a knee pressed to my spine. My left arm was wrenched behind my back. My attacker grabbed for the other.

A keening sound came from Belle. I had never heard such a strangled cry out of her in all our years together. Out of my periphery, she launched through the air, knocking my attacker off my back.

Feral sounds emanated from her throat. "Get off my Master!" She kicked a man who had a scar traveling from his ear to his jaw. In their struggle, she dislodged a gun from his hand. The weapon went sailing through the air to land ten feet away.

Who the hell were these guys?

I rolled to the side. Belle was a wildcat, all hissing and spitting—so damn beautiful. She gave me exactly the distraction I needed to get free.

I spared a glance to my right. My Queen dragged herself away, hand pressed to her knee. Her brows pulled together, and her forehead creased with pain.

A fist connected with my jaw, bringing my attention back to the man with the scar. He tossed Belle off his back, but she was already lifting herself off the ground and attacking again. As she flew at him, I rolled to my feet, a little unsteady, but prepared to defend or attack.

Belle was on his back, biting his shoulder. He struggled to remove her.

To my left, Scott faced off against another man who raised the barrel of his gun. Scott leaped forward, swinging with his knife and ignoring the gun. A shot fired, but Scott's momentum propelled him forward. He sliced across his attacker's forearm, wresting the gun from the man's hand.

I couldn't spare any more of my attention for Scott. I turned back to the scarred man in front of me who had been disarmed thanks to Belle. He peeled Belle off his back and slammed her to the dirt. She landed with a thud and scrambled back to her feet.

I didn't have time for this. I pulled out the gun I'd taken from the fools locked in my dungeon, pointed and pulled the trigger.

Nothing.

I pulled the trigger again. Nothing! The damn thing was a dud.

I tossed the pistol and reached for my knife.

"Belle, get his gun!"

I lunged with my knife, intending to make quick work of him.

He sidestepped, leaving me slashing at the air. Using my momentum, I pivoted and readied for another strike. I jabbed in a downward arc and was rewarded with a hiss and a stripe of crimson over the man's bicep.

I thrust my knife forward, but he caught my wrist. Twisted it.

Pain shot through my arm, but I wasn't releasing that knife. I stepped forward, the bastard wasn't expecting that, and I head-butted him—our skulls connected with a crack.

He released my wrist, and we faced off, me with my knife and him with bare hands.

To my left, Scott aimed the gun he'd taken from his opponent, but nothing happened when he fired. What was up with the guns? He did what I had done, fired again, but when the gun failed, he threw it over his shoulder with a snarl. He came at his opponent in a furious whirl. I'd been worried about Scott, but there seemed to be no need. Perhaps I had misjudged Scott's skill with a knife.

My fears assuaged, I focused on the asshole before me.

A tall man, his muscular frame climbed from here to forever. He had more muscle than me, but I was faster with a longer reach.

We lined up and prepared for the devil's dance.

SIXTY-THREE

A Hero

MELISSA

Something popped inside Melissa's knee, sending shards of pain shooting through her leg. She crawled away from the mayhem, a nearly impossible task with an injured leg and hands cuffed behind her back. Still, she managed to find a place of safety against the left side of the van. When she was far enough from the fighting, she wiggled her good leg through her cuffed hands. Biting against the pain, she stretched to get the cuffs around her injured leg, thanking long hours of yoga practice for excellent flexibility.

With her arms now to the front, she pulled herself up the driver's side door. The effort exhausted her, and she leaned against the van, panting with exertion. She tried to leverage herself to standing, but a brief test of her leg found her knee buckling beneath her weight.

Behind the van, the men fought.

She spared a quick glance. Scott and Pierce had knives. Pierce's opponent parried with bare hands, while the other man faced off against Scott with a wicked blade of his own.

Scott's face had lost all his sophisticated elegance, his enraged visage, feral and wild, was not something she would ever forget. He and his opponent circled, each man looking for an opening to attack. Their steps brought Scott closer to where she cowered against the van.

With her hands clutching the side mirror, Melissa forced herself to balance her weight on one foot. She couldn't undo the cuffs, they were locked tight, but she didn't need her hands free to drive.

Those men, whoever they were, had to be with CJ. He wouldn't have let Scott take her if he hadn't had a backup plan.

Was CJ still trapped in that hellhole?

Scott's knife slashed. Droplets of blood spattered. The man fighting her ex-husband cursed, and a stripe of red bloomed on his shredded shirt. He came at Scott with a swipe of his blade cutting into Scott's arm. Scott staggered back.

Scott lunged, driving his opponent back with a thrust. But he aimed too high. His knife hovered in front of his opponent's face; his wrist captured in the grip of his opponent.

Melissa grabbed the door handle, intent on climbing inside and away from Scott, but a mass of flailing arms came at her. Belle pulled her to the ground.

"No! You belong to him. You serve him!" Belle's brand of crazy filled the air. She kicked and spat and clawed at Melissa's face.

"Get off me!" She slapped at Belle.

Belle flipped Melissa onto her stomach, and a shock of pain lit her knee on fire.

"You will not run." Wildly insane eyes blinked at Melissa.

With her good leg, she kicked, connecting with Belle's gut. Pierce's slave doubled over, clutching at her belly. Melissa kicked a second, and then a third time, scooting herself further from the psychotic woman and moving away from the van, closer to where the men fought.

And then she saw him. CJ sprinted across the field with Mac and Jenny by his side.

How had they escaped that dungeon?

Melissa bit her lower lip and swallowed an excited cry.

A fist caught her jaw, swinging her head to the right. Stars filled her vision. Belle was back on her, kicking, screeching, and scratching again.

With a curse, she defended against the madwoman. Her knee throbbed, the pain making her want to retch. All fists and arms, she couldn't throw Belle off, and with her hands bound, it was impossible to restrain the raving lunatic.

Grunts sounded to her left. Flashes of steel glinted in the fading light of early dusk. Belle straddled Melissa, holding one hand on her wrists and the other pressing into her wounded knee.

Melissa screamed.

"Do. Not. Move." Belle's eyes danced with madness.

Melissa stopped resisting and panted against the pain.

Belle's hand eased up on her knee.

Pierce danced with his opponent, circling. Scott did the same.

CJ scrambled for one of the discarded guns. "Don't move!"

Pierce laughed. "Go ahead, that damn thing doesn't work."

"Ever heard of an RFID trigger lock, ass-wipe?"

A surge of strength flowed through Melissa. She didn't understand what a trigger lock was, but she didn't care. Belle's mouth gaped, and she shifted her weight as if intending to run at CJ. Melissa took advantage of Belle's distraction and bucked Belle off her stomach. Belle launched forward and hit her head on the edge of a sharp rock. A loud crack sounded, and Belle didn't move.

CJ's eyes hardened. He leveled his gun at Scott, who took a step back.

"It's over," CJ said.

The chaos of the battle quieted with a sudden and profound hush.

Pierce froze, his knife raised before him.

Scott's chest heaved from his exertion, blood dripping from his blade. More seeped out of the gashes across his chest.

Melissa's vision sharpened. Breath eased into her chest, no longer constricted by fear. Strength followed. The clamoring of her heart stilled, replaced by a steady beat.

This horrible nightmare was over.

Mac searched the ground and retrieved his gun. He aimed at Scott.

No one moved.

"Drop your weapons," CJ ordered with a flick of his gun. "Kick them away."

Pierce glanced at Scott, his visage dark and ominous.

"This is all your fault." Scott glanced at his hand, his brows drawing close. He made a move as if to drop his knife, but then he lunged toward Melissa.

CJ fired his weapon. The shot blasted her eardrums.

Scott took a step, his face set in a frozen mask. His chin dipped down to stare at a widening stain on his chest. His eyes seemed frozen with surprise, and then he crumpled to the ground.

She should have felt something, some relief in his death, but she felt numb and distant. Less than three feet away, Scott's soulless eyes stared unblinking and dead into the sky.

Pierce worked his jaw side-to-side, his fingers clenching the grip of his knife.

CJ turned his weapon on Pierce.

"Cuff him, Brett." He tossed a pair of cuffs in the air.

The man Pierce had been fighting snagged the cuffs. "Drop that knife."

Pierce glanced at Melissa, his eyes soft and round. His gaze cut to the unmoving form of Belle. His Adam's apple bobbed with his swallow. "You were always meant for me, my Queen. We would have been great together. I would have served you well." He sighed. "We will meet again."

Brett lunged as Pierce sliced across his throat. A red fountain bubbled up and spurted down the front of his chest. He landed in a sprawl of limbs on the dirt.

CJ ran to Melissa, his breathing smooth and easy.

Her ears still rang from the gunshot.

"Are you okay?" he asked.

"I will be." Her entire body shuddered. She gripped his hand.

CJ cupped her cheek. The warmth of his fingers soothed her and eased her breathing.

He wrapped his hand around her waist and pulled her close.

"You saved me," she said.

"I thought I'd lost you." He tangled his fingers in her hair. "Are you hurt?"

She couldn't answer because in the next breath his lips found hers. The horror of the past moments fled in the heat of his touch and the press of his mouth against hers. He pulled back, their lips lightly brushing, and then he yanked her against him.

Desperate.

Hungry.

Needful.

She needed more.

With a sigh, she parted her lips and welcomed the taste of him. He broke off the kiss and pressed his brow against hers, tangling his fingers in her hair.

He breathed out a sigh. "Never do that again."

"Do what?"

"Leave."

Bright lights flashed down the road. She squinted against the glare.

Mac's shadow fell over them. "Sam's arrived," he said.

"He's a bit late." CJ huffed a laugh. "Do you think he's going to be pissed?"

"If he doesn't fire your ass, I'll be surprised." Mac's smile twisted.

"Yeah, but you and I both know he won't." He jerked his chin toward the van. "The crazy chick is knocked out cold, but breathing."

Three black SUVs skidded to a stop, tires crunching against the gravel. Their headlights blinded her until she looked away. Men spilled out of the vehicles, and deep voices shouted commands. Mac went to greet the newcomers, his deep timbre filling the night with a recap of the scene.

A stranger approached, swinging a flashlight. He shined the light at CJ. Early fifties with a face scarred by acne, his expression was dark and stormy. "Never fucking listen, do you," he said.

"Late to the party again, Sam," CJ teased.

"Ma'am." He tipped the brim of his hat. "You must be Melissa."

Melissa swallowed, unable to find her voice, but she managed the slightest nod.

"Found Charlie at the house. We're calling a victims' response unit." He glanced around. "What a fucking shit storm the paperwork on this one is going to be."

CJ rocked her, and she relaxed. Within the fortress of his arms, she felt safe, the nightmare at an end. Scott was dead. He could no longer hurt her. A weight lifted off her shoulders, and she curled into CJ's embrace.

SIXTY-FOUR

An Ending

MELISSA

The events following her rescue blurred in Melissa's mind. All the women in Pierce's dungeon were taken to Saint John's Community Hospital, where they were examined, treated for their injuries, and met with specialists from a Victim's Response Unit. While their physical wounds would heal with time, many of the psychological scars would likely persist for a lifetime.

The last time she'd been to this hospital, CJ carried her in his arms. He was with her this time, too, overprotective and refused to be separated during the ride in the back of the ambulance.

He greeted the doctor at the emergency department with some familiarity and asked about a dog. Melissa didn't understand except the dog had pulled through, and a baby and his mother were doing well.

It was morning, and her knee had been wrapped in a brace. She had an MRI and an orthopedic visit scheduled in a week. There was concern about a tear of one of the ligaments, but it wasn't anything that would keep her in the hospital. Fortunately, her injuries were limited to her knee. The same could not be said for the other women.

The woman Pierce had called Gretel went to surgery and was recovering in intensive care. All the other women were admitted to the general medicine ward, where they were being tended to by a team of psychiatrists and internal medicine physicians.

CJ stayed with her, refusing to leave after visiting hours ended. He spent the night by her side, holding her hand, and soothing her when nightmares brought her screaming awake. Her pulse went ballistic and triggered the alarms on the monitors, but he soothed her fears.

"How do you feel?" CJ pressed his lips against her forehead. He finger-combed her hair, straightening out the knotted mess.

"I'm so tired." And scared. She was deathly afraid of going home, but where else could she go?

"Hey," he said. "Don't worry. We'll sort everything out together." The deep tone of his voice pulled her from her concerns.

Together?

"It's just…" She felt incredibly lost, but free at the same time. As if that made any sense. With Scott's death, a huge weight felt like it had been lifted from her shoulders. And she made a decision. She didn't want to live in this town anymore. She definitely never wanted to go back to her house. Sell it, or burn it, she would never step foot back in the house where Scott killed his last victim. But where would she go?

"Shh," he said. "Let me help." He placed a finger over her lips.

She didn't know how he could help. He had a life to get back to, and her life was a mess. They barely knew each other, although it felt as if she'd known him forever. They connected on a level she didn't understand, but with everything that happened…

She didn't want to think about letting him go.

The nurse came into the room, interrupting their conversation, and went over Melissa's discharge instructions. CJ took the papers and tucked them into a pocket of his jacket.

"Do you have any questions?" the nurse asked.

"No, thank you for everything." Melissa had spent too much time in hospitals and was ready to go.

"You have our number if any questions come up. You're good to go, Miss Evans. You can leave at any time."

Melissa took in a breath.

"You ready?" CJ asked.

Melissa adjusted the straps of her leg brace and grabbed the crutches she'd been provided.

"I'm more than ready, but if you don't mind, I want to check in with Henrietta."

She'd never forget Henrietta's strength. They didn't know each other but had bonded in that dungeon. Melissa needed to make sure Henrietta was going to be okay and wanted to make sure they had each other's contact information.

CJ's phone buzzed. Whatever he read on the text brought a smile to his face.

"I think that would be perfect," he said. "There's something I need to do. Do you mind if I slip away for a bit and meet you at her room?"

His consideration for her feelings astounded Melissa as if he understood she needed time with Henrietta alone.

"That would be great," she said.

He hovered beside her while she worked her way down to Henrietta's room. After a quick check with Henrietta, CJ excused himself.

Melissa gave Henrietta a hug. "Hey."

Henrietta's smile came slowly. "Hi."

"Any idea when they're going to let you go home?" She knew Henrietta had two girls waiting for her and couldn't imagine the worry her new friend had for her daughters' well-being.

"They have a few more tests, I think."

"Did you talk with the psychologists yet?"

"I did. They're coming back later, but I'm hoping I'll be discharged tomorrow." Henrietta clasped her hands and brought them to her chest.

"You're going to be okay." Melissa placed her hand over Henrietta's.

"I know. My dreams…"

"They'll fade with time." Melissa understood about the nightmares.

A soft knock sounded on the door. CJ peeked his head inside.

"Mrs. Jones?"

"Yes?"

A broad smile filled his face and made him look even more devastatingly handsome. Oddly, the twinkle in his eyes wasn't for Melissa, but for the woman lying in the hospital bed.

"I have a surprise."

"Mr. CJ," a small voice screeched. "I wanna see the surprise."

Henrietta gasped, and her eyes teared up.

A little girl barreled into the room, and then she stopped in her tracks, her eyes widening with shock, and her mouth gaping wide.

"Mama!" The little girl launched herself at the bed and crawled on top of Henrietta.

"Anna!"

Another girl, a little older, poked her head around the door. Her eyes widened, and she tugged on the front of her shirt. "Mama?"

"Angela! Come here!" Henrietta gestured the girl forward.

Angela's eyes watered. She closed the distance slowly and climbed into the bed beside her sister. The three of them hugged and kissed and cried. Melissa took a step toward the door, wanting to give them space.

"Come, let's let them get reacquainted." CJ's arms wrapped around Melissa's waist, and he whispered in her ear.

Melissa waved to Henrietta and gestured for her to call her later.

As they left the room, CJ swept her into his arms, scooping her crutches into his grasp.

"How about we make this official, Miss Melissa Evans?"

"Official?"

"How about a first date?"

"First date?" She laughed. "CJ, we've kind of moved past first date territory." She'd never think about a shower the same way with CJ around. That clinical and traumatic event had turned into the most unforgettable experience of her life.

"I want a first date and take my girl out in style." His eyes crinkled with mirth. Perhaps he'd been thinking about that night, too. "All this…" He made a vague gesture. "It's not the way I like to woo a woman."

"Woo me?" Melissa laughed. "Careful, you're dangerously close to stepping back into the nun-zone."

"Hey, I'm trying to be serious here." By the look in his eyes, she knew that to be the truth. His stubble tickled her fingers as she traced the angle of his jaw.

"Well, you can start by apologizing."

"Apologizing?"

"For calling me a drowned rat."

"I'll never apologize for that." CJ threw his head back and roared with laughter.

"Well, then you'd better find a way to impress me."

"How about we take a trip across the country? I'm thinking a few weeks to drive, take in the sights."

"A cross-country trip as a first date? That's a bit unconventional."

"And yet, perfect. I want to show you my home, and someplace that's a bit unconventional, but might be the perfect place for you to recover after all of this."

"Recover?"

"Wrong word?"

"No, recover is the right word. I guess I thought…are you saying… do you want…" She couldn't get her words out. Too afraid to voice what she wanted from him.

"Wow, that's painful to listen to. Let me save you from tripping all over your words."

"I wasn't tripping over my words."

"You totally were." He tapped the tip of her nose. "Let me make this really easy. I'm not ready to let you go. I like you, like I like, like you, and I want you in my life if you'll have me. But my life is with the Guardians, and we're headquartered in Northern California, just below Monterey. I don't know if anything is holding you here, but I'm hoping a little vacation away from here is something you'd consider. I'd also like to get to know you better, you know…without all the kidnapping stuff going on. I want time with just you alone with me. And I want to show you a place I think can really help you after all of this mess."

"A place?"

"Yes, a place. We call it the Facility."

"The Facility? Not a very original name."

"Not really, but it's amazing. It's a place for the people we help to receive the services they need to recover. It also helps them develop the life skills they need to move on. It's free, you can stay as long as you like. I'm literally right across the street. I mean, you can stay with me. I'd love it if you stayed with me, but I don't want to put too much pressure on the living together thing, considering we haven't officially had a first date yet."

"Is that so?"

"I'm serious, Melissa. I want to get to know you better. By whatever twist of fate, you and I, we're meant to be together." A smile filled his face, and his eyes twinkled with mirth. "But not in a creepy psycho-killer kind of way."

"Definitely not in a creepy psycho-killer kind of way." She couldn't help it. She laughed, and like magic, her laughter unloaded the miasma, which still clung to her after the ordeal with Pierce and Scott. "So, you're asking me out on a first date, which is to drive across the country and shack up with you at the other end?"

He locked eyes with hers and dipped his head. His exhales washed over her, searing her skin with the heat of his desire. There was a tingle in her breath, and a hitch in her chest as her entire body became painfully aware of his presence.

His bulging biceps held her. His powerful shoulders supported her. Every inch of this wonderful man protected her. He was her hero. He rescued her from a deadly tornado and from the unimaginable evil of Pierce and her dead ex-husband. In CJ's stare, he promised much more. He promised to give her his heart.

"Is that a yes, Miss Evans?"

"Yes." She looped her arms around his neck. "Most definitely, yes."

He seized her with a kiss. There was nothing tender as he claimed her with his possession. His desire for her, his bruising aggression, pushed past her fears, obliterating them in the grinding of their lips.

Fate twisted their lives together, and she wanted to find out what would happen next. It looked like CJ wanted that, too. And she couldn't wait for their official first date to begin.

***

Enjoyed reading about CJ?
Interested in more about the Guardians?
If so, you're in for a treat!
More Guardian Hostage Rescue magic is on its way.
Grab Your Copy of Rescuing Zoe, book 2
The Guardians: Hostage Rescue Specialists
CLICK HERE to get your copy.

FLIP the page for a SNEAK peek!

SIXTY-FIVE

Rescuing Zoe Sneak Peek

SNEAK PEEK OF RESCUING ZOE

Guardian Hostage Rescue Specialists

Once upon a time, there was a girl.
A happy, vibrant girl
Who didn't believe nightmares were real

But the girl woke up
A terrified, frightened girl
Trapped in a living nightmare.

That girl is me.

Zoe

It's been two days since they added the last girl. Anna arrived much as we all did, struggling, snarling and full of fight. She survived her first beating. She's quiet now. Recovering from her injuries. Now she whimpers and cries, much like me. Just like the rest of us.

Like Anna, I fought when they took me, and like her, I suffered.

I'm smarter now.

We all are.

In the oppressive silence, and cloying blackness which smothers all hope, we're not ready to die. And while nobody knows where we are, or where we're going, we are headed somewhere.

We're fed, watered, and they remove the foul smelling bucket of waste once a day. I think. Measuring time is difficult, but we know one thing. They want us alive when we get to wherever it is they're taking us.

To monsters who wait for us.

To the beginning of a living hell.

After Anna's arrival, the metal floor of our prison vibrated. A low, persistent drone shook the shipping container. Sometime later, hours maybe—It's hard to tell how much time passes in here—a soft up and down, side to side, rolling motion confirms our fears. We're being shipped to the next destination in our descent into hell.

The days pass with the relentless march of time. We can't stop it, slow it, or reverse it.

Time is meaningless when minutes last hours, hours last days, and the world no longer makes sense. With only suffocating darkness to pass the time, each day I lose more and more of my sanity.

My fingers plait a tiny braid. I make one for each day, or at least I think the time between one opening of the shipper container and the next is one day. It's when they feed us and water us like the chattel we've begun.

There are ten braids now.

A loud bang and I nearly jump out of my skin.

Men's voices rumble outside.

It feels like a lifetime when they shoved me kicking and screaming into the darkness.

I scurry back, not wanting them to touch me. To hurt me. The girls who got too close were dragged out. Not all of them returned. Those who did, are shadows of their former selves. We lost three girls before Anna. She was the last to be shoved inside this box.

That was two days ago.

When the doors open, all we see is more darkness. Light from the moon penetrates the towers of stacked shipping containers, casting shadows upon shadows. I prefer the formless blackness to the shifting shadows. Not once do they open the door during the daytime. It's always night.

Always dark.

A hand reaches in and takes the waste bucket. Footsteps recede while someone else places a large bowl of water just inside. We wait for the man with the bucket to return and toss it back inside.

Covered in filth and grime, the bucket no longer bothers me.

When water comes, no one touches it. We fear what might be in it more than dying of thirst.

We wait.

We wait until the doors close. Until the metallic thunk of the locking lugs tells us we're safe, once again locked inside our stifling prison. Only then do we move.

One girl.

One girl finds the bowl in the blinding darkness.

One girl takes a sip.

And we wait.

If she doesn't pass out from whatever drug they may have laced it with, we share the water. Small sips which do nothing to quench our thirst.

But it keeps us alive.

We survive together, thirteen strangers bonded by a nightmare.

Each girl takes her turn to test the water.

Today, it's my turn.

I lift my head from my knees and reach for the bowl. Dipping my finger into its contents, I croak out a scratchy, "W-water." There is no food. Gnawing hunger claws at my belly, but it's thirst which drives me.

Sighs sound all around me in the dismal darkness. It's been too long without water. The only thing carrying me through, the only reason I hold onto hope is that I believe we're more valuable alive than dead. I know what fate awaits us. We all know. But it's still better than death.

I take a long pull, swallowing water down a scratchy throat which still hurts from all the screaming during my abduction. It feels as if I broke something inside, because my voice is nothing but a breathy whisper now.

As the first girl, I'll drink more than the rest. That way the drug, if it's there, will be more likely to take effect on me, thus saving the others. I scoot back against the wall and slide the bowl to Bree. She came the day after I arrived. Our fingers interlock as I tip my head back to wait.

If nothing happens, Bree will take a sip and pass it to Chloe. Chloe will pass it to Dawn, and Dawn will pass it to Eve. On down the line, we'll share until the last drop is gone.

Then we'll wait for the door to open again.

We don't have the strength to fight. Not that I'll waste my energy on these men. I'm saving mine for the real monsters to come.

Not sure if my eyes are open or closed, fetid darkness folds around me. My thoughts wander, like they do every hour of every day, to the last moment I was happy. But I struggle to remember happier times.

I don't focus on the men who snatched me off the street.

Instead, my thoughts go to brilliant blue skies and white sand beaches of Cancun. Crystal clear, tropical waters sparkle beneath a bright sun. The festive Spring Break party atmosphere lets a smart girl lower her guard. I lost my freedom in the span of a heartbeat, on my very first night in paradise.

I thought I could walk from the beach to our hotel by myself. I gave no thought to the vulnerability of a pretty young girl walking alone. But I didn't think I was alone. People were all around me, partying, with far too much liquor flowing in their veins.

I felt safe.

But I was too easily separated from the crowd. They yanked me into a filthy van. Took me to a filthy house on a filthy street. There I was stripped, examined, and left to huddle on a filthy floor with a filthy flea-infested blanket. Then they shoved me inside a filthy shipping container twenty feet long with ten other girls.

Has it really been ten days? The braids in my hair don't lie.

What are my friends doing now? Did they call the police? Do Mexican police even care about an American girl who disappeared? Or do they think I got drunk and passed out in some foreign bed with some nameless boy?

I'll never know. What about my overly protective brother? Austin must be going ballistic, worrying about me? And my father? He must be out of his mind.

"How do you feel?" Bree keeps her breathy voice soft. We aren't allowed to speak to one another. That freedom, among many things, was violently taken from us.

"Good so fa…" I struggle to complete my thought as darkness overtakes me. My eyes droop. My muscles relax.

"It's drugged." Bree's voice sounds far away and defeated.

Hands reach for me and drag me over a rough metal floor as I dream of a happy, vibrant girl who doesn't believe in nightmares.

Axel

"ALPHA-ONE TO ALPHA-THREE," MAX'S VOICE CRACKLES THROUGH the radio. "Axel, you gotta see this." His tone makes my skin crawl.

"Copy that." I hold my position, weapon leveled on four men lying face down on the dirty floor. Zip Ties bind their wrists at the small of their backs and tie their ankles together.

Legs bent. Backs painfully arched. Shoulders straining. They're furious with my handiwork. Took less than thirty-seconds to truss them up, but I've been hogtying cattle all my life. For the record, humans are much easier to subdue than a calves.

"You got this?" My attention shifts to my teammate, Griff.

"Go ahead. I got this." He spits into the eye of one of our prisoners. Bastard curses in Spanish. "Sorry bud, a little spit in your eye is the least of your worries." Griff gives the shithole a love tap to the kidneys with the tip of his steel-toed boot.

Our angry friend's thick muscles bunch. Fury darkens his face. He, and his buddies, aren't going anywhere, and I think they're finally figuring that out.

I don't move until Griff gives the okay.

We're a six-man team. Knox and Liam stand outside, guarding our retreat. Griff's with me. Max and Wolfe moved through, looking for the target.

"Alpha-three to Alpha-one, headed to you." My radio squawks as I radio my intention to move my position.

"Copy that." Max sounds frustrated, it vibrates in his clipped reply.

Two days we've been on assignment while our target suffered at the hands of these men.

Our target? I grind my molars until my teeth throb and the muscles of my jaw ache.

Our target is my best friend's little sister, an annoying little scrap of a girl who made my life miserable with her hopeless crush. Last year, I finally set Zoe straight. I was a dick about it.

Firm.

Callous.

Mean.

I was an asshole about and broke her heart, but there was no other way. She needed to move on.

And now she's been taken.

"Status." That voice belongs to our mission commander.

CJ's been at this game twice as long as any of us. Famous for bringing a serial killer down, along with his copycat wannabe, he freed half a dozen women while on vacation. In our community, CJ is a legend.

I work my way deeper into the building, knowing he follows our progress via the helmet and body cams streaming our every move. Our successes and failures are broadcast in realtime back to command.

It's dark. We cut the electricity to the entire block. The flashlight mounted on my helmet provides all the light I need as it pierces the dimly lit hall.

"Do you have the package?" CJ's voice crackles with impatience, locking my molars tighter together. We can't afford to be late and this feels all kinds of too fucking late.

Cancun is famous for kidnapping rich Americans and pretty American girls. Zoe is exactly what they look for, a willowy blonde knockout with bright bottle green eyes. It's her most striking feature.

I pass down a hall. Weapon up. Scanning left to right. Finger on the trigger guard.

Max and Griff cleared these rooms on their way in, but I never assume. Those who do don't last long in our line of work.

Methodically, I scan the long hall, clear each room as I go, and make my way to the last room at the end of the hall. I meet Wolfe there with a lift of my chin. He responds in kind.

The room's empty.

"Fucking hell." My nose wrinkles at the smell of blood, sweat, and human excrement. The stench is enough to make me gag. Breathing through my mouth only makes it worse. Now I taste the foulness as it floods my senses.

Zoe was in this room.

Past tense.

Mission failure.

Ratty blankets form amorphous lumps on the dirty floor.

Lumps.

Pleural.

Not unexpected. We know the men who took Zoe are part of a human trafficking ring. That's why we're here. We're the hostage rescue specialists paid very well to bring stolen girls home, preferably safe and sound. Although we were only hired to recover Zoe, we'll save them all. Forest won't have it any other way.

There's easily a dozen or more blankets strewn about. A dozen lives taken. The foul taste of failure coats my tongue. I'm not used to the bitter tang.

Guardians never fail.

Tell that to Zoe. Tell her how this isn't a colossal fucked up failure.

If she's still alive.

My helmet light pierces the gloom, revealing dried blood and fetid urine stains. They kept the girls in here like animals. The blood comes in various forms, dried pools on the floor, stains on the blankets, and splatter marks on the wall. Urine stains are everywhere.

These men are sloppy. Damaging their merchandise cuts into their bottom line. By the looks of this place, all of the girls suffered. Some more than others. Zoe suffered.

In my six years as a team guy, I've seen a lot of fucked up shit. When I left the Navy, I thought the worst of human depravity was behind me. How wrong I was. This is some fucked up shit.

I used to hunt dangerous men, relieving them of the burden of their pathetic lives, or returning them to whichever prevailing authority waited to extract their pound of flesh.

Now, I retrieve the fallen, the broken; those who've been taken. I'm a Guardian, a hostage rescue specialist dealing with a catastrophic mission failure. The girls are gone. From the looks of it we're hours late, maybe even a whole day late.

This job isn't any easier than my team days. In many ways, it's far worse. Revulsion coils in my gut, thinking about what these girls endured.

Girls. Young women. Innocent victims.

That's not an emotion I ever felt for the targets I disposed of during my time in the Navy. I dispatched lives without a bit of compassion or lick of guilt cluttering my conscience.

"What did you want me to see?" I turn my attention to Max, our team leader. He could've told me about this shit instead of dragging me from my position.

"You tell me." He gestures to another room. The door sits off its hinges, propped haphazardly against the wall. The low beam of his flashlight barely lights up the doorway. I push past and look inside.

"Christ!" My heart rate quickens before I can force it back to its slow plodding pace. The veins in my temples bulge as fury fills me. "Fucking pigs."

Max follows me into the room. He ordered me to tell him what I see.

"It's a procedure room." My nose wrinkles at the stench. There's more blood here than in the other rooms. Layers of dried blood pool on the floor beneath an examination table. It tells the tales of multiple victims enduring unspeakable acts.

"Well? What do you think?" Max watches me closely. Like the rest of the team, he's aware of my personal connection to this mission.

"It's a gynecologic exam table."

"No shit Sherlock."

As team medic, my medical skillset comes in handy in the rare instances when one of us needs a little patching up in the field, but there's no reason for my medical skills here.

The back of the exam table is set at an incline. Two metal poles with heel cups extend from the end. Unlike a normal exam table, this one comes with shackles. Shackles bolted at the high end for the chest. Shackles to secure wrists a little lower down. Another runs across the hips to hold an unwilling patient as they thrash. Finally, there are two more straps at the feet.

"What were they doing? Rape?" Max growls, and I echo his rage.

"Could be. The table definitely places a woman in a vulnerable position, but I doubt their customers would pay for damaged goods." I glance around the filthy room, looking for anything which might explain what they did in here. "Check the trash can."

Max heads over to a waste container. Instead of checking, he picks it up and brings it back to me. I'm smart enough not to reach inside. Who knows what might prick me and transfer disease.

Disease?

My eyes narrow and I pull out my knife. Using that, I dig through the contents.

"You seeing this?" My question isn't for Max, but for our Doc Summer watching from command.

"Yes." Doc Summers' crisp voice tightens. A tough cookie, nothing phases our indomitable lead physician.

"See what?" Max peers into the trash can.

"Those are STD kits. Tests for gonorrhea, chlamydia, and…" I sift through the contents. "IUDs? Doc, am I correct?"

Static over the coms crackles then clears. "Looks like they tested the girls for sexually transmitted diseases and inserted IUDs." Her voice softens. "At least that answers one question."

"What's that?" Max turns the can over and dumps the contents on the floor spreading them out. He does this to send better pictures back to base.

I glance at the trash and count IUD wrappers. "Looks like thirteen."

"Sixteen chlamydia swabs. Thirteen IUDs." Doc Summers confirms. "I'd mark that at sixteen victims."

"Not thirteen?"

"If some of the girls already had IUDs, they wouldn't place a new one."

"How fucking considerate." My stomach twists. They want the pleasure of raping their victims without the unwanted side effects pregnancy brings.

"Search the place." A new voice rumbles through our comm channels. Forest Summers' deep baritone is unmistakable and elicits an ass-puckering gluteal clench.

What the fuck is the CJ's boss' boss doing on Overwatch?

My team worked with Forest Summers on an operation in the Philippines that went to hell in a handbasket in the blink of an eye.

That had definitely been a FUBAR moment. We lost the head of our organization. I'm surprised we weren't all fired on the spot. A couple months later, we rescued him in a brilliantly executed raid, but still that's not something a person ever forgets.

Forest continues, thinking out loud. "There must be something which says where they took the girls. See what the prisoners have to say."

"With pleasure." Not a fan of torture, per se, I love a good interrogation.

"We're on it, boss." Max gives a nod. He's our team leader. All final orders come from him. I tap the button for the team only comm channel. "Alpha-four, we need to know where they took the girls."

With Forest Summers' interest in the mission, need means necessity.

"Copy that." Griff loves getting his hands dirty.

If we can get the intel we need, we might be able to salvage this operation.

Grab Your Copy of Rescuing Zoe, book 2
The Guardians: Hostage Rescue Specialists
elliemasters.com/RescuingZoe

Please consider leaving a review

I hope you enjoyed this book as much as I enjoyed writing it. If you like this book, please leave a review. I love reviews. I love reading your reviews, and they help other readers decide if this book is worth their time and money. I hope you think it is and decide to share this story with others. A sentence is all it takes. Thank you in advance!

Click on the link below to leave your review

Amazon

Ellie Masters The EDGE

If you are interested in joining Ellie's Facebook reader group, THE EDGE, we'd love to have you.

The Edge Facebook Reader Group
elliemasters.com/TheEdge

Join Ellie's ELLZ BELLZ.
Sign up for Ellie's Newsletter.
Elliemasters.com/newslettersignup

Books by Ellie Masters

The LIGHTER SIDE

Ellie Masters is the lighter side of the Jet & Ellie Masters writing duo! You will find Contemporary Romance, Military Romance, Romantic Suspense, Billionaire Romance, and Rock Star Romance in Ellie's Works.

Sign up to Ellie's Newsletter and get a free gift. https://elliemasters.com/RescuingMelissa

YOU CAN FIND ELLIE'S BOOKS HERE:

ELLIEMASTERS.COM/BOOKS

Military Romance

Guardian Hostage Rescue

Rescuing Melissa

(Get a FREE copy of Rescuing Melissa when you join Ellie's Newsletter)

Rescuing Zoe

Rescuing Moira

The One I Want Series

(Small Town, Military Heroes)

By Jet & Ellie Masters

EACH BOOK IN THIS SERIES CAN BE READ AS A STANDALONE AND IS ABOUT A DIFFERENT COUPLE WITH AN HEA.

Aiden

Brent

Caleb

Dax

Patton

Rockstar Romance

The Angel Fire Rock Romance Series

EACH BOOK IN THIS SERIES CAN BE READ AS A STANDALONE AND IS ABOUT A DIFFERENT COUPLE WITH AN HEA. IT IS RECOMMENDED THEY ARE READ IN ORDER.

Ashes to New (prequel)

Heart's Insanity (book 1)

Heart's Desire (book 2)

Heart's Collide (book 3)

Hearts Divided (book 4)

Hearts Entwined (book5)

Forest's FALL (book 6)

Hearts The Last Beat (book7)

Billionaire Romance

Billionaire Boys Club

Hawke

H.R.H. Richard

Brody

Contemporary Romance

Firestorm

(KRISTY BROMBERG'S EVERYDAY HEROES WORLD)

Contemporary Romance

Cocky Captain

(VI KEELAND & PENELOPE WARD'S COCKY HERO WORLD)

Sweet Contemporary Romance

Finding Peace

Romantic Suspense

The Starling

~AND~

Science Fiction

Ellie Masters writing as L.A. Warren

Vendel Rising: a Science Fiction Serialized Novel

About the Author

ELLIE MASTERS is a multi-genre and best-selling author, writing the stories she loves to read. Dip into the eclectic mind of Ellie Masters, spend time exploring the sensual realm where she breathes life into her characters and brings them from her mind to the page and into the heart of her readers every day.

When not writing, Ellie can be found outside, where her passion for all things outdoor reigns supreme: off-roading, riding ATVs, scuba diving, hiking, and breathing fresh air are top on her list.

Ellie's favorite way to spend an evening is curled up on a couch, laptop in place, watching a fire, drinking a good wine, and bringing forth all the characters from her mind to the page and hopefully into the hearts of her readers.

FOR MORE INFORMATION
elliemasters.com

facebook.com/elliemastersromance
twitter.com/Ellie__Masters
instagram.com/ellie_masters
bookbub.com/authors/ellie-masters
goodreads.com/Ellie_Masters

Connect with Ellie Masters

Website:
elliemasters.com
Amazon Author Page:
elliemasters.com/amazon
Facebook:
elliemasters.com/Facebook
Goodreads:
elliemasters.com/Goodreads
Instagram:
elliemasters.com/Instagram

Final Thoughts

I hope you enjoyed this book as much as I enjoyed writing it. If you enjoyed reading this story, please consider leaving a review on Amazon and Goodreads, and please let other people know. A sentence is all it takes. Friend recommendations are the strongest catalyst for readers' purchase decisions! And I'd love to be able to continue bringing the characters and stories from My-Mind-to-the-Page.

Second, call or e-mail a friend and tell them about this book. If you really want them to read it, gift it to them. If you prefer digital friends, please use the "Recommend" feature of Goodreads to spread the word.

Or visit my blog https://elliemasters.com, where you can find out more about my writing process and personal life.

Come visit The EDGE: Dark Discussions where we'll have a chance to talk about my works, their creation, and maybe what the future has in store for my writing.

Facebook Reader Group: The EDGE

Thank you so much for your support!

Love,

Ellie

Dedication

This book is dedicated to you, my reader. Thank you for spending a few hours of your time with me. I wouldn't be able to write without you to cheer me on. Your wonderful words, your support, and your willingness to join me on this journey is a gift beyond measure.

Whether this is the first book of mine you've read, or if you've been with me since the very beginning, thank you for believing in me as I bring these characters 'from my mind to the page and into your hearts.'

Love,

Ellie

Books by Jet Masters

If you enjoyed this book by Ellie Masters, the LIGHTER SIDE of the Jet & Ellie writing duo, and aren't afraid of edgier writing, you might enjoy reading BDSM themed books written by Jet, the DARKER SIDE of the Masters' Writing Team.

The DARKER SIDE
Jet Masters is the darker side of the Jet & Ellie writing duo!

Romantic Suspense
Changing Roles Series:

THIS SERIES MUST BE READ IN ORDER.

Book 1: Command Me
Book 2: Control Me
Book 3: Collar Me
Book 4: Embracing FATE
Book 5: Seizing FATE
Book 6: Accepting FATE

HOT READS

A STANDALONE NOVEL.

Down the Rabbit Hole

Light BDSM Romance
The Ties that Bind

EACH BOOK IN THIS SERIES CAN BE READ AS A STANDALONE AND IS ABOUT A DIFFERENT COUPLE WITH AN HEA.

Alexa
Penny
Michelle
Ivy

HOT READS
Becoming His Series

THIS SERIES MUST BE READ IN ORDER.

Book 1: The Ballet
Book 2: Learning to Breathe
Book 3: Becoming His

Dark Captive Romance

A STANDALONE NOVEL.

She's MINE

THE END

Made in United States
North Haven, CT
18 September 2022